Praise for Lynn Cahoon and Her Irresistible Cozy Mysteries

AN AMATEUR SLEUTH'S GUIDE TO MURDER
"The prolific Lynn Cahoon starts another winning cozy series!"
—*Criminal Element*

"Cahoon launches a promising new series with endearing characters and a charming locale."
—*Kirkus Reviews*

"Plan a cozy day by the fire with a cup of tea, snuggle in, and enjoy. The day will be over before you know it. And there may even be time to make Lynn's Yummy Murderous Mac and Cheese for dinner."
—Nancy Coco, author of the Candy-Coated Mysteries

"If you love cozy mysteries, you will love *An Amateur Sleuth's Guide to Murder*—a delightful mixture of a practical guidebook and a clever fictional mystery."
—Valerie Burns, author of the Mystery Bookshop Mysteries

FIVE FURRY FAMILIARS
"A fun read for those who enjoy tales of witches and magic."
—*Kirkus Reviews*

THREE TAINTED TEAS
"A kitchen witch reluctantly takes over as planner for a cursed wedding . . . This witchy tale is a hoot."
—*Kirkus Reviews*

ONE POISON PIE
"*One Poison Pie* deliciously blends charm and magic with a dash of mystery and a sprinkle of romance. Mia Malone is a zesty protagonist who relies on her wits to solve the crime, and the enchanting cast of characters that populate Magic Springs are a delight."
—Daryl Wood Gerber, Agatha winner and nationally best-selling author of the Cookbook Nook Mysteries and Fairy Garden Mysteries

"A witchy cooking cozy for fans of the supernatural and good eating."
—*Kirkus Reviews*

A FIELD GUIDE TO HOMICIDE
"The best entry in this character-driven series mixes a well-plotted mystery with a romance that rings true to life."
—*Kirkus Reviews*

"Informative as well as entertaining, *A Field Guide to Homicide* is the perfect book for cozy mystery lovers who entertain thoughts of writing novels themselves . . . This is, without a doubt, one of the best Cat Latimer novels to date."
—*Criminal Element*

"Cat is a great heroine with a lot of spirit that readers will enjoy solving the mystery (with)."
—*Parkersburg News & Sentinel*

SCONED TO DEATH

"The most intriguing aspect of this story is the writers' retreat itself. Although the writers themselves are not suspect, they add freshness and new relationships to the series. Fans of Lucy Arlington's 'Novel Idea' mysteries may want to enter the writing world from another angle."
—*Library Journal*

OF MURDER AND MEN

"A Colorado widow discovers that everything she knew about her husband's death is wrong . . . Interesting plot and quirky characters."
—*Kirkus Reviews*

A STORY TO KILL

"Well-crafted . . . Cat and crew prove to be engaging characters and Cahoon does a stellar job of keeping them—and the reader—guessing."
—*Mystery Scene*

"Lynn Cahoon has hit the golden trifecta—Murder, intrigue, and a really hot handyman. Better get your flashlight handy, *A Story to Kill* will keep you reading all night."
—Laura Bradford, author of the Amish Mysteries

TOURIST TRAP MYSTERIES

"Lynn Cahoon's popular Tourist Trap series is set all around the charming coastal town of South Cove, California, but the heroine Jill Gardner owns a delightful bookstore/coffee shop so a lot of the scenes take place there. This is one of my go-to cozy mystery series, bookish or not, and I'm always eager to get my hands on the next book!"
—*Hope By the Book*

"Murder, dirty politics, pirate lore, and a hot police detective: *Guidebook to Murder* has it all! A cozy lover's dream come true."
—Susan McBride, author of the Debutante Dropout Mysteries

"This was a good read and I love the author's style, which was warm and friendly . . . I can't wait to read the next book in this wonderfully appealing series."
—*Dru's Book Musings*

"I am happy to admit that some of my expectations were met while other aspects of the story exceeded my own imagination . . . This mystery novel was light, fun, and kept me thoroughly engaged. I only wish it was longer."
—*The Young Folks*

"*If the Shoe Kills* is entertaining and I would be happy to visit Jill and the residents of South Cove again."
—*MysteryPlease.com*

"In *If the Shoe Kills,* author Lynn Cahoon gave me exactly what I wanted. She crafted a well told small town murder that kept me guessing who the murderer was until the end. I will definitely have to take a trip back to South Cove and maybe even visit tales of Jill Gardner's past in the previous two Tourist Trap Mystery books. I do love a holiday mystery! And with this book, so will you."
—*ArtBooksCoffee.com*

"I would recommend *If the Shoe Kills* if you are looking for a well written cozy mystery."
—*Mysteries, Etc.*

"This novella is short and easily read in an hour or two with interesting angst and dynamics between mothers and daughters and mothers and sons . . . I enjoyed the first-person narrative."
Kings River Life Magazine on *Mother's Day Mayhem*

Books by Lynn Cahoon

The Bainbridge Island Mystery Series
An Amateur Sleuth's Guide to Murder * Confessions of an Amateur Sleuth

The Tourist Trap Mystery Series
Guidebook to Murder * Mission to Murder * If the Shoe Kills * Dressed to Kill * Killer Run *Murder on Wheels * Tea Cups and Carnage * Hospitality and Homicide * Killer Party * Memories and Murder * Murder in Waiting * Picture Perfect Frame * Wedding Bell Blues * A Vacation to Die For * Songs of Wine and Murder * Olive You to Death * Vows of Murder * Merry Murder Season

Novellas
Rockets' Dead Glare * A Deadly Brew * Santa Puppy * Corned Beef and Casualties * Mother's Day Mayhem * A Very Mummy Holiday * Murder in a Tourist Town

The Kitchen Witch Mystery Series
One Poison Pie * Two Wicked Desserts * Three Tainted Teas * Four Charming Spells * Five Furry Familiars * Six Stunning Sirens * Seven Secret Spellcasters

Novellas
Chili Cauldron Curse * Murder 101 * Have a Holly, Haunted Holiday * Two Christmas Mittens

The Cat Latimer Mystery Series
A Story to Kill * Fatality by Firelight * Of Murder and Men * Slay in Character * Sconed to Death * A Field Guide to Homicide * A Killer Christmas Wish * Caught Dead to Write * Murder on a Snowy Evening * Formal Fatality

Novellas
Body in the Book Drop

The Farm-to-Fork Mystery Series
Who Moved My Goat Cheese? * Killer Green Tomatoes * One Potato, Two Potato, Dead * Deep Fried Revenge * Killer Comfort Food * A Fatal Family Feast

Novellas
Have a Deadly New Year * Penned In * A Pumpkin Spice Killing * A Basketful of Murder

The Survivors' Book Club Mystery Series
Tuesday Night Survivors' Club * Secrets in the Stacks * Death in the Romance Aisle * Reading Between the Lies * Dying to Read * Sleuthing with the Stars

CONFESSIONS of an AMATEUR SLEUTH

LYNN CAHOON

KENSINGTON PUBLISHING CORP.
kensingtonbooks.com

KENSINGTON BOOKS are published by

Kensington Publishing Corp.
900 Third Avenue
New York, NY 10022

Library of Congress Control Number: On file

ISBN: 978-1-4967-5212-3

First Kensington Hardcover Edition: May 2026

ISBN: 978-1-4967-5214-7 (ebook)

10 9 8 7 6 5 4 3 2 1

Printed in the United States of America

The authorized representative in the EU for product safety and compliance
is eucomply OU, Parnu mnt 139b-14, Apt 123
Tallinn, Berlin 11317, hello@eucompliancepartner.com

To the ones I confess to—you know who you are.

Meg's Tips and Tricks

1. Interviewing is a conversation, not an interrogation. Especially when you don't wear a badge.
2. Sometimes what you wear says a lot about a person. Check your clothes when you're investigating to make sure the other person doesn't start to look for you.
3. Going undercover is a lot like dating. You leave out the warts until you know you want this stranger to know your secrets.
4. Sometimes you find out information you'd rather not know. It's all part of the job.
5. People tell you things without realizing what else they're saying. Don't miss these opportunities to find out more.
6. You need to be aware of what's going on, but not so close to the investigation that people start to know you.
7. Don't become part of the conversation. Or worse, a suspect.
8. Sometimes it's hard to figure out who's an ally in your camp. Be quiet until they show the real person behind the mask.
9. Even professional detectives need to take a break. Stepping back lets the clues marinate in your mind.
10. Admitting you have a filter helps you put the world in perspective. Try to see things from someone else's point of view.
11. Having a partner around when you're out investigating is Safety 101. Even if they just think they're having lunch with you.
12. If you don't know a business or community well, make sure you find a subject matter expert to help you interview. You'll understand the nuances of conversation more clearly.

13. And the Most Likely to Murder Award goes to . . .
14. No use crying over missed opportunities.
15. Family connections sometimes complicate investigations.
16. Who did the victim hang around with? Now and in the past.
17. Not everyone a dead guy knew is a suspect, but they could be.
18. Sometimes the way you look at a clue makes a difference. You could be putting your own filter on the information.
19. Memories are like flowers, they're better when they're fresh.
20. Be careful when you dig into the past. Sometimes you find things you don't want to see.
21. Sometimes what you seek is right in front of your eyes.
22. Beware of free information. It might not be worth what you pay for it.
23. Sometimes the answer is right in front of your face.
24. It takes a village to raise a child and to solve a murder.

Chapter 1

Interviewing is a conversation, not an interrogation. Especially when you don't wear a badge.

Something was missing. Okay, a lot of things were missing. Meg Gates stared at the local authors shelf as she stood at the front door of Island Books, her mother's bookstore. She'd made the display eye-catching, but the shelves were almost empty. Three weeks ago, her mom had promised she'd get Meg the list of books she'd been curating since she'd opened the shop. Right now, only L. C. Aster's books inhabited the bookcase. Of course, Lilly Aster, Meg's other boss, had been writing for years, so she had a lot of books to showcase.

Meg wanted to highlight other local authors as well. She typed out a text to her mom since her phone calls had gone unanswered that morning.

As she clicked "send," the bell over the door alerted her to a customer. "Welcome to Island Books, may I help you?"

"Where's Mom?" Stephen 'Junior' Gates beelined directly to the counter. "She usually works Tuesday mornings."

"Good morning to you." Meg rolled her eyes as she addressed her brother. Junior dressed like an accountant. Even on days off, he wore a polo shirt and chino shorts. He still worked for their dad at his accounting firm, and the job fit his personality. Junior liked his life orderly. "Why aren't you at work?"

"I take off the second Tuesday of every month to take Mom to Seattle for lunch. I called her when I got on the ferry this morning. But she hasn't answered." Junior tried to peek around Meg. "I guess she must have gotten my message since you're here to cover her. Is she in the back?"

"One, it's not the second Tuesday, it's the first. And no, she's not here." Meg leaned back on the stool. "Funny, I haven't been able to reach her by phone this morning either. She emailed me on Monday with my hours for the week. She didn't explain, but I'm working the day shift on Tuesday, and then on Thursday I have the entire day from open to close. She said I could close when it got slow Thursday night. Maybe she has appointments this week."

Junior seemed to analyze the information as he read the back of a memoir of an English prime minister that a customer had left unpurchased on the register counter. "But that doesn't explain her not picking up her phone. And why would she have appointments on two different days? You don't think she's sick, do you?"

"I saw her Sunday at church. She looked okay." Meg thought about how her mom had acted that day. She'd eaten her entire lunch at the restaurant and even ordered dessert. Something Mom never did. "She even had a tan."

"So you think it's just a checkup?" Junior set the book down. "I wish she'd called me back so I wouldn't have wasted a ferry ticket."

"You were already heading here when you—" Meg started but then stopped. Explaining to Junior that the world didn't work on his schedule was a waste of breath. She watched as he pulled his phone out and started texting someone. "So why did you come this week and not next week anyway?"

Junior's face turned red.

"Junior?" Now Meg was curious. Her older brother had always been the steady one. Meanwhile, Meg had been a three-time loser—she failed to finish college, then the tech startup she'd joined went bankrupt, and, of course, her wedding was canceled due to her fiancé's lack of understanding of the definition of the word *faithful*. Meg had returned to Bainbridge Island to live in an apartment over her aunt's garage and work at her mom's bookstore. Junior, on the other hand, had finished his degree and went to work for their father in Bellevue at his accounting firm. She loved her family, but she hated that she was always seen as the needy one.

He kept his gaze on his phone. "I've got plans next week."

"Plans. At work?" Meg noticed he'd turned even redder. When he didn't answer, she asked again, "What plans?"

"I'm going to a conference in San Francisco if you must know, nosy." He looked up and met her gaze. "Are you happy? Or do you need the rest of my schedule?"

"Why are you blushing about a conference?" Meg searched his face for clues. "Unless you're going with a woman. Don't tell me you're dating someone at Dad's firm. Please don't let it be your secretary."

Now Junior's face turned scarlet. "We don't have secretaries anymore. We have assistants. Besides, I'm not Dad. Anne works in corporate accounts. She's an accountant. We've only been dating for a few weeks. We'll be staying in separate rooms. Now can we stop the third degree?"

Meg felt bad about bringing up their father. His new wife, Elaine, had been his secretary, but they both claimed that the relationship had changed from work friends to something romantic only after the divorce. Meg wanted to believe him, but he'd been the first of her parents to start dating. Mom still hadn't gone out with anyone. At least as far as Meg knew.

She realized Junior was watching her. "I'm sorry. I shouldn't have brought Dad into the conversation. So, Anne, huh? She's an accountant and what else? Is she from Seattle? What does she look like? Is she nice?"

The door to the shop opened and with the bell's announcement, Dalton walked into the shop. "Hey Junior, are you ready?"

"What's going on?" Meg looked from Junior to Dalton. The two men had been friends since middle school.

"Mom's not here so I checked in with Dalton to see if he had time for lunch." He picked up the memoir again. "Put this on my account. Tell Mom I'll call her later. When you see her."

Watson, Meg's tan cocker spaniel, had roused himself from his morning nap and started circling Dalton for attention.

Dalton leaned down and gave the excited pup head rubs. Then Dalton looked up at Meg. "Do you need me to take him out before we leave?"

"Would you?" Meg glanced at her watch. "He's been asleep for almost three hours now. I'm sure he needs a walk."

"Sure. And do you want me to bring you something back from the restaurant for lunch?" Dalton walked over and grabbed Watson's leash from behind the counter.

Junior groaned as he perched on the edge of the couch. "You've been spending too much time here with my sister. Her dog loves you and you know where everything is."

"Maybe you've just been spending too little time here." Dalton stood and headed to the door. "I'll bring him back in a few and you can answer my lunch question."

"No lunch," Meg said as a group of tourists came into the bookstore. "I'm going to a writers' meeting this evening over at Island Diner. I brought a lunch."

"I'll come with you," Junior declared as he followed Dalton out the door. "Just tell Mom I was here."

"When I see her," Meg muttered, then she smiled at a woman walking toward her. "What can I help you with?"

When Dalton brought back Watson, she had a line of customers at the register. He tucked the leash back under the counter as the dog headed to his water dish to refill. "Junior's waiting for me at Island Diner. Do you need me to stay?"

She handed a credit card receipt and a bag to the customer she'd been helping. "No, I'm good, but thanks for taking him out."

"My pleasure," Dalton responded as he made his way out of the shop.

The next customer watched Dalton leave, then handed Meg her card after she'd rung up the book purchase. "Your boyfriend's cute and thoughtful. You need to keep that one."

Meg smiled as she ran the card. She turned the screen toward the customer for her signature. "Dalton's not my boyfriend."

"Oh?" The woman turned and looked out the window where Dalton had disappeared seconds before. "Does he know that?"

Mom hadn't called back by the time Meg needed to close the shop. She could get dinner at the meeting, but she couldn't take Watson inside the restaurant. She needed to take him home and feed him. And turn on his favorite movie.

Yes, her dog was spoiled. But he was also good company and kept Meg from talking to herself. She'd found him on a rescue website one day and had gone down to the shelter the same day to adopt him. She did one thing right—take care of her dog.

By the time she got back into town, the meeting had started. She grabbed a waitress and gave her order, then sat down at the back of the banquet room to wait for food while she listened to the presenter.

A man leaned over and held out his hand. "Hi, I'm Lee Anderson. I'm a freelance food writer."

Meg leaned closer so she could lower her voice. "Meg Gates. I guess I'm a nonfiction crime writer. I'm working on my first book. Who's talking today?"

"That's Crissy Lorde. She writes cozy mysteries and she's talking about her experience self-publishing versus the more traditional route." He held up his notebook to show Meg. The page was empty except for the date that Lee had written on the right corner. "I'd share my notes, but so far, I've got nothing. She's just talking about her own journey in writing. But she promised ten comparisons between the two options sometime tonight. The way she's going, we might be here until midnight by the time she hits number ten."

Meg suppressed a giggle. The speakers at the writers' group ranged from people who were just there to sell their book to professional writers like L. C. Aster, who'd come to talk to the group about her thrillers last month. Meg was Lilly's author assistant and had recently told her boss that she was trying to write a nonfiction book about solving mysteries. Lilly had suggested that Meg join the local writing group to meet other writers and learn about the industry.

Writing a book was harder than Meg had imagined. Sometimes she felt like she had control of the nonfiction book about how to become your own Nancy Drew. Sometimes she thought the book was controlling her. The good part of the process was that it gave her an inside look at what authors like Lilly went through when creating the product. The bad part was she felt like an imposter a lot of the time. Lilly's advice. One page at a time. Don't look back until it's done, then you can see if it works or not.

Meg was beginning to think the "or not" advice was what eventually would happen. But she was going to finish it, mostly because she was tired of changing lanes when things got hard. Whether or not it eventually sold was out of her hands. But she could help it along. Like by attending and learning from the local writers. Which was why she was here tonight.

This presenter may not have been worth the time to attend the meeting, but as her mother always said, "You get what you get and you don't throw a fit." Besides, Meg could probably find at least one tidbit in the talk to get her excited about writing.

Apparently, Lee Anderson hadn't had the same upbringing. He pulled out his phone and started scrolling through his emails. He looked over at Meg when her food was delivered. "Wake me when she's done."

Meg had finished eating when the speaker finished her presentation. Crissy *had* presented them with ten comparisons, and Meg had written them down, wondering if her amateur investigation book would be appropriate for self-publishing. She wanted the book in bookstores. And that meant an agent and a publisher.

Lilly had read the first chapter of Meg's guidebook and told her it was promising, so at least one person thought she might be on the right track. Besides, she wasn't going to worry until she finished the book. She took notes on marketing ideas and wrote down any editors who seemed to be accepting queries in her area. But she was mostly there for the hour of sprint writing and the happy hour afterward. She'd already met several nonfiction writers and they'd been friendly. She just hadn't made any new friends. Yet.

The group transitioned into a quick write-in. Thirty minutes of uninterrupted writing. Meg opened her laptop and got busy.

Lee found her again during the happy hour. "Did you get any words?"

"Four hundred new words and a chapter read and tweaked. I swear, every time I look at a page, I find a typo or something I want to say differently. Does the editing ever stop?" Meg sipped her wine as she scanned the group. Crissy was still holding court over by the bar talking about how she published.

"That's why I write for local papers. I have a deadline, so once it's out of my hands, I'm done. I can't play with it forever. So many people go over the first three chapters of a project and never move on. I'd love to write a book someday. Maybe like Anthony Bourdain, an exposé on the state of restaurants in the Pacific Northwest." Lee shrugged and looked around the room. "Someday, I guess."

"I don't know about Someday," Meg said.

Lee turned toward her, a frown narrowing his eyes. "What?"

"There's Monday, Tuesday, Wednesday . . ." She tapped her fingers as she listed off the days of the week. "And it all ends with Sunday and starts over. But Someday? I've never heard of it."

"Okay, fine. You got me. I need to just shut up and do it. Like in the Nike ads." He grinned and finished his beer. "I've got to catch the ferry, but I like you, Gates. Why don't you come with me to dinner tomorrow night? I'm reviewing a local restaurant. But we can't let them know that's why I'm there. You can be my cover. No one ever expects a food critic to have a sidekick. And we can talk more about writing nonfiction. I've got a few contacts you might want to interview. And my paper will buy your dinner."

"Sounds good." Meg glanced at her watch. She had a new project from Lilly she needed to start tonight. Especially since now she wouldn't be home tomorrow night. "I'll meet you at the restaurant. Which one and what time?"

He opened his phone. "My reservation is for eight at the Local Crab. Do you know it?"

"Yeah, I've met the chef before. Maybe I'm not a good sidekick for this one." Meg hoped Lee didn't have a reputation for trashing restaurants.

"Don't be silly. You're perfect. I'm just a friend from Seattle. He'll never suspect anything, and I can get a clear reading on the meal without them trying to impress me." He snapped a picture of her as she was taking a drink. He laughed at her widened eyes. "I like to remember where I meet people. That way I don't forget their names. Although you seem pretty unforgettable."

Meg shook her head. "No sweet-talking your writing partner. This is just about writing. I'm not looking for a relationship."

"Good, because I'm not either. I just got out of a long-term relationship a few months ago, and my head is still not clear from her games. So we're just friends, right?" He scanned the room as he talked.

"Exactly." Meg finished her wine and set her glass on the counter. "I've got to run. Watson is probably waiting for me."

"Oh, so there's a boyfriend?" Lee called after her.

She shrugged and headed out the door. If Lee was looking for something more, Watson would keep him from misinterpreting her agreeing to go to dinner. She liked Lee, as a possible friend. Besides, one of the rules of investigating was to find out more about others, not give out all your personal information. It was a skill she was still working on.

Meg didn't want to be an open book. Especially when she was working on an investigation, she needed to learn to be more invisible. It said so in her book.

As she left Island Diner, a small blonde waved at her. Meg waved but didn't go back inside.

She'd practice her casual interviewing skills on Lee tomorrow night. Maybe she'd find out more about the food critic. And he could be her second writing friend. Lilly Aster was her first. Even if the famous author didn't know they were friends.

Meg was playing the long game.

She was almost home when she realized who had waved at her as she left the meeting. Irene Olsen. The cruise salesperson who she'd been avoiding since she'd had coffee with her months ago.

The woman was relentless. As Meg hurried up the stairs, her phone buzzed with what was probably the first of many messages she'd get from Irene.

This day wasn't turning out to be one of Meg's favorites.

Chapter 2

Sometimes what you wear says a lot about a person. Check your clothes when you're investigating to make sure the other person doesn't start to look for you.

Mom was still at the bookstore when Meg arrived for her shift the next day. Felicia Gates had been a stay-at-home mom for years, raising her two children, Meg and Junior. Then, when Meg was in high school, she'd bought the local bookstore. Mom seemed happier then, but three years later, Meg woke up to the news that her parents sprung on her and Junior the morning after Meg's graduation party.

Good morning, Congrats on your life achievement. Here's your favorite muffin to celebrate. By the way, your Dad and I are getting divorced.

It shouldn't still hurt, but it did. Her father, Stephen, had remarried and lived with his new wife, Elaine, in Bellevue. Meg got invitations to dinner at their house often, but seeing them together, happy in their new life, made her feel unwanted.

The feeling was stupid, she knew. Especially since she was approaching twenty-seven this year. She let Watson off his leash and tucked her tote in the back room. When she came out, her mom was getting ready to leave. "Hey, I tried to call you yesterday."

"Sorry, I had my phone off." Her mom grabbed the offending phone and tucked it in her purse. "What did you need?"

"I wanted to see if you had that list of local authors for me. I know Skyler Johnson and Lilly, of course, but you said there were others?" Meg glanced at the list of sold books her mom kept in a notebook so they could reorder. "You haven't been very busy today."

"No, walk-in customers were slow." Mom put her purse over her shoulder and held out a task list. "I'll get that list to you on Friday unless I have it on my laptop at home. Make sure to do a bank drop sometime today or tomorrow. Just put the receipt in my box."

Meg didn't understand why her mother was rushing out. "Don't you have dinner with Aunt Melody tonight?"

Her mom shook her head as she looked at her watch. "I rescheduled. I have something else tonight."

Before her mom got to the door, Meg called out, "Oh, and Junior was here to take you to lunch yesterday. He seemed put out that you weren't here waiting for him. He's such a smuck."

"Don't talk about your brother that way." Mom turned back toward Meg. "Wait, why was he here yesterday? Our lunch plans are for next week."

Meg grinned as she leaned over the counter. Her forearms supported her body. "He is going to a conference. With a girl from work. And, Mom? He blushed when he told me about it."

"Your brother is very sensitive. Did he say what her name is?" Her mom stood by the door, watching her.

"Anne, in corporate accounts. He said they had been on a few dates." Meg thought about her brother's history with women. "Maybe he just has a crush. You should ask Dad."

Her mom raised her eyebrows. "Maybe *you* should ask your father. He texted me and said you haven't accepted a dinner invitation from him since you moved home."

"And that's why I don't call him about Junior." Meg sighed when her mom stared at her. "Fine, I'll make plans to have dinner with him soon. So what are you doing tonight?"

"Heading to Seattle," her mom answered. "Sorry, I need to go."

Before Meg could tell her about seeing Irene again, Mom opened the door and hurried out of the store. Junior's question about Mom going to a doctor popped into Meg's head. If her mother was having some sort of procedure where she needed to stay overnight at a hospital, she'd effectively cleared her schedule to do that.

Meg texted Aunt Melody and asked if she knew where her mom was going tonight.

The answer came back quickly. **A visit to Seattle**.

Meg waited for more information. When it didn't come, she asked her what was going on.

This time her aunt's response was even more vague, if possible. **Don't worry, she's fine**.

Whatever was going on with Meg's mom, her aunt was in on it. Before she could ask any more questions, a customer came into the store and Meg was busy until it was time to close and meet up with Lee Anderson.

Dalton texted just before she left the store, asking if she was free tonight. He probably was getting off work soon and wanted to hang out.

She texted back saying she had a dinner meeting with another writer. She added a question to the end. **Tomorrow?**

Sure, I'm beat tonight anyway. Tell Watson I miss him.

Meg loved the way Dalton liked her dog almost as much as he liked her. They'd talked about changing their relationship from friends to dating a few months ago, and besides adding some amazing make-out sessions to their dates, their life felt the same. She knew he was waiting for her to make the first move, but she couldn't push through yet. She hadn't been traumatized when Romain broke off their engagement. Well, after she'd cut up her wedding dress in little squares. Surprisingly, that had helped a lot. Mostly, she'd missed the idea of the man. A man he never was and would never be. Dalton had been the same since he'd arrived on the island as a kid. He wanted stability. And he wanted a life with Meg.

Someday.

She closed the bookstore early and took Watson home. She grabbed a short sweater to throw over the sundress she'd worn to work. The Local Crab was usually chilly inside. She also threw a notebook in her purse just in case Lee had some contacts in nonfiction or ideas on classes. You never knew where you might learn something important for your career. Then she headed back into downtown Bainbridge, enjoying the sunset and cool evening air.

The sidewalks on Winslow Way were busy but not crowded with tourists like they were during the day. People still on the island were looking for somewhere to eat, the shops were closing up, and the air felt soft. Maybe it was the light that made it seem just a little magical, or the lights on the buildings. Flowers bloomed in planters as she walked through town toward the Local Crab, giving off a sweet smell. Meg let the day's busyness and stress flow off of her shoulders as she walked.

Lee Anderson stood outside the restaurant when she walked up, dressed in a suit jacket over a colored T-shirt and jeans. Fancy, but not over the top. He leaned in and hugged her lightly. "Thanks for coming with me. I hate eating alone."

"Well, I know you won't be disappointed in the food here. Emmett is amazing." She nodded at the door. "Should we go inside? Aren't our reservations at eight?"

"Actually, they were at seven thirty and I didn't tell them I was bringing a guest. We'll see how their on-the-fly customer service is here." He opened the door for her and ushered her inside.

She turned around and stopped just inside the doorway. "Are you trying to give yourself something to complain about? By arriving late, we're messing with the kitchen's flow."

"Not my problem." Lee took her arm and turned her around. He dragged her over to the hostess stand. "Anderson, party of two?"

The hostess frowned as she scanned the computer reservation sheet. "I have a seven-thirty pm reservation for one for an Andersonville. That party was a no-show."

"You must have gotten the name wrong." He shrugged.

"Let me see if we can still accommodate you and your guest." She disappeared and went over to talk to a waiter. The guy looked at us, then the two of them went into the kitchen.

"It's hard to use that you got the name wrong excuse anymore. Most restaurants have online reservation systems. Luckily, they don't." He smiled at Meg. "You look lovely tonight."

"I came straight from work," Meg replied. She was starting to regret saying yes to this invitation. "So you write for a newspaper?"

He put his finger to his lips and shook his head. "We can't be showing our hand. We can talk about my career path some other time."

Meg wasn't sure there was going to be another time since tonight seemed to be a complete waste of time. Right now, all she needed to do was make sure everything was great at the restaurant, so Lee didn't have anything to complain about. She thought it might be harder than she expected.

Thirty minutes later, they had been seated at a second table. Lee had complained about the sun over the harbor at the first spot. And that was just the beginning of the train wreck. As they ate their entrees, Lee complained about the temperature of the plate. The appetizer had been served on a chilled plate, and it had been too cold according to Lee. Now the entrée plate was too hot. Maybe dessert would be just right, but she doubted that Lee Anderson had ever even been a child, much less one who had a loving parent to read bedtime stories. He probably had been raised by wolves, not humans who taught their children morality fairy tales.

"I like my pasta," Meg responded to his tirade that went on long enough the plate was probably already cool.

He rolled his eyes. "You aren't trained in culinary expertise. When you throw food in front of most restaurant slobs, they all say it was great."

Meg grabbed her purse and stood. "Lee, I can't continue even pretending that this is a pleasant dinner. You can tell the waiter that I loved everything but I had a family emergency. I hope this isn't a precursor to how the article is going to look."

"You're leaving?" Lee frowned as he looked up at her. "You haven't finished your pasta. And we're going to have dessert."

"Thanks, but I've had enough of the company. This restaurant slob said the food was amazing." Meg walked out of the dining room and past the hostess. She wanted to let them know that Lee was a food critic, but he might not even be one. She'd taken his word for it at the writers' meeting. This was one mistake she wouldn't make again.

A woman grabbed her arm on the way out. "Meg, how are you?"

She turned to see Irene Olsen standing next to her with a guy. They were on their way into the restaurant just as Meg was storming out.

Man, her luck was really tanking tonight.

She smiled at both of them. "Hi, Irene."

The man held his hand out. "I'm Mark Thomason. Irene's date for the evening."

"Nice to meet you, Mark. Meg Gates." She shook his hand.

Then she laughed as he made the required "Gates" joke. She felt a headache coming on. "Sorry, I'm just heading out."

"Oh, well, I hope we can talk at the next Island Writers meeting. I saw you there last night. Didn't you hear me call out?" Irene pushed her bottom lip out, a testament to Meg's rude behavior.

"Sorry, I didn't. Watson hasn't been feeling well lately so I don't like leaving him for long. That's why I need to go now," Meg lied. She felt kind of bad, but after having a disastrous dinner with Lee, all she wanted was to get home. And if you gave Irene an opening, she'd talk for hours about the cruises she marketed. She should have just told Dalton to come get her and they could have gone out on his boat.

As she moved away, Irene called after her. "We need to talk about your mom one of these days."

Meg waved and headed down the street. Irene probably wanted Meg to buy her mom a cruise for her birthday. Irene's mom was in the same women's group at church and according to Mom, she was always talking about how Irene was sending her to Mexico all the time. Under her breath, Meg muttered, "Probably sometime, never."

As Meg walked home, she hit something with her foot and knocked over a sign in front of the city hall. Groaning, she stopped and righted the sign, reading it aloud. "GOOD LUCK THURSDAY TO OUR ISLAND'S SENIOR PICKLEBALL TEAMS THAT MADE IT TO REGIONALS."

A woman passing by grinned and said, "I love Pickleball. It's such a great workout. Did you know it was invented here on the island?"

"Sorry, no. I don't play," Meg admitted as she smiled and walked away.

Meg needed a restart. She'd go home and pull the covers over her head. Tomorrow had to be better. She'd just ignore both Lee and Irene at the next writers' group meeting. She sent good wishes to whoever was playing Pickleball and hoped her wishes might add some karma coins to her balance.

She needed them.

The next morning before leaving the apartment, Meg double-checked the supplies in Watson's tote bag for the day. They'd be at the store longer, so she didn't want him to run out of anything. She decided to head down to A Taste of Magic, her friend Natasha Jones's bakery, for coffee and a chocolate croissant for breakfast. She deserved the treat because she hadn't had any dessert last night. Besides, she needed to vent about how horrible last night had been. She was still upset about Lee's behavior. And, if she thought about it, worried about his review for the Local Crab. Emmett Harding was a top-rated chef and a nice guy. Maybe she'd warn Dalton tonight since he knew Emmett better than she did.

Natasha brought over coffee and croissants for two as well as a roll and water for Watson. "Why are you out so early? I thought you'd be working on your tasks for Lilly today."

"I should be, but Mom changed my hours. She has me covering the bookstore all day today. I should have some time in between customers to work on the tasks Lilly left for me." Meg broke off a bite of the roll and fed it to Watson. "I'm so mad that I agreed to meet up with another writer last night at the Local Crab. I could have been done with it by now."

"You went on a date?" Natasha looked around and lowered her voice. "Without Dalton?"

"It wasn't a date. This guy needed someone to eat with him for his restaurant review. I didn't know when I said yes that he was going to spend all night trashing Emmett and the restaurant. He was horrible." Meg rubbed her face. "Now, I have to tell Dalton about it so Emmett won't be blindsided."

"He's going to think it was a date." Natasha broke off a piece of croissant and ate it while she stared at Meg.

"No, he's not. I told him I was having dinner with another writer. I was hoping to pick his brain about writing for newspapers but all he wanted to talk about was the imaginary errors the waitstaff were making, how the plates were the wrong temperature, and that he hated everything he ordered." Meg broke open the croissant and took a bite. "This is amazing."

"You would be a horrible food critic. You like food too much." Natasha smiled as the bell over the door sounded. "I've got to get Serena to handle this. She said she'd cover the front while you were here, but she was taking out the last batch of bread. Hold that thought."

Instead, Meg called after her, "I like good food too much."

The woman who had just walked into the bakery smiled at her and gave her a thumbs up, agreeing with her statement.

When Natasha came back, Meg's croissant and Watson's roll were gone. "Anyway, Dalton's coming over to the bookstore tonight to help me close. Do you want to grab some food, and we can eat and talk before?"

"I actually have a real date. And not just as a placeholder for a food critic." Natasha leaned her head down. "I met him here. He came in every day for a week until I said I'd go to dinner with him. He's taking me to some steakhouse in Seattle."

"Oooh, fancy." Meg was happy for her friend. Natasha didn't date a lot. She had spent a lot of years getting the bakery going, but now she had Serena, who baked for her in the early mornings, and Candi, who worked afternoons so Natasha could have a normal life. Now, it looked like she might be getting one. "Now I'm jealous. Maybe we should double date? I can talk Dalton into going."

"On the first date? Are you kidding? I don't know if I like this guy enough yet. Give me a few weeks, and maybe then we'll set something up. If it lasts that long." She crossed her fingers. "I really think we have a spark, though. And he's so cute."

Meg and Natasha talked about her date, including what she was going to wear, for a few more minutes. Then Meg finished her coffee and stood. "I better go open the bookstore. It was nice having time together. We haven't just sat down to talk for ages."

"You're always off with Dalton. Or working," Natasha reminded her as she hugged Meg. "Wish me luck tonight. And if I disappear, I wrote his name off his credit card and put it in the cash register. Just in case."

"Better safe than sorry," Meg replied as she grabbed Watson's leash and his tote bag. She left the bakery and was already opening the door to the bookstore when she realized Natasha hadn't told Meg her date's name.

Chapter 3

Going undercover is a lot like dating. You leave out the warts until you know you want this stranger to know your secrets.

At exactly ten thirty, Meg decided that the day shift at the bookstore was not her favorite job. She'd had three customers, two that were just looking and one homeschool family with a kid who took out every book on the picture bookshelf before finally making his decision. Watson had hidden behind the counter as soon as he'd heard the first yell from the kid, who had to show his mom every book. Maybe it was just a boy thing since his sister had come in, chosen her book, and sat on the couch reading while her brother destroyed the kids' section of the store.

She hadn't brought a lunch, so she ordered something for pickup, closed the store with a BE RIGHT BACK sign and headed down the street with Watson to get a sandwich from the Bay Bistro. The restaurant's hostess came outside to greet them as soon as she walked into the small patio area.

Ever since the time someone had untied Watson's leash when she went into Island Diner, she'd avoided going any place where she had to go inside to pick up her food. She didn't want him to get hurt.

While she was waiting, she scanned the community bulletin board. Maybe she could join a class or group. She was taking a required English class on Monday mornings, but most of the people in it were younger and lived on campus. Meg saw an advertisement for a tarot reading class starting in two weeks. And an announcement looking for more Pickleball players for a Tuesday morning league. That flyer had FREE LESSONS on the top. And a picture of a match with two older players smiling and posing with their paddles by the net.

The picture was really fuzzy, but Meg swore the woman in the shot looked like her mom. She took a picture of the flyer and was about to text it to her mother when she heard someone behind her.

"I tried to join a league but never could find a partner to play with," the hostess said as she brought out a bag with Meg's order. "If you decide you want to play, let me know."

"Are you available on Tuesday mornings?" Meg thought it might be fun. And she certainly needed the exercise since both of her jobs were sedentary unless her mom had her shelving books or cleaning.

"Most weeks. They play from eight to ten. Most of my friends are still asleep at that time. My shift starts at eleven thirty. I'm Brooke, by the way. Brooke Hastings. I think I saw you at the Local Crab last night with Anderson. I work server shifts there when I can get them." She took out her pen and an order pad she had in her purse. "This is my number. If you want to join, we can start next week. The guy that runs the league at the community center is hoping to find another team or so."

"Sorry about the scene at the restaurant." Meg decided to make a quick decision. How hard could this be? She ripped the paper in half and asked to use Brooke's pen. "I'm in. Here's my number. I'm Meg Gates. Do we just show up on Tuesday at eight? At the community center?"

"Probably, unless we get the late game. I'll call you as soon as Derby tells me the schedule. He'll send out one too, so I'll need your email to give it to him. This will be fun." She smiled down at Watson. "I wish you could come with us, but the community center doesn't let dogs inside the courts."

Meg added her email address. "I'm looking forward to this. How long is a season?"

"Nine weeks. Then we'll be in the fall league. It runs twice that long, if you still want to play. It's a good excuse to get out of the house on a rainy day." She glanced over at the door. A line had formed. She reached for the paper and her pen. "Sorry, work calls. See you Tuesday. Oh, and enjoy your lunch. I love the turkey avocado."

Meg tucked the paper with Brooke's number into her pants. Perhaps Natasha or Dalton might want to substitute, or they could even form their own team for fall. Between the two of them, someone should be available to be her doubles partner on a Tuesday morning. As long as her mom didn't need her at the bookstore that morning. Or her new fall school schedule had her in class.

"Tomorrow's worry," Meg said to Watson as he sniffed the bag. "Let's go back to the bookstore and eat lunch."

She'd show her mom the picture of her doppelganger when she saw her next. And tell her she was joining this league. Mom was always pushing Meg to do more things on the island and to meet more people. Like she had time.

As soon as she got back, she blocked out the time on the next nine Tuesdays on her calendar, added Brooke's number to her contacts, and wrote it in her planner. Then she dug into her sandwich, hoping she had enough time before the next wave of customers from the ferry arrived.

Later that afternoon, Dalton called her. "What time are you off today?"

"It's been dead most of the day, so I was thinking I could

sneak out early. Maybe six?" Meg closed her laptop. She'd had time to finish and send off her work to Jolene, Lilly Aster's personal assistant. Now that Lilly knew Meg better and trusted her more, Meg had regular tasks to complete each week in addition to the odds and ends that the author sent her way. Lilly had even been hinting that by next year, she might need Meg full-time. Meg's mom would probably love it if she cut her hours at the bookstore. She felt like her mother had created Meg's job to keep her on the island.

"I'll come by and get you and the mutt then. Can we drop him off at the apartment? I've been dying to eat at this restaurant in Seattle for months. Emmett got us in with a seven-thirty reservation. They had a cancelation."

"Come at five thirty then. I'll need a little time to dress up if this is an actual date." Meg was glad that Natasha had bailed on Meg's suggestion to eat all together at the bookstore. Rescinding the offer would have been awkward.

"No heels. We'll be walking from the ferry to the restaurant," Dalton reminded her. "I've got to run. See you later."

When Dalton arrived, she and Watson were ready. She'd explained to her dog that he was staying home alone for a while, but he didn't seem to worry about it. A full day at the bookstore had worn him out. Especially that one little boy. Watson seemed nervous around kids. They moved fast, they were loud, and they tended to grab at him, rather than gently pet. Meg thought it better that sometimes Watson just stayed home.

Meg told Dalton about her day as they walked the few blocks to the apartment. Then as they were climbing the stairs, she asked how his day had been.

"Fine." He shrugged as he answered. Dalton worked for the Washington Ferry Service since he left the Coast Guard. He worked on the ferry that ran from Bainbridge to Seattle. Usually, he had a fun story or two about his day. Today, he seemed less enthused. "Some days are just blah. I don't get a lot of time to talk to the ferry passengers, even when I'm a clicker. I've been waiting for this promotion for a while, but they haven't had an opening yet. I'm beginning to wonder if they ever will. And if I'll even be considered."

"Your boss loves you. He's always saying how happy he is when he can send you to a new task without worrying about how you'll do it. It just takes time." Meg unlocked the door and handed Watson's leash to Dalton before he could ask what she knew about moving up in an organization since she hadn't done it. Ever. "I'll hurry and change. Can you feed him and make sure he has water?"

"He'll probably have to go outside after he eats." Dalton unclicked the leash and headed to the kitchen. "If you're still getting ready after he's done, I'll take him out again."

"You're the best," Meg called from the bedroom. She thought about her failed relationship with Romain. He wouldn't have even agreed to feed Watson, much less been concerned about him needing a walk before they left. In fact, Romain would have griped about her even asking him. How many times had he said to her, "It's your dog."

A few minutes later, she was ready. Watson had eaten, been walked, and his favorite channel was running on the television. He and Dalton were watching a show, sitting together on the couch. Meg smiled as she watched Dalton rubbing Watson's ears as they sat there. They were two peas in a pod. She glanced over to the water dish, and it was full. And it looked like Dalton had cleaned the dish and the area around the water dish where Watson tended to drip water as he drank.

Dalton was a keeper. And Watson loved him.

"I'm ready if I can break up the bromance," Meg said, then kissed the top of Watson's head.

Dalton stood and rubbed Watson's belly. "Sorry dude, your mother is making me leave for a stupid dinner."

"Whatever." Meg laughed as she slipped on a light jacket. She'd worn a favorite midi skirt with a light sweater on top, but she knew when they were walking, she'd need the extra layer. Even with boots and tights.

"You look amazing." Dalton took her keys and locked the door. She tucked them into her crossover and zipped the pocket closed. She had her wallet, keys, and her phone. Just in case.

"It feels good to dress up. I don't think I have worn this in forever." The outfit was one of her favorites, but Romain had thought it too casual and called it her fortune-teller outfit. She gently tapped her wrist, a reminder to banish all thoughts of he-who-must-not-be-named. She rarely thought of him, but when she did, it was usually a comparison to how good her life was now. "Did I tell you that I heard Rachel dumped Romain last month? I need to follow up and see if that's true."

"Uh oh. Is this your way of telling me he's been looking to reconnect? Don't tell me he was who you had dinner with last night," Dalton asked, looking at her, uneasiness filling his face.

"God, no. Besides, it's a rumor and it's Rachel. They're probably back together by now." Meg probably shouldn't have brought it up, especially since Dalton had said this was an official date. She just liked sharing every part of her life with him. "I went to the Local Crab with another writer I met at the writers' group. It was a disaster. I'm glad you brought it up. I wanted to let you know so you could warn Emmett."

"Warn Emmett? I'm confused. Was dinner less than satisfactory? I always love whatever he makes." They started down the road to the ferry terminal.

"The food was great. The dinner companion, less so. He's a food critic and told me if I'd go as his plus one, he'd pay for dinner. Or his paper would. And I thought it would be a nice opportunity to talk about writing. Boy, was I wrong." Meg pulled her coat around her. She didn't know if she was cold or just shivering from the memory of dinner with Lee.

"Are you okay? He didn't try anything, did he?" Dalton lowered his voice, the tone concerned.

"Oh, no. He was just so horrible about the food, where they

sat us—he even had us arrive thirty minutes late, which I didn't know, and he used a variation of his name, saying the hostess must have gotten it wrong on the reservation. Then he made them move us because of the setting sun. I offered to switch seats, but he wanted to see how they handled the request.

"After that it was a Goldilocks story. Plates were first too cold, then too hot—I didn't stick around to see if he liked anything, but I doubt he did. I felt sorry for our waiter." Meg looked around as she and Dalton paused on the bridge to the ferry. A small line of people was going into Seattle tonight. "I think his review is going to be mean. I'm sorry I even went with him. Tell Emmett it wasn't my fault."

Dalton hugged her. "Serves you right for going to dinner there without me. I love Emmett's place. I'll mention that a review might be coming. What was your date's name again?"

"Not a date," Meg clarified. Again. "Anyway, his name is Lee Anderson."

"Seriously? You didn't know him?" Now Dalton looked amused. "He's trashed most of the island restaurants he's reviewed. It's a kind of joke around here. Emmett will think he's finally been accepted into the local fold. Natasha got a three-star from the guy and thought she was getting off easy. And he gave no stars to the farmers market. The mayor was going to ban the guy from even getting off the ferry, but my boss told him he couldn't. Not unless he wanted to get your uncle to arrest him."

The line started moving. They didn't need tickets to walk on at the Bainbridge Island side of the ferry, but the department still tracked the number of riders. Dalton waved at the clicker standing by the entrance. "Hey, Tom."

They went to the front of the ferry and found a seat inside. Meg took off her coat and set it in her lap. "I'll be glad when I know all the islander things. Every time I do something, I wind up with a jerk or doing something only a tourist would do. So, what do you know about Pickleball?"

Dalton shook his head. "You are the master of changing subjects. Is this for your guidebook?"

"Pickleball? What does that have to do with investigation techniques?" She didn't tell him that she hadn't been keeping her weekly writing appointment with herself. She'd told Lilly last week, and she'd told her it was normal. And to keep going to her writers' meetings. Which had led to the disaster with Lee. "Never mind. I joined a league and am wondering if I made a mistake."

"It's a big thing here in the area. Pickleball started on Bainbridge Island. Did you know that?" Dalton went on to tell her what he knew about the history of Pickleball on the island. "The local community center is probably where you'd play. They have leagues running all the time. A lot of older people join them."

"You're calling me old." Meg poked him in the side with her finger. "If that's so, my partner and I should kill our league because we're both under thirty."

He took her hand. "I didn't mean that. I'm sure there are different age groups. I'm glad you're trying out new things. With my work schedule, I never know what days I'm getting off."

They talked a little more about Pickleball and about Dalton's job. As they got ready to disembark the ferry, she looked up at him. "You could go back to school and get a degree in something else. Dad would hire you in a heartbeat if you went into accounting."

"You must have been talking to Junior about me." He waved at another crew member as they walked through the crowd. "He probably tells me that same thing once a month now, if not more."

"How was your lunch with my brother?" Meg wondered if Junior had told his best friend about this Anne girl.

"You're fishing about Junior's dating life and I've been sworn to secrecy." He nodded toward the corner where they would cross the road. "If we hurry, we can make the light."

She smiled as they joined the crowd crossing the street. When Dalton turned her left, she let herself wonder where they were going that Emmett would have contacts to get them in so fast. Or maybe Dalton had been working on this for a while. She wouldn't put it past him. He was thoughtful. "So, does he like Anne a lot? Is she pretty? She's probably smart. My brother always loved smart girls."

"What part of confidentiality don't you get? I think I should call Lilly Aster and let her know you're a loose cannon and she shouldn't trust you with any book secrets." His threat came with a smile. "Or I'll call Jolene. She's more tightly wound than Lilly."

"You think?" Meg laughed and as she did, Dalton steered her through a doorway. She found herself in a large hotel lobby. People were sitting around, drinks in their hands. A registration desk was in front of them. "Dalton, I don't know what to say. You know I can't leave Watson overnight."

"Ha, ha." Dalton walked past registration, and then they turned down a hallway. "This way is just warmer than walking to the street entrance. It's chilly tonight."

"And that's why I brought the coat. It's supposed to be close to seventy this weekend." She put her arm in his and stepped closer. "This is fun. We should come to Seattle more."

"Between our work schedules and your classes, I'm surprised we even fit tonight's adventure in." He looked down at her as he replied. "Besides, I don't care where we are. Just as long as we do it together."

"You're sweet," she said as they turned into the restaurant. The table was dark, and candlelight sparkled on the tables.

Meg thought even the walls were painted black with a tinge of midnight blue. It looked like a clear night sky. "Wow."

The hostess smiled and nodded. "We get that a lot. What's the name on the reservation?"

"Dalton Hamilton." He stepped closer, taking Meg's coat as the hostess scanned her computer screen. He handed it to the woman at the coat check and got a ticket.

"Mr. Hamilton and Miss Gates, we have a table near the window. It's quiet over there." The hostess smiled and started walking them to the table.

As they passed through the dining room, Meg recognized someone sitting at a table. She paused at the table with the man and woman sipping wine. She should have kept walking, but she just couldn't.

"Mom? What are you doing here?"

CHAPTER 4

Sometimes you find out information you'd rather not know. It's all part of the job.

After they were set at their table, Meg's phone buzzed with a text message. It was from her mom.

Don't freak out and don't get the wrong idea. We'll talk tomorrow.

Meg looked over at the table where she met her mom's gaze. She nodded and put her phone away.

Dalton saw the exchange. "I can't believe I'm saying this after all the trouble Emmett went to getting our reservation, but if you want to go, we can."

Meg shook her head and turned away from where her mom was eating dinner with a man who was a complete stranger to Meg. "No, I'm good. Sorry about the outburst. You didn't need drama added to your night."

"Being with you is always an adventure," Dalton teased. "Let's just enjoy the meal. You can say all the things you want to say on the way home on the ferry. But for now, what do you want to drink? Wine, a cocktail, coffee?"

"I'll take a glass of wine. Chardonnay, please. And a soda water. With lemon. It's all about staying hydrated. A rule that the bonfire regulars should start implementing." She smiled at him, pushing all the questions about her mom out of her head. She could deal with them later. Except . . . "I'm just going to say this one thing. I was worried she was in the city having some sort of surgery, and instead, I find she's been spending time with a man. It's disconcerting for a daughter."

"You had to realize she'd start dating sometime." Dalton rubbed the top of her hand. "Your dad's been married for years now."

"I know." Meg took a deep breath. "Let's stop talking about it and focus on dinner. Did Emmett have recommendations on what to order?"

They ordered appetizers and the next time Meg looked over at her mom, the table was empty. She turned back and saw Dalton watching her.

"They left about ten minutes ago," he filled her in. "The man she was with paid the check and then held out a hand to assist her. He seems nice."

Meg shook her head, chuckling. "I thought we were going to ignore them."

"You needed to ignore them. Your parents practically raised me once Junior and I became friends. I wanted to make sure he was treating Felicia right." He shrugged. "Sue me, I'm a nice guy."

Meg sipped her wine as she watched him. Dalton was a nice guy. He liked and respected her parents. And he was good to her. How come she'd never seen him in this light before now?

As they rode home on the ferry, she took out her phone and texted.

"I thought your mom said you'd talk tomorrow," Dalton said from the bench across from her where she'd thought he'd been sleeping.

She looked up from the text and saw him watching her. "I didn't text my mom. I texted Junior. Maybe he knows who she was out with."

"Isn't he at a conference?"

Meg tucked her phone away. "He leaves tomorrow, I think. Once I started asking him about Anne, he clammed up. Cupid's been busy this week."

"Oh?" Dalton's eyes twinkled against the backdrop of the night sky from the window.

"I just meant that Junior and now Mom are dating. Or kind of dating." She blushed as she turned her head to look out the window.

Flashing lights at the ferry terminal caught her eye. "Uh oh, something's happened," Meg said, trying to see through the smudged glass.

Dalton leaped up and leaned toward the wind. "Stay here, I'll be right back."

He hurried upstairs to see what was going on. When he came back, the ferry was beginning to dock at the terminal.

"A guy was reported sleeping in his car, so the security guards went out to the parking lot to check on him. He wasn't sleeping." Dalton lowered his voice as he added, "It looks like a suicide."

Dalton walked her home. The sidewalk near the parking lot was closed, so they were diverted to the other side, with security directing foot traffic around cars coming off the ferry. Since it was late, the ferry was almost empty, but Dalton kept an arm around Meg until they started up the hill toward her apartment.

Uncle Troy's truck was gone and the lights were still on at Aunt Melody's house. Meg heard Watson barking upstairs. "I need to take him out. Do you want to come in, have some coffee?"

Dalton shook his head. "I've got an early shift tomorrow. And with this new investigation happening, tomorrow's going to be a zoo with the press. Thank you for coming to dinner with me. I know, it wasn't what you were expecting."

"Life is always filled with surprises." Meg looked over and saw that her aunt was turning off the lights in her house. She must have seen Meg and Dalton return. "I need to see Lilly tomorrow morning anyway, so I guess I should get some sleep."

He kissed her gently, then took off for home. Meg went upstairs and got Watson on a leash. Then she walked him around the block before heading home. It gave her time to think. She felt bad about whoever had died at the ferry parking lot, but seeing her mother dating had *really* thrown her for a loop. Why hadn't she just told Meg? She thought they were close, but no, Mom would rather have Meg worry that she was sick or dying than just tell her she was going on a date.

The guy had been handsome in an everyman way. At least from what she'd seen before she'd realized his date was her mom. With dark hair sprinkled with gray, he appeared to be tall, and he had a nice face. He could have been a hundred different men if Meg was forced to try to pick him out of a lineup. At first, she hadn't recognized the well-dressed, laughing woman as her mother. She'd even been wearing makeup. And she knew that had to be a new dress.

Watson barked and she realized they were back at the garage. "Are you ready to go to bed? I know you've probably been sleeping all the time I've been gone."

All Watson had heard was *bed* and he started pulling on the leash toward the stairs. She followed him upstairs and got ready, trying not to think about her mom. She turned on her alarm and tried to sleep, waiting for the next day when Mom said she'd tell her what was going on. *Maybe he's her lawyer or something.* Meg's last thought before she fell asleep calmed her.

The next morning, she was surprised to see her mom coming up the stairs with a paper bag. She opened the door and greeted her. "Coffee's on. I didn't expect you this early."

"I know you're going over to Lilly's soon, but I wanted to

explain," Mom said as she greeted Watson. She rubbed his head as she asked him, "Have you been outside?"

"I don't know what he's going to say, but yes, we took a short walk this morning after I got out of the shower." Meg set a freshly poured cup on the table. "I don't have any creamer, but there's sugar."

"Black's fine," Mom said as she set the bag on the table. "Pastries from Natasha's. That girl has a strong customer base. I had to wait in line to get those."

"Plates or napkins?" Meg asked as she refilled her cup. She knew they were both avoiding talking about the real reason for her mother's early-morning visit. When her mom said napkins, Meg finally sat down and asked, "How was your dinner?"

"The restaurant is wonderful, the food amazing, but I'm thinking you're more interested in my dinner companion." Meg's mom sat, then sipped her coffee. "It's new, so I didn't tell you. We've been friends for a while, and he's divorced. His ex-wife and daughter live on the island, so it's complicated."

"Mom, you didn't have an affair, did you?" Meg asked, then regretted the question. She didn't want to know.

"Heavens, no. We know each other through the Pickleball league. Like I said, we've been friends for years. He's a big reader, so he came to the bookstore a lot. After the divorce, he'd stay and have coffee if it was slow. Then last year, he invited me to be his doubles partner. We won the Senior division this week. Last night's dinner was a celebration." She opened the bag and took out an apple turnover. "And our first real date."

"So you didn't stay together." Meg felt her face flush. "I thought maybe you were getting outpatient surgery or something. Then I saw you and him, and my mind went somewhere else."

"In the gutter, apparently. No, I am not sleeping with Derby." Mom paused before she continued. "However, it's likely we will. And it's none of your business."

"Like Dalton being a friend wasn't your business when you told him to leave me alone?" Meg immediately felt bad for pointing out her mom's meddling. Water and bridge. "Anyway, Derby? Is that his last name?"

Now Mom's face turned scarlet. "No, it's Derby Olsen. He attends my church, or he did."

Meg tried to remember seeing him in church or seeing her mother talking to anyone at church. "Wait, Olsen? Please don't tell me he's Irene Olsen's dad."

Mom nodded. "Yes. And before you say anything, Irene is a sweet girl."

"Irene is a bad salesman who doesn't know the word *no*." Meg had been avoiding Irene since one get-together at the coffee shop. "Is that why she's been trying to talk to me? She knows about you two?"

"Irene doesn't know, and neither does her mother. Derby is telling them about us this weekend. We want to make sure there's no confusion." Mom tore off part of her croissant. "We were going to wait until a few months had gone by, but I told him I had to tell you."

"After I caught you at dinner," Meg replied, looking at the clock. "Sorry, I need to run. Thank you for being honest with me."

"Meg, I know seeing your parents as people can be difficult," Mom started, but stopped when Meg stood and put her cup in the sink.

"I'm not mad that you're dating," Meg interrupted. She stood there, staring at her mom, her arms crossed. "I just wish you'd told me. Like I said, I need to go. I'm sure Aunt Melody's waiting to hear all about your date. She knew where you were, right?"

Her mother turned bright pink.

"Yeah, I thought so." Meg grabbed her jacket and her tote. She filled Watson's water dish and turned on the television for him. Then she held the door open for her mom. "I'll see you at three at the bookstore."

"Meg," her mom started, then stopped. She stood and dumped out most of her coffee. Then she walked over to Meg and kissed her on the cheek. "I'll see you later today."

Meg took her time locking the door, letting her mom get down the stairs and go into Aunt Melody's house. She was being childish, but it hurt that her mom hadn't trusted her enough to tell her about what was going on in her private life. Not a peep.

As she biked to Summer Break, Lilly Aster's house on Puget Sound, she realized that the woman in the pictures playing Pickleball was her mom. Now Meg was supposed to play too. Would they run into each other? Or did the different leagues play at different times? And what was she supposed to say to Irene? What if they got married? Irene would be her stepsister.

The questions kept haunting her as she pedaled harder and harder. Finally, she reached Lilly's and pushed the thoughts away. She had to be in work mode. Lilly deserved her best. Especially the way she was paying her.

Jolene, Lilly Aster's assistant and house manager, swung open the door. "Okay, spill it. What do you know?"

Meg's eyes widened as she thought about her mom's confession less than an hour before. Bainbridge Island was a small town, but Jolene couldn't have heard gossip about Mom and this Derby guy yet, could she? "Know about what?"

"The guy they found in the parking lot. First, I heard it was a suicide, but now they're thinking it was murder? The news crews have been camped out at the ferry for hours, waiting for your uncle to make a statement. Are you sure you don't know anything?" Jolene held the door open as Meg came inside.

"Dalton and I saw the police lights last night as we were coming home from Seattle, but everyone on the ferry said it was a suicide. That was about ten. Other than that, I don't know anything. I have a few things going on," Meg admitted.

Jolene narrowed her eyes. "For someone who is supposedly writing a book about investigating, you're not very nosy."

"The day's young," Lilly Aster said from where she stood at the door to her office. "Jolene, stop browbeating Meg and bring us some fresh coffee and some of those muffins. Meg, let's talk about the next release. I need your input on this tour schedule."

Meg followed Lilly into her office, grateful for being rescued from Jolene's inquisition. "I'm happy to help, but I don't know much about touring a book."

"Sure you do, you just don't know what you know yet." Lilly sat down at her desk and moved her computer so Meg could see the screen. "I want you to give me three to four different tour options. Look at where I've been in the last five years. Jolene should have the number of books sold, or at least the attendees, at each stop. She might have already given that information to you for the bookstore list. Then, map out a possible tour schedule, lumping places together so I'm not flying back and forth. I want three different choices for the tour to last ten, twelve, or fifteen days. If it's the longer one, please schedule a few days at home where I can breathe in the middle. I can do ten without coming home, but much longer than that, I tend to get sick."

Meg was writing everything down in her notebook. Lilly went on about alternating stops, but if one event had done extremely well, she wanted to include that bookstore in the new tour. Meg asked some clarifying questions and then glanced at her notes. "What about hotels? Do you want to fly? Rent a car? Taxis?"

Josh Aster came into the room and walked around the desk to kiss Lilly. "We want to fly, but if you find a nice, romantic bed and breakfast back east where we can hole up for a weekend, that would be nice too. Maybe a beach? Oh, and maybe we can hit some major league baseball games while we're out?"

"Don't listen to him. If he comes with me, he'll be locked in our hotel room finishing his book that's due the end of the month during my release." Lilly smiled up at the man now standing behind her.

"Maybe I'll already be done and in my creative development time. Authors have to fill the well, you know that." He wrapped his arms around her, sitting on the arm of her desk chair.

"There's no way you'll be done because you keep bothering me when I'm trying to work. I know you're not getting your words in." She glanced at her watch. "It's only ten. Have you even started writing?"

He kissed the top of Lilly's head. "This woman's a hard taskmaster, Meg. You need to be careful what you agree to. I'm going back to my little office without this amazing view and writing until my fingers bleed. Will that make you happy, princess?"

"Extremely. If you start bleeding, Jolene has Band-Aids." She smiled as he left the room. Then she rolled her eyes. "I can't believe I let this happen again. He's so needy. Seeing him once a week was fun. Then, I could get back to work. Now, he's everywhere."

"I heard that," Josh called from the hallway.

"Whatever," she called back, laughing. "Anyway, let me know what you come up with and we'll talk again next week. How's your writing going?"

"Slow. But I've blocked out time and I've been writing at least five times a week. Or I had until the last few weeks. Taking that class really cut into my free time, especially since it's on campus. And next quarter, I'll be taking more classes." Meg didn't want to think about what her schedule might look like starting in August. "I'm not complaining, I'm just adjusting."

"Good catch." Lilly opened her planner and wrote down their next meeting. "How's the social media working? The posts you're making are really cute. Are they getting engagement?"

"Yes, a lot. Do you want to see stats weekly? Or is once a month good?" Meg explained what she'd been seeing using a broad brush, comparing the different social media sites.

"Since you just took over this task, send me weekly reports. Next Monday is fine for the first one. I'd like to see if they're effective. And once you get comfortable with that process, I'd love to hand off my newsletter. Of course, I'd increase your hours when that happens."

As Meg and Lilly finished up their discussion, Meg watched the boats on the sound. Josh was right. Lilly's office was beautiful. They said their goodbyes and Meg left with a good idea of what she needed to get done that week. How long it might take her was the question mark. She didn't have plans this weekend, and Dalton was working, so she'd block off time then.

Somehow, Meg's life had gone from only being focused on planning a wedding that didn't happen to running two jobs, going to school, spending time with friends and family, and maybe a boyfriend. Not to mention the time she spent with Watson. Or the book.

She liked this life.

Her phone rang and she glanced at the number before answering. Uncle Troy. She stood by her bike and put her tote in her basket. She needed to answer it. Was she being chastised for the way she ended things with Mom today? Only one way to find out. "What's going on, Uncle Troy?"

"Tell me why you stormed out of the Local Crab on Wednesday night. And why you were on a date with my victim, Lee Anderson. Tell me you didn't dump Dalton. I liked that kid."

Chapter 5

People tell you things without realizing what else they're saying. Don't miss these opportunities to find out more.

Meg glanced at the window of Summer Break where Jolene was watching her. She smiled and waved as she answered her uncle's questions. "One, I wasn't on a date. Two, Lee Anderson was out to do a hatchet job on Emmett's restaurant and was causing the problems he was going to put into his column. And three, did you say victim? Was Lee the suicide?"

"Not a suicide, unless he lived long enough after shooting himself to hide the gun somewhere not on the ferry terminal property. And the coroner says that is unlikely. I take it you've heard about the incident?"

"Dalton and I saw the police lights coming home from Seattle last night. The rumor going around the ferry was that it was suicide." Meg repeated the information she'd given Jolene. She hadn't liked Lee Anderson, especially after having dinner with him at the Local Crab, but that didn't mean someone should have killed him. "This is awful."

"So did you know him well?"

Meg shook her head, even though her uncle couldn't see her. "I met him this week at my writers' meeting. He invited me to have dinner. I thought we'd talk about nonfiction writing and how he got on with the paper. Then he was a total jerk at the restaurant."

"Okay, so people saw you together at this writers' meeting and the restaurant. Were you with him any other time?"

"Besides the writers' meeting? We sat at the same table, but no. Like I said, it wasn't a date. I just wanted to find out more about nonfiction writing. Dalton knows, if you're worried about that." Meg noticed that Jolene was still watching her from the window.

"Dear, your love life is none of my business. I'm trying to keep you off the suspect list." He said something that was muffled and Meg assumed he had his hand over the phone. "Where are you? Home?"

"No, I'm just leaving Summer Break. Then I'll be home. I work the bookstore at three."

He sighed. "Just don't leave the island until I get your official statement."

Meg didn't realize for a few seconds that he'd hung up. She tucked the phone into her tote, then got on the bike. Jolene was still at the window. Meg smiled and waved again as she pedaled off.

Today wasn't going as well as she'd hoped.

By the time she got to the bookstore, word had gotten out. Both Dalton and Natasha had texted her, and they planned to meet for dinner after Dalton got off work. He'd started his texts with **Are you okay?**

Meg stared at the message. It wasn't like she and Lee had even been friends. She'd only met him a few days ago. She assured Dalton she was more than okay and that she'd talk more tonight. Hopefully, the store would be slow and they'd have time to eat the take-out Chinese she would order later.

Her mom was helping a customer when Meg arrived, so she got Watson settled and her stuff tucked away. She poured herself a cup of coffee from the pot, wondering if it was one too many but not caring. When she came back out to the front, her mom was sitting on the couch, waiting for her.

"Come talk to me." Mom patted the seat next to her. "I want to clear the air. I didn't think this morning went well."

"There's nothing much to say. You were dating someone and didn't feel it was my business. Yet when I came home you basically strong-armed Dalton into handling me like I didn't have a mind of my own." Meg set her cup down on the table and then sat next to her mother. "Oh, and you told Aunt Melody everything, so she had to lie to me when I was worried about you."

"I never told her to lie." Mom sighed. "Look, I admit I handled this wrong. I was scared to tell you. You hate your dad because of Elaine. I didn't want this to be something that came between us, especially if there wasn't anything there. But I have to admit there is. I like Derby. He's kind to me. He's smart. And he makes me laugh."

Meg rubbed her face. "I'm being a brat, aren't I?"

"A little, but I'll take my share of the blame. I should have told you what was happening. We were at a tournament in Seattle. We all got separate rooms, well, except for the married couples, of course. Derby and I took first in our division. We get to go to Nationals in Atlanta, next month."

Meg smiled at the image of her mom playing Pickleball. She opened her phone and found the picture she'd taken. "You and Derby are on the league flyer. I guess you must be good at it."

"They did not!" Mom took my phone and stared at the snap of the flyer. "This was after a match, even. I'm all sweaty and my hair's standing up."

"You look good." Meg took her phone back. Her mom was right, she did look like she'd just finished playing. "I said I'd play doubles with a girl from the Bistro. She was looking for a partner and it's Tuesday mornings. Does that interfere with your playing? You seem to be the professional with this thing."

"I am not a professional, and yes, it will be fine. Unless you need the time for class or Lilly's work." Mom patted Meg's leg. "I am sorry I didn't tell you. I just didn't want to look foolish."

"For falling in love or playing Pickleball without telling me?" Meg pulled her mother into a hug. "I'm the one who came back into your life full force after the failed wedding. I should be apologizing to you for getting upset."

"You are always welcome here, no matter what my marital status is or what sport I'm playing," Mom said as she glanced at her watch. "And speaking of that, I need to go. Derby's taking me to Seattle for dinner and a show tonight. I need to go home and change so I don't smell like a book."

"There's nothing wrong with smelling like a book." Meg took a sip of her coffee. "Oh, and I better tell you before you hear it from Aunt Melody. I had dinner, which ended in a fight, with the guy who was murdered at the ferry parking lot."

Her mom froze. "You what? I thought you were dating Dalton now."

"It wasn't a date and Dalton knows all about it." Meg was a little tired of explaining what had happened between her and Lee. But she'd just confronted her mom for not sharing, so she told her what happened. She wrapped it all up by saying, "Uncle Troy called me this morning and asked all the questions. I just didn't want you to be blindsided by anything."

She almost added *like I was*, but thought better of it. Her mom had apologized when she didn't have to, and Meg needed to just get over it.

After her mother left, the bookstore was quiet, so she ordered food and texted Dalton and Natasha to let them know what time it would be arriving. Natasha gave her a thumbs-up. But Dalton didn't answer.

She started to worry, but then he came in the door with Natasha just before the food arrived.

"I stopped at the store and brought sodas. Is there ice in the fridge?" He held up a bag. "They should still be cold, but when I stopped by to pick up Natasha, she had to yell at her employee."

Natasha rolled her eyes as she took off her jacket. She grabbed a soda from the bag and felt it before she opened the top. "I wasn't yelling at Candi. I just needed to do some course corrections before she keeps doing things wrong."

"You mean, not your way." Dalton held out a lime sparkling water to Meg. "For the princess."

"Just because I like sparkling water, it doesn't make me a princess," she said as she took the drink. "The fact I can sleep on ninety-nine mattresses and still feel the pea is the telling factor."

"Whatever," both Dalton and Natasha said in unison. Their conversation was interrupted by the food delivery. And for a few minutes, they all focused on filling their plates and eating.

"What has your uncle told you about Lee's death?" Natasha asked as she set her fork down and scooted back in her chair. "Are there any suspects?"

"Besides me?" Meg chuckled. "I don't know. He failed to give me that information. I know if Emmett's review had come out, he'd probably be on the list."

"Anyone who had that guy review their restaurant will be on the list," Dalton countered. He was friends with Emmett and didn't want to see him get labeled a killer just for a review.

"I should be on the list," Natasha said as she took another egg roll. "A couple years ago, he gave me faint praise, which is worse than trashing the bakery. Told people my place should be a witch's house since I used sugar not as an ingredient but instead as a weapon. He didn't like my scones. Which I think is my best product. Then he gave me three stars and a 'meh.'"

"He did not," Meg said. She loved Natasha's scones.

"He did. I can't believe you even let him talk you into dinner. No one on the island likes him." Natasha took a bite of the egg roll, watching Meg's reaction.

"I didn't know that. I wasn't here when you had problems

with him," Meg deflected. "So why don't the two of you list out all the people I shouldn't trust on the island? That way, if I run into one of them, I'll know better than to assume that they are nice people."

"Don't get all huffy," Natasha said, trying to defuse the conversation. "I guess you're right, there are probably some things that have happened here while you were off to college or in Seattle that you don't know about."

"Like did either of you know that my mom was dating Irene Olsen's dad?" Meg watched their faces as she let out that bombshell.

"She is not." Natasha blew out the statement. "Tell me you're kidding."

"She is. Dalton and I saw them together in Seattle at a restaurant." Meg turned to Dalton for backup.

Dalton didn't say anything. He focused on his fried rice. His face was red, up around his blond hair.

"Oh, my God. You knew before we saw them." Meg pointed her fork at him. "You weren't surprised at all now that I think about Thursday night. You knew."

He set his plate down and shook his head. "I suspected. I saw your mom on the ferry a couple of times alone and then a few more times with him. They just had that vibe, you know. Excited. Chatting about everything and nothing. Your mom's happy. You shouldn't try to mess with that. Even if the package comes with Irene."

Meg finished her dinner, thinking about what Dalton had said. Finally, she sipped her water and set it down. "Fine, I agree with what you said. I'll leave it alone. Let's change the subject. What else do you two know about our murder victim?"

Natasha told them more about the column he'd written about her bakery. She'd never even met him, but someone had pointed him out once on the ferry.

Dalton mentioned seeing him there a few times too. "I

promise, I didn't go over and yell at him. But I wanted to push him off the boat."

"Don't mention the wanting to push him off the boat if Uncle Troy interviews you. I think that's called motive." Meg curled up on the couch, watching her friends.

Dalton shrugged. "If that's the motive, all of the restaurants he reviewed would be on your uncle's list. Other than reading his column and hearing people complain about how mean he was, I am not involved with this guy or his death."

"Except he took Meg to dinner," Natasha pointed out.

Dalton looked at Meg as he answered. "Meg's free to have dinner with anyone. She told me she was going out with a writer friend before she went and made a scene at the Local Crab that night. I think I'm far from being on Troy's list for that."

"So he was mean in his reviews. Is that all we know about him?" Meg looked from Dalton to Natasha, who both shrugged. "Well, I hope Uncle Troy is having better luck with this one."

They started cleaning up the mess from dinner when the doorbell announced a customer.

"Come on in, we're still open," Meg called out.

"I should hope so, your sign is still up." Irene Olsen stepped around the bookcase and stared at the three of them. "Having dinner here? I'm glad someone can eat since your mother is a homewrecker!"

Meg had avoided getting into a fight with Irene before she left the bookstore, but not by much. As Dalton walked Meg home, she was still upset at the woman bursting in and ruining their evening. Her shoulders were tense, and she rolled them as they arrived at the apartment.

"You okay?" Dalton leaned against the garage, watching her. "Irene was out of line. Her folks are divorced and her father is free to date whomever he wants."

"I know that. Mom even said they didn't start hanging out

until after the divorce was final, but I guess part of me knows how Irene feels. I was blindsided by my parents' divorce too. Irene still thought they were going to get back together." Meg laughed. "I go from hating Irene to feeling sorry for her. I guess she won't be trying to pin me down for a cruise plan now."

"That's my girl, always looking at the bright side. Changing the subject, I'm off tomorrow. Do you want to take the boat out with me?" Dalton watched as Watson sniffed around the garage, finally deciding to water a lilac bush.

"I should work on Lilly's stuff, but sure. I need a break. It's been a little crazy around here this week." She stepped closer and squeezed his arm. "Thank you for dinner Thursday night. I don't think I said that yet. I was a bit distraught."

"You were totally freaked. Emmett asked how we liked the food and I told him it was wonderful, even though I'm not sure you tasted anything you ate. Not after that shock."

"Which is horrible since he went to so much trouble to get us a reservation. Now I feel really bad." Meg dropped her head on Dalton's chest. "I'm a horrible person."

"No, Irene is a horrible person and we all have to say our prayers and hope she won't be having Thanksgiving at your mom's house this year. I mean, I'm rooting for your mom to find true love and all that, but Irene's dad? If she's that bad, he has to have some faults your mom needs to find out about, and soon."

"Maybe we'll have to go to Dad's." Meg grimaced as she shook her head. "Then we'll have to play the 'what we're most thankful for' game with Elaine. And I just can't. No, our only hope is to break up this romance sooner than later."

"I hate to say this, but maybe we can get Irene to help."

Meg lifted her head off his chest and stared at him. "Sometimes I wonder about you. You have a devious side. I've got to crash. What time are we going out?"

"I'll come get you at seven with a bag of goodies from the bakery. So don't worry about making breakfast." Dalton watched as she walked up the stairs to the apartment. "Can you make us some coffee?"

She turned and stared at him again. "Seriously, dude, do you even know me?"

As she entered the apartment, she saw her aunt had been busy again. A basket filled with baked goods and a two-layer cake were sitting on her counter with a note. Meg opened it and read, *Sorry about not telling you about your mom, but she asked me not to. I put some frozen dinners in your freezer and went on a grocery run for you.*

Watson barked at his bowl that was filled with dry dog food and then brought her a large bone that had been laid on his bed.

"Aunt Melody must have really felt bad." She reached down and gave Watson a rub. "I wonder if she felt bad enough to clean the bathroom and do my laundry?"

She texted Dalton to let him know he didn't need to stop by the bakery because she'd have food here, and she got a row of question marks in return. She laughed and texted back that she'd explain in the morning.

Then she turned on the television. The local channel was running a story on Lee Anderson's death. Someone had sent a picture to the station of Meg yelling at him at the Local Crab. She stared at the headline: MYSTERY WOMAN ARGUES WITH ANDERSON JUST A DAY BEFORE HIS DEATH. She changed the channel. Uncle Troy knew what had happened.

That was all that mattered.

Chapter 6

You need to be aware of what's going on, but not so close to the investigation that people start to know you.

Meg lay in bed the next morning, unable to sleep long before her alarm went off. She made mental notes about what she could do about the station showing that picture. It was too early to call the station to complain. After tossing and turning for a while, she got up and tried calling anyway, only to be disappointed by the message machine telling her to leave her complaint at the beep. It had been bad enough that she had been on the news leaving Summer Break a few months ago during a prior investigation. Now she'd been linked to a second murder. People were going to start talking.

She guessed writing the investigation book was getting serious. What was the saying, *bad news is as good as good news*? Or press. Or something like that. She made a pot of coffee and heated up a muffin in the microwave, not waiting for Dalton to arrive before she ate breakfast.

She looked at her week. She worked tonight at the bookstore, but she was mostly caught up with her other work. She had class on Monday morning, so she pulled out the course book and read the assignment.

A knock on the door and Watson's barking pulled her out of the reading just a few pages before she was done. She slid a bookmark in and put the book away on her desk as she stood to open the door for Dalton.

Watson greeted Dalton first, and he rubbed the dog's head. "Hey, buddy. Are you keeping your mom from murdering someone else?"

"Not funny. I guess you saw the news?" She pulled another cup out of the cabinet and filled it, setting it on the table. "Aunt Melody supplied our treats this morning."

"Wow, the woman likes to bake. Is she missing having a job?" He sat down and grabbed a piece of banana bread and the butter dish.

"Maybe. But this is because she's feeling bad she kept me in the dark about Mom's dating." Meg pointed to the cake. "I'm letting her. She put frozen dinners in my freezer, so I'm good with groceries until next week or even longer."

"How are you feeling about Derby and your mom? From last night, it's clear Irene isn't dealing well." Dalton took a bite and groaned.

"I'm okay with it. I knew that it was going to happen sooner or later. Mom and Dad are never going to see the error in their divorce and get back together. The problem is they never fought. At least not in front of me or Junior. So here we are." Meg shrugged as she looked at another muffin. *I will not eat my feelings*. She sipped her coffee instead.

Dalton set down his banana bread. "Your folks were my role model on how to have a good relationship. I never knew my dad, and Mom, well, she was flaky from the moment she came to get me after my grandmother died. I must have been about six then. A lot of times, she would be so high, she wouldn't even remember I was there. I spent a lot of time at the library. My grandma used to take me there every Saturday. I learned to read early."

Meg sat and listened. This was the most Dalton had ever talked about his life before moving in with the prior police chief and his wife on Bainbridge Island. "I'm sorry you lost your grandmother. Is your mom still alive?"

Dalton finished his coffee. "Don't know and don't care. Who knows if she even remembers I exist? The Kings raised me right. I got through high school, went into the Coast Guard, got a steady job, and here I am. A fully functioning member of society."

"You're a good person, Dalton Hamilton. That's all that matters," Meg added to his list of accomplishments.

"You only love me for my boat. And speaking of, are you ready to go? Should we pack a cooler with water and some snacks?" He stood and took his plate and cup to the sink, taking his time to rinse and put them into the dishwasher.

Meg gave him some space and grabbed Watson's tote. "I've got the pup all ready. The drink cooler is in the laundry room. I'll go grab a jacket and shoes."

When she came out of her bedroom, the cooler had been packed, and everyone was ready, just waiting for her. Dalton was talking to Watson and laughing. The world had been put right and the demons that had chased him as a kid were all tucked away.

She squeezed his arm as she got closer. "I meant what I said. You're a good man."

"If you make me cry, I'm leaving you home and taking Watson on the boat," Dalton threatened as he kissed the top of her head.

Then they put aside everything that had been bothering them and went out to the boat to relax.

As Dalton worked the sails, Meg and Watson watched the shoreline. Sunlight sparkled in the waves around the boat and she let her fingertips dangle over the side, feeling the coolness of the water around them. As the sun warmed her face, she could only think this was the perfect spot to relax. Let the challenges of the last few days melt away and just be in that moment. A meditation practice that Watson was much better at than she was. All he wanted to do was lean on her and watch what was going on. Gulls flew around the boat and Watson seemed to be watching them as well. After a while, Dalton slowed the boat, then threw out an anchor and came to sit by her, handing her a bottle of water.

"I heard what you said when I left the bookstore the other day. Do you want me to be your boyfriend?" He ran his finger, wet and cold from the ice in the cooler, up her bare arm.

"Isn't this where you pass me a note with a check box for yes or no?" She took a sip of the ice-cold water. "It's beautiful out here. I can't believe I never went out on boats before."

"You used to go when we were in high school. We'd borrow the chief's boat and go out after school. You, Junior, Natasha, and me. You and Natasha wore those bikinis and tanned most of the time." He smiled at the memory. "Junior was in love with Natasha for years and she never saw him. And you're trying to get me off topic. Do I need to find paper and pen to get my answer?"

Instead of answering, she turned toward him and kissed him. The magic tingled through her lips as she pulled away. "I'd always mark yes."

On the way back, they stopped at the Bistro for lunch and their official first date since checking the imaginary box. Watson and Meg found a table on the patio and Dalton went inside to order. As she was sitting there, the hostess, Brooke, came up to greet her. "You're back. Please don't tell me you changed your mind. I bought a new tennis dress to wear on Tuesday. I know it's not tennis, but the dress was so cute. Anyway, we're playing at eight. I was going to email you, but I thought with everything going on, you might have changed your mind."

"Nope, I'm excited to play. I'm just wearing a tank and

shorts, though. I have court shoes." Meg figured Brooke had to be talking about Lee Anderson's death and the picture.

"Great, I'll let Derby know and he'll send you a schedule." Brooke stepped back when Dalton came back with two beers from the bar. "Oh, hi, Dalton. Did you get your order in?"

"We're all set here, Brooke. Maybe we could get a couple of glasses of water? Meg, you have a bowl for Watson, right?" He sat down and moved a bottle over to Meg.

"Always." Meg smiled. "I'll meet you at the community center on Tuesday morning."

Brooke nodded, then snuck another look at Dalton. "I'll have someone bring your water out."

After she'd gone back inside, Meg turned toward Dalton. "Don't tell me you dated Brooke."

"Once and done. It was years ago. Do you want a complete list of the women I dated between you going to college and now?" he teased as he sipped his beer. "I'm willing to make one, just as soon as I find some paper. You'd think I would keep some on hand when I'm with you."

"It might help, since I'll be playing Pickleball with this one for nine weeks. Was she heartbroken?"

He shook his head. "I don't think so. She went to a concert with Nate Baldwin the next night."

Meg laughed. "Boy, did she choose wrongly."

"I've always known that," he said, his grin cocky. "Anyway, this dinner with Anderson. You're sure your uncle knows everything? I'd hate to have to visit you in prison. Gig Harbor is over an hour away."

"Funny, but at least I'd have time to finish my book," Meg teased. "Between the bookstore and working for Lilly and classes once a week, my schedule's slammed."

"Maybe you should have stayed home this morning and worked." Dalton raised his eyebrows. "I'll stop tempting you with boat rides if you're too busy."

"Then I'd have no balance in my life and I'd be depriving Watson of time with his favorite guy. He's just started getting used to the boat, I think." Meg reached down and gave him a rub. "It's all a juggling act. Besides, I'm almost done with Monday's homework. Well, at least I've done most of the reading. I still have an essay to write. And I need to do a report for Lilly on social media hits."

"It's a big change from you being at Romain's beck and call all day." Dalton studied her. "You know, if we're going too fast, I can slow down."

"I love spending time with you, stop trying to be sensitive," Meg said as a young man came out with three glasses of water, two with ice.

"One for each of you, and one for that precious dog." He grinned at them, then turned back to the restaurant entrance. He called out as he walked away, "Your food is almost up."

Meg filled Watson's water dish. Then she looked at Dalton. "Are you sure Brooke wasn't upset seeing you with me?"

"I don't care if any of the women I used to date are upset with our relationship. The only person whose feelings I care about is you." He moved his water glass out of the way. "And your mother. She can be a little scary at times. Junior will get over it eventually."

"I brought up her meddling with you when we talked about her and Derby." Meg thought for a moment, then groaned. "The Pickleball leagues are run by a Derby. Do you think my luck is good enough that it's not the same man who's dating my mom?"

"You really think the universe is that kind? We're a small town. Even I know there's only one Derby here, and that's Irene's dad and your soon-to-be stepfather." He leaned back as the same man delivered their food.

"Don't even think that," Meg whispered after the server had left. "I'm just getting used to using the *dating* word with my mom. And you get to sit next to Irene at family dinners if it happens. I call 'not it.' "

"We'll make Junior do it. He's not here to object." Dalton took a bite of his sandwich.

Meg's phone rang and she answered the call from her brother. Since there weren't a lot of people nearby, she put the phone on speaker. "And speak of the devil. Do you have Watson's collar bugged or something?"

"What are you talking about? Do you have me on speaker?"

"Yes, she does," Dalton answered. "But it's just me and a dozen of our closest friends listening."

Meg laughed. "He's kidding. It's just me and Dalton. We're at the Bistro eating lunch. What's going on? Aren't you supposed to be at a conference now?"

"We just got here. I checked into my room and finally returned Mom's call. She's dating?" Junior sounded stunned. "Are you pushing this?"

"No, I was as shocked as you are. Why would you think I put her up to this?" Now Meg was miffed. "It's not my fault she's dating."

"And it's not my fault either that Dad married Elaine," Junior snapped back.

"Okay, kids, let's just calm down here. The cat's out of the bag. Your mom is dating. So, how's Anne?" Dalton asked, trying to change the subject.

"I don't want to talk about it." Junior paused. "Oh, and I just got a text from Dad. You were on the news fighting with a murder victim? Are you trying to ruin your life, Megs?"

"He wasn't dead when I was yelling at him. Besides, he was a jerk," Meg tried to clarify. "Anyway, I've talked to Uncle Troy and told him everything. There's no smoke or fire there. Tell Dad I'm fine."

"Maybe you should call Dad and tell him yourself," Junior said, his voice softening. "He misses you."

"Oh, look at that, our food's here," Meg lied. Dalton made a face at her. She stuck her tongue out before continuing. "Junior, I'll call Dad, but you need to tell me about Anne when you get back in town. And be careful."

"Yes, Mom," Junior responded. "I'll see you next Friday night for the game, right, Dalton?"

"Sounds good," Dalton responded. "Have a good time, dude."

"It's a work conference," Junior sighed. "Not a vacation."

"The conference doesn't run twenty-four-seven," Dalton called out.

"Whatever," Junior said as he disconnected.

Meg put away her phone. "You didn't tell him about Irene."

"Neither did you," Dalton said as he smiled, a dimple showing in his cheek. "It will be a nice surprise, right?"

Meg got to the bookstore at three. Her mom and aunt were whispering at the counter when she and Watson came inside. "Good afternoon, family. What's going on?"

"We're just worried about you. You weren't home when I came over for breakfast at Melody's this morning." Her mom straightened a pile of books that was already straight.

"I went out on the boat with Dalton. Then we grabbed lunch at the Bistro. Thanks for the goodies, Aunt Melody. But you didn't need to do all that. I'm glad to take any pastries you don't need but don't bake on my account." Meg decided not to mention the cleaning and laundry.

"Oh, a morning on the boat must have been calming." Aunt Melody smiled at her. "And I love baking for you. Unless I'm bothering you."

"It's fine." Meg felt guilty about enjoying the pampering her aunt was providing. "Hey, has Uncle Troy said anything about Lee Anderson's death? He was shot, right?"

Aunt Melody and her mom shared a look. Then Aunt Melody said, "Troy doesn't like me sharing information with you, but if he didn't want people to know, he shouldn't tell me. Anyway, Anderson was shot and it was made to look like a suicide, but someone threw the gun into the sound, right by the ferry terminal. Someone found it and turned it in. The gun wasn't registered."

"The killer isn't very good at what he does." Meg read between the lines. "From what Natasha and Dalton told me about Anderson, most people who own or work at a local restaurant should probably be on Uncle Troy's suspect list."

Aunt Melody nodded. "That's the problem. I don't think there is a local restaurant around that hasn't been scathed in one of Anderson's columns. The media wants to know your name and connection, but he's told them that he's talked to and cleared you. I don't think that's going to stop Miss Chin, though." Vi Chin was the local investigative reporter on the television channel everyone watched. "So watch out. Someone is going to tell her you work here at the bookstore sooner or later."

"Maybe you shouldn't work for a bit," Mom said. "Just until this settles down."

"I didn't do anything wrong. In fact, that's why I was yelling at him in that picture. I told him I wasn't going to take any part in trying to ruin Emmett's business." Meg tucked her tote in the back and filled up Watson's dish. "Anyway, I'm here to work. You should leave and have a life. Work-life balance is all the rage nowadays."

"You're a little snot sometimes." Aunt Melody hugged me. "We just worry about you."

"Tell Irene not to come by and yell at me, then." Meg looked at her mother. "She's not happy with you."

"I know. Derby told me she didn't take it well. I don't think her mother did either. I never once wished that Stephen would come back. But then again, I was the one who asked for a divorce. We weren't happy together anymore." She smiled at Meg. "And no, he wasn't cheating on me with Elaine. The two of them are more compatible."

"I never said—" Meg started, then stopped. She *had* wondered. And held it against Elaine.

"So, since you want to work, can you take Glory's shift tomorrow? One to four and then you can close. I'm taking the day and going to Seattle with Derby. We need some time to talk." Mom grabbed her purse. "Oh, and I won't be at church, so if you decide to skip, I won't be there to notice."

"I don't just go to church because you want me to," Meg said as Mom and Aunt Melody headed to the door.

Mom turned back. "Oh? So you'll be there tomorrow?"

"No. I go to spend time with you, Mom." She waved them out of the bookstore. If she knew her mom and aunt, the two were heading to a restaurant to gossip about her, Junior, Uncle Troy, and probably Derby. The sisters were close.

She'd brought the other half of her sandwich from lunch as well as another muffin. She made herself a cup of tea and opened her laptop. She wanted to crank out at least a few words of her manuscript today. She was writing a chapter on making assumptions. Sometimes the simple answer was the right one—like how the sound of running hooves on Winslow Way usually meant horses, not zebras.

Vi Chin was seeing zebras if she thought Meg had anything to do with Anderson's death. Maybe she should call the television reporter and tell her that.

Meg looked back over what she'd written. Part of being a good investigator was staying out of the limelight. If you're fighting for your own innocence, people aren't going to tell you what you need to know.

No, Meg would wait for Vi Chin to find her. Then she'd tell her story.

CHAPTER 7

Don't become part of the conversation. Or worse, a suspect.

Meg didn't have to wait long. Sunday afternoon, she'd just opened the store when Vi Chin walked in. She scanned the shelves, pretending to shop, then grabbed a popular romantasy and strode up to the counter. Watson looked up at her, then dropped his head again. Apparently, he didn't sense the reporter was a threat.

Meg thought he was wrong. She turned over the book and checked the price, then rang it up. "I'm surprised you haven't read this. I thought you did a story on the rise of romantasy last month on the Sunday morning show."

Vi Chin smiled and handed her a credit card. "It's a gift for my niece. She just finished all the Sarah Maas books and needs a new series. So, you know who I am. Good."

"I know you didn't come to buy a book." Meg ran the card. She wasn't going to talk the reporter out of buying the book even though she knew she had come to get Meg's story.

"You were very hard to find. You and your mom are well-liked here on the island. I got a call from someone in Seattle who wanted to know if they'd be rewarded for the information. When I said no, they huffed but told me your name and where you worked."

"Male or female?" Meg had two guesses.

"Female, why?"

"It was probably Rachel. She and my former fiancé went on the honeymoon I planned after he broke it off before the wedding. It's a long story."

"Man, you have the worst luck. So, the police chief is your uncle, right?" She pulled out her notebook.

"Uncle Troy." Meg nodded.

"Yes, Troy Miller. He said you were just having dinner with the victim, Lee Anderson, and that you had an alibi for his time of death." She met Meg's gaze. "Correct?"

Meg explained the dinner and why she was mad at Anderson. "I didn't want to be part of him trashing Emmett's restaurant. He set them up to fail."

Vi tapped her pen on her notebook. "Would you be willing to say this on camera?"

"No. I would not. And I don't think it's fair for you to use the photo you did. Maybe I should consult my attorney about it. I didn't give you permission to use it." Meg leaned on the counter and thought she saw the reporter flinch.

"The public has a right to know," Vi Chin started, but Meg shook her head.

"No, they don't. Me being upset at a guy who's badmouthing a good man's restaurant? My opinion wasn't for sale. Wait, did you buy the picture?"

Now the reporter was sweating. "What makes you say that?"

"I've heard about tabloid news before." Meg narrowed her eyes. "I better not see that picture on the news again or I am going to call my attorney."

The woman hurried out of the bookstore. She stopped to talk to a man who had been shooting the outside of the bookstore as well as the street around it. As Meg watched through the window, Vi told him to put the camera down. They headed back down Winslow Way toward the ferry terminal.

Watson looked up at her as Meg walked back to the counter.

"Well, that was interesting," she said as Watson stretched and laid his head back down on his bed. "Well, I thought it was interesting."

She went back to working on her manuscript. The local writing group was meeting on Tuesday for their weekly write-in. Maybe someone there would know something about Vi Chin's history of getting information. Or even just the general rules around news reporting. The reporter had backed down so quickly when Meg mentioned an attorney. And Chin had practically run out when she asked if the picture was purchased. Was that a no-no?

Four o'clock came fast. No wonder Glory liked working on Sundays. A few minutes after Chin had disappeared, a ferry had docked, and soon a wave of customers arrived. The process repeated itself right up until the three o'clock ferry left. She'd seen more people during this Sunday shift than in most of her evening shifts in a week combined.

Meg texted both Dalton and Natasha to let them know she was heading home but no one responded. Dalton was probably still working. And Natasha might be sleeping if she had to bake last night. Her schedule was all over the place.

She gathered her things, checked the back door locks, and clipped on Watson's leash. "Let's go home and see what Aunt Melody left us in the freezer."

Watson just heard *home* and stood patiently waiting for her to punch in the alarm code and lock up.

As soon as Meg was done, she turned around and saw a small blonde standing there staring at her. "What do you want, Irene?"

"Dad said I was supposed to leave you alone, but I had to ask. Are you okay with your mom dating him?" Irene asked.

"They're adults, and it's not our business." Meg knew how she was feeling, but she wasn't going to admit it to Irene.

Irene nodded slowly. "My dad said the same thing. Why were you at the writing club? Are you writing a book?"

Meg leaned against the bookstore wall. She guessed it must be Share Your Secrets Day. "I'm trying to write one. What about you?"

"My boyfriend took me there. He's writing a book. A spy novel. He knew that guy who was killed. He went to school with him. We heard what you said to Lee at the restaurant. At least part of it. Mark said that Lee just used people. I told him you were dating someone and he shrugged and told me that 'Anderson doesn't care. He stole my first girlfriend in college and never blinked an eye.'"

"It wasn't a date." Meg blew out a breath, frustrated. "We were talking about writing nonfiction. I thought maybe I'd learn something."

"Oh." Irene thought on that for a moment. "I thought you were on a date. It's an expensive place for a casual dinner."

"His newspaper was going to cover it. He was a food critic. Heavy on the critic part of the title." Meg glanced at her watch. "I need to get Watson home so I can feed him. Do you want to walk with me?"

"I'm heading into Seattle to meet up with Mark. I just wanted to tell you I was sorry about what I said." She blushed a little. "About your mom."

"Your dad made you apologize, didn't he?"

Now Irene grinned. "Let's just say I had a financial incentive to be a nice person today. It was lovely to talk to you. I'm still not okay with them dating, but I guess you're right, it's not my business."

As Meg and Watson headed home, Meg wondered if Irene wasn't so bad after all. When she heard the ding of a text on her phone, she pulled it up. It was Irene. She had texted a link for a sale on a cruise leaving next week.

"Okay, maybe she is that bad," Meg said aloud as they arrived at the garage and started up the stairs. Watson gave her a look. If he could talk, he would have said, "duh."

"No judgment from the peanut gallery," Meg said as she unlocked the door and proceeded to get ready for her quiet evening in.

Monday morning, Meg was driving to class when her phone rang. Using Bluetooth, she answered the call through her radio speakers. "Hi Dalton, what's going on?"

"Junior just called and he's coming for a week. He's staying with me, but I think he plans to break up your mom and Derby."

When Meg didn't say anything, Dalton continued. "You can't think this is a good idea."

"He'll have an ally with Irene. She came over yesterday and gave me a lukewarm apology, but she's not thrilled about them dating. Junior's just blowing off steam. There's nothing he can do to change Mom's mind. Is he bringing his girlfriend?" Meg focused on the road ahead.

"To my tiny house? I don't think so. As it is, he's sleeping on the couch. Okay, well, I just wanted to warn you that your brother was going to be here. Are you on your way to class?"

"Yep. Class today. Then Pickleball tomorrow with Brooke. Then I go back to work on Wednesday." I listed off the big items on my weekly schedule. "When are you off?"

"Today and Wednesday. I'll come get you tonight and we can take your brother to dinner. Will you behave if we go to the Local Crab? I don't want you to get kicked out."

Meg rolled her eyes as she pulled into a parking spot. "Funny guy. I wasn't fighting with Anderson, I was just tired of his shenanigans. What time are you picking me up?"

"Emmett got us a table at six. I know it's early, but it was a favor."

Meg turned off the car, gas was expensive enough without

letting it sit and idle. “Six is fine. I probably won’t go out for drinks with you guys afterward, but oddly enough, I know my way home.”

“Now who’s being funny? Besides, you’re not on anyone’s suspect list for the Anderson killing that I know of, right?”

“I think Irene and Rachel would love to see me there, but no. Oh, and I forgot to tell you about Vi Chin.” Meg sat in the car and relayed the incident from Sunday, switching the call from the car to her phone.

“You think Rachel called and told them where they could find you?”

Meg thought about it. “Rachel or maybe Irene. But I didn’t think Irene hated me so much. I think she hates Mom.”

“True, but do me a favor and don’t go off with either one of them until your uncle solves this murder. I’d hate to be the one they interview after your death who says, ‘I was worried something might happen.’ ”

“Whatever. Go clean your house. I know that’s what you’re doing.” She climbed out of the car and grabbed her backpack. “I’ve got to get to class.”

As Meg headed to the Language Arts building, she texted her mom.

Junior’s coming for a visit.

Just as she started to put her phone away in the classroom, the response came.

I know. Dinner tomorrow night at the house?

Meg responded that she’d be there, then turned off her phone and put it away. It was only later, during class, that a thought hit her. *What if Mom’s inviting Derby to meet her family?*

And Dalton worried about her going to the Local Crab.

When she got home, she curled up on the couch and read the assignment for the next week while she ate a sandwich for lunch. When that was done, she went to her desk, logged in to her computer, and started her work for Lilly Aster. She checked her email in case Lilly, or more likely Jolene, had added a task. When she didn't see anything, she started working on the book tour.

First, she set up three different schedules, making sure she had listed the details Lilly liked to know, like the last time she'd visited each store and any additional information. Lilly always started her release tours at Mom's Island Books, which had equaled—if not exceeded—the bigger events. Mom's bookstore always sold more books since people knew that Lilly always held a release party on the island. After she made the three potential schedules, each one longer than the last, Meg started checking flights, rental car costs, hotels, and the distance between stores, to ensure the travel was logical.

She had just gotten up for a soda when she noticed the time. Dalton and Junior would be here in ten minutes. She saved her working documents, closed her computer, and ran to the bathroom to get ready.

Dinner at the Local Crab wasn't formal, but it wasn't jeans-and-a-grubby-T-shirt casual, either. Which is what she'd changed into after class.

She was just finishing styling her hair when a knock sounded. She set down her curling iron and hurried to answer. Dalton and Junior came inside, and Watson went crazy. "I'm almost ready. Can you take him out and check on his food and water? I got busy with Lilly work and lost track of time."

"Of course." Dalton grabbed Watson's leash. "He knows who loves him, anyway."

"Whatever." Meg hugged her brother. "Did you get the summons for dinner tomorrow?"

"Yes." Junior squeezed her back. "Mom and her dinner parties. I'll help get the mutt set up. Go finish getting ready. You only have makeup on one eye."

Leave it to her brother to point out her flaws. "It's a new trend. I'll be ready in a few minutes."

"Don't hurry. Our reservation is at six thirty. I told Dalton to pad thirty minutes so you'd be almost on time." He smiled at her, then turned and went to fill Watson's water dish.

Sometimes Meg didn't like her brother. Okay, most of the time. She thought when they grew into adults that he might mellow out, but he was still as bossy and judgmental as he was as a kid. Her interactions with him over the last two weeks had proved that.

She considered only putting makeup on one eyelid, just to spite him, but she didn't want to look foolish in front of Dalton or Emmett. Especially since they were friends. Besides, the waitstaff probably already thought she was rude since she'd stormed out of the restaurant that night. She went back into the bathroom and finished her preparations.

She returned to the living room, where Junior and Dalton were eating the cookies that Aunt Melody had left her. She listened to their conversation for a few minutes and no one noticed she was there. She cleared her throat and Dalton turned.

"Hey Meg, are you ready? You look amazing." Dalton stood and brushed the cookie crumbs off his hands. "Watson is all set, walked, watered, and fed."

Watson sat by the door watching them. He knew something was up. "I've got to go out for a few hours, but I'll be home soon and we'll watch television together," Meg said as she rubbed his head.

She went over and turned on the TV. "Okay, I'm ready."

"You're leaving the set on for the dog? That's a waste of electricity," Junior said as he stood to leave.

"I guess I don't have to ask about your date with Anne since you're saying such stupid things, there's no way you'd go all night without putting your foot in your mouth." Meg grabbed her shawl and slipped her keys, phone, and several twenties into a small purse.

"Let's get going. I'm starving," Dalton said, trying to defuse the situation, his arm around Meg.

Junior went out the door first. "I can't get over seeing the two of you together. Dalton's so different than Romain. Did you have a brain fart then or are you having one now?"

"You're such a jerk," Meg responded as she locked the door. Maybe dinner with her brother wasn't the best idea. Especially at the one place where she'd already made a scene last week. Even though it was perfectly justifiable, she had still yelled in the middle of the dining room.

"I'm going to turn this car around if you two kids don't stop fighting," Dalton said as he waited at the bottom of the stairs for Meg to come down.

A chuckle came from the house near the carport. "I thought that was my line," Dad said as he stepped out of the darkness. "I came to visit Meg but I see it's a bad time."

"Hey, Dad. I didn't know you were coming to the island." Junior stepped over and the two men bro-hugged.

Dalton followed suit. "You're more than welcome to join us for dinner. We're heading to the Local Crab."

Meg stared at her father as she walked down the stairs. When she got there, she said, "Hi, Dad."

He walked over and pulled her into his arms. Then, he looked at her face. "I think I will accept your invitation to join you kids for dinner, Dalton. Thank you."

Chapter 8

Sometimes it's hard to figure out who's an ally in your camp. Be quiet until they show the real person behind the mask.

Things could be worse. Mom could be also here eating dinner with us. Meg glanced at the menu and ordered a cocktail. She might even have two. Dalton squeezed her hand under the table.

"Order what you want. The check's on me." Meg's father scanned their faces as they sat at the table. "I can't remember the last time I had dinner with you three kids. And yes, I'm including you in that mix because face it, Dalton, you were always at the house for dinner."

"Mrs. King liked having TV dinners when her husband was working." Dalton smiled at the memory. "The food wasn't bad, there just wasn't enough of it. I'd wind up eating a bag of chips after dinner or a package of cookies. I'm so glad that you and Mrs. Gates invited me to eat with your family."

Meg hadn't known this was why Dalton was there. Natasha ate a lot with the Gates' family too, mostly because her mom didn't like to cook. If Natasha didn't make dinner, they ate snacks.

"Well, we loved having you there." Dad smiled at Meg as

the drinks were delivered. "Although it's strange to see you all drinking alcohol with dinner."

Meg was about to say that having a drink or two was the only thing keeping her sane right now, but instead, Junior spoke up. "Yep, we're all adults. Are you here to deal with Mom and this foolishness?"

Pain crossed over Dad's face as he turned toward Junior. "Son, your mother has every right to date anyone she wants to. I just came by to see how Meg was dealing with the changes. You've already made your feelings clear."

Junior started to speak, but then the waiter came by. "Hi, I'm Frank. I'll be your server. I see Angelica has already gotten you some drinks. Can I tempt you with an appetizer?"

He looked around the table and focused on Meg. "Oh, it's you. I'm so glad you came back. I have something you left. That man was horrible, wasn't he? I sure hope he's not family or something. I would feel like a jerk saying that aloud."

Meg glanced at Dalton when the waiter hurried away. "I don't know what he's talking about."

"It has to be the night you were here with Lee Anderson. Did you forget something?" Dalton asked, lowering his voice. Junior and Dad both looked confused. "Meg was here recently with a . . ."

"With a friend. Kind of. I thought he might become a friend, but it was a bad match. It wasn't a date, and Dalton knew all about it." Meg cringed at her explanation. It sounded as bad as if it had been a date.

The waiter came back with a manila envelope. "We kept this for you. So, what can I get everyone to eat? Appetizers? The crab dip is our most ordered."

Meg put the envelope into her purse even though it stuck out. She'd check and make sure it was still there before she left.

She took a long sip of her margarita. Strawberry, and on the rocks, not frozen into some summer blast. She realized her father was watching her. Had he asked her something after the waiter had left? "I'm sorry, what?"

"I wanted to know how you were doing here on the island. I know you were a little broken up after the whole Romain thing. Are you better now?" Dad was twisting his wedding ring on his finger as he talked.

"I was more upset that I'd planned this lovely wedding, honeymoon, and life that I didn't get to enjoy. I'm sorry you lost money." She smiled at her father. He'd been there for her when Romain had dumped her.

"Don't worry about the money. I can always make more. Besides, we didn't go much in the red. Your dress, of course," he said, blushing. "But again, it's not about the money. I just want you to be happy."

"Did you have to cut that dress into a thousand pieces? I'm sure you could have sold it online or something." Junior sipped his gin and tonic. The same drink Dad had. Later, when he hung out with Dalton, he'd drink beer. But when he was with Dad, Junior always matched his father's drink.

"I felt like it, okay? Besides, it wasn't your dress or wedding. Why do you care?" Meg shot back.

"Meg," Dad warned. "Let's stay civil."

Meg pushed down all the other things she wanted to say. Why did she have to stay civil when Junior started it? She used the box breathing method she'd learned from some class. Breathe in for four, hold it for four, out for four, then hold it again. She'd promised Dalton she wouldn't make a scene. She hadn't thought her making a scene might even be a possibility until this very moment. Her anger flared for totally different reasons, but if she blew up again, it would look like she was the problem.

Family. It drove her crazy at times.

"Sorry, let's just not talk about the wedding, okay?" Meg felt

Dalton pat her leg. She'd made it through one trial tonight. Hopefully, there wouldn't be more. "So how have you been, Dad? The business doing well?"

"The business is fine, dear. Thank you for asking." He turned to Junior. "This guy is killing it with the new creative arts section," he said, slapping him on the back. "He's brought a lot of business into the company this year."

Of course, he has. Junior was a superstar in their dad's eyes. Always had been and always would be. Meg sipped her drink and spooned some crab dip onto her plate, taking a few slices of fresh bread from the basket before handing it to Dalton.

"You should introduce him to your boss," Dad said as he scooped crab dip.

It took a minute to realize her dad was talking to her. "My boss? Mom?"

Dad chuckled. "Your other boss, L. C. Aster. I bet she needs a good accountant. I hear she's coming into some money from her rogue agent that died."

"I'm sure Ms. Aster has an accountant, Dad," Meg said as she stared at Junior. Had he asked their father to pave the way for his introduction? Maybe getting out of here without raising her voice was going to be impossible. No wonder she didn't go to Belleville for family dinners.

"But everyone should be aware of—" Dad started, but Junior put a hand on his arm.

Shaking his head, he said, "Meg said no, Dad. It's not an issue. I don't need her help building my book of business. Dalton, how's the ferry business? Have they promoted you to captain yet?"

"Ha, that's a few years off, if ever. First, I need to be promoted to an actual crew member. I'll get there. Besides, being outside on the ferry all day? It's the best job ever. Too bad you all work inside." He leaned back and let the server take his appetizer plate, replacing it with his dinner. "Time to focus on what a genius Emmett is with food. Did you know about his California restaurants?"

For a few minutes, Dalton praised his friend and the new restaurant. As he transitioned the conversation, they all ate, talking about food and memories. When it came time for dessert and coffee, Meg stood and excused herself to the bathroom.

"Do you want chocolate cake for dessert?" Dalton held her hand so she couldn't leave as he asked.

"Perfect." Smiling at him, she took her purse and headed toward the restroom.

She pulled out the envelope. The contents had been bothering her all night. She knew she hadn't left something. Was this something that Lee had dropped?

A small sitting area lay just inside the ladies' room. A place with a mirror and chairs to make a call or just ignore what was happening out in the dining room. Did women often sit here and wish things were different? Or hide from the men in their lives? Meg would have to ask her mom and aunt what the purpose of these sitting areas was.

But for today, it was a perfect place to open this envelope. She glanced at it. No writing on the outside. She opened the clasp and ran her finger between the sticky label and the main section.

She turned the envelope over. A tennis bracelet fell out. A diamond tennis bracelet. She held it up and let it sparkle in the light. She looked back into the envelope and saw a note.

To Meg, thank you for saving me from ruining my life. L

She put the tennis bracelet and the note back into the envelope, then folded it so it would fit into her purse. The envelope had been for her. The tennis bracelet had been a gift. From a man whom she'd barely even known.

As she returned to the table filled with the men in her life, she wondered, how had she saved Lee Anderson? And from whom?

Junior offered to walk with Dad back to the terminal, but Meg and Dalton begged off to go back to Meg's apartment and let Watson out. As her father said goodnight, he hugged her. "We need to do this more often. I've missed talking to you."

"Me too, Dad," although she hadn't felt like they had really talked tonight. Except about how well Junior was doing. Meg decided she'd be the better person here. Besides, it allowed her to justify not going to Dad and Elaine's family dinners. Or at least she could postpone going for a while.

She didn't say much as they started to walk up the hill. "I opened the envelope." Meg paused and took it out of her purse, handing it to Dalton.

He slid the contents out and whistled. "Wow, I need to up my game if random strangers are throwing jewelry at you just for dinner."

"Read the note, smartie." She loved that Dalton wasn't getting upset over this.

He put the bracelet back, then opened the note. "I don't understand. What did you save him from?"

"I have no idea. But it's weird, right?" She took back the note and put it and the envelope in her purse. "I guess there was more to our meeting than just chance."

"I wanted to ask if you were okay, until you dropped that bombshell," Dalton said after they'd walked quietly together. "Your dad seemed a little pushy tonight."

"I'm used to it. I guess you don't remember how much family dinners were the Junior show growing up. Or maybe the pushing only happened when you weren't there. 'Meg, you don't mind if we go to Junior's game rather than your concert, right? Meg, I know you got fewer gifts this year'—translation, every year—'but Junior needed a laptop. Or a phone. Or a car.'" Meg laughed as she lifted her face to the night sky to see the stars. "I'd forgotten a lot, but sitting there tonight, it all came rushing back. Junior always had favorite child status with my dad. I think Mom saw it too, but she's never talked to me about it."

"I'm sorry. He never talks bad about you. Maybe some of your decisions, yes, but I shut that down pretty quickly. He was mad you cut up the dress, though. He griped about it all the way from your place to the ferry the day we moved you. I told him I thought it was funny." Dalton took her hand. "This is why you don't visit your dad?"

"Mostly. I blame it on Elaine, but I just don't feel like he wants me there. Not really. He says all the right things. Until Junior is in the room with us. Then I disappear." Meg swallowed back the tears that were trying to escape her eyes.

Dalton squeezed her hand but didn't say anything as they kept walking.

Finally, she turned to him. "You think I'm wrong."

"Oh, no. I'm just wondering how my ideal family turned into this. I never saw any of it, until tonight. You don't think he planned the whole dinner to get you to convince Lilly Aster to hire Junior as her accountant, do you?"

"The dinner's going to be expensed. And there has to be a reason." She started walking again. "At least my mom's pretty normal. Except for the whole dating Irene's dad thing. Tomorrow you get to see the other side of the family dynamics. Aren't you excited?"

"I don't want to sound like a poor little orphan boy, but at least you have parents. They're dysfunctional, I'll give you that, but deep in their hearts, they love you. Maybe deep, deep in your father's heart. Past his worship of Junior. He has a small, tiny square of love for you."

Meg laughed. "I'm sorry. I know this isn't funny, but that's just cruel. True, but cruel."

"Family is hard, but I believe each and every member of yours loves you the best way they can. And as adults, it's up to us to acknowledge it and find friends that fill in the gaps. Like you, me, and Natasha. We're family." He looked up at the apartment. "Oh, and Watson. He's probably ready to go out. Let's go upstairs and I'll walk him. You can get into comfortable clothes."

They walked upstairs together. "Aren't you meeting Junior for a few drinks?"

"He can wait a minute. Watson's more important. Besides, your feet are probably killing you after walking in those heels."

Meg slipped them off as soon as they crossed the threshold. "I hate being a slave to fashion."

The grin on Dalton's face said everything.

"Just go, I can take Watson out," Meg said, but then the dog made a run to the door. "Hold on, buddy. Let me get some shoes on."

"I've got him. Go relax. You need to girth your loins to go to your mother's for another family dinner tomorrow night."

"You don't have to go, you know. You kind of paid your dues tonight," Meg said as she watched him click the leash on Watson.

Dalton stood and winked at her. "I live to serve the noble house of Gates."

"Oh, my goodness, are you on a fantasy kick? Or did you fall and hit your head?" She laughed as he shrugged and left the apartment with her dog.

Meg went into her bedroom and found some sweats and a tank. Then she put on cozy socks and shuffled out to the living room. Watson was already back inside, sitting on the couch. Dalton had left a note on the desk. She reached for it and read, *Lock up and I'll see you tomorrow.*

Watson was watching her.

"Dalton's not the boss of me," Meg said as she locked the

door. Watson barked. "Okay, I know. You're the boss of me. Let me get some popcorn started and we'll find a movie."

After she put the popcorn in the microwave, she took the envelope out of her purse. She looked at the bracelet and note again. "So, Lee Anderson. Who were you, really?"

She opened her notebook and wrote down everything she knew about the guy. Then she opened her laptop and started searching online to verify if anything she'd known was true. She moved over to the couch and snuggled with Watson as she worked.

After thoroughly scouring the internet, she closed her laptop and grabbed the bowl of popcorn that Watson was watching but had given up on ages ago. She curled her feet under her and thought about the contents of the envelope. The internet had let her down this time. Maybe she needed to add more parameters.

Grabbing her laptop one more time, she looked up the tennis bracelet's value. If it had real diamonds, it was worth a few thousand dollars. Why would he give it to her, someone he'd met less than a week ago?

She thought about the note. How had she saved his life? She knew they hadn't dated, not even once on a blind date. She'd been with Romain for four years. Before that, she'd dated off and on in college, and at the start-up, but nothing serious.

Too many questions for this late at night. Tomorrow, she had Pickleball, then she needed to spend the rest of the day on Lilly's work. Putting the laptop away, she grabbed her planner and scribbled a note for tomorrow. She was going to be late for dinner. She had to stop by the writers' meeting and see if anyone knew the real Lee Anderson.

She'd met him there. It had to be the key.

Meg forgot the murder and her family issues as she focused on the movie. With Watson at her side, the world seemed to make sense in that moment.

As long as she didn't dig too deeply or question the premise.

She was where she was supposed to be. Living in her aunt's apartment and working for her mom. Well, and Lilly. Maybe this was the cocoon stage before she turned into a butterfly. What would she become? A famous nonfiction author? Someone who worked in the book business?

All she knew was she needed to build her own boat to be able to survive another flood like the one Romain caused. Maybe she was smarter now, and there wouldn't be another Romain in her life. She and Dalton were doing well.

She focused on the movie. She wasn't going to lift any rocks tonight or look at any horse's teeth. She tried to recapture the calm she'd just been feeling.

It wasn't working.

CHAPTER 9

Even professional detectives need to take a break. Stepping back lets the clues marinate in your mind.

After an hour of Pickleball, Meg felt like she was ancient. How had she gotten so out of shape? And why did chasing a ball around a half-sized court make her feel like she'd run a marathon?

Maybe she should have gone to the doctor first. Wasn't that what they said in the disclaimer? And if the saying *you're as old as you feel* was real, Meg was in real trouble. She drained what was left of her water bottle.

"That was amazing. I know they say Pickleball isn't real exercise, but I love moving first thing in the morning, don't you?" A barely sweating Brooke leaned on the wall next to Meg, sipping her water. "You did great for your first time. This was your first time, right?"

Meg nodded, not trusting her voice. "Yeah, I'll do better next week."

"You need to stretch more. You could have hit some of those shots if you would have leaned into them." She took another bottle of water out of her bag and handed it to Meg. "You should bring two bottles of water, just in case. Of course, there's tap over there."

Meg nodded, looking in the direction of the fountain. There

was no way she was telling her doubles partner that she had brought and already drunk two bottles. Brooke didn't need to know. Meg dug into her bag and brought out a cereal bar she'd bought at a store on the way since she hadn't eaten before the match.

"And those are just sugar." Brooke frowned at the bar. "But I guess it's better than nothing. Next week, I'll bring you a protein bar that will make you feel better after the sugar high goes away and put some nutrients in your body besides sugar and carbs. We're going to have fun, I can feel it. Oh, there's Carly. I've got to go. See you next week at eight."

Meg waved and then opened the water bottle Brooke had left her. By the time she'd eaten the bar and drunk most of the water, she was feeling a little stronger. She was about to get up when a man squatted next to her and held out a Gatorade bottle.

"Water's great, but this will give you some electrolytes," he said gently. "You did great out there for your first time. Brooke's a machine and your opponents have been playing together for five years now. You gave them a run for their money. Once you get your game, you two might be the power double pair for your age group."

"If I can ever stand up again." Meg laughed. She took the bottle and sipped the lemon-lime drink. Then she peered at the man talking to her. "You're Derby Olsen."

He smiled and nodded. "I'm afraid I was a little taken back on Thursday when our paths crossed. It's nice to meet you, Meg."

She studied him and took another sip. "Thanks for the drink."

"Derby, we've got a problem with the next match." Another man came up behind him. "Do we need a medic here?"

Meg rolled her eyes and shook her head. "I'm fine. I'm just resting."

"Okay, then." The man turned back to Derby. "Can I get your help, please?"

"Sorry, Meg. I'm sure we'll run into each other again soon," Derby said as he stood up and left with the other man.

Meg decided it was time to leave. She had work to do and it might take her most of the day to hobble back to the apartment. She groaned lightly as she made her way to her feet. Besides, Watson was waiting for her.

The only good thing she could think of as she walked uphill to her apartment was that she only had eight more weeks of this torture.

As Meg's thighs burned from exertion, she noticed she was passing by a jewelry store. She decided to pop in since she didn't have to worry about bringing Watson in. She scanned the glass cases and found a bracelet that looked like the one she had in her desk. She blinked at the price.

"Oh, are you interested in that beautiful bracelet? I've already sold one this month. It's my most popular item lately." A man stepped up on the other side of the case. "Can I show it to you?"

"That's okay," Meg said as she thought about Lee's gift. "Did you sell the other one to a man, about six foot, dark hair with a beard?"

He frowned. "How did you know?"

"I think I have the bracelet. I'm just not sure why he gave it to me." Meg stared at the bracelet and noticed the sparkles. "Did he say anything about why he was buying it?"

The clerk rubbed his hand on his chin. "Let me think. He came in here last Monday, looking for a gift. He said he had found out that he had something in common with an island resident and wanted to thank her. I told him that was quite the thank-you."

She tapped the glass case. "Thanks for the information. Chief Miller might come by and talk to you. Show you a picture, that kind of thing."

"Oh, my. Is the bracelet part of an investigation?" The clerk's eyes widened. "He didn't steal it, he paid with a debit card. The charge went through. We had him come pick it up the next day just to make sure. We always do that with a large purchase."

"You might want to pull up those records," Meg said as she stepped out of the store.

What was it with men and jewelry? She wasn't even that big of a fan of baubles. Now she had a bracelet to put in her safety deposit box, to collect dust along with her old engagement ring.

Later that night, she hesitated as she approached Island Diner. She'd promised her uncle that this time, she'd stay out of the investigation. But the look on his face when he came to pick up the note and bracelet earlier that afternoon had told her that she might be in trouble.

For nothing. She couldn't control what men thought or tried to do. And if Lee Anderson had tried to give her the bracelet directly, she would have turned it down. Or at least she thought she would have. She needed to know the story and figure out why Lee had singled her out.

She'd go back to the beginning, where she'd met him. The writers' group.

She set Watson up for the night. It was beginning to be a routine: take him out for a short walk, fill water and food dishes, get out a chewy, and then turn on the television. He knew he was being left behind. The look he gave her was worthy of an Oscar nomination.

"I'll come and get you before I go to Mom's for dinner. This is just a short trip to Island Diner. You know you can't go in and I don't want someone untying you like last time." Meg hugged the cocker spaniel, rubbing his tan ears. "It's for your own good."

How many times had her parents used that line on her? Had they felt the emotional manipulation from her reaction like she did from her dog?

She grabbed her tote and put it over her shoulder as she tried not to jingle the door keys. No use pouring salt into the wound that Watson was already feeling. She paused at the door, making eye contact. Hope filled his eyes, and she crushed it by saying, "I'll be back soon."

She locked the door and hurried down the stairs. She didn't hear him barking, just the banging of hammers from the destruction phase of the home improvement show she'd turned on the television.

Rolling her eyes, she headed down to the meeting. They would gather at six, then start a writing sprint at six thirty. Then break and repeat the exercise. So she needed to get there before the writing began or no one would talk to her. She wanted to start with the person who'd set up the group and served as its official president and leader: Alice Monroe. If Alice didn't know Lee, she might know someone who did.

Opening the door to the conference room, she saw that her plan had worked and Alice was alone. "Hey, can we talk a minute?"

"Of course. You're Jolene's friend, Meg, right? She was insistent that you should join our group. Usually, we have someone come and visit for a few weeks before we invite them. But you're here on Jolene's recommendation alone." She sat down and rolled her eyes. "And I'm oversharing. Can you tell I've been home alone with the two-year-old for a week? My husband comes back on Friday. Then I'm heading to Mexico with my sister for the weekend. Margarita heaven. Anyway, still oversharing. What can I help you with?"

"You gave me some of the background I was looking for on how someone gets into the group. Can you tell me how and when Lee Anderson joined? Is he a local?" Meg sat next to her. She took the offered treat. Only to be nice. Then she almost groaned when she bit into the salted chocolate chip cookie.

"Good, huh? One advantage of being home is that I have time to bake." She took another cookie and broke it in half.

"Honestly, Lee Anderson had been coming by for a few months, asking about you. I guess he heard you were writing a book and wanted to meet you. I was about to tell him to pay up or stop coming, but then he officially joined a few weeks ago. He used to live on Bainbridge Island, so he met the eligibility criteria. We're a little loose with our criteria, which lets the tourists come too. Especially those who rent a house for a month or so. Anyway, back to Lee. I mentioned that Seattle has several writer groups that would have probably been closer for him. I thought he had a crush on you. Meet-cutes happen here more than you'd expect. Writers are more likely to find our soulmates in a group like this rather than in a noisy bar. At least you'd have something in common."

"He was asking about me?" Meg was sure she'd never met Lee Anderson before last week. Why would he have been looking for her?

"Yes. Although it's funny. The night he joined was the same week Jolene sent me your information and annual dues. Maybe he knew Jolene, too?" Alice looked up at a few people coming in. "And here come the rest. I don't see your laptop. Are you staying to write?"

Meg told Alice about the family dinner but promised to be there next week. As she walked out, she saw Irene walking in. Luckily, she hadn't seen Meg. She ducked out of the banquet room and headed to the main entrance.

Lee Anderson had known about her for months before she'd met him. Who was this guy? She blinked as she stepped out into the bright light of the day. The light in the diner had been muted. Now, even with the sun setting, the sun's rays enveloped her as she turned to go back to the apartment and pick up Watson. She didn't have time to write down what Alice Monroe had said unless she wanted to be late. Since Irene wasn't invited to dinner, she didn't mind going. Even if she'd have to talk to her brother.

Okay, maybe she had a few minutes to write down the encounter before she had to leave. Less time with Junior meant less biting her tongue so she wouldn't say what she wanted to say.

Meg opened the kitchen door at her mom's after letting Watson off his leash in the backyard. Someday she'd have a real house with a real backyard for Watson. But first, she needed a real job that paid her real good money.

"Hey family, I'm here," Meg called as she opened the door. "And be careful going out the back gate. Watson's in the yard, so don't let him out."

"He could have come inside with us, dear," her mom said, hugging Meg as she looked out the door window and saw Watson wandering. "Of course, this is probably the only place he gets to roam without being on that leash. He's probably thrilled."

"We go to dog parks and he gets out when I'm visiting Aunt Melody." Meg corrected her mom, then set her tote on a chair. "Are she and Uncle Troy coming tonight?"

"No, just you kids and Dalton," Mom said as she glanced at the clock. "Now that you're here, we need to get dinner on the table. I want to talk to you all about something."

"Mama's new beau?" Meg teased as she went to the half bath and washed her hands. "I think we all already know about Derby."

"I want to talk but not without your brother. Please go get the boys from the living room." Mom pointed in that direction. "They're watching some news program."

When Meg got there, she realized that the television wasn't tuned to the news. Some stock show was playing, in which some guy yelled and hit things with a mallet. Meg went over and grabbed the remote. She turned off the television.

"Meg, what the heck?" Junior stood and reached for the remote.

Meg held it high and away from his reach. "Mom said to come to the table. Supper's ready."

"Great, I'm starving." Dalton stood and hugged her. He whispered in her ear. "Thank you for saving me."

"Dalton, we still need to examine how your retirement portfolio is set up. You don't want to wait years to pass just to realize you've missed the stock wave." Junior was still focused on the financial discussion.

"You guys can talk about all those fun things and your high school highlight reel after dinner. Mom's waiting." She took Dalton's arm, and they walked toward the dining room. "Watson's outside, so don't let me forget him when I leave. He's already mad I went to town without him earlier."

"I didn't realize you were heading to town today. Shopping?"

Meg could hear the tension in Dalton's voice, but just because they were dating, it didn't give him the right to tell her what she could and couldn't do. She decided to be the bigger man or woman and tell him. "I went to the writers' group to see what they knew about Anderson."

Dalton pulled a chair out from the table and held it for her. "Any answers?"

"No. More questions, though. He was looking for me," Meg said, and let that sit with Dalton.

"Dig in," Mom said, and started passing food.

The one thing about Meg's childhood was that food was always around. Mom baked a cake every week for Sunday dinner. If the boys didn't destroy it, they had dessert at least through Tuesday, and then Mom would bake again. Tonight's feast included baked ham, scalloped potatoes, corn, rolls, and a salad. The cake appeared to be a two-layer chocolate with chocolate frosting. If Meg was to guess, she'd bet there was some vanilla ice cream in the freezer, to top it off. A perfect Sunday dinner. On a Tuesday.

Something was definitely wrong.

Junior and Dalton didn't seem to notice, but Meg saw her

mom watching them all eat. Throwing out conversation starters. She asked Meg if she was enjoying her class and Junior how his trip went.

In answer, he blushed and said it was very productive.

He didn't mention Anne and quickly moved the topic to Dalton's boat and his sailing lessons. "This guy's making as much in his side hustle as he's taking home from his job. Or he was, before he got distracted."

Now Junior stared at Meg. Dalton kept his head down and eyes on his plate.

"I knew you were giving Emmett lessons, now you have a business?" Meg asked Dalton.

He shrugged and looked up at her. "I work with a few people."

"And you could do more. I'm telling you, I've got a ton of clients I could send you from people I work with. Everyone wants a sailboat when they come into money, but nobody knows anything about them." Junior elbowed Dalton. "You'd be doing Seattle a public service. Keeping idiots off the water. Or at least training them to be safe. Did you hear about the guy who stranded his family last weekend?"

As Junior went off on his story, Meg looked at Dalton. He smiled back. They were going to have a conversation about this. Especially since Junior was apparently convinced that Meg was the distraction.

Dinner ended, then Meg's mom served the cake with ice cream, as Meg had expected, along with coffee. She brought Watson inside and gave him a bowl of dog food she kept on hand for him. Finally, her mom sat down and looked at each one of them.

"Kids, and Dalton, I wanted to tell you all in person about what was going on in my life. I've started dating someone and I don't know if it's going to last, but it just might. They say older folks like us tend to make faster decisions when we move into a new relationship. I guess we know what we want." Mom paused and sipped her coffee.

"Do you know what you want, Mom?" Meg asked. Watson trotted over to the table and rested his head on Meg's leg.

"I think I do. Anyway, that's what's happening, so I told you and now you know." Mom checked her watch. "He'll be here in five minutes. So be nice."

"Wait, that's the discussion? You don't want to know what we think?" Junior asked. "I guess I knew you and Dad wouldn't get back together as long as Elaine was in the picture, but I thought someday."

Mom looked puzzled for a minute. When she started talking, it was slowly and carefully. "Elaine wasn't the cause of our breakup. We were just different people than the two who had made vows together. We needed to move on. Your dad has, now it's my turn. And yes, no discussion. I'll repeat myself. Be nice."

The doorbell rang and Watson went crazy, running to the front door to greet Mom's visitor.

"I'll get it." Meg stood up and followed Watson. She needed to corral him anyway. She opened the door and Derby stood there, a bouquet of flowers in his arms. She shouldn't have been surprised at his appearance. "Come on in. Watson, hush."

Chapter 10

Admitting you have a filter helps you put the world in perspective. Try to see things from someone else's point of view.

Looking back on the night before, Meg drank her coffee, wondering where things had first gone wrong last night. Had it been when she invited Derby inside? Or when she'd accepted the invitation from Mom in the first place?

As soon as Derby walked into the dining room and handed Mom the flowers, Junior exploded. He stood, not even finished with his favorite dessert. He stared at Mom, then Derby, and announced he needed to leave. Urgent business engagement.

Dalton followed him outside, and when he came back in, he shrugged. "He's still getting used to the idea."

The rest of them had finished coffee, made small talk, and soon, Meg, Dalton, and Watson had left too.

Watson was still sleeping on his bed on the floor. He'd been annoyed at Meg's restlessness during the night, so he'd left his favorite spot by her feet and moved to his bed.

Meg refilled her cup. Maybe Watson had the right idea. Just ignore all the politics and history and accept Derby as he was. A person dating Meg's mom.

Besides, if she could deal with this, she'd be the favored

child. At least in her mom's eyes. She wasn't convinced that she could do anything about the situation anyway.

She took out the notes she'd made in the murder book on Lee Anderson. He'd specifically come to the writers' meeting to meet her. But she hadn't joined until a few months ago. So why did he think she'd be there, eventually? And what or who did he think she'd saved him from? That part didn't make sense.

She wondered if her uncle had found Anderson's laptop—or accessed his writing. It might explain Anderson's fascination with her. But the direct approach, asking her uncle point-blank, would just get her a lecture about staying out of his investigation.

A truck engine started, and Meg stood to look out the window. Uncle Troy was heading out to work. She could run down and ask him about Anderson. But she'd just got herself off his suspect list after the fight at the Local Crab. Did she want to shine a spotlight back on herself?

No, she needed to ignore what Alice had told her and focus on who could want Anderson dead. She opened her laptop and started reading his online column. With every disparaging review of a restaurant on the island, another suspect had been uncovered. Why had Lee Anderson hated the restaurants on Bainbridge Island so much?

She looked deeper. Had he been born here? Did he have family here? What was Lee Anderson's story?

After an hour of researching, she gave up. She had several leads, including the fact that Lee had gone to the same college she now attended. He lived in Seattle. And one thread linked all of the restaurant reviews he'd done for the *Seattle Times*. If the restaurant was located in Seattle, it usually received a good review. If it was on Bainbridge, the review was always less favorable. She was surprised that no one had seen the pattern before. But it was clearly there.

Lee Anderson had hated Bainbridge Island. But why? Alice

had mentioned that Lee grew up on the island. Did he still have relatives here?

Her sleuthing hit a dead end, so she dived into work for Lilly Aster. She almost had the author's travel schedules ready to review and ready for her boss to make a choice.

When she got to the bookstore, she felt good about the work she'd completed that day. Mom was in the stacks, adding new arrivals, when Meg and Watson came through the door. "We're here," Meg called out to the sound of the ringing bell.

Aunt Melody was sitting on the couch, reading. "Oh, hi Meg. I didn't realize it was so late. Felicia, we have a reservation at four."

"I remember," Mom said as she came out of the shelves. She hugged Meg. "Well, last night was a disaster even with my special chocolate cake. Your brother hates me."

"He doesn't hate you. He's just trying to deal with seeing you as a woman rather than his mother." Meg squeezed her mom before letting her go. She wiped tears off her mother's face. "You deserve to have a life."

Her mother looked up at her expectedly. "So, you like Derby?"

Now Meg felt on the spot. Both her mom and Aunt Melody were waiting for her answer. "Actually, I don't know if I like him or not. I've only met him twice now. Three times if you count seeing him in the restaurant with you that first night. I know he seems to like you. Those flowers were beautiful."

"Derby's very thoughtful," Mom replied as she went over to the counter. "He's a good man, Meg."

"I'm glad he's good to you." Meg came around the counter and tucked her tote away. Watson was already curled in his bed, tired from the walk from the apartment. "Aunt Melody, has Uncle Troy said anything about Lee Anderson's death?"

"Nope, I'm not getting involved in this. Troy asked me if

you had said anything about the murder this morning. I told him you were probably still dealing with Felicia's news and ignoring his investigation." Aunt Melody stared at Meg. "You are staying out of it, right?"

"Sure, but do you know anything about Lee Anderson living on the island? He seemed to have a vendetta against restaurants here. Nobody got a good recommendation from him."

Aunt Melody laughed. "Troy said the same thing. But he didn't ask about Lee living here. There were some Andersons around several years ago. Felicia, you'd know better. We had a Grant Anderson in school with us, didn't we?"

"Grant was a bit of a scoundrel. He asked you to prom when he was still dating Beth Millings, remember? You didn't know they were dating and told him yes, and then she marched in the library during study hall and yelled at you for stealing her man. Very dramatic." Mom smiled at the memory. "You were so mad, you found him at basketball practice, walked out onto the court while they were playing, and told him you wouldn't be going with him to the dance. Then Troy stepped in between you two and asked you to go with him to the dance. It was the start of your romance."

Aunt Melody smiled. "Thank goodness for Grant Anderson, then. What happened to him?"

Mom sat down on the couch, next to her sister. "Let me think. You went off to college and then New York to intern for a book agent. Oh, Grant and Beth got married. The marriage didn't stick. Last I heard, he had moved to the coast."

"Did they have kids?" Meg watched the sisters as they walked down memory lane. They'd shared a lot of living together. Was this Lee Anderson's connection to Bainbridge Island? He had been a resident as a child. Maybe his memories here weren't happy, which had affected his reviews.

"I'm sorry, I don't remember. Your dad and I had just gotten married and Junior was on the way. I was too busy to keep up with island gossip. And after that incident with your aunt, Beth wasn't a close friend."

Aunt Melody broke out in laughter. "It's always my fault, right? Well, if Beth chose someone who would do something like that, I don't think you would have wanted to be friends with her anyway."

"Probably true." Mom stood and held out a hand for her sister. She helped Aunt Melody off the couch. "All I ask is that you give Derby a bit of a break and get to know him. I hear you're part of his Tuesday young adult teams. I didn't know you were interested in Pickleball. We could have played women's doubles."

"I thought I'd try it. And before this week, I didn't know you were playing because you didn't tell anyone. Remember? Maybe it would have been easier for Junior to accept Derby if you were honest about your relationship at the beginning."

"We didn't know if it even was a relationship," Mom started, but then she backed down. "Sorry, Meg, you're probably right. It was important for you and Junior to see us as friends first. I messed that up."

"Wow, you're human," Meg teased. "I thought you were Supermom?"

"Maybe I'm only Supermom when I'm just a mom. When I add in my personal life to being a wife or mother, I seem to fail." She shook her head when Meg started to object. "I'm just thinking aloud, dear. No need to pad my fragile ego. Come on, Melody, let's go eat. I'm starving. I don't think I ate a bite last night at dinner. I was that upset."

Meg knew for a fact that her mother had eaten well the night before, but she might be remembering it differently. Her mom tended to eat when she was worried and then forget that she ate at all. Last night had been stressful, for all of the family. "Have a fun night."

* * *

Dalton showed up at seven with pizza. He set the box down and hugged her. "I thought you might need some food. You didn't eat much last night."

"Funny, I was just talking about last night's dinner with Mom and Aunt Melody. I feel bad for Mom." Meg collapsed on the couch and opened the box. The smell of the fresh crust and tomato sauce hit her first, and her stomach grumbled at the thought of pizza. "Thank you. I am hungry. But I'd rather not talk about that fiasco. Is Junior okay?"

"He packed up this morning and headed back to Seattle. I don't think he's dealing with your mom's new dating life well at all. You know your brother—out of sight, out of mind." Dalton handed Meg a napkin. "But that's his problem. Your mom's a classy lady and she deserves some happiness. No matter what the kids think."

"No, go ahead, tell me what you really feel," Meg teased as she finished off her slice. She wiped her hands and stood to grab sodas from the fridge in the back. When she returned with two root beers, Dalton took the offered can. "Honestly, my head agrees with you. My heart is just a little scratched. I know Mom and Dad aren't getting back together but tell that to my inner child. I didn't realize that I was even holding out hope until the flame was doused by Mom's announcement."

"Okay, then we'll talk about something else. How's the book coming along?" Dalton sipped his soda and then went back for more pizza.

"Fine, let's talk about Mom and Derby." Meg laughed as she grabbed another slice, then set it down on the napkin. "Okay, let's talk about writing. Honestly? I'm in a funk. I don't know if what I'm writing is all dribble or if it works. I think it works, but then I read it, and I hate everything. Lilly said going to this writers' group and making friends should help, but so far, all I've gotten out of the meeting is going to dinner with a guy who was later murdered and, tada, I'm a suspect. Not quite the help I needed."

"And you got to talk to Vi Chin. That must have been amazing." Dalton pointed out a bright side. "Developing trusting relationships takes time. You can't go to a few meetings and find your perfect writer friend. Maybe you need to try a group from the college. There have to be a ton of writers there."

Meg picked back up her slice and ate it, thinking about Dalton's points. When she finished, she wiped her mouth with a napkin. "Did I tell you that Irene's in the writers' group here? Her and her new boyfriend? Maybe you're right. Maybe I need to check out another group. I'll look at the college's bulletin board online. You always have an answer."

"That's me, the answer guy. And I only charge for my very best answers, these ones are only so-so. I'll give you them for free." Watson came up to the coffee table and barked at them. Dalton laughed and stood. "I'll take him outside for a walk, but don't eat all of the pizza when I'm gone. I want another slice."

After Dalton and Watson left, Meg was left sitting and thinking about the group. She hadn't told Dalton that Lee Anderson had started coming to the meeting to see her. She wondered if Lilly had known him. Maybe Lilly had asked him to talk to Meg about writing. That could be plausible. But Alice said Jolene was the one who recommended her to the group.

And she wanted to know who told Vi Chin who she was and how to find her. A woman had left a tip. Who hated Meg enough to see her on the hook for a murder she didn't commit? The actual murderer? Or just a disgruntled friend or acquaintance? Like Irene.

She grabbed her phone and texted Irene, asking if she'd leaked her name to Vi Chin.

The text she got back was brief and to the point.

I didn't know about your mom and my dad then. Why would I tell Vi Chin about your dinner?

Okay, so Meg had broken one of her own rules of investigation. She'd forgotten to make a timeline of what happened.

She texted a short **sorry** message back to Irene and got back a terse answer.

Whatever.

Then she went into the back and retrieved a box out of the recycling pile. Using tape, she tried to fashion it into a large rectangle, but it still folded. At least it would be easy to conceal and carry.

She cleared the pizza and other remnants of dinner off the coffee table and then cleaned it with the spray her mom kept under the counter. She carefully dried the top and set the cardboard on the table.

Using a black marker, she drew a thick line across the cardboard rectangle. She scrawled a cross point about fifteen percent down the line, which represented the day Lee Anderson's body was found. Then, she added the day she met him at the writers' group. And finally, their not-date dinner. The evening he had planned to give her expensive jewelry for an action she didn't remember taking. She put Vi Chin's visit on the board, too.

Then in her murder notebook, she added some questions. Who had called the news about her? It could have been anyone on the island except Chin had made a point of saying she'd tried to get people to talk, but no one had volunteered the information.

Until she'd gotten a call. A call that told her exactly where she could find Meg Gates and the most likely times she'd be at the bookstore. Information that Irene knew since she'd been stalking Meg, trying to get her to buy a cruise a few months ago.

She needed to talk to Irene. Face to face. As much as she didn't want to, she knew it was the only way to figure out if Irene was the leak. Then she needed to know what exactly she had told Vi Chin that had sent her on the ferry to Bainbridge.

And if it wasn't Irene that talked? If she'd been truthful in her text? Well, Meg would cross that road when she came to it. Besides, there was always Rachel. Although her ex-sorority sister and ex-bridesmaid had gotten the last laugh on Meg—she'd got Romain. Rachel probably didn't care enough to send Meg's name in to the news, unless she'd gotten money for the tip.

When Dalton came back, he helped her finish putting the points they knew on the timeline. Standing back, looking at the whole picture, Dalton whistled. "When we made a timeline for Meade's murder, we knew so much more than we do now. I think life is getting in the way of your investigation."

"Probably true, much to Uncle Troy's joy. I have been focusing on other things. Like work, school, and my mother's love life. My priorities have been jumbled." Meg glanced at the timeline. "Something happened before I met Anderson that fueled his murderer to go to this extreme. I made a list of all the island spots that Lee had trashed in his column. Maybe one of them was hurt enough to blame the column for their demise."

"I'm off tomorrow if you want some help talking to people. I don't like the idea of you running around the island asking about murderous intent all alone." He stepped over to the counter and grabbed the last piece of pizza.

Meg thought about her day. "I'll go over to Lilly's to drop off some work first. I can ask her if she knew Anderson then. Meet me here at ten and we'll go visit some of these restaurants to see what we can find out. Natasha has already spilled her guts about her feelings on the charming article he wrote on her bakery."

"And the attack piece on Emmett's restaurant hasn't happened yet. Let's hope he didn't get time to write the piece. I'd hate to give your uncle both Natasha's and Emmett's names again as suspects. One of these days, he might think we're serious."

Meg folded up the timeline. "I don't think Uncle Troy takes anything I say about his investigations seriously. He just tells me to stay out of the line of fire."

Dalton walked over and pulled her into a hug. "I have to say I agree with your uncle on that point."

Chapter 11

Having a partner around when you're out investigating is Safety 101. Even if they just think they're having lunch with you.

Thursday morning, Meg sat drinking coffee in Lilly's office, chatting about books and writing. She'd dreamed about this scene when she first came back to the island and Aunt Melody had set up her job. Meg wanted to be part of L. C. Aster's writing world. Except today the dream was descending into bleak reality. Meg had a book started that she had no idea how to finish, and Lilly was complaining about her ex-husband, Josh, and how needy he was, especially regarding his writing.

Even the amazing view of Puget Sound from Lilly's office windows was gray and foggy.

"You know, I knew this would happen, and yet, somehow, he drags me back into the relationship. Honestly, I liked it much more when we lived apart and came together just for sex." Lilly laughed at Meg's shocked expression. "Please don't judge me. I didn't like the sneaking around part, just the fact I had more 'me' time. I'm telling him to stay at his condo in Seattle more. He's always busting into my office when I'm writing to ask me about a sentence. Seriously? A sentence? Just write the story, then do the edits. The way he writes, he'll never finish the first draft of the book. And since he's without an agent right now, he needs a strong book to go out on submission."

"You sound like you're talking about me." Meg sighed as she sipped her coffee. "I'd love to have you next door to question a word or a phrase. I promise, I'm going to the writers' group, well, except for this week. I couldn't go because Mom had a mandatory family meeting."

"Life goes on around your writing, it always will. The successful writers among us make sure they carve out time for sitting and staring at the blank screen. We all suffer for our art. The magic is in the doing. Not the planning or thinking about the book. You must sit down on a regular basis and fight with the words. It can be every day or once a week—but it needs to be consistent. It's why dancers practice the same move over and over. Muscle memory. In this case, the muscle you're training is your mind. No one is going to hold your feet to the fire. Or ask if you got your homework done, including me."

"I get the message. One more question, though." Meg tucked her notebook and pen back into her backpack. "The writers' group. Did you attend it when you started writing? I guess I'm asking why you sent me there."

"Is it not working out?" Lilly asked.

"I was just wondering what pointed you there." Meg wasn't asking the right question, she knew, so she dived in. "I met Anderson there and wondered if you knew him."

"I didn't realize that. Jolene found the group online, I think. You'll have to ask her." Lilly tapped her fingers on her lips, a giveaway that she was thinking. "Actually, the idea of a writing group came up when my agent, Sarah, was around and we were talking. I mentioned you were writing and would need a nonfiction editor soon. She doesn't do nonfiction, but she knows some people. Then she asked if you were in a group. She's very supportive of writers' groups. She says they weed out the people who aren't serious about the craft."

"On that note, I better get back to the apartment, I'm meeting Dalton at ten. And I have writing times blocked on my calendar, I promise." Meg finished her coffee as she stood.

"Why are you asking about the writing group? Is something wrong?" Lilly leaned forward.

Meg pressed her lips together. She could just let it go, or she could use Lilly's wealth of information to learn more. She decided to tell her everything, from meeting Lee Anderson to the disastrous dinner, and, finally, the gift he left her with the cryptic note. "I talked to Alice Monroe, who runs the meeting, and she said Lee's been looking for me there for a while. Not many people know I'm writing a book or that I'd be attending, so how would he know to find me there?"

"Talk to Jolene, but I'm sure that she didn't tell anyone. She's very good at the confidentiality piece." Lilly paused, and then her computer beeped. It was time for her next appointment. "And look at Sarah's stable of writers. Maybe he was one of hers. I hate to think she broke confidentiality, but maybe she didn't see the harm in it. Especially if she thought the two of you could help each other."

"That makes sense." Meg nodded and headed to the door. "Where's Jolene?"

"She's in Seattle this morning. I'll tell her you need to talk to her when she gets back." Lilly turned to her computer and was on to the next task before Meg left the room.

Meg let herself out and rode her bike back to the apartment. Dalton was already there, playing with Watson near the garage. Dalton was the only one who could get Watson to chase a ball. When Meg threw it, he just lay down and watched her go after it.

He threw the ball one more time, then helped her store the

bike in the garage. His truck was parked on the street. "How did your meeting go?"

"Fine. She's keeping me busy with work. Which is great. But apparently, she told me to attend the writers' group because her agent said I needed one. Jolene found the group online." Meg nodded to Watson as he ran back toward them with the ball. "My list is upstairs. I guess we should leave him here?"

"Yeah, we'll be going into places he can't come. The first restaurant is on the other side of the island, so I thought we'd drive there, then park in town to hit the other five." Dalton took the ball that Watson dropped at his feet. "Come on, killer, let's get you settled in for a morning nap."

Within ten minutes, they were parked outside the Steakhouse, the first restaurant that Lee had torched in his column. Meg had never been, but the restaurant was an island tradition, especially for special occasions. Tourists loved the place, so the owner enforced a special rule to always leave at least one table open for a local. Especially if they called for a table and mentioned that it was an anniversary or birthday.

"They don't open until three," Meg pointed out.

Dalton climbed out of the truck, and when Meg met him in front of the long brown building, he nodded to the door. "Emmett called ahead for us. The chef, Jon Michael, is expecting us."

"You asked Emmett for help?" Meg was impressed. Usually, Dalton liked to keep his friends out of investigations. Or at least out of the last one.

"All the chefs have been talking about Lee Anderson's death. They know your uncle is going to come along sometime or another to chat with them. I think they just want to be ahead of the curve and let you know they weren't involved."

"Somebody killed Anderson," Meg pointed out. "And he damaged their businesses."

"Hardly." A man in chef's whites appeared next to them in

the foyer of the restaurant. “Lee Anderson’s negative reviews became a rite of passage around here. You weren’t a real restaurant until he speared you with his words.”

“Chef Jon Michael, thank you for talking with us.” Meg held out her hand and they shook and made introductions. A framed copy of Anderson’s article was hanging on the wall next to a James Beard nomination. Someone had written *WRONG* in red on the glass, covering the article. “So, this is it?”

“One night, he visited the restaurant. The next month, I received my James Beard nomination. The culinary community thought he was a joke. Even the chefs from Seattle restaurants he liked. I’d heard that his paper was considering firing him a couple of months ago. We were planning a get-together to toast the end of an era. But then he died.” He nodded to a nearby table. “Would you like to sit? Maybe something to drink? I don’t think we have any food ready, but we could make you a cheese plate or maybe a quick pasta dish.”

“We won’t take up much of your time.” Meg sat down at the table, already covered with a white cloth.

“At least let me get you some coffee or water.” He nodded to a server.

“Water, please.” Meg smiled as the young waiter looked at her. Dalton ordered the same, and Chef Jon Michael asked for coffee.

“I drink coffee all day and I still sleep like a baby. Of course, I don’t get out of here until ten or so.” He rubbed a wrinkle out of the tablecloth as he talked. “So, Lee Anderson is dead. The boy never was happy. I knew him when he used to come in with his parents. I thought maybe he’d become a chef—he loved food. And had an amazing palate. Then his father died, and I heard his mom moved him closer to her family. Near the coast. I welcomed his return with open arms, then he bit me with that article. I couldn’t believe it.”

Meg was taking notes in her notebook while Chef Jon Michael talked. It wasn't quite the story that her mom had told her, but if Anderson's dad had died, it explained the move. As the chef continued to talk, she thought about what Lee had told her about being a food critic. He'd thought he'd been incognito during his restaurant visits. "So, you knew Lee wrote the review. Did everyone else recognize him when he came into their restaurant?"

"Of course. It's a small town. We talk among ourselves and he puts his picture on his column. Not smart for a food critic. Others who come act like normal patrons, so we usually don't spot them. That's why we are always training the staff on customer service and quality. We want to be the best. We want to celebrate your big days with our amazing food and service. I wouldn't have kept doing this if I didn't treat every customer like I would my own family."

"He said he liked to bring people along to help hide his being a critic." Meg wondered if anything Lee had told her was true.

Chef Jon Michael shrugged. "He might have on other reviews, but here, he came in all by himself. I even came out and talked to him that night. Asked if he was visiting or returning home. He said he'd moved to Seattle for a girl, so who knew how long that would last. I told him to bring her with him, but he never did."

"Did he say who his girlfriend was?"

The chef shook his head. "Sorry, I don't remember. He did say she was out of his league, though."

Meg wrote down *Girlfriend?* Then she finished her water. "Thank you for talking with us. We'll have to come back soon. It smells amazing in here."

"I learned that trick from the grocery store. They always pump the smell of their freshly baked bread into the store make you buy more. Here, I just want you to enjoy the food.

And come back anytime." He stood and nodded toward the back where someone was waiting. "My absence from the kitchen has been noticed. I enjoyed talking with you, even if it was about a sad subject. I hope whoever killed Lee is found quickly. Murder on the island is never good for the tourist business."

After they got into the truck, Meg turned to Dalton. "What do you think? Was he being honest?"

"Totally. I think it's interesting that Lee blew his cover on his first assignment on the island. I wonder if his newspaper would talk to us."

"Or his former newspaper." Meg thought about the night they'd met. "I don't think he'd just lost his job. He told me that the paper would pay for my meal. Or he was lying to me."

"That bothers me too. If he was working on that book he talked about, wouldn't he just say that? Why tell you he was doing a column for the newspaper? I wonder why the newspaper was considering firing him. Budget cuts or malfeasance?" Dalton looked over at Meg. "What's the next place on your list?"

By one, they had talked to everyone on the list. Every chef seemed to be in on the joke of getting a bad review from Anderson. Several had framed the review and posted it, like at the Steakhouse. A few were still visibly upset about the rating, but most shrugged it off. Meg and Dalton decided to have lunch at Proper Fish, the last restaurant on Meg's list.

"As Chef Jon Michael said, Lee's reviews were treated as a joke." Meg sipped her soda as they waited for their fish and chips to be delivered. "I'm thinking his job isn't why he was killed. And no one else said anything about him being fired."

"If it's not the job, then maybe it's that girlfriend who was so out of his league?" Dalton adjusted the salt and pepper in the table carrier.

"And there's still the note to me about saving him. Was he

talking about the girlfriend? Maybe I sold him a self-help book? I just don't remember ever seeing him before."

"Maybe he got the wrong Meg Gates?" Dalton leaned back as the server brought their food. "And saved by the bell. I'm starving."

"There was no bell." Meg rolled her eyes. "What, are you getting tired of playing detective?"

"A little bit. Especially the boring parts, like this. On television, the sleuth finds the killer by the end of the hour and is involved in at least a car chase or shoot-out. We've been at it for three hours and no one has even thrown a cross word at us, let alone a knife." He waved a French fry at her for emphasis. "Unless our food is poisoned. Although, right now, I'm too hungry to care."

"We haven't been poisoned." Meg sprinkled malt vinegar on her humongous serving of fish. "But maybe I was the wrong Meg. He thought I was someone else. Think about that."

They spent the rest of the meal talking about food and life and avoiding the subjects of Meg's family and the current investigation. She finished her meal as Dalton took a call. When he came back to the table, he finished her fries. "I need to drop you home, then come back to help Kirk move out of the marina. He and Elaina have made up and she's letting him back into the house."

"I can walk home." Meg glanced at her watch. She had plenty of time to get home, change, and get Watson ready before her shift at the bookstore.

"Are you sure? I don't want to kick you out of the truck."

She stood and leaned over to kiss him. "You didn't kick me out. I chose to leave. Tell Kirk good luck."

"Third time might be the charm," Dalton said as he put a hand on her back as they weaved their way out of the small dining room. Even after the noon rush, the restaurant was still busy. "I'm sure he's going to be back living on the boat sooner than later, but what are you going to do? Love always wins."

Since Meg had a few minutes, she swung by the bakery on the way home. Natasha was at the front, clearing off a table. The dining room was empty. "Hey, you're slow."

"The ferry just docked. I've got about twenty minutes to clean up and restock before the next wave comes in. However, since it's Thursday, it won't be as bad as tomorrow. What are you doing? Aren't you working today?"

"I'm heading up to the apartment to get Watson, then walking back to the bookstore to relieve Mom. I don't want to be early, in case she wants to talk about Derby." Meg sank into a chair and watched her friend work.

"You didn't call after the family dinner. Was it so horrible?"

"Yes. I'll tell you later. But I have a question to ask you. When Lee Anderson reviewed your bakery, were you mad?"

"Of course." Natasha grabbed two chocolate cookies from the case. "I wanted to smack him. I think sometimes getting a 'meh' review is worse than a bad one. I never saw him around. And I wasn't here when he came in. At least, not that I noticed."

"All of the chefs I talked to today said they knew he was reviewing them and that his column was a big joke." Meg said the thing that had been bugging her all afternoon. "Everyone said it didn't bother them."

"They're lying."

Meg almost choked on the bite of the cookie. "What?"

"Chefs are extremely protective of their brand and their food. If they said they didn't care what Lee Anderson said about them, they lied to you. Maybe they're lying to themselves, too. But they cared. They cared a lot."

Meg thought back on the interviews they'd done today. The chefs had been happy to talk to her, maybe a little too happy.

"You're right. I should have brought you with us. You would have gotten to the bottom of it."

Meg took a cookie for the road and headed back up the hill to her apartment. When she arrived home, she pulled out the notebook she only used for writing ideas about the guidebook. She sat down at her desk and wrote a paragraph about making sure that you either knew the business or had a subject matter expert with you when you interviewed, if possible. Neither she nor Dalton knew anything about opening a business or feeling protective over it afterward, a natural aspect of the process. The chefs had been bothered by Anderson's columns, but they might have hidden it from themselves. No one was that confident at all times.

She put the notebook away and gathered everything up for her bookstore shift. Hopefully, she'd have some quiet time to work on Lilly's book tour proposal as well. She'd gotten some clarifying details this morning from Lilly. As well as more than she'd wanted to know about her love life with her ex-husband.

Meg hurried back into town and made it into the bookstore just before another ferry was due to disembark. Not that she expected a lot of people. This late on a Thursday, any visitors to the island were probably heading to a restaurant for a meal or a bar to meet up with friends. Window shopping at the little shops on the main drag happened mostly in the morning.

Her mother stayed away from small talk, probably afraid of what Meg might say about her new relationship, and hurried out the door as soon as Meg settled in. Meg hoped it wouldn't be this awkward for long.

As she shelved the new books that had arrived that day, the bookstore door opened and Emmett Harding walked in. The man strutted. Not in a bad way, but he knew who he was and what he wanted. When he saw Meg at the counter, he took off the fedora hat he'd been wearing and stepped over to greet her.

Meg set down the book she'd been working on. "Good evening, Chef Harding."

"Please, call me Emmett. I hope I'm not disturbing your work tasks, but I needed to talk to you. I got several calls from my fellow chefs today after your visits. I'm afraid we left the wrong impression with you and Dalton. I called him first to ask where I could find you. I need to explain."

CHAPTER 12

If you don't know a business or community well, make sure you find a subject matter expert to help you interview. You'll understand the nuances of conversation more clearly.

Chef Emmett Harding picked a cookbook off the counter where Meg had been unpacking new arrivals. "I find the cookbooks I enjoy are a mixture of recipes and memories. Like this one. I hear she talks a lot about her childhood growing up in Tennessee."

"Yes, I like those cookbooks best as well." Meg climbed on the stool behind the counter. She didn't think this was going to be a fast conversation. "So, some of the local chefs called you today? I hope they didn't think I was being intrusive."

"Oh, no. They said you were sweet." Emmett set the book down. "Look, I don't think they were completely honest with you about how they felt about Anderson's reviews. Most of us want to murder anyone who says something bad about our restaurants, but we'd never act on the feeling. We're just overprotective. I'm sure a review from Anderson lost a local eatery some business, especially when it was first published, but we always win people back. We all cook great food. What else matters?"

"Exactly. It's like those people who say that chocolate is bad. They don't know what they're talking about." Meg pointed to the book on southern cooking that he'd picked up a few minutes ago. "And some people don't like southern food. It's not that it's bad, it's subjective. So why weren't they just honest with me?"

"No one wants to be on your uncle's suspect list. Getting a bad review is one thing. Going to trial for killing someone? That can tank a business. We're all about the relationships. You, as a customer, should feel like you're at home or a friend's house, eating the best meal you've ever had."

"Even being accused of killing someone puts a bad vibe out there." Meg nodded, understanding now why they hadn't been honest, and why she felt that something had been off. She wasn't any closer to finding out who had killed Lee Anderson, but she understood the restaurant business a little better. "Do you mind if I ask you some questions about food critics in general? Or about Lee?"

"Of course." Emmett glanced at his watch. "I have a few minutes before I need to be in the kitchen. What do you want to know?"

When Chef Harding left the bookstore, he had a new cookbook in his hands. And Meg had a good understanding of opening a restaurant, as well as how food critic reviews brought people in or kept them away. She kept writing notes long after he left, but eventually she stood and stretched, returning to finishing shelving the books.

When Dalton arrived at nine to walk her home, he asked, "Did Emmett find you? I would have been here, but I promised your aunt I'd help her move some furniture into one of her rentals. Troy was going to help, but he got called to the station."

"Why? What's going on?" Meg asked as she tucked the keys away in her pocket after locking the door.

"She didn't tell me." He took Watson's leash. "But he was back at the house when I dropped her off a few minutes ago, so it couldn't have been anything big."

Dalton might be right, but Meg thought her uncle had been way too quiet on Lee Anderson's death. Although he hadn't been found on a very well-known author's beachside. Maybe that was the difference between this investigation and the last one, where Lilly's agent was the victim. The news even seemed to have quieted down about Anderson's death. Maybe Vi Chin would leave Meg alone now.

Now that she knew exactly how the local chefs felt about Anderson, she'd look back on the interview notes she'd taken to see if anyone stood out. Emmett wanted her to know the truth, but he hadn't believed that any of his friends could have actually killed Lee.

Maybe he was wrong.

"Penny for your thoughts," Dalton said to her right.

She blinked, then shook her head. "Still thinking about what would lead someone to kill Anderson. He wasn't very likable, so I could get the sentiment, but murder seems so intimate. It had to be more than just a bad review, right?"

"A human life should be worth more than just an exchange of words." Dalton paused at the bottom of the stairs. "I need to get home. Early call-out tomorrow."

"You didn't have to walk me home," Meg said. Then she leaned in to kiss him. "But I'm glad you did."

"Shucks, ma'am, I was already in the neighborhood," he quipped as he ran a finger down her cheek. "I hate the thought of you walking alone at night. I know it's not a big city, but bad things happen everywhere."

"Not if you think good thoughts," Meg said as she called to Watson. "Thanks again for walking me home. Have a good day at work tomorrow."

"I'll be on the ferry. It's always a good day, even when bad things happen." He raised his hand as he went over to his truck, and he waited for her to get inside before starting the engine.

Meg refilled Watson's water bowl and watched out the kitchen window as Dalton drove away.

It was nice of him to walk her home. She paused in that thought. "Unless he knew why Uncle Troy was called to the station and he was worried about me. Why would he worry about me unless the person who Uncle Troy suspected was one of the chefs we talked to earlier?"

She went to the door and saw the lights were mostly off at her aunt's house. They were upstairs. She wouldn't bother them now, but she set her alarm for six. She needed to do her work for Lilly, and if her aunt saw she was up, she might come over for some coffee and gossip after Troy left.

If Aunt Melody didn't come by, Meg would go to her.

With a plan for tomorrow, Meg curled up on the couch with Watson and turned on a movie.

Her brain wasn't good at letting things go, so she brought her notebook to the couch. Having it close by helped her relax, and she finished the movie.

The next morning, Aunt Melody came up with a loaf of zucchini bread still warm from the oven. She unwrapped the dishtowel that covered the basket and took the loaf out. "Get out the butter. It's still warm. I hope you like walnuts."

"I love walnuts." Meg grabbed small plates and moved the butter and a knife to the table. "Coffee?"

"Please. Troy has me freaking out, so I didn't get much sleep last night." Aunt Melody cut two thick slices from the bread and then rewrapped it with the cloth. "You'll need to put it away in a ziplock after it cools to keep it fresh."

"Okay." Meg set her coffee in front of her, then sat down. She focused on the bread and took a bite. "Yum. You know you're making it really hard to move out of here."

Aunt Melody laughed. "Then don't. I like having you nearby. Especially now that your mom is in the lovey-dovey stage with Derby. I never see her anymore. He called during our dinner on Wednesday to make sure she had time for dinner last night. Now that they aren't hiding it from anyone, they are together all the time."

"I guess she was lonely." Meg didn't want to disrespect her mom or Aunt Melody's feelings.

"Felicia had a full life. A man should never take up all your available space. You lose yourself. That's what happened between your mom and dad. Stephen had a busy life, but Felicia was just left at home. Which, when you kids were little, was fine. But when you guys got your own lives, well, she was lonely. So, she bought the bookstore and started attending different clubs. But by then, it was too late. Your parents didn't have anything left in common." Aunt Melody looked up and frowned. "I shouldn't be dumping all of this on you. I'm just worried she'll go all in again and lose herself in the process."

Meg took in the information. "I did the same thing with Romain. I had just lost my job, so when he proposed, he told me to wait until after the honeymoon to start looking again. And then, wham. He fell for someone else."

"We do like to jump in feet first." Aunt Melody laughed. "Look at me. I'm a full-time homemaker. Of course, I have our rentals, and they keep me busy. I'm thinking about getting back into the agenting business. Taking on a few clients. Not a full stable, but some new hopefuls."

"Well, let me know and I'll beg you to take on my proposal to shop. I've been reading up on agents, although I want to write the book first. Just to make sure I can."

"Darling, I'd love to rep you. Just let me know." Aunt Melody sipped her coffee.

"What's going on with Uncle Troy? Dalton said he was called to the station last night?" Meg hoped her question sounded casual.

"Just someone to interview. I guess Troy had him flagged in case he came on the ferry, and he showed up last night." Aunt Melody looked up at Meg and must have seen something in her face. "And no, I don't know who it was or why he wanted to talk to him. Let's change the subject."

Aunt Melody left a few minutes later, after they'd finished the bread and coffee. Meg went over and got her timeline from the bedroom closet. She added yesterday's mystery interview. So far, she was the most likely suspect in killing Anderson when she looked at the plotted points. It was a good thing she had been in Seattle with Dalton. And Mom and Derby. It was strange that the night when she'd had a huge shock about her mom was also the perfect alibi for not being in town to kill Anderson. Typically, she would have just closed up the bookstore and walked home, alone.

Pushing the thought away, she refocused on the case. She needed more information on the victim. Maybe his murder had something to do with his past here on the island. Or maybe it had something to do with the note he'd attached with the gift. Had Anderson been engaged before, and if so, to whom?

Maybe this was the lead that her uncle was chasing. A thought occurred to her. She'd never heard anything from him about the bracelet and the note. She knew it would muddy the waters as far as her innocence was concerned. But finding out why he would buy her an expensive bracelet had to be a clue, right? One more thing on her to-do list. Uncle Troy hadn't returned the bracelet, so she had an excuse to stop by the police station to see if she could get it back. Then she'd stop at the bank and put it in the safety deposit box until she decided what to do with it.

At this rate, she'd have enough jewelry stowed away for a small down payment on a house. She didn't see herself as a woman men threw jewelry at, but she'd read about it happening. She bet it happened to Rachel. That girl knew what she wanted and got it. Like Romain.

Meg had heard rumors about Rachel being engaged several times, with several rings in her jewelry box to prove it. But at least she hadn't gotten Meg's ring. Once Meg heard that Rachel had wanted it, she was determined not to give it back or let Romain buy it from her. It was her trophy. She might not have gotten the man, but she still had the ring.

And, she thought as she got busy with the work Lilly had assigned, she had still gotten the better deal.

"I'm glad you stopped by. I've got some more questions on this gift. When did you get the note?" Uncle Troy asked as he stared at her. Meg sat in a visitor chair in his office as he paced back and forth, looking from the bracelet to her. His face was getting redder by the minute.

"Let's see, Tuesday, Mom had us over at the house to tell us she was dating, so it had to be Monday when Dad showed up. Dalton and Junior had set up dinner at the Local Crab, but then Dad appeared and joined. I think Junior knew all along, but it was a surprise to me. At least, Elaine didn't come . . ." Meg saw that her uncle had stopped pacing and was staring at her. "What? Okay, short answer, it was Monday at the Local Crab. The waiter recognized me and said that my date had left the envelope. It wasn't a date, but the package was left the night Anderson took me on the food critic adventure at the restaurant."

Uncle Troy held up his hand to make Meg stop talking. Then he sat down in his chair and took a couple of deep breaths. "So, before Monday, when this waiter gave you the envelope, you didn't know anything about the bracelet, and you'd only met Lee Anderson once. Yet you agreed to have dinner with him?"

"We were supposed to be talking about writing. Or at least

that's what I thought the dinner was going to be. Writers get together and talk. It's like being around a water cooler for office people. I knew he was doing the food critic thing, but I didn't think he'd be a jerk to the waitstaff. After he complained about the temperature of the main course, among a trail of other issues, I stood and told him he was rude and I wasn't staying." Meg took in a breath. "Sorry, I know I tell a long story, but you need to know the full picture. These aren't yes or no answers. I had dinner with him. I would have dinner with any person, male or female, that I find interesting and want to talk about writing and marketing with. I need to learn this stuff."

Uncle Troy rubbed his face. "Can't a book or a class teach you this stuff? You have to do the stories-around-the-fire methodology of learning?"

"I think you're talking about the Socratic method. What can I say, I learn best by doing. And if someone else has tried something that works, I want to know. Especially if it only costs me time and my dinner," Meg added.

"I wish you liked gardening. Your aunt has a lovely spot for a garden out behind the garage." He picked the bracelet up with a pen and studied it. "You think these are real?"

"I talked to the jeweler who sold them to Anderson. They're real, all right. He told me how much they cost and that Lee intended the bracelet to be a gift." She dug in her purse and pulled out a business card. "This is the guy I talked to at the jewelry store. I told him you might call, then I forgot to give the card to you."

Uncle Troy took the card and put it with the note. "Do you mind if I hold on to these for a bit? I'll get the bracelet back to you as soon as the case is closed. It's clear he wanted you to have it. Do you know why?"

"Not a clue. Like I said, I had just met him. But Alice Monroe, who runs the writing group, said he'd been looking for me there for months. It sounded like he was stalking me but didn't know where to find me."

"Not a local and not trustworthy." Uncle Troy nodded. "That's what everyone is saying."

"But he was a local, once." Meg hadn't planned on telling her uncle about her and Dalton's trip to the restaurants that Anderson wrote bad reviews on, but she had loose lips. She told him about her visit to the Steakhouse and what the chef had told her. "All the other chefs blew off the bad review, but this guy? He was hurt. You could hear it in his voice."

Uncle Troy handed her a piece of paper. "Please list off everyone you talked to that afternoon. And anything you remember them saying that felt off to you. I'm going to kick myself for saying this, but you have a good instinct for when things seem off."

While Meg jotted down what she remembered, Uncle Troy pulled out a file and started sifting through papers. He buzzed his assistant and when she came in, he handed her the envelope. "Please log this as evidence and bring me back a copy of all the pictures."

Meg finished the list of restaurants and chefs. She knew them by heart, since she had compiled the original list of restaurants to visit in the first place. "I visited everyone from the island who had a bad review. Well, except Natasha. But we know she didn't kill the guy. And her review wasn't horrible."

Her uncle just nodded. He tucked the note into his folder and closed it. Then he stood. "Don't you need to be at work? Thank you for telling me about this."

The other part of his statement went unsaid. The part where he griped about Meg getting involved in the investigation. Meg heard his unspoken message loud and clear.

"Thanks, Uncle Troy. Let me know if you have questions or need to run something by me." She flashed him a big smile, hoping he wouldn't throw something at her, or worse, throw her out of the station.

"You're lucky you're cute and related," he grumbled in reply. She snorted into her hand and burst out laughing. Meg was still laughing when she walked out of the station and almost ran into a tourist.

CHAPTER 13

And the Most Likely to Murder Award goes to . . .

Mom was pacing when Meg arrived at the bookstore. "Good, you're here. You're late."

Meg looked at the clock. Only two minutes had passed since the top of the hour. "Sorry, I stopped by to see Uncle Troy and then Watson had some issues. I figured you wanted him walked before I came in to work so I don't have to close the shop to take him out again."

"I don't care if you take him out." Mom reached down and rubbed Watson's back. "Sorry, I'm just nervous. Derby is taking me into Seattle tonight for a show."

"Sounds nice. Why are you nervous?"

Meg's mother shrugged. "I don't know. What if he thinks we should spend time together now that people know?"

"Time? As in overnight time?" Meg closed her eyes and tried not to picture it. "Mom, you should be talking to Aunt Melody about this."

Her mother laughed. "I can't believe I've embarrassed you. Do we need to have the talk again?"

"The one that starts when mommies and daddies really love each other? Are you telling me you want another baby?" Meg didn't know why the thought surprised her.

"No, I mean, being intimate isn't just about procreating. It's a natural part of life." Mom pulled on her jacket.

"One you don't talk about with your daughter," Meg added. Boy, she wanted to get off this topic. "Look, I know if your relationship continues, this is going to happen. I'm not stupid. I just would rather not hear about it."

"Okay, message received. No girl-to-girl talk about our love lives. Are you sure there's nothing you want to tell me about Dalton?" Her mother paused at the door.

"Mom!" Meg's face heated.

Her mother smiled as she left. "Payback is so much fun."

A customer came in right as her mom left, so Meg had something to distract herself from images of her mom and Derby kissing. Or worse. Kids shouldn't have to deal with this from their adult parents. There should be a law.

By the time she'd calmed down and the shop was quiet, she glanced over her mom's to-do list. Tonight, she had ordering to complete, so she grabbed the notebook her mom kept a manual list of book sales in and started replacing the books that had sold during the week. A few had question marks, which meant her mom wasn't sold on restocking, but Meg thought they could sell the replacement books, too. She ordered the full list. Then she turned to the back where Mom kept special orders and completed those as well.

By the time she finished ordering a few romantasy books for a new display she had designed, the bell over the door went off and Irene came inside.

She nodded to Meg and went straight to the romance section, quickly picking out several books. She came up to the counter and took out her wallet. "Hi, Meg."

"Hi, Irene. How are things going?"

"My boyfriend stood me up for dinner last night, then called and said he'd been pulled into the station to talk to your uncle. What is this, retribution on my father?" She shoved a credit card at Meg.

"I'm sorry. Was this the guy I met the other night? Mark Thomason?" Meg rang up the books as she talked.

"Who else? You think I'd have two boyfriends?" She signed the receipt and tossed the pen back at Meg. "Just tell your uncle thanks for ruining my date night. Now he can't see me until Sunday. He works nights."

Meg tucked the books into a bag. Mark Thomason had to be the guy that Uncle Troy interviewed about the Anderson murder. She needed to keep Irene talking. "I'm sorry about your date, Irene. Do you know what Uncle Troy was asking him about?"

Irene picked up a book, then set it down. "He wouldn't tell me. He said it was nothing. They wanted to talk to him about a project he had worked on with Lee Anderson. But if it wasn't a big deal, why did he cancel our date afterward?"

"I don't know." Meg remembered something Irene had said about Mark and writing. But not much. Now, she wished she'd listened better. On the other hand, Irene was hard to listen to. "Wait, I thought you said Mark wrote fiction."

"He does. Spy novels. But he and Lee were working on a compilation of Lee's reviews. Kind of a what to eat in Seattle guidebook. He complained that Lee thought all he needed to do was provide the reviews. That Mark would be doing all the hard work." Irene looked at her watch. "I've got to go. I'm playing Pickleball with my dad early tomorrow. He thinks everything can be worked out over an activity. When I was a teenager, he always took me hiking whenever I was upset about anything. I guess it could be worse, but I'm still mad at him for leaving Mom."

Meg almost said, *I know how you feel*, but she didn't want to form a connection with Irene. She hesitated after Irene left, reconsidering her standoffishness. What if Mom actually married Derby? Then Irene would be in Meg's life all the time. That would be horrible.

Maybe Irene murdered Lee.

Meg shook her head. Just because someone was annoying, it didn't mean they were a murderer. Besides, Irene going away to the women's prison would just delay the awkward family dinners if Mom married Derby.

Something Irene said about Mark was bumping around in Meg's head. They'd gone to school together. High school? Or college? Had Mark bowed out of the review project before Anderson was killed?

Could working on a book be a motivation for murder?

Meg was frustrated with the whole writing process, but her gut reaction was to ignore the problem. If Lee and Mark had fought about the division of work, maybe they'd fought about other things. The murder could have been an impulsive act. The straw that broke the camel's back sort of thing.

She ordered herself some dinner, then put the idea of Mark killing Lee away in her head. She'd write him down as a suspect, but the motive was really lame. Her uncle had probably done the same thing.

No, her better suspects were in the chef pool. The ones who pretended that Lee Anderson's bad review hadn't pierced their heart. Like Chef Jon Michael. He'd known Lee and his family for years. He'd welcomed Lee home with open arms. Then the guy had stabbed him with his bad review. James Beard nominee or not, that had to hurt.

Meg opened her laptop and started researching the Steakhouse and the chef that had run it for more years than she'd been alive. When her food arrived, she closed up the shop, ate, then took Watson for a short walk.

Walk-in traffic had been slow tonight. She wondered why the bookstore didn't host a book club or writers' group at least one night a week. Having people in the store might spur impulse purchases.

She'd brought this up to her mother before, but nothing had come of it. Now Meg thought maybe it was the Derby distraction. She decided to talk to Alice Monroe next week about what might be a collaboration between her group and the bookstore. Perhaps the bookstore could host authors that wrote in genres chosen by the writers' group. Maybe someone who wrote a book on the process of writing.

After cleaning up the remnants of dinner, she emailed Alice about some possible joint adventures. She cc'd her mother on the email since she was acting as a bookstore rep. Meg went over and pulled some books from the shelf and looked up the authors. A couple had recent releases and lived in the Pacific Northwest.

She reached out to three authors, asking if they would be interested in presenting and what that might cost. She'd need to figure out how many books they'd need to sell to make this doable. As she closed up the shop later that night, Meg felt like she'd actually earned her wages that day. Mom had started expanding the shop's reach by hosting Lilly's releases, but she'd stopped there. Meg knew that if the bookstore could become a gathering place for local and regional readers and authors, it could withstand any storm.

As she and Watson walked home, she realized she'd started another project. Maybe she actually would be able to make a living here on the island. If not, it wasn't because she didn't have enough irons in the fire.

She'd been through so much this year but as she looked back, Meg wondered if her reaction to Romain's betrayal was more about her idealized idea of what life should be rather than just dealing with life day to day.

"Maybe it's my follow-through," she whispered to Watson as they climbed the stairs to the apartment. As soon as they got inside, she pulled out her calendar and blocked off time to work on the book. Even if she just sat at the keyboard for thirty minutes a day, she was going to touch the manuscript daily, like she had when she first started the project. She estimated what she needed in words for a first draft and then divided it by what she knew she could write. At a rate of five hundred words a day, she'd have a rough draft by the end of the year.

Then she could start editing. By next summer she'd either have a book or a book contract. Solid, reachable goals.

She glanced at the clock. "No time like the present to start a habit."

Then she opened her manuscript and wrote a few pages about leads that didn't go anywhere, using Mark Thomason's interview with her uncle as an example.

Except as she wrote, she realized she didn't know exactly what had pointed her uncle to Mark in the first place.

She'd text him tomorrow. The lights were out at her aunt and uncle's house since they both were early birds. She didn't want to wake him with a text. She wrote down the question on tomorrow's agenda and noted that she needed to go shopping for food before work.

And she put a big note on her day planner. *WRITE FIRST.*

With that in place, she closed down the computer and got ready for bed. Watson was already cuddled on the couch, thumping his tail to invite her to sit with him

"Just one show." She gave in and turned on the station Watson liked to watch. Then they both became immersed in the problems the television hosts always ran into refurbishing old houses. "You would think that they'd expect to have to pull up the wood flooring after a while."

Watson barked and then laid his head on her lap, agreeing with her assessment.

Meg slept in a little later than she'd expected, but it was Saturday. Dalton was working the day shift, so they'd agreed to have dinner at the bookstore. She texted Natasha the details and told her to let her know so they could order enough food. Then, with coffee cup in hand, she opened her laptop. Her goal was thirty minutes and five hundred words. She'd exceeded the word count yesterday, so she was hopeful.

Watson barked after ten minutes. She realized she hadn't taken him out yet, so she stopped her timer and grabbed his leash. As they came down the stairs, she saw her uncle step out of his truck. She smiled and waved. "Hold up a second, I have a question."

Uncle Troy stood outside his truck and offered Meg a weary smile as he waited. He was a handsome man, maybe a little less fit, but Meg knew that her aunt's cooking was to blame for that. He looked a little tired around the eyes. "What's up, buttercup?"

"Okay, I know you don't want to talk about the case, but I have a question. Irene told me that you questioned Mark Thomason about the murder. What made you even think of interviewing him? The book writing partnership? Or the fact that they went to school together?"

Uncle Troy swore under his breath but then refocused his gaze on her. "I shouldn't humor you but as your aunt reminds me, you are writing a book. And maybe this isn't your way of sticking your nose in my investigation. Right?"

Meg nodded. "Actually, I was shocked when Irene told me you'd interviewed Mark. I met him once and he seemed nice. Irene thinks you're messing with her life because of Mom and Derby."

"Now why would I—" Uncle Troy chuckled as he rolled his eyes. "Never mind. Irene Olsen has one way of looking at everything in the world. Anything that happens is all about how it affects her."

"You got that right. I found that out the second time I talked to her," Meg admitted.

"Anyway, Mark Thomason was interviewed because his name was in Lee Anderson's planner. In fact, they had a standing appointment listed twice a week for three months. Then his name suddenly disappeared from Anderson's ongoing meetings. I wanted to know why."

"So, Mark told you he was working on co-authoring a book with Lee."

Uncle Troy nodded. "He said he found out that Lee had been talking to agents without him, and he realized that he was going to be given a thank you in the acknowledgments rather than being a co-author. He told Lee he wanted a fifty-fifty deal, and Lee laughed at him. So, he stopped helping. And he called an attorney who told him that if Lee published the book, they'd sue. He had plans to be compensated. I don't think he'd kill him before the book was even finished."

Meg came to the same conclusion. Lee's greed toward his co-author wasn't excessive enough to kill him. "Thanks for sharing your thoughts. I'm writing a chapter about weeding out the unlikely suspects first so your final few are the ones most likely to have committed the murder."

"That's an interesting way to look at it, but basically, yes. That's a lot of what I do as a law enforcement officer. Weeding out the ones who didn't do it." He got into his truck, waving as he left.

Watson was done, so she hurried upstairs and started her timer again. First, she went back to the chapter and added a heading. *Weeding out the unlikely suspects.* She'd change it later, but it encompassed what she wanted to write about.

When her alarm went off, she'd gotten over six hundred words. Two days in and she was meeting her goals. She should have implemented this write-first motto when she started the book. She could have been done with the whole thing by now.

No use crying over missed opportunities.

She went back into her manuscript and added that as a possible chapter heading. Then she shut down her computer. She had cleaning stuff to do before she went shopping. Then she took her calendar and went to the counter to meal plan so she wouldn't buy too much stuff. She would eat at Island Diner on Tuesday night since she'd be at the meeting. And, looking at her calendar, she had Pickleball.

As Meg went through her planner, she made notes about all the meals she needed for the week and where she might eat out. Then she went to the fridge and figured out what she needed to buy to supplement the frozen meals her aunt had made for her. It wasn't much of a shopping list.

At the store, Meg was deciding between sparkling water brands when she saw Chef Jon Michael. He was at the meat case, talking to the butcher. She moved closer after grabbing a package of her favorite water, even though it wasn't on sale. The two were discussing an order. The butcher thought he was buying the wrong cut for a recipe.

"I am the chef, not you. Between you and Anderson, I'm tired of people telling me what I should be using at my restaurant. Just stay in your lane." Chef Jon Michael pointed to the case. "Give me ten porterhouse steaks."

"Yes, chef." The butcher responded in a snide tone but did what he was asked.

Meg pretended not to hear what had just happened and in a bright, cheerful voice asked, "Chef Jon Michael. How nice to see you again."

He turned, his face still flush with anger. When he recognized Meg, he nodded. "Meg Gates, right? How's the investigation going? Have you caught your man, or woman, yet?"

"I'm just asking questions," Meg clarified. "My uncle is the one in law enforcement. It was so nice of you to give us some time, though. I didn't know Lee Anderson well before he died, but I'm learning so much more about him now."

"Lee Anderson was a blowhard who thought the world revolved around him." The butcher laid a package wrapped in brown paper on the counter. "Much like some other people I know."

He glared at Chef Jon Michael, who rolled his eyes, then grabbed the package. "It was nice to see you again, Miss Gates."

After the chef had left, the butcher turned to Meg. "Can I get you something?"

"Two chicken breasts and two servings of salmon. Can I get them packaged separately?" Meg glanced after Chef Jon Michael. "He seems upset."

"Don't mind him. He's been a grump since his wife, Mary, died. She was an angel. Him? He was born mad but since she left I think it's been getting worse." He patted the top of the case. "Salmon and chicken packaged separately, coming right up."

Meg used the time to cross items off her grocery list and to think about where the chef fit into her list of suspects. He was the only one of the chefs they'd talked to who had a personal relationship with Lee Anderson. Did that make him more or less likely to kill someone?

CHAPTER 14

No use crying over missed opportunities.

Natasha came into the bookstore around six but from the way she was dressed, Meg knew she wasn't staying around for Chinese food.

"You have a date?" Meg asked.

Natasha broke into a large grin. She twirled in the new fit and flare dress. "Too much?"

"Depends. Who is he and where are you going?" Meg offered Natasha a bottle of water but she turned it down. They went over and sat on the couch.

"I'm not saying, yet. It's too early to get excited and I don't want you hating on him if this doesn't go well." Natasha pushed Watson down off her dress. "Besides, you don't know him. He's picking me up at the Seattle terminal to go to that place you and Dalton went last Thursday. I'm really excited."

"Well, hopefully you won't get surprised like I was that night." Meg smiled at her friend. Natasha had been going through a dry spell in men for a few years. She'd date, then drop them when they did something stupid. Natasha had a low tolerance for idiots. Or men who didn't call after the first date. You didn't get a second chance with her. "Tell me about him."

"He's tall. Dark brown hair and piercing green eyes. And

smart. He was reading the book that's the retelling of Huck Finn? I can't remember the name now. But he told me all about the story and why it was so engaging. I love a man who reads. Like Dalton. He reads a lot."

"It keeps him busy on slow days on the ferry," Meg pointed out. "So, handsome and smart. Did he ask about you? What you like?"

Natasha nodded. "I talked about the bakery and his eyes didn't glaze over. Tonight is our second date this week. He took me out for coffee in Seattle one night after I closed down the bakery. Like I said, I don't want to jinx this, but it's looking promising."

"Are you taking the next ferry?"

Natasha nodded. "I just stopped over to see you and let you know where I'm going. In case, you know, serial killer."

"Text me if you need an emergency phone call to get out of the date. You know the code."

"I remember," Natasha said as she giggled. They'd made up the codes years ago, long before Romain. And they each had a separate one. Natasha's was **Buy muffin mix** and Meg's was **The book you ordered is at the store**. "Anyway, I better get going. I'll come by tomorrow. I'm not working."

"I'm not either. Glory wanted a few more hours." Meg didn't mind not working on Sundays. She had church with her mom. Then family brunch. And now, she'd be free all afternoon. Well, except for Natasha's visit and her thirty minutes of working on the book. And homework for Monday's class.

Maybe not working tomorrow was a blessing since she also still hadn't finished the book tour options for Lilly.

Irene stared at her all during Sunday school. Meg was trying to pay attention to the lesson from Reverand Sage about being more open to meeting others, but every time Meg looked up, Irene glared at her from across the table. After class, Meg tried to grab her to see what the problem was, but she disappeared into a different room and locked the door behind her.

"That's the basement. We've had some problems with kids breaking in through the cellar, so we keep it locked, unless there's a special event and we need the room." Reverend Sage came out of the adult Sunday school classroom and stopped next to Meg. "Are you looking for a restroom? They're near the chapel."

"No, I just saw someone go in there." Meg saw that Reverend Sage was staring at her. Kind of like Irene had been, but with less malice. The minister looked like she thought Meg was losing it. "Anyway, I'm looking forward to your sermon today."

"I always love the sermons that speak to friendship. It's such an important part of our lives, don't you think?" Reverend Sage took Meg's arm as they walked through the now empty hallway to the front of the church where the chapel entrance was located, as well as the restrooms.

"My friends got me through many of my worst moments," Meg said, realizing the truth of her words.

"Then you'll appreciate the sermon. I'll leave you here. I have some things to finish up before we start." Reverend Sage squeezed her hand. "I'm so glad you're back in the flock here. I've missed seeing you."

Guilt about not attending here or anywhere when she lived in Seattle hit hard. Romain had complained that he didn't like adjusting his weekend for family or religious services. He needed her with him. Another red flag she should have paid attention to. Dalton used the work excuse for not attending. But his soul was his business. She had enough trouble keeping her own path to salvation clean.

Meg saw her mom in the chapel and walked toward her. Then she realized that Derby stood next to her. And on the other side of the room stood Irene and her mother. Both were glaring at Derby and Mom. It was like a showdown at a ghost town, sides had been taken. No wonder Irene had been in a snit at Sunday school. Meg thought about turning around and going home to stay out of the fray, but that would leave Mom alone. She put a fake smile on her face and headed to greet the new couple.

Derby smiled at her. "Thanks for supporting your mom and me. I didn't realize it would be such a big deal for us to attend Sunday service together. Martha and I have been divorced for three years now."

"Have you told Irene yet?" Meg mumbled but still got a sharp elbow in her side from her mother.

"We're going to your aunt's house for brunch after service," Mom told her like she didn't already know the drill. "I hope you can join us."

"I was planning to," Meg said. The music changed, notifying the congregation that the service was about to begin. They passed by the pew where her family always sat. Derby motioned the women into a pew farther up and on the wrong side. This adjustment was more than just Mom dating. Now it was affecting her routines. Meg took a breath. "Just wait until Junior visits on a Sunday."

Mom turned and glared at her. In a whisper, she said, "Derby and I talked about this before we came. We're starting a new tradition. It's just a pew, not a marriage."

Meg felt shame at her comment. "You're right. Sorry. Irene has me on edge. She glared at me all during Sunday school."

"Irene is having trouble dealing with the change," Mom said as she looked over to where Martha and Irene were sitting. "They both are."

After a really uncomfortable service, Meg was glad to be walking back home alone. She'd declined a ride from Derby and Mom. Mom and Derby. She needed to get used to the grouping. Mom had waited until they were both sure that the relationship was going somewhere before springing it on the kids.

Now, they looked too comfortable with each other, at least in Meg's mind. She rubbed her arms. They hadn't run off and eloped. Not yet.

At home, she changed into comfortable clothes before heading down to brunch with Watson. She wondered if Uncle Troy had known about the relationship before she did, and groaned. Of course, he'd known. If Aunt Melody had known, she would have told Uncle Troy.

Watson stood at the door waiting. He needed to be let out, and she thought he also somehow knew that he'd get to spend some time in the fenced backyard while they ate. Dogs knew stuff.

"Okay, let's go get this done. If I wasn't starving, I'd stay home." Meg clicked his leash on his collar.

Watson winked at her. Like he knew she was totally fibbing.

"Whatever." Meg headed down the stairs. When she came into the dining room, Uncle Troy was bringing out the egg strata. No one else was around. "Happy Sunday, Uncle. Where's everyone else?"

"Your aunt is taking the new guy around to see the house. I guess I should be thankful that anyone who tours the place also sees the gun safe. The guns should deter them from coming back later to rob the place."

Meg stared at him, then giggled. "She does like to show off her home."

"Everyone on the island, including the guys who drive the delivery trucks, knows that." He glanced around the table, then went and poured two mimosas. He handed one to Meg. "I'm off today. No matter what. I told the mayor I had to have every other Sunday totally off, no on-call, no nothing. I was thinking we'd go into Seattle for a show. Instead, we're hosting your mom's new boyfriend."

"Welcome to the family." Meg took the drink and sipped it.

"Mom likes everyone to be on the same page. She's had a rough week. Junior isn't dealing well."

"He'll get over it. He needs his own girlfriend to push him around. Then he'll get it." He sat at the table. "Come sit by me and tell me what's going on in your life. I see you up and around a lot in town. I hear you visited several restaurants recently."

"I told you that, right?" Meg shrugged. "Unless it's true that revenge is a dish served ice cold, I think I'm on the wrong track. Hey, what did Mark say about dating Irene?"

"He didn't mention that at all. I thought I saw him with someone else recently. Oh well, dating doesn't mean exclusive, right?" He grabbed a roll and buttered it. "I know, no food until grace, but your aunt is taking her time."

"Because we were talking about how we're redoing the master suite." Aunt Melody took one half of the roll from her husband's hand and ate it. "You could have tagged along."

"Then I wouldn't have been here to open the door and chat with Meg," he responded, standing to pour more mimosas.

"Hi Meg, I'm glad you came." Derby stepped over to where she stood. "I was afraid I'd frightened you off with the whole switching pews idea. I thought making a symbolic clean break might send a message."

"I've tried that method, and sometimes it actually works," Meg said. She knew he was trying. And she appreciated that.

Still, it was hard to see the couples getting along like the past, her childhood, had never happened. The only thing worse than this brunch, Meg thought, would be to have her dad and Elaine here as well, drinking mimosas and talking about the recent television season.

Meg excused herself right after brunch and took Watson back up to her apartment. She had work to finish, and even though she saw the hurt in her mother's eyes, she smiled and tried to convince herself that next time would be better.

Life as a grown-up was hard, man.

She sat down with her laptop and focused on her thirty minutes of writing.

What had she learned that she needed to pass on to a new amateur sleuth? That family connections sometimes complicate investigations. She reached for a piece of scratch paper and wrote.

Where is Anderson's family? And, more to the point, how close were they to Chef Jon Michael? Was this murder about family? Or a failed relationship?

The problem with investigating a murder is everyone's a possibility until they aren't. And as an amateur sleuth, you can't just ask to see the videotape from the ferry parking lot at the time of the murder. If it was available, the police would know if the killer was short, tall, male or female, and maybe even young or old.

Meg had to look at the victim and say, *Why would someone kill you?* The issue with looking at the problem from the victim's perspective is that Lee Anderson was a jerk. He'd made her mad enough to walk out on a free meal before dessert, and she'd only met him twice.

She tried to focus on the chapter she was writing rather than the who-killed-Anderson puzzle. All she had to do was thirty minutes, every day. She could do that.

Reluctantly, she turned over the sheet of paper where she'd written her questions about Lee's death and focused on the chapter outline. Then she wrote until she thought thirty minutes had gone by. She checked the clock on her computer.

Instead of thirty minutes, she'd been working over an hour. She had made good progress on the chapter. Smiling, she wrote down her time and the word count and closed out her

Word program. Then she got up and stretched, getting a soda from the fridge.

She took out the murder notebook and wrote down the questions she'd had on the scrap paper. Then she went back to the computer to see what answers she could find. She already knew the restaurants and chefs on the island that he'd written bad reviews on. But what about Lee Anderson's history? Was there anything more on the internet she could find about him?

Since she'd focused on social medial connections then, now she went to his newspaper's website and located his bio. She screenshotted the page, just in case they replaced him sooner than later. Then she broke down the information in her notebook. As of today, he was still listed as employed. Maybe Jon Michael had been wrong.

Lee went to U-Dub, the same university she was now attending. Did someone at the college remember him? He'd been an English major, so she went to the school's website and found the program. Then she wrote down all the professors, noting when they'd started. Maybe she could find out when he'd attended, which would weed out professors to talk to. Perhaps she could also find prior professors who had left since Anderson had graduated.

Maybe the school had yearbooks, or at least a listing of the students in each class.

She logged into the college system with her student identification. There, she found Lee Anderson's alumni bio and years attended. She wrote the information down in her notebook. This profile hadn't been updated with Lee's death, yet. Did a student intern update the alumni information?

She was getting sidetracked.

Meg went back to the list of professors and started crossing off ones who hadn't been teaching during the time Anderson was a student. She was down to five.

She navigated to the online reference section of the library, but the college yearbooks ended in 1994. She needed to spend time on campus Monday to see if she could find out more.

Checking out his college experience was probably a waste of time, but at least it was something she could do.

A knock brought her head up. Hopefully, it wasn't Mom checking on her. She didn't want to deal with her feelings today. Besides, Meg didn't quite know what she was feeling.

She opened the door to find Natasha holding a bag of what smelled like burgers and fries from Island Diner. "I hope you're hungry, because I also bought onion rings."

"I could eat." Meg glanced at her watch. It was already five. She'd been working for over four hours. "Let me take Watson out for a few minutes. I'll be right back."

Watson didn't need a few minutes. Apparently, he'd been waiting for Meg to notice him for a while.

"Sorry, buddy, I got lost in work. Bark at me next time." Meg said as she rubbed his head before going back up to the apartment.

The food waited on the table, but Natasha was staring at the timeline that Meg had created for Lee Anderson's murder.

"I need to do a murder suspect board, but I don't know how to narrow down the suspects. Right now, the list includes nearly everyone who has ever met Lee Anderson. I'm checking out his college connections on Monday. I'm trying to find out if anyone there knows why he turned into such a grinch. Or maybe he was born that way. Let's eat."

But Natasha didn't move. She pointed to an entry on the board. "Meg, why do you have Mark Thomason's name on this board?"

"Uncle Troy interviewed him last week. He's Irene's boyfriend. He was with her at the writers' group and the Local Crab the night I stormed out on Lee." Meg grabbed sodas from the fridge. "Is Coke okay? Or do you want sparkling water?"

“He was at the writers’ group? With Irene? And then dinner the next night?” Natasha said, not turning around.

“Yeah, why?” Meg sat down and realized her friend still hadn’t moved to come to the table. “Natasha, what’s wrong?”

“My amazing date last night, the one I was going to tell you all about? It was with Mark Thomason. Apparently, he’s dating both me and Irene. What a weasel.”

Chapter 15

Family connections sometimes complicate investigations.

Meg convinced Natasha to sit down at the table, and then she watched as Natasha pulled out her phone.

"Here's a picture of the two of us at dinner last night. The waiter took it. Please tell me it's not the same man you saw with Irene." Natasha's hope poured out of the look she gave Meg.

Meg stared at the photo. Then she handed the phone back to Natasha. "You look great."

"And?"

Meg closed her eyes and sighed. "It looks like the same guy. Maybe they had a fight and he's single again."

"Maybe. Or maybe he likes playing games. I'm so glad I came home alone on the ferry last night. I was thinking about staying the night. I thought he was just being old-fashioned when he agreed we should wait. I almost went to his place, but I needed to be up early to bake since Serena is off this week. That's why I'm not working now."

"Okay, so tomorrow, call this guy and see what's going on." Meg leaned back into her chair. "What else is happening in your life?"

Natasha closed her eyes, then took three deep breaths. "You're right. No use going through all the things that could be happening. I'll call him tomorrow and calmly ask if he's also dating Irene. Of course, it is Irene. She might have just been selling him cruises."

"True." Meg knew her friend would be okay, but she hated that Natasha had gotten her hopes up on this guy working out. "Derby came to church and brunch with Mom today."

"They are moving fast," Natasha said as she leaned forward. "Tell me everything."

Grateful for the distraction, Meg gave Natasha a blow-by-blow of the morning's events. She ended it by saying, "I guess it's a real relationship now. I want Mom to be happy, but did she have to choose Irene's dad?"

"Yeah, that woman is all over our business now," Natasha joked. "Do you want to go to the park and walk Watson? I've got a lot of angst to burn off and if I sit here, I'm going to eat that plate of cookies on the counter."

"Aunt Melody strikes again. I swear, she just gives them to me so she won't eat them." Meg snapped her fingers at Watson, who was sleeping on the couch. "Want to go for a walk?"

The dog looked up, looked at the television, then laid his head down again.

Natasha laughed. "Clearly, he thinks it's couch potato Sunday."

"He does like his home remodeling shows. But it's not his decision." Meg got up and grabbed Watson's backpack. "Being a dog mom is preparing me for the real thing. We don't leave the house without his stuff. Water, dog bags, a few treats. Do you want a bottle of water, too?"

"Sure. Let's walk to Hawley Cove Park, then return and hit the Dock Bar. We can sit outside with Watson and I can drink away my sorrows." Natasha stood and waited for Meg to finish packing Watson's bag.

As they walked, Meg talked to her about her lack of progress in the investigation.

"You realize it's your uncle's case, not yours," Natasha reminded her.

Meg snorted. "I'm not sure a book on leaving the work to the professionals would sell a lot of copies."

"Is this just about the book then? You're not putting yourself in danger?" Natasha didn't look at Meg as she walked down the street.

"I don't want to do anything dangerous or tell anyone to do risky things. It's like solving puzzles but with real-world consequences. Lee Anderson dragged me into his world for a reason. I'd like to at least know why he thought I saved him and what from. He made it personal by giving me that bracelet. Now I need to connect the dots. I'm going to do some research tomorrow after class. I found two professors who taught Anderson and still teach on campus. And I'm going to search for clues in the yearbooks. Uncle Troy doesn't have the manpower or time to do little things like this anyway."

"If you say so." Natasha paused at the trailhead. "I was serious about stopping at the Dock Bar on the way home, but I can't stay long. I'm baking tomorrow morning."

"I figured as much," Meg said as she hugged her friend. "Besides, two dates, no matter how great they are, aren't worth damaging your kidneys for."

"You don't know how great the dates were," Natasha said as they headed on the trail toward the beach. "I'll give him a chance to explain, but he's out of here if I don't like what he says. Plenty of fish in the sound."

When they got to the Dock Bar, they ordered an early dinner to go along with their drinks. And they were surprised to see whales out in Puget Sound. Meg thought the whales were a good omen. They were on the right track—both Natasha with her planned discussion with Mark and Meg with her investigation.

Meg got home just before six, so she fed Watson, then took out her laptop. She'd already marked off her writing time, so she dug into her author assistant chores. One of her tasks was to make social media posts for Lilly, then she or Jolene would fine-tune or reschedule them as needed. She was a few weeks ahead, but she liked having a month's worth of content ready for Lilly.

She still needed to make images for the next book release. She'd create one with all the stops, one with a month of stops, and one with the week's events. Until she got approval to start booking, she could only make the templates, but they would save time later.

She loved working with Lilly. The work was always changing. It wasn't what she'd expected at the beginning of the job, but at least she wasn't just being used as a researcher.

Her mouth was dry, so she saved her work to get a drink. As she checked the time, she was surprised to see that it was already after eight. Watson popped his head up when he saw her move and ran to the door. "Sorry dude, I got caught up again. Let's take a walk."

She grabbed his leash and headed downstairs. While they wandered around the block, she noticed that her uncle's truck was still parked at the house. He must have been serious about not working today. The lights were on in the living room and Meg imagined her aunt and uncle cuddled together on the couch, watching a movie, or, more likely, talking about the day. And Mom's new boyfriend.

Living at home was hard. If she was still in Seattle, she might know about the dating, but she wouldn't see it in action, like she had today. Derby was different than Dad. He and Mom seemed to make decisions together. Dad usually surprised her mom and the family on a whim with his plans. Like the summer they went to California for a week to visit Disneyland and Sea World. It was fun, but she'd missed a week of summer reading and the start of cheer camp. Mom had rescheduled the camp and they'd gone to the library early to get her books to take along. Dad acted and Mom reacted to his plans, fixing things as she went.

It sounded like Derby and Mom talked about their steps together as a couple, like telling the family about their relationship and moving pews at church.

They might seem like little things, but Meg bet they were big to Mom.

Back in the apartment, Meg noted her time for Lilly's work in her day planner. Then she opened her notebook for her class to complete the readings and assignment.

Meg thought about her first attempt at college. She'd been a mess. She missed classes and hung out too late with friends. She'd had so much free time, she hadn't prioritized her studies, and her grades that first quarter had shown it. She'd come out with a B average, with two classes with A's and two classes with C's, but she hadn't felt like she'd learned much. Now, with two jobs and the book, she prioritized her time better. Fall quarter she was jumping in feet first with full-time classes and both jobs.

She needed to learn to fit everything in. If she finished the book this summer and just be in editing mode during the fall, she thought she could do it.

Satisfied that she was ready for tomorrow's class, she pulled out her investigation notebook and made a to-do list for tomorrow's campus research trip. She would be gone longer than normal so she texted her aunt to see if she could let Watson out at ten and again at one.

She hadn't expected to get an answer back until the morning, but her aunt responded asking that Meg drop him off in the morning at her house for doggie daycare.

She looked over at Watson, who was watching television again. "You want to go to Aunt Melody's tomorrow while I'm at class?"

A wag of his tale gave her the answer, and she sent her aunt a thumbs-up emoji. Since she still wasn't tired, she opened the manuscript again and started writing.

For a day that had started out rocky, she'd gotten a lot done when she set her alarm and turned off the lights later. Consistency didn't mean boring.

The next morning, Meg was up and ready early.

When she dropped off Watson for his playdate with Aunt Melody, Uncle Troy was at the breakfast table, reading on his phone. Meg sat next to him. "Hey, did anyone look into Lee Anderson's past? Did you know he went to the University of Washington? I'm going to look him up in the alumni information on campus today to see if there's anything strange, and I'll try to chat with his old professors."

"You think he made someone angry in college and they killed him?" Uncle Troy was trying not to smile. "That's really cold revenge."

"No. Not exactly, but I do think that knowing your victim is the first step in solving his murder." Meg took the bag Aunt Melody handed her along with a purple travel mug. "What's this?"

"Breakfast burritos and coffee for the trip. I figured you didn't eat anything yet." She leaned down and gave Watson a kiss on the head and a command. "You go lay by the door, and we'll go outside and play after everyone leaves."

To Meg's amusement, Watson did just that. "Thank you for letting him hang out. He's used to me being around all the time. I need to break him of that."

"No, you don't. He can come over here anytime I'm home. He's not a bother at all." Aunt Melody sat down and sipped her coffee.

"You heard the woman," Uncle Troy said, a grin on his face. "Besides, having Watson around keeps her from going out and getting a rescue."

Meg saw the twinkle in her aunt's eyes. "I'm not convinced of that logic, but thanks. And thanks for the food."

"Meg." Her uncle's voice stopped her at the door.

She turned around. "Yes?"

"Thank you for telling me what you're doing but be careful. Some secrets are hidden for a reason." Then he went back to scrolling on his phone.

Meg backed her car out of the garage and headed to school. Aunt Melody had put not only the foil-wrapped burritos in the bag but also napkins. Once she was on the ferry, Meg unwrapped one of the burritos and took a bite. *Heaven.*

How had she ever lived anywhere else? Or why?

In the parking lot at school, she finished eating as she listened to the radio. A news announcement about Anderson's death came on and ended with "officials are still looking for leads. If you have any information, call the Bainbridge Island police department." Then it listed off the phone number.

Meg made sure everything was in her backpack, grabbed her half-empty coffee cup, and headed to class. She threw away the bag and leftovers at the first trash can she found and walked to the Liberal Arts building. She still had some time, so she went up to the floor that held the English professors' offices to search for Dr. Amy Allcot and Dr. George Deary, who had both taught Lee Anderson. Neither were in their offices, but Dr. Allcot had office hours today after Meg's class.

She wrote a note to Dr. Deary and put it in his mailbox. She kept it vague but mentioned Lee Anderson. She said she was looking for background information. Hopefully, it sounded like she was writing an article on the late student. Not investigating his death.

Huh. Maybe she should include examples of written correspondence to gather information in her book. Notes that worked and those that didn't. She hurried back downstairs to the classroom and, before the lecture started, scribbled a note for her writing ideas file. She put a purple sticker on the page so she could find it later, then turned the page and got ready for the class.

A lot of students took notes on their laptops, but Meg liked the old-fashioned process of writing things down. It helped facts stick in her head better.

As the professor lectured, her mind kept wandering to Anderson's professors. Finally, she turned the page and scribbled down her questions for them. Then she could focus on the class.

At the end of the session, she hurried up to Dr. Allcot's office. The door was open and the professor was just taking off her blazer and sitting down at her desk. When Meg knocked, the woman looked up with a smile that turned into a frown as Meg stepped inside. "I'm sorry, are you in one of my classes?"

"No, and I won't take up much of your time. I'm Meg Gates, and I knew Lee Anderson. He was just killed in Bainbridge. I was wondering if he was in any of your classes when he attended here." Meg sat down without being asked and pulled out her notebook. "I know it's a stretch, but I saw you were teaching at the same time Lee got his degree. I'm heading to the library to look at the yearbooks and any student projects they might have. Like I saw that he was part of the newspaper staff."

"Lee Anderson. I haven't heard that name here in ten years. Yes, I had Mr. Anderson in several classes. I wasn't his adviser, but even back then, Lee liked to use his writing to inform others. I hear he became quite a food critic. I've discovered several restaurants from his column. But I think he got several wrong, especially those on Bainbridge Island."

"Oh? Can you think of any ones specifically?" Meg focused on her notebook, trying not to give away her excitement. Maybe this professor knew about Lee's personal life too.

"The Steakhouse for one. It's a lovely, if dated, restaurant with amazing food. Lee seemed to focus on the atmosphere rather than the dishes. My husband and I love going to see what Chef Jon Michael has created. We go at least once a year, if not more often."

Meg let the silence fall between them as she could see the professor thinking.

"The strange thing was, I swore Lee told me he grew up on Bainbridge Island and he was the one who suggested the restaurant in the first place." Dr. Allcot shook her head. "I know things change, but why would he trash the restaurant in his column if he loved the place just a few years ago?"

As Meg and the professor continued to talk, she wondered the same thing. Why had Lee's view on restaurants on Bainbridge changed?

It didn't seem logical. Especially after what Chef Jon Michael had told her a few days ago about how the Anderson family had been frequent customers.

Maybe she'd find something in the yearbooks that would help her pin the problem down. Or maybe she could talk to someone else about Lee Anderson. After thanking the professor for her time, Meg checked her phone as she walked to the library, but she hadn't missed any calls. If Dr. Deary had seen her note, he hadn't called her back.

She was on what her uncle would call a fishing expedition, but she wasn't sure what she was even fishing for. Maybe she'd know it when she saw it. They said that all the time in murder mysteries. Maybe this time, they were right.

CHAPTER 16

Who did the victim hang around with? Now and in the past.

After two hours of looking through the materials in the special collection, she turned to the university's website. Nothing she hadn't seen before. She found a paper from the English department, but it explored what professors in the department and other universities were doing. Nothing on student activities or written by students. She keyed in a more general search term and discovered a newspaper. *The Daily*. Now she could do some research. She found the microfilm for the paper in the years that Anderson attended and started scrolling.

What seemed like hours later, she stood and stretched. She had one more year of films to scroll through, then she needed to head to the research area to see if there were any yearbooks covering the time Lee Anderson was a student. She'd decided to do that last since the noncirculating section was on the first floor and she could run out to the mini café in the lobby between tasks for a soda. And maybe a cookie.

She wasn't hungry, thanks to Aunt Melody, but she was feeling tired. A sugar hit would help. She sat back down and loaded the next film into the viewer.

At one point, she realized Lee Anderson didn't have any by-lines in the paper. She scrolled back a week and nothing. Then another week. Finally, she found a column by Lee. It was on the change of companies for the upcoming year to manage the cafeterias. The kitchen staff he'd interviewed were angry that their jobs had been outsourced. He said he'd tried to talk to the college leadership but found them less than helpful in explaining the change. Budget cuts was their short answer.

As Meg scrolled through, she noticed that three weeks after that column, Lee Anderson's name dropped off the masthead. Had he been taken off the newspaper's staff? Or had he quit?

She wrote down the name of the newspaper's sponsoring professor. Maybe he'd have some answers.

Then she went downstairs and got a soda and a candy bar from the café. A sign near the cash register said THIS CAFÉ IS BROUGHT TO YOU BY BAKERS AND SONS.

That was the company that had taken over the campus food program back in Anderson's day. She went over to sit in the sunshine and pulled out her notebook. Then she wrote a note to look up the company.

After finishing her snack, Meg headed back into the library's noncirculating section. Or in other words, books you couldn't check out. She guessed everything had its special terminology, even libraries.

She found the college yearbook up to 1994. Then nothing. This wasn't helping. She opened her laptop and pulled up the alumni section. Here someone had posted the pictures taken for the identification cards that each student got at the first of the year. Listed were the years Lee had attended, his extracurricular activities, and his current employer and job. A note stated that the information was provided by the graduating student. She focused on the four ID snapshots first. Sometime between junior and senior year, Lee had grown a beard. He looked less like the wide-eyed, excited freshman from his first photo. Meg took a picture on her phone of all four years. Just because.

Then she dug into the listed activities. He'd been a member of the Honor Society the first year, but he wasn't listed in the next three years. Had transitioning from high school to college been an adjustment for Lee too? Meg could sympathize. Maybe all college-bound kids should have to work a year in a real-world, minimum-wage job. Just to let them know their choices. Meg regretted leaving school for the start-up, but then again, things happened.

Sophomore year, he had become part of *The Daily*. He seemed to blossom there. He had several writing-related club memberships. One additional picture was included. A snap in what looked like a newsroom with another guy and a girl. Meg leaned in closer to see, then checked the caption. Lee Anderson, John McGee, and Brooke Michael.

Meg wrote John McGee's name down and took a picture of the trio together their senior year. She didn't have to find Brooke Michael. She'd see her tomorrow to play Pickleball. Brooke Michael was now Brooke Hastings, her doubles partner.

As Meg drove back to her apartment, she thought about the connection between Brooke and Lee. Bainbridge Island was a small community. It wasn't odd that she knew someone who had gone to school with Lee Anderson. Especially since he'd grown up here. But she hadn't known Brooke until she'd invited her to play Pickleball. She'd seen her here and there around the island, but that was it. Then, a couple of weeks after Lee Anderson had been killed, all of a sudden, Brooke had come into her life.

It could be a coincidence, but Meg didn't think so. Pickleball would be interesting tomorrow.

She'd stayed later at the library than she'd planned, so she got caught in afternoon traffic. She needed to get Watson from Aunt Melody, then jump in the shower and be ready at six for Dalton to pick her up. She turned up the radio, trying to drown out her thoughts about Lee and Brooke. And who was John McGee? If anyone. Just because they were close in college, it didn't mean they were still friends. Brooke should know. And was she related to Chef Jon Michael?

Meg had thought the chef went by two first names, but if Brooke was his daughter, that would explain their connection. He'd said Lee had been at the restaurant a lot. Were Lee and Brooke high school sweethearts or just friends?

Meg had expected nothing to come of her fishing expedition. And she assumed her uncle had expected the same since he hadn't balked at her mission. But maybe she had found something. At the least, she'd come back with more questions and suspects.

After collecting her dog and dodging Aunt Melody's questions, Meg hurried upstairs to spend a few minutes going over her notes and listing out the questions that had come to her while she was driving home. Why did she always think of things she needed to do while she was driving? Or walking? Or even showering? Was her mind somehow free to wander when her body was doing something else?

Meg put that question on hold for a few minutes. She wondered if Dr. Deary would call. If not, she'd reach out during his office hours. She'd written down his schedule in her notebook when she'd left the message in his mailbox.

Meg put her notebook away and hurried into the shower. Dalton would be here soon, and she wanted to be ready as soon as he arrived. She was starving.

They sat out on the deck of the Whale Fin as Meg talked through her day with him.

He sipped his iced tea and listened. When she was done, he

focused on eating his salad for a few minutes. "I don't remember ever hearing about a John McGee on Bainbridge. Of course, Lee Anderson was older than us. I met Brooke a few times at the bonfire. She works for Emmett, and she'd seen me at the restaurant."

"Seen? Does that mean dated?" Meg wasn't jealous. What happened before she'd come home was water under the bridge, for both of them. But if he'd dated Brooke, maybe he knew more.

"No." Dalton smiled his slow, hot smile. "I would say *dated* if that was the situation. No, she was there with a group of servers from Emmett's place, and she invited me to go with them to an afterparty in Seattle. Since I had to work the next day, I politely declined. We went out one time, then she went out with Nate the next day. She asked a few other times, but I think she got the message after a while. I wasn't interested."

"Not your type?" Meg wasn't sure if she was happy that they hadn't dated more or disappointed that he didn't have information to add to the notebook.

He smiled at her. "You're my type."

"That's the best answer." She laughed as they turned their attention back to the meal.

Later, at her apartment, they worked on a murder board for the case. She printed off a few pictures. "Isn't this romantic?"

Dalton lifted his gaze from where he was gluing suspects to the board. "I must have missed the signals. Did you want romance tonight?"

She shook her head. "I was being sarcastic. I don't have time for romance. We need to figure out Lee Anderson's murder and his connection to me. That still feels creepy. Besides, I have homework and Lilly's work to finish before I have to go back to the bookstore on Wednesday. I can't do everything, every day."

"Which is why you have a planner and a week. But you can write every day. Did you write your thirty minutes yet?"

Meg groaned as she sorted out the pictures. "No, I went to class and then I was in the library, researching."

"Okay, then you go sit at your desk, and I'll work on this by myself." He pulled over Meg's notebook. "Everything's in here, right?"

"You don't have to do that," Meg told him, but then she saw the look in his eyes. "You're right. I committed to this. I need to do it. I just hate leaving you alone to work on this."

"If I get stuck, I'll take Watson out for a walk. I think I can entertain myself for thirty minutes without your help," he replied. "Wasn't it Seinfeld who did the one-joke-a-day chain on his calendar? Maybe you need to get an I WROTE sticker like those I VOTED ones. Or maybe a gold star. You could give yourself a gold star every day."

Meg rolled her eyes, but really, his idea had merit. "Okay, I'm going to write, so leave me alone for thirty minutes."

"I'll do my best to keep my hands off you." He turned back to the murder board. "If you're ready, I'll start my watch timer."

Meg sat at her desk and opened the laptop, booting up the system and finding her document. Then she opened the notebook with the book ideas and notes she kept on her desk and grabbed a pen. "I'm ready, so start the timer."

She read a few paragraphs to reacquaint herself on where she was, checking the notebook as well. She always wrote down a few starter ideas when she stopped writing for the day, to give her a jumping-off point. Or, if she thought of something after she'd written, she'd jot it down in her notebook to revisit the next day. The chapter she was currently writing was on what to do when you aren't friends with the coroner. She had a list of ways to look up causes of death even when the police reports were less than forthcoming. She still needed to try a few, so she grabbed a stickie note and wrote down *bullet markings, casings, powder marks?* Then she continued writing the book.

When Dalton called time, she blinked and finished her sentence. Then she wrote notes about what she wanted to write tomorrow and marked her word count on the chart. She could keep writing, but that would be rude. She took the stickie note over to the table where Dalton had finished updating the murder board. "Thanks for pushing me. I would have told myself I was too tired after you left."

"I'm here for you. If you need motivation, I'm good at it. I took a goal-setting class the first of the year at work."

"Oh, what did you wish for?" Meg asked as she checked out the murder board.

"Goal setting isn't wishing. I have a plan. It may or may not happen, but I'm working on it." He pointed to the stickie. "What's that?"

"We need to find out more about how Lee was killed. I know it was a gunshot, but was it a small pistol? Large? Close up? Would he have seen his killer? I don't know enough about guns to even picture the scene. Maybe I need to take a class on guns and other weapons." She went and put the kettle on to make tea. "Do you want some?"

"Please, but no caffeine. I need to sleep tonight. I'm up early tomorrow for work."

"Peach too girly?" She held up a tea bag.

"Sounds great." He looked at her notebook. "I didn't put this John McGee on the suspect list. I figured we needed something more, like a motive or opportunity, to put someone on. I didn't put Brooke on it either."

"I'm going to talk to my new doubles partner after Pickleball. If I go missing tomorrow, you'll know where to start." Meg filled the cups with hot water, pouring it over the tea bags, and took them to the table. "She seems really nice. I hate to question her about Anderson."

"You're just asking about their relationship. And if she knows how he knew you. It would be logical to ask after finding out they went to college together."

"True." Meg curled her legs up on the chair and hugged them tight with her arms. "I'm not sure I'd even recognize anyone I went to college with. Not even my freshman-year roommate. By sophomore year, I had moved out of the dorms into an apartment with friends. I hated dorm life. Too many people and too much noise. I used to go to the library to study."

Dalton checked his tea, then stirred in a couple of teaspoons of sugar. "I still keep in contact with my Coast Guard buddies. I didn't mind the close quarters, but I'm more of a people person than you are."

"I'd be offended at that statement but it's true. I like some people. I like being home with Watson more. Especially if you or Natasha are here. Her date last night was strange, by the way." She went on to tell him about Natasha seeing Mark Thomason, who Meg had met as Irene Olsen's date a few weeks ago.

"That's not good. Do I need to have a talk with this Mark guy?" He sipped his tea, ruining his enforcer status image.

"Not unless Natasha brings it up. I probably shouldn't have told you, but she tells you things about me all the time." Meg uncurled from the chair as she leaned to check on her tea. "It's just weird, isn't it? Natasha doesn't date in forever, and when she does, the guy is also dating Irene."

"And he shows up at your writers' meeting, as well as your 'not-a-date' with Lee Anderson, with a girl whose dad is dating your mom. And now he's seeing your best friend." He broke a cookie in half, handing her one side. "Is it just me or am I seeing too many connections that lead directly to you?"

"Great. Yesterday, I had no suspects besides the local chefs in Anderson's murder, and today, we've not only added more people but also widened the motives list. Just once, I want to investigate a case where the killer raises his hand and says, 'Me! I did it. I hated him since fifth grade when he pushed me down on the playground.'"

"Your book wouldn't sell many copies if killers just walked around introducing themselves and their motives. And your uncle would be out of a job." He finished his tea. "I hate to call an end to tonight, but I'm beat. I'll text you tomorrow. Do you want to go to the bonfire and watch people get drunk and stupid?"

"I've got the writers' meeting tomorrow night. Sorry. It sounds like fun. Not." She stood and followed him to the door. "Watson, let's go out one more time."

As they followed Dalton down the stairs, he paused at the bottom and kissed her. "Have a good night."

"Thanks for pushing me to write. Usually, the men in my life are less supportive of my dreams." She didn't mention Romain by name.

"You need to up your standards and only date awesome men like me." He rubbed her cheek. "Or maybe only me."

Chapter 17

Not everyone a dead guy knew is a suspect, but they could be.

Brooke handed Meg a bottle of water. "See? You're already twice as good as you were last week. Did you get in any practice?"

"No. My life is combusting all over everything. I walk most places, and I have a dog to keep me company, but I need to join a gym or something. That's why I'm here once a week. To make sure I work out." Meg took a sip from the water and considered pouring the bottle over her head.

"Pickleball falls into that doing something category, but it's not a full workout. The gym here isn't bad. A few CrossFit guys train there, but they go into Seattle when they're off work to a real CrossFit gym. People mostly go in to use the treadmills, which I don't get at all. Why walk there and not outside? Well, unless it's raining." She walked over to the reception desk and picked up a flyer. "They have all kinds of classes. I'm always looking for a session to work around my jobs since my shifts are all over the place."

Meg took the flyer and glanced at it. Maybe she could fit in a class, like on nights when Dalton was working. She held up the flyer before tucking it away in her bag. "Thanks. For this and the water. Can I ask you a weird question?"

"Why I work at the Bistro and the Local Crab?" Brooke smiled as Meg reacted to the response. "Even sharing a small house with two roommates, I need two jobs to live on the island. And I love it here."

Meg knew the story. "Me too. I'm cobbling together jobs and school. So I get that. But that's not what I wanted to ask you. I saw some pictures of you and Lee Anderson together on his alumni page at the school yesterday. I didn't realize you knew him."

Brooke nodded slowly, then drank some of her water. "Lee Anderson. He was a complete jerk and a good friend, all at the same time. We grew up together. He used to come over after school and we'd play outside my dad's restaurant. He owns the Steakhouse. I don't work there anymore, because, well, family. It's a long story. Anyway, Lee and I did go to college together. I wasn't as convinced that English was my jam, but he loved working on the school paper."

She paused for a minute, staring at the floor. "After graduation, he got that job at a Seattle paper as a food critic, and he changed. He was never mean before that. In school, he even wanted to fight the 'man' when the college fired all the kitchen staff and contracted out the food service. He tried to set up protests on campus, but no one was as committed as he was to the cause. We stopped talking soon after."

"You don't know why he changed?" Meg knew there had to be more to the story. Brooke was leaving something out. She could see it in her eyes.

Brooke glanced at her watch. "Look, can we talk about this later? I need to get to work."

"Oh, sorry, sure." Meg watched as Brooke sprinted out of the community center.

Derby walked over, his gaze on Brooke. "Something wrong?" He sat next to Meg.

"I think I hit a nerve." Meg turned away from the door. "How are you?"

"Doing good. I didn't realize how hard it was to keep my relationship with your mother on the down low. Now that it's all out, I feel like a weight has been lifted off my shoulders." He smiled and met her gaze. "I should be asking you how you are doing."

"Seeing you together was a shock at first, but I knew Mom and Dad weren't getting back together. It's been too long, and he's happy with Elaine. All I want is for my mom to be happy. And to not have too many things in my life change for change's sake," Meg said, smiling as she stood, putting her backpack on her shoulder. "I need to get home. I'm working tomorrow at the bookstore, and I have other things to finish up if I want to go to the writers' group tonight."

He stood as well. "Irene's been attending those meetings. She thinks she wants to write a fantasy book. All those times I read *The Hobbit* at bedtime must have stuck."

Meg didn't mention that Irene had told her that she was just going because of Mark. Especially now that Mark had moved on. An idea niggled at the back of Meg's brain. "Maybe I'll see her tonight."

She didn't say anything about seeing Mark or confronting him about dating both Irene and Natasha. It might be a fun evening after all. And at the next family get-together, she could ask Derby about his reading choices. Being a fantasy reader was a commitment. Not something anyone decided on a spur of the moment. Maybe she was going to like having Derby around after all.

It was guest lecturer night at the writers' meeting, so Meg wouldn't get words in. She needed to start coming to the write-ins to increase her word count. Tonight, Meg's mission was to find out more about Mark Thomason.

The event room in the back of Island Diner was already crowded. They'd set it up like a classroom so everyone would have room to eat as well as take notes. She had just slipped into a chair at the last table in the room when a waitress touched her shoulder.

"Are you ordering dinner?"

Meg nodded and glanced over the menu on the table in front of her. "Soda water and a club sandwich. With fries."

She handed the waitress her card. They always paid upfront at this event so the serving staff didn't have to wait for the meeting to finish. If a writer wanted something else, they went to the bar to order.

"You're Meg Gates? I expected someone taller." The waitress held her card up and smiled at her. "I'm Charli. I'm friends with Jolene."

"Oh, nice to meet you." Meg held out her hand. "I don't think I've seen you here before."

"I just got back from a trip to see my mom. Well, to help out after she . . ." The woman paused and wiped at her eyes. "I'm not going to be able to say it, I guess. I was back home in Idaho for a few months. I'll get this rung in so you'll have food before the meeting starts. It was nice to finally meet you."

Now Meg knew how Jolene had found this group. She had a friend on the inside. She wondered if Charli knew anything about Mark, or Lee for that matter. She took out her notebook and pen and zipped up her backpack. She left her wallet on the table since Charli still had her credit card.

"Hey, I hoped I'd see you here. I've been trying to call Natasha but she's not answering. I hope everything's okay." Mark Thomason came up and tried to give Meg a hug. She shrugged him off.

"Are you here with Irene?" She glanced around the room, trying to find her almost-stepsister. Okay, maybe not yet, but she felt a loyalty to her and Natasha. Mostly Natasha. Mark, she wanted to punch in the nose.

"Irene? No." He stared at her. "Is that why Natasha isn't answering my calls? She thinks I'm dating Irene?"

"You told me you were dating," Meg reminded him.

"No, I told you I was Irene's date for the evening. We work at the same company. I'm in logistics. We were going to a company event, and she asked if I wanted to get dinner first. The date thing was a joke because we knew everyone at work would assume we were dating if we came to the event together."

"You work for the cruise line?" This wasn't the answer that Meg had been expecting.

Mark nodded and then repeated, "Logistics. I move boats from one port to another. Well, the captain actually steers the ship, but I tell him when the ship can move and where. That line works better with women after a few drinks. You didn't tell Natasha I was dating Irene, did you?"

"Yes. I did. And in the future, being upfront with everyone is a better idea. Irene called you her boyfriend," Meg pointed out.

He rubbed the side of his face. "I know. I told her it was just one night. And she came to the writers' meeting to see if the group would work for her. And—" He paused. "She thought it was a real date. I'm an idiot."

"Men usually are," Charli said as she gave Meg her credit card back with a receipt to sign. She set a large club soda with a lime perched on the lip on the table. "Food should be up in a few minutes. What did Mark do now? Try to hit on you? Everyone and his dog knows that you're dating Dalton."

Mark threw a ten on her tray. "I didn't know. Charli, can you get me a beer?"

"Sure," Charli said as she met Meg's gaze. "Everything else okay here?"

The question wasn't just about food. Charli was offering Meg a way out of the conversation. Charli would get him to leave, or at least leave her alone. But Meg thought she had it. Of course, she had thought the same thing when she first talked to Lee Anderson. Maybe it took time to see the crazy. "I'm fine."

"Okay, you just let me know if you need anything else," Charli said. "Mark, I'll get that beer in a second."

After she left, he paused. "Look, I just want a chance to explain myself to Natasha. I really like her."

"I'll tell her what you said. What she does with it is up to her." Meg shrugged as a server brought her food.

"That's all I can ask. Thanks, Meg." He turned and left, heading back to the front where he was sitting between two men Meg didn't know. As he sat down, one turned back and smiled at her. He lifted his hand to wave, but Mark pushed it down.

The fact that she was dating Dalton, not here looking for a relationship, was circulating the writers' group. At least she wouldn't have to worry about being hit on. Now she just had to figure out why Lee Anderson had been looking for her.

Oh, and who killed him. Easy peasy.

The speaker talked about writing a synopsis or an outline for your book. Meg figured most of the people at the meeting were writing fiction. Maybe she needed to find a nonfiction writers' group, but that might be divided up between short-form freelancers and long-form authors. At least this group talked about publishing and reviews. All things she needed to learn.

She spent the first part of the next morning going over last night's notes and looking up the books and research materials the speaker had mentioned. She sat at the table with her laptop, digging into a muffin and sipping on coffee. Right now, in this moment, life was good.

Maybe that was all anyone could get out of life. Moments of pure contentment.

Then Watson ran to the door, barking.

So much for contentment. Meg hurried over to see who was outside. Dalton waved when she looked out the window. She unlocked the door and let him inside. Watson went crazy, jumping up on him until he acknowledged the dog's presence.

"He's mad at me because I didn't take him with me last night." Meg poured a cup of coffee for Dalton. "What are you doing today?"

"I have the morning off, so I thought I'd come by and see how your meeting went." He sat down and took the coffee she offered. "Did you learn anything?"

"Besides Irene might be a big fat liar?" Meg shook her head. "Mark said he didn't know they were dating. He even explained both times I saw him with her. Do I believe Irene with all her faults or the guy who Natasha is falling for?"

"I don't know." He rubbed Watson's ears. "Maybe neither one right now. No new information about Lee Anderson or who would want to kill him?"

"No, nothing to report on that scale. But I did learn the importance of having a newsletter long before your first book is published. These people are sharks. They know everything about publishing." Meg reported what she'd learned. "Sometimes they make me feel stupid with all the things I don't know. It could take years to be good in this group."

"Everyone has to start somewhere," Dalton said. "You're working tonight, right?"

"I start at three. This morning, I was going to write my thirty minutes, then finish up my reading for next week's class. What time do you go in?" Meg asked. She wanted to have an excuse to hang out this morning, even if it meant she'd miss out on her writing time. She would probably have time at the bookstore.

"No way, you're not going to use me as an escape hatch to not write. I have the morning free. Why don't you write, and I'll take Watson on a long walk? We'll be back around eight. Then you and I can walk on the beach until it's time to have lunch at the Steakhouse to clear up some questions about Lee and Brooke." He looked down at Watson. "You can come, too. The Steakhouse has great patio dining."

"You sure he won't be in the way?" She stood and walked over to her laptop. Then, after not hearing any response to her question, turned back to Dalton. "Are you okay?"

"Sure, I'm fine." He seemed a little distracted as he studied the murder board that Meg had gotten out from under the couch this morning. "Go on, write. I'll take Watson out as soon as I finish this coffee."

At the Steakhouse, Meg was surprised to see Brooke walking out of the restaurant as they arrived. She waved at her, but Brooke either didn't see her or didn't want to talk. She seemed a little put out. When Meg went inside to see if they could sit on the patio, Chef Jon Michael was standing by the hostess stand, staring at the door. He blinked when she came in, then a smile crossed his face.

"Miss Gates, so good to see you. Are you by yourself today?" He held out an arm toward the dining room. "We should have a nice table for you for lunch."

"Actually, Dalton, my boyfriend, is outside with my dog, Watson. Can we sit on the patio?"

His smile widened. "Of course. Aimee will get you seated. Just walk around the building to the left."

As Meg exited the restaurant, she saw Brooke pulling out of the parking lot in a red sports car. Her face was set. Did she have a fight with her father? And did it have anything to do with Lee Anderson?

Meg saw Dalton walking Watson around the parking lot. She caught his attention and pointed toward the path leading to the patio.

As they settled into the table in the corner of the patio, Meg glanced at the menu. Chef Jon Michael was watching them through the window. When he saw her looking, he disappeared back into the restaurant.

"I think Brooke and her father must have gotten into an argument just before we got here," Meg said after the waitress had brought water for all three of them and took their drink order.

"She took out of here fast. I was going to walk over and say hi, but she flew out of the parking lot. I wonder what they were talking about."

Meg shook her head. "I don't know, but I would bet it was something about Lee Anderson. I wonder if Uncle Troy has talked to Chef Jon Michael yet about knowing Lee."

"I'm sure your uncle knows what we know. Although, I have to admit, I didn't know that Brooke grew up here. That never came up during our date. In fact, she didn't talk about living on the island at all. I thought she was a new resident."

Love made people do all sorts of crazy things. Like give restaurants bad reviews. Had Lee been reacting to a possible failed relationship with Brooke when he trashed the Bainbridge restaurants? Who had Brooke worked for in the past? Maybe that was the clue to why Lee Anderson had hated Bainbridge Island restaurants so badly. He could have been reacting to one person working there. Brooke.

Was Brooke working at the restaurant during the bad review? Had Lee Anderson been that petty?

Brooke couldn't have been the person that Meg had saved him from. She'd never even met Brooke until a few weeks ago. She'd probably seen her around the island, but she swore that they never had a real conversation until they talked about Pickleball.

Was she trying to squeeze a square peg into a round hole? Or were the clues all there for the picking?

Chapter 18

Sometimes the way you look at a clue makes a difference. You could be putting your own filter on the information.

At the bookstore that night, Meg had been surprisingly busy with walk-in customers until about five. After the ferry left the harbor, the store was dead. She locked up and took Watson for a quick walk with a BE RIGHT BACK sign in the window. She waved and nodded at a few island residents who were either coming back from a day of work in Seattle or heading to dinner at one of the local restaurants. Somehow, in the last year, she'd regained her island resident status. Probably because of her mom and her bookstore.

She thought about her to-do list on the counter. She'd finished the bookstore list for the day, but she had brought her own work, just in case it was slow. Gloria, Mom's other employee, used the slow times to read. Meg filled it with one task or another from school, her job with Lilly Aster, or more recently, the book she was writing.

Tonight, she'd already finished her class work. Thanks to Dalton's insistence that she do her writing before they went to lunch, she had already worked on the book. But maybe she'd take another thirty minutes to review what she had and plan forward. She still hadn't mapped out a few chapters. But the book was getting close.

And she was getting nervous. What if she'd done all this work and no one wanted to publish it? What if she couldn't get an agent? What if she had to haul her aunt out of retirement to shop the book? And the question that haunted her dreams: What if, after all this work, it wasn't any good?

Lilly said it was normal to worry. And to not even try to sell her first book. But did she even have an idea for a second one? Amateur sleuthing had been her hobby for as long as she could remember. If she didn't write about that, what would she write about?

As she turned the corner to the bookstore, she saw a woman standing by the door waiting with her back to Meg. She hurried over, digging her keys out of her pocket. As she arrived, she focused on unlocking the door. "Sorry, I needed to take my dog out for a walk. Come on in."

The person followed her in, and said, "I thought you were supposed to work night shifts. Can you just lock up anytime you want?"

Meg knew that voice. She unhooked Watson's leash and grabbed a bottle of water to fill his bowl. "Hi, Irene. What can I help you with? Romance? Or slasher mystery?"

"You could help by not scaring off my boyfriend. Why is your friend trying to steal Mark from me? First, your mom goes after my dad, now this. Why does everyone hate me? All I want is my happily-ever-after." Irene rattled off all the injustices of the last week with a scattershot cadence.

"I didn't have anything to do with any of those things. I found out about my mom and your dad about the same time you did. Mark says you weren't even really dating." Red bloomed on Irene's face, but Meg kept going. "His relationship with Natasha isn't my business. Unless he's still dating you, which he assures me he isn't and never has dated you. He said you guys just hung out."

Irene rolled her eyes. "And you believed him?"

"Not my problem," Meg repeated. "This is between him and Natasha. And you, I guess. How much do you know about Mark Thomason? Is he a decent man?"

Irene sank into the couch and leaned forward onto her knees. She wasn't a very big woman to begin with, but now, she looked like a kid. Trying to figure out life. "Mark and his sister lost their parents a few years ago in a car accident. He's been devoted to her since. She's spoiled and conceited in my view. But then again, my view doesn't count for much. I hoped Mark would see me as something more than just a friend. However, that hasn't happened. Why is dating so hard? According to my plan, I was supposed to be married by now and having my first child. Not hanging around with guys who are just killing time."

Not for the first time, Meg felt sorry for Irene. "Do you want some coffee or tea?"

"Tea would be great. Green if you have it." Watson went over to snuggle with Irene, sensing her emotional upset. Irene absently rubbed his back as she talked. "How do you like playing Pickleball? My dad says you're playing doubles with Brooke."

"It's more of a workout than I expected," Meg said as she brought out the cups of tea on a tray with spoons and sugar. "Brooke is interesting."

"She's quiet. Kind of hard to get to know." Irene stirred sugar in her tea, then sat back, letting the tea bag steep in the water. "She grew up with Lee Anderson. At least that's what my dad told me. They were as thick as thieves before something happened in college."

"She told me that story. Lee went off to fight for the little guy and they didn't talk afterward. It seems like a poor excuse to end that kind of friendship. Her dad's Chef Jon Michael. Did you know that?"

"Duh, everyone knows that." Irene rolled her eyes before she heard how she sounded. "And now I know why I don't have any friends. Sorry, it just slipped out. My dad says I need to work on being more likable, whatever that means."

Meg agreed with Derby Olsen. And not for the first time. Irene needed to learn how to be a nicer person. Derby probably didn't lead with that to his only child. She knew Irene was waiting for her to disagree with her dad, to tell her she was fine just the way she was, but Meg couldn't bring herself to lie. "Sometimes it takes a while to change your personality."

"So, you agree with my dad. I'm unlikable. Nice, Meg. I'm trying to be open with you and you just stab me. You could have waited and just stabbed me in the back when you were talking about me to your friends. I'm sure it's not the first time." Irene pushed Watson aside as she stood. "Thanks for the tea. I think I need to go before I say something my dad will regret."

Irene swung her purse over her arm and left the bookstore.

Meg swore under her breath. "That didn't go as well as I'd hoped," Meg said as she stood to put Irene's cup and the leftover sugar on the tray. "But it's a start." She knew her mom wanted her and Irene to become friends. Meg wasn't sure that would ever happen. She left the tray on the table. She was going to finish her tea.

Instead of worrying about the possible future of Irene being a part of Meg's family, she grabbed her laptop and focused on what Irene had told her about Brooke and Lee. She didn't know if their relationship, or lack of one, had been a factor in Lee's death, but it was a lead. And with this murder, she didn't know if she had any leads she could even try to investigate.

What happens when you run out of leads? That should be a chapter heading. She thought about the question, then wrote down a single sentence.

You go back to the beginning.

So that was what she was going to do. Go back to the beginning. She might not have been able to find much on Lee and Brooke in college, but what about their growing-up years? Chef Jon Michael had said that Lee had moved away with his mom after his dad died. When he came back here for college, was he trying to reconnect with Brooke? And if so, what had happened to prevent that from occurring?

Meg didn't think a change in college cafeteria staff would cause such a change in personality in Lee Anderson, unless it was personal.

Had that changed something for Lee or someone he cared about?

Watson's bark brought her out of her thoughts. It was time to close the shop and go home. Her musing about Lee Anderson would have to wait.

Dalton walked up to her as she left the bookstore. He took Watson's leash and kissed her on the cheek. "Sorry, I thought I'd catch you before you closed."

"Almost. I was going down the rabbit hole on Lee Anderson's life and death," Meg admitted as she took his arm, leaning into him as they walked. "Have you eaten?"

"Not since lunch," Dalton replied. "Do you want to stop somewhere and grab a bite?"

"No, I've got soup frozen at home, Aunt Melody's take on Zuppa Toscana. And I have some fresh rolls." She thought about Lee's personality change but decided to leave it alone for the night. "And I could make a salad."

"You had me at soup," he said as they turned the corner to

the street where Aunt Melody's garage and Meg's apartment resided. "How was work?"

Meg talked about Irene's visit, ending with a sigh. "I think Irene's lonely."

"She brings it on herself." Dalton grabbed Meg's keys and opened the apartment door. "From what you're telling me, this guy was just being nice and she turned it into a white house and picket fence dream."

"It just doesn't seem fair. I know, she does it to herself." Meg waved away what Dalton was going to say. She took the soup out of the freezer and grabbed a pan to heat it in.

He stared at her, then laughed as he filled Watson's food dish and gave him fresh water.

"What?" Meg crossed her arms, staring at him.

He shrugged as he got out the stuff to make a salad to go with dinner. "I think you're starting to defend your new sister. It's kind of cute."

Meg threw a roll at him. "Bite your tongue."

Dalton turned the kitchen radio on and continued working on the salad. Meg unpacked her tote and repacked it for tomorrow's shift at the bookstore. She set her laptop on the desk and plugged it in. As she did, she turned Lee's childhood back and forth in her head. Surely, a clue from his childhood or his time in college could explain how a fun-loving kid turned into a man who hated Bainbridge Island and everyone on it.

A thought hit her. She needed to find out more about Lee's mother. She opened her laptop and looked up something. Then she met Dalton's gaze. He'd been watching her for a few minutes. "What are you doing tomorrow?"

"Nothing. I have a night shift, so I start at five. Why?"

She wrote down the information she'd found online. "Do you want to go to a funeral with me? It's in Seattle, so we'd have to leave at nine."

"Lee Anderson's?"

When she nodded, he glanced at his watch. "I'm sure my suit's clean, but I'll need to iron a shirt."

"Let's get dinner done, then, and get you home. I need to figure out what questions I want to ask his mom. I'm sure something happened in college that changed him." She didn't want to bring up the food service change, but somehow, she knew it was a clue. Lee's life was focused on food. Good and bad.

"There's no rush, I know how to iron a shirt." He finished the salad and put it on the table. "The soup looks like it's done. Butter for the rolls?"

They talked about anything but Lee Anderson's funeral as they ate. Dalton always had a fun story about someone riding the ferry or something around town. For someone who arrived on Bainbridge Island as an orphan, he had built a good life here. He was liked by everyone. He had a good job and friends.

He had made Bainbridge home. Whereas Meg had run from the island as soon as she could. She'd wanted to explore the world. He'd wanted to make a home. She thought he'd been the one with the right idea.

After dinner, she suggested a movie and even found a package of microwave popcorn in the cabinet, but he begged off. He needed some sleep since he'd be working late tomorrow. Unless she wanted him sleeping at the funeral.

After he left, she popped the popcorn anyway, and she and Watson curled up with the movie. She could sleep tomorrow night while Dalton worked. It might not be a fair deal, but she didn't have a job that could keep her up late. Thank goodness.

She stood and grabbed her laptop again. She took out her murder notebook and copied Anderson's short obituary onto a blank page. She then listed his relatives on the page. His mom and grandmother. No one else.

She looked up both names, but every hit led her back to the obituary. They seemed like normal people. She then Googled his father's name and found several articles on him about cooking. He'd been a teacher at a local culinary institute until he was killed in a car\pedestrian accident on his way home to Bainbridge. The roads had been wet, and the rain had prevented the cab from seeing him on the crosswalk. The cab driver had done time for manslaughter and the case had been closed.

Probably for everyone but Lee Anderson and his family.

CHAPTER 19

Memories are like flowers, they're better when they're fresh.

Walking into the small chapel, the smell of cold flowers hit Meg and she involuntarily grabbed Dalton's arm a little tighter. They'd been given a flyer when they'd walked in. A picture of Lee Anderson from his column. A copy of his obituary was on one side and an agenda of today's service on the other side. On the back, a Robert Frost poem talked about taking the road less traveled.

As they sat down, she studied the poem. What was the road that Lee Anderson had turned away from? Had he wanted to be a chef? Or a novelist? Or was he exactly where he wanted to be as a food critic?

The chapel was about half full and the service was about to start. Was this all the friends and family that Lee had? Or had he burned the bridges of his personal life as well as with the Bainbridge Island community?

An older woman in a wheelchair sat near the coffin at the front of the chapel. Her hand rested on the polished wood. Another woman came and leaned over, whispering in her ear. She handed her a tissue, then wheeled her back to the front pew. Soon afterward, a minister stepped up to the microphone and welcomed the small group.

As the service continued, Meg let her gaze wander over the attendees. No one she knew, until she hit the last row on the other side.

Brooke Hastings sat alone. Ramrod straight, with tears streaming from her eyes.

Whatever their differences had been, Brooke missed her friend. Maybe they hadn't been friends anymore, but they had been in the past. And maybe, Brooke missed the opportunity to return to that status.

Meg tried to focus on the music. Grief was often about the things that never would be, rather than the loss of what you had. Now she kind of wished she'd gotten to know the real Lee Anderson. Not the man who had complained about everything that night at the Local Crab.

After the service, they stood as the coffin and Lee's family left the chapel on the way to the cemetery for the private graveside service. One woman stepping toward the chapel door stood out to Meg. Dark hair, black dress, and a freaking veil over her face. Over-the-top glamour apparel for a funeral. Meg would bet that the shoes were designer from the red soles.

But it wasn't the shoes or the outfit that had first caught Meg's attention. She could have sworn that the woman was Rachel Midler. Her sorority sister and bridesmaid that had run away to Italy with Romain and ruined Meg's wedding.

Was she seeing things or had Rachel known Lee Anderson?

She felt Dalton's hand on her elbow and realized it was their turn to exit the pews. She followed the small crowd to the end, then Dalton led her back to the chapel doors.

"Do you want to stay and talk to people? They have coffee and probably cookies in the reception room." Dalton paused by the exit door and glanced around the room. Then he looked down at her. "Meg? What's wrong?"

She smiled and shook her head. "I think I'm seeing things. I think we should pay our respects to his mom and grandmother and then leave. I don't think today's the day for answers."

They stepped in line, and when they got to the front, Dalton reached out and squeezed the mother's hand. "I'm very sorry for your loss."

"Me too," Meg added on. She felt a little foolish using words that meant so little for an emotion so large. "I didn't know Lee well, but I hate this."

The mother smiled sadly. "Thank you for coming. It would have meant a lot to Lee for you to be here."

Meg started to ask if she could stop by another day, but something in the mother's demeanor told her it was the wrong day and time. Today was to mourn Lee. Not to question his actions that might have gotten him killed.

They stepped out into the rare Seattle sunshine. Meg looked up and held out her hands. "It doesn't seem appropriate that the sun decided to shine on Lee's burial and commitment to the ground, does it?"

"I don't know. Sometimes the universe blesses even the oddest of ceremonies." He held her arm as they walked down the sidewalk. "If we want, we have time to eat in the city before getting on the ferry."

"It's up to you." Meg wasn't sure she was even hungry. Dalton put his arm around her and she leaned onto him. She hadn't known Lee well, but his funeral had been draining.

"Let's get some food down at that little restaurant by the Market. At least some chowder. You look like you need a boost." Dalton glanced at his phone. "We can walk or grab a rideshare."

"Let's walk. It will give me some time to clear my head. The service was emotional." Meg pulled her shades out of her purse and slipped them on. "His mom looked wrecked."

"Losing a child must be hard." Dalton pulled her closer, away from a jogger on the street. "Did you see anyone you knew?"

"You're going to think I'm crazy, but I thought I saw Rachel

Midler. The woman who's now with Romain. Or was. I still haven't verified the rumor of them breaking up." Meg met Dalton's gaze. "She was in the back and left as soon as the doors opened. I could have been wrong, but it looked like her."

Dalton didn't say much as they made their way to the restaurant. Once they had ordered and were settled at a table by the window with a view of the sound, he stared out the window. Finally, he asked, "Why would the woman who wrecked your wedding be at a funeral for Lee Anderson?"

"Good question. Or do you think I'm losing it?" Meg was glad she'd added a glass of white wine to her chowder order. She'd burn it off long before she had to work tonight.

"Just asking a question, Magpie. No need to be touchy." Dalton smiled as he watched the sound. A few minutes later, after the waiter had brought their order, he turned back to her. "It might explain the bracelet, though. You need to talk to his mom. Brooke has been less than upfront with her emotions or the truth. Maybe his mom can tell you if that was Rachel at the chapel or not."

Meg buttered some of bread as she thought about what she might ask Mrs. Anderson. Then she looked up at Dalton. "Will you go with me to talk to her?"

He squeezed her hand. "Of course. Just tell me when."

Meg made a note to call Mrs. Anderson tomorrow morning. She'd gotten her number from Brooke when she'd called her a few minutes ago to ask if she was okay. Brooke tried to hide her pain, but she'd given Meg the phone number without questioning why.

As Meg shelved books that afternoon, she thought about her call with Brooke. She'd been at a bar, Meg was almost certain from the background noise. Not drunk, but not sober either. She hoped she was close to home and not still in Seattle. Getting home to Bainbridge Island had its hiccups, including riding the ferry. The area around the ferry terminal wasn't the best neighborhood when you were on alert and sober. Drunk, you could look like a target.

Concern made her go back to her phone. Her mom wouldn't mind if she closed up the bookstore to go save a friend. She texted Brooke. Asked her where she was at.

The message came back fast. **Island Diner. Don't worry. I can walk from here.**

Meg smiled as she read the message. Brooke had known exactly why Meg had followed up the phone call. And she'd been smart. She had waited until she was on familiar territory where she knew people before she'd started drinking.

She texted back a snarky reply, hoping it would make Brooke smile. **Just don't want to have to replace my doubles partner.**

The message was read, but no response was returned. Meg put her phone back under the counter. Watson was curled up on his bed behind the counter and lifted his head when she came near. When he realized she wasn't going anywhere, he put his head back down and went back to sleep.

Meg returned to finish her book shelving, and when Natasha came by after closing the bakery with a bag with something sweet, Meg was ready for a break. "I can smell the calories from here."

"Dalton told me you had a rough day, so I brought the magic elixir, chocolate cake with chocolate frosting. Do you have coffee to go with it?" Natasha held up the bag.

"Of course, I do." Meg moved to the back room. "Black?"

"Is there any other way?" Natasha called back.

When Meg returned with the cups, Natasha already had the cake sitting out. Watson had been aroused from his nap by the smell of food and now sat at Natasha's feet, begging.

"Dude, you can't have chocolate," Meg told her dog.

Natasha smiled. "No, but he can have this peanut butter biscuit that I'm starting to sell for my canine customers. Do you know how many people travel with their dogs? I was missing out on a huge customer base."

"So, he's a test taster?" Meg watched as Watson quickly took the biscuit and headed back to his bed. "He seems to like it."

"That's the plan." Natasha picked up her fork and took a bite of the cake. "Was Anderson's send-off emotional? Chapel filled with tearful women who wanted to be more than friends?"

"The opposite. The room was about half full. His mom and grandmother were his only family there. Brooke Hastings was there." Meg paused before adding, "And I think I saw Rachel there."

"Your sorority sister? The woman that ruined your wedding but probably saved you from a later divorce? That Rachel?" Natasha put the cake down.

She nodded. "Romain wasn't with her, if it even was her. Dalton's going with me if I can get Lee's mom to talk to me. Maybe she can tell me if Lee knew Rachel."

"Maybe they worked together?" Natasha offered an answer.

"No. Rachel was a legal assistant at a law firm in Bellevue. Lee's newspaper was headquartered in downtown Seattle. I don't think they ran in the same social circles either." Meg took a bite of the cake. It was heaven. "I could have been seeing things."

"I've never known you to be wrong or see things. You are the most levelheaded person I know. If you say Rachel was there, I believe you. Even if you don't believe yourself." Natasha curled her legs under her. "Now, what else has been going on?"

They talked together for another hour, but when she saw Natasha yawning, she told her to go home. Meg decided that she'd close up early as soon as she'd cleaned up and finished off her closing chores.

As she made some notes for her mom, the bell over the door

tinkled and a woman walked in. "Hi, welcome to Island Books. Are you looking for something specific?"

"Are you Meg Gates?" The young woman smiled and touched the books as she walked toward Meg. Then she held out her hand. "Hi, I'm Anne Blackwell. I'm dating your brother. I thought we should meet."

Anne wasn't what Meg had expected. Her red hair was pulled back in a messy bun. She was wearing jeans, a sparkling top, and cowboy boots. Not the fancy ones that were only worn for show, but a solid brown pair that appeared to be well-worn. Meg smiled and shook her hand. "Welcome to Mom's store. It's nice to meet you."

Anne smiled and looked around. "I was in the bookstore a few years ago. I knew it was your mom's store because your dad is always talking about how proud he is of her and what a success she made of her life. It's strange. My folks are divorced and they rarely talk to each other, let alone talk so positively about the other one. You guys must have dealt with the divorce well."

"My parents dealt with the divorce well," Meg corrected. "I think I'm still in a bit of shock. And it's been three, four years? Do you want some coffee?"

"No thanks, I can't stay long. I just wanted to put a face to your name. Your brother talks a lot about you. How he's so proud of you for taking charge of your life after that guy." Anne picked a book off the new release pile Meg had put on the counter for impulse buys. She read the back copy, then pushed the thriller toward the cash register. "I've been meaning to get this one. I'll take it."

Meg rang up the purchase. She wasn't quite sure what she was supposed to say to the girl who was dating her brother. "It was really nice to meet you. Are you doing something on the island tonight?"

"Meeting up with a few friends. We were all in the same

sorority at college, so we take turns picking a spot for dinner and some drinks every month. I chose the Local Crab." She frowned as she signed the credit receipt. "Sorry about your wedding. I guess I shouldn't have brought up my sorority sisters."

"No worries, I can deal with the word." Meg laughed a little. "People were touchy around me for months when I first moved back. All that pity wears on you after a while. But now, I'm just another islander."

"Well, I probably shouldn't tell you this, but we ran into your ex-fiancé a few weeks ago at a restaurant in Seattle. He was with that Rachel. Or at least that's what Steve said her name was. Your brother excused himself from our table, then went over and told Romain what a piece of dog poop he was for doing what he did. Then he told Rachel she was just as bad. His final words were 'you two deserve each other.'" Anne's eyes shone with pride at the memory. "Then Steve came back and apologized to me for disturbing our night out. He's such a sensitive man."

Meg smiled at the story. It felt good to hear that her brother had stood up for her, even when he didn't have to. "I'm glad it didn't ruin your evening."

"Actually, I wasn't sure about dating Steve until that moment. He's a hard worker and so smart, but I worried he was a little cold. Unemotional, if I'm saying it right. When he stood up for you, I knew he cared deeply about his family. That's the type of man I want to build my own family with. Someone who will make a scene in a restaurant because it's the right thing to do."

They exchanged numbers and Meg told her to come back anytime when she had more time to talk.

After Anne left, Meg looked over at the sleeping Watson. "Well, that was unexpected. Ready to head home?"

Watson lifted his head from his bed at the word *home*. He

was ready. Meg closed up the shop and made her way to her apartment, thinking about the woman Junior had finally found. Maybe her brother was on the right track after all.

Uncle Troy was sitting out on his porch when she walked up. He stood and leaned on the gate. "Got a few minutes to talk?"

Meg turned a confused Watson away from the steps to the apartment. "Were you waiting for me?"

"I heard you were at the funeral today. Anything I need to know?" Uncle Troy opened the gate and leaned down to greet Watson.

"If you already know I was there, you already know who else was there." She met his eyes. "Brooke Hastings for one."

"Yes, I know about Ms. Hastings's relationship with our suspect. Childhood friends who stopped being friends after an argument in college. Seems a long time to hold a grudge. Then there's the question of why she was so upset about his death." Uncle Troy stood after one last pat to Watson.

"I think it was the fact that they'd never healed the rift. If you want my opinion." Meg wondered if her uncle could verify something else for her. "Did your spy see Rachel Midler there as well? I thought maybe I was seeing things."

"Rachel Midler was at the funeral. My officer missed talking to her after she left the chapel. We don't know why she was there." He met my gaze. "I was just wondering if you knew. And if you were okay."

"I don't want to hit her anymore. That's a positive step forward, right?" Meg grinned at her uncle's facial reaction. "Seriously, I'm joking. But there was a time."

"Well, I'm glad that time has passed. If you think of anything else, let me know." Uncle Troy closed the gate after giving Watson one last pat on the back. "Have a good night, you two."

As Meg went upstairs, she decided that she needed to know

more about her former sorority sister and almost bridesmaid, Rachel Midler.

Rachel was vain enough that most of her life should be posted on her Facebook page. All Meg had to do was look. Meg hadn't taken the time to unfriend her after the breakup. It seemed like too much work. Maybe that oversight would work in her favor today.

CHAPTER 20

Be careful when you dig into the past. Sometimes you find things you don't want to see.

After fifteen minutes of scrolling through pictures of Romain and Rachel on their "impromptu" Italian vacation, or what should be more accurately named "Meg's stolen honeymoon," she closed the laptop and went to the couch to cuddle with Watson. She'd try again later.

The next morning, a message popped up on her Facebook page. Lee's mother was inviting her to lunch today at the Steakhouse. Meg texted Dalton to see if he could go with her but got a **sorry, working,** with a promise to bring pizza to the bookstore that night. She confirmed her lunch appointment with Mrs. Anderson, adding it to her schedule.

Meg thought the bookstore might be busy tonight since it was Friday, but she'd been wrong before. Besides, if it got crazy, she'd have Dalton to help with Watson. She wanted to focus on Lee Anderson more, but instead, she refilled her coffee and opened her laptop to work on her book.

At eleven fifteen, she drove to the other side of the island. She'd dressed in her work clothes, putting a blazer over the polo to hide the Island Books logo. She didn't look too casual, or at least she hoped not. She hoped that it wouldn't be hard to get Mrs. Anderson to talk about her son. Before she left, she texted Uncle Troy and told him about the lunch invite.

His response was short. **She invited you?**

Meg grinned as she honestly answered, **yes.** Brooke might have called Lee's mom and told her that Meg wanted to talk to her, but she hadn't reached out besides asking Brooke for her number. She checked the water in Watson's dish and told him she'd be back to get him before she went to work.

He looked up from his spot on the couch where he was watching television, gave her the guilt stare, then dropped his head.

Her dog was not happy, and he knew how to let Meg know.

When she got to the restaurant, it had just opened and only a few cars sat in the parking lot. One was a newer BMW sedan. She'd seen it at the funeral chapel too. Maybe it was Mrs. Anderson's? She wondered what she did for a living. Whatever it was, she was able to take time off work in the middle of the day to have lunch. Or she might have taken the week off due to the death in the family. Meg shouldn't judge.

She walked inside and a hostess greeted her. "Meg Gates, right? I know Natasha, so I've seen you around town. And your mom's bookstore is just the cutest."

Meg smiled and thanked her. "I'm meeting a Mrs. Anderson for lunch?"

"She's back here. Chef was just chatting with her. He asked me to seat her before you arrived because of the situation. Did you know Lee?" The young woman chatted all the way to the table, where she waited for Meg to sit and then handed her a menu. "Kelly will be right over to assist you."

Meg took in the woman across the table. She looked about the same age as Meg's own mother. Her hair was blonde with highlights and cut chin length. Her eyes were bright blue, but Meg could see the dark circles, even under the makeup. The woman reached out a hand to grasp Meg's. "Thank you for the invite. I've been wanting to talk to you."

"My dear, me too." Hope filled the woman's eyes. "I wanted to ask you about your relationship to Lee. I know I might be overstepping, but he said he was dating someone last year and it was getting serious. Was it you, dear?"

"Me?" Meg squeaked. "No. I just met him a few weeks ago. I was hoping to find out more about him. He left me a present that I don't understand."

"Lee was very generous. I haven't worked for years now. I used to be a line cook. It's hard work, especially on the back and knees, for someone my age. I thought maybe I'd move up or open my own restaurant, but life happens. First, Lee's birth, then his father's accident. I had to move us away from Bainbridge. We just couldn't make it here on my salary. I started thinking about the future, so I began working at the university. Free tuition for family members was part of our benefits."

"So that's how Lee got through college." Meg understood his anger about the university contracting out the food service department now.

Kelly came and took their order.

"You get whatever you want, dear. It's my treat. I enjoy being able to talk about Lee to someone. He had so few friends." Mrs. Anderson's gaze scanned the dining room. "We used to come here as a family, then Jon Michael hired me. Lee hung around here after school. He and Brooke were two peas in a pod. I always thought they'd end up together, but life happens."

Life happens seemed to be Mrs. Anderson's favorite saying. Especially when she talked about bad things occurring. Meg gave the waitress her order, refused wine, and asked for an iced tea instead. When the waitress left them alone, she turned back to Mrs. Anderson. "I'm sorry that I wasn't the person you were looking for. Do you know anything about who he was seeing?"

Mrs. Anderson sipped her wine. "He was always so secretive. I didn't even know his friends. He was embarrassed in school since I was cooking at the food service. He said he didn't want anyone to know I was a lunch lady."

"No." Meg winced at the term.

"He was young, what can I say? His father was a lawyer, so when he was alive, my income was just mad money. Thank goodness Jon took me under his wing and taught me so much. I never went to culinary school, but with his recommendations, I never wanted for work. Lee had what he needed, but I know he was lonely. He missed his dad. I worked long hours to keep a roof over our heads. The house sale gave us enough to live on, but not much more." She sipped her wine again. "When he got his job, he told me I wouldn't have to worry about money again. But he didn't make much the first few years. Then, he started working a second job—that money put him onto another level. He was secretive, but I assumed he was ghostwriting for someone. And with his life insurance, I'm set as long as I manage the money well. But you didn't come to hear an old woman talk about her money troubles. Tell me about you. When did you meet Lee?"

They talked through lunch, and even though Meg enjoyed spending time with Mrs. Anderson, the lunch hadn't answered any questions for her about who could have killed Lee. In fact, it had opened up more questions. What was this second job that had brought in so much money? And why had Lee tried to meet her?

As she ended the lunch, an idea hit her. "Where was Lee living? Have the police been there?"

Mrs. Anderson nodded. "They went through his condo a week ago. Someone from the police department called me and said I could have access now. I'm going to have to clean it up and sell it, I guess. What do I need with a condo in Seattle?"

"Mrs. Anderson, this is a strange ask, but do you think I

could walk through the condo?" Meg held her breath as the woman studied her. "Lee was trying to find me for some reason. I'd like to know why. Maybe there's a clue in the condo. A lot of writers have journals."

"It's a possibility, but honestly, I think he did most of his writing on his computer, and I don't have his password. Besides, the laptop is still with the police." She paid the check, then pulled out a set of keys. "These are my extra keys to the apartment. Please return them to Chef Jon Michael. He'll get them back to me."

"Thank you." Meg held the keys in both hands. "I promise I won't take anything or mess up the apartment in any way."

"You're a Bainbridge girl. I trust you." She stood and gave Meg a hug. "And let me know when you find out why Lee was looking for you. Or if you find his girlfriend. I'd love to talk to her. At least once."

Meg had guessed right. The bookstore was slammed right up until just after seven, when it was like someone had turned off the waterspout of tourists. The ferry bell rang a few minutes later. There must have been more people getting on the ferry than getting off. Or if they were getting off, they were heading to dinner or a night out. Meg watched them walk by the bookstore window.

The smell of tomato sauce and bread crust hit her as soon as Dalton opened the door with a large everything pizza. Natasha followed him in, and they set up the food on the coffee table. Meg grabbed sodas from the fridge and a roll of paper towels. Then Watson sat and watched the three friends devour the food.

He did whine a little.

Dalton pulled off a piece of plain crust and handed it to Watson. "You're going to get fat if you keep eating bread."

"He likes bread." Meg sighed as she finished her slice. "Just like his mom. I'm glad you're both here tonight. I've got an adventure, and I'd love it if someone would come with me."

"Does this adventure have anything to do with what Mrs. Anderson told you at lunch?" Dalton asked.

"You ate lunch with Lee's mom?" Natasha leaned forward and grabbed a second slice of pizza. "Tell me everything. I mean, us."

"Thanks for remembering I'm here, since I brought the pizza," Dalton teased.

Meg brushed pizza crumbs from her hands and leaned forward. "Okay kids, we're not there yet so stop fighting. Here's what happened."

Meg recounted his mom's story about Lee's childhood and how she worked as a line chef for the Steakhouse. Then she explained the rest and finally pulled out the keys to Lee's condo. "I need a partner in crime to go with me to the condo. Maybe tomorrow?"

"I'm working in the morning. I can go at night," Natasha offered, wiping the pizza sauce from her face.

"I'm back here at three, so it has to be early. Sorry. Unless we want to put it off until Sunday." Meg really wanted to go tomorrow and get Lee's keys back to Chef Jon Michael as soon as possible. Lee's mom had written down his address on a piece of paper for her.

"I can get you at eight tomorrow morning and we'll be back long before three. We'll probably have to leave the mutt home. Especially if his condo building isn't pet friendly," Dalton offered. "But I'm working Sunday."

"Dalton wins." Meg grabbed his hand and raised it in the air. "Next week's going to be busy. Mom and Derby are going to play Pickleball next weekend, so I'm opening and closing Thursday through Saturday."

"A weekend alone? Where are they going?" Natasha handed out the dessert she'd brought. Cupcakes, each in its own little box. A fork was taped to the top of the clear box.

"Idaho. A city in the northern part, Coeur d'Alene? If they place in the top three, they'll go to the nationals in Miami. Mom's super excited. I guess she's never been to Miami before." Meg thought Mom's Pickleball obsession took a lot of time. But maybe she just liked spending time with Derby. "So anyway, between the store, Lilly's work, and school, I'm going to be swamped."

"And your book," Dalton added.

Meg frowned as she turned to look at him. "What?"

"And your book. You have to write thirty minutes a day, even when you're busy, or the plan doesn't work." He shrugged as she gave him a death stare. "Hey, I don't make the rules, I'm just pointing them out."

"Fine. And my thirty minutes a day of writing. And walking Watson. And whatever time I have for friends and family. And maybe a shower." Meg dug into her cupcake. After a couple of bites, she widened her eyes, remembering last night's visitor. "Speaking of family, guess who stopped by last night."

After they'd cleaned up the mess from dinner, Natasha left to meet some friends at Island Diner. She invited Meg and Dalton to come along.

"If we do, I'll have to take Watson home first and change so I don't look like I work at an appliance store." Meg glanced down at her outfit. "I don't think even adding the blazer would help me fit in at the bar."

"Glitter. You need to sparkle." Natasha laughed as she hugged Meg.

"She already sparkles enough. She has strangers throwing jewelry at her feet." Dalton stuffed the empty pizza box, dessert carriers, and soda cans into a trash bag. "I'm just a working man. I can't keep up with competition like that."

"Good thing you don't have to." Meg tucked a wayward napkin into the trash bags. "I'll see how I feel after I'm done. I still have a big day tomorrow."

"You sound like the old folks," Natasha teased as she headed to the door. "I need to get out there and find a guy since the last one was Irene's castoff. I'm not sure how I feel about that."

"Technically, not Irene's castoff," Meg called after her, but if Natasha heard, she just waved a hand behind her. "She'd keep Mark if Natasha doesn't want him."

"Even Irene can do better," Dalton said as he went to dump the trash outside. Then he sat on the couch reading while Meg finished her shift. As they walked home, he was quiet until they got off the main sidewalk. "Do you want to go hang out with Natasha at the bar?"

Meg sighed. "Not really. But if you want to go, I'll go. I get overwhelmed by all the noise and people."

He chuckled. "I don't want to go. But I don't want you to stay back if you want to go. I'll go."

"You'll hate it but you'll go," Meg interpreted.

"Basically. Going to the bonfires is nice since we're outside and can look at the stars. We live in a beautiful area. Why spend time inside when we don't have to?" He paused to let Watson sniff a tree.

"And I don't have to sparkle and attract barflies. Are they called barflies if they are guys?"

Dalton chuckled as he shrugged and Watson started walking again. "It's the same principle. Hanging out to see if anyone is available or attracted."

"You are a homebody, Dalton Hamilton. I'm shocked no one grabbed you before I came back to town." Meg breathed in the cool night air.

"You assume I was looking to be grabbed." He reached for her keys as they arrived at the apartment. "You too tired or are you up for some popcorn and a movie?"

"I thought you didn't want to be inside," she said as she dropped the keys in his hand.

He leaned down to kiss her. "It depends on who I'm inside with, I guess."

CHAPTER 21

Sometimes what you seek is right in front of your eyes.

Dalton knocked on her door at seven thirty the next morning. He had a bag of what smelled like donuts in his hand as well as his Mariners travel mug. "Good morning, Magpie. Did you write yet?"

She narrowed her eyes at him. "It's seven thirty. In the morning."

"I know. I came early so you wouldn't have an excuse. I'll take Watson out if you sit down at your computer. You can have a donut when you're done."

"I'm not a kid. Bribing me to do my homework won't work." Meg eyed the bag. "Is there a maple bar in there?"

"Of course there is. I'm not a savage." He clicked the leash on Watson. "Are you writing?"

"Yes, let me grab some coffee. I just got out of the shower." She smiled as she went to fill up her cup. It was nice having someone who cared, even if it was a pain at times.

"Okay, I'll just put these up here." Dalton tucked the bag above the cabinet where Meg couldn't reach without a step stool. And as she watched, he grabbed that too and set it outside on her small front deck. "We'll be back in thirty minutes."

He left laughing as she sat at her desk and opened the laptop. She checked her email first, just in case someone needed her this morning. She found another message from Mrs. Anderson on her Messenger app.

Her eyes teared up as she read the message.

Thanks for having lunch with me yesterday. I only wish you had been the woman my boy had fallen in love with. We would have been a nice family. Take your time at the condo. I'm planning on starting the cleanup late next week. I'll need to get boxes and more tissues first.

Before she could stop herself, she offered to help pack up Lee's condo with the warning that she couldn't start until the week after next. But the offer stood if Lee's mom needed help.

She closed out her social media accounts and opened her word processing program. She set a timer on her watch and opened the notebook that held her notes and progress. Then she started writing about how having an open heart can lead people to trust and give more information than barreling into a situation. She wrote a fictionalized version of the conversation between her and Lee's mom and what she hoped she'd find.

As she wrote those words, she wondered what she did hope to find in Lee's home. A dining room wall filled with pictures and notes and strings going all over? A larger version of her murder board but this one with the answer on why he'd given her the jewelry? What favor had she done for someone she'd never met until a week before he was killed?

Anything to do with the case would have already been bagged up, labeled, and shipped off to Uncle Troy's evidence locker. What did she think she'd find as an amateur?

She'd thought drafting the book would be easier when she was actually investigating a crime. Instead, the crime was getting in the way of her logical thought process for the book. So many times, it took a while for her to see the whole picture. In her writing and in the investigation.

Maybe checking out Lee's condo was her way to see the whole picture. A way to give her a fuller portrait of the man and, hopefully, the reason he'd been killed. Of course, having someone turn over the keys to their private residence just because she had a good feeling didn't happen a lot. People needed to be able to trust you. And if they just met you, trust would naturally be in short supply.

She wrote down a question that had been bothering her since Mrs. Anderson had put those keys in her hands. Why had a woman who'd just lost her son in a violent incident trusted a stranger? Maybe she could find out that answer, too, by visiting Lee's condo.

She just hoped it wouldn't be a waste of time.

The alarm on her phone went off as Dalton and Watson came back inside.

She saved her work and closed her notebook, tucking it away in her desk. She looked up the directions to Lee's condo and pivoted the laptop so Dalton could see them. "I think we can walk from the ferry terminal."

"Sounds good." Dalton filled Watson's water dish, then brought the donuts down from their lofty perch. "Let's get going so we can get you back in time for work. Depending on what we find, we might have to grab hot dogs on the ferry for lunch."

"Well, at least I have a maple bar to keep me on a sugar high." Meg opened the bag and pulled out the fresh donut. "Let me fill a travel mug and scarf this down and I'll be ready."

He sat down at the table and opened the bag again, pulling out a second maple bar. Watson watched him closely. "Sorry dude, fried bread and sugar aren't on your diet plan."

"It's probably not on mine either, but who cares? This is amazing. Was Natasha working?" Meg filled her travel mug even though she still had some coffee left over from this morning. "I hope this trip isn't a total waste of time."

"If it is, then at least you can check one thing off your list. Look, I know the fact that Lee Anderson stalked you and left you that bracelet is bugging you. But maybe he had the wrong Gates." Dalton took a big bite of his bar. "Sometimes people get things wrong."

"Maybe." Thinking about getting things wrong led her to wonder about Natasha and Mark. She hoped he was being honest with both Natasha and Meg when he said he liked the local baker. She saw that Dalton was watching her. She drained her coffee cup and put it in the sink. "I'm ready anytime you are."

The condo building was a few blocks away from the ferry terminal. A few uphill blocks away. Meg grinned at Dalton. "At worst, we can count this as our cardio for the day."

"I'm thinking I'll need two hot dogs when we get back on the ferry." He pointed to the next street. "According to the map, we take a left on Fourth Avenue and go past the library. Pretty upscale area for a food writer."

"His mom said his second job brought in the money. She thought he was ghostwriting for someone." She stood by him as they waited for the light to change.

"Well, it's something. I guess we'll see what his condo looks like. Has Troy said anything about Anderson's financials?" Dalton asked, taking her arm as they crossed the street.

"Yeah. He came over last night, gave me a copy of his case file, and then went over it step by step with me." Meg looked up at him. "Of course he hasn't said anything. I noticed that Lee's mom drives a nice car, and she said Lee set her up."

"And the condo's in a nice part of town. But he could have bought it a while ago," Dalton speculated as they made their way through the crowd of people on the sidewalk. Tourists walked slow, pointing out the architectural highlights of the buildings. Residents and those who worked in the area were more focused on getting where they were going or talking on their phones.

When they reached the building, Meg took a breath. "Lee would have had to get it in a foreclosure sale or in horrible shape to afford it on his regular salary. How much do ghost-writers make?"

"That is a question for your friend Lilly. Although I don't know if she'd even know unless she had hired one before. But she might have heard rumors." Dalton nodded to the lobby doors, where a UPS delivery man was coming out. "There's no doorman right now. Maybe we should take advantage of his absence."

They entered the large glass doors and headed straight to the elevators. As they waited, Dalton poked his head inside a small room to the side. The bell announcing the elevator buzzed and he hurried back, taking her arm to quickly step on the elevator.

As the doors closed, Meg saw a man in uniform step out of the room Dalton had just looked at. "The doorman?"

"I think so. That looked like a package room. He must have walked the delivery back just as we came in. I think we got lucky. Your uncle probably told the building owners about Anderson's death. I'm not sure just having the keys would have gotten us upstairs." He stepped out of the elevator as the doors opened on the ninth floor. "Here we are. What was the condo number?"

"905," Meg said from memory. She had the address on the little piece of paper that Mrs. Anderson had given her at lunch, but she'd memorized the apartment number. Later, she'd look it up on a real estate website to see if she could find when Anderson bought it and maybe the sale price. It depended on how long ago the unit had sold.

The units in the building definitely weren't in her price range. Or anyone she knew. Except maybe Lilly. And she already had her dream home.

They opened the door and stepped into a starkly furnished living room. They walked through the apartment, and Dalton narrated. "Two bedrooms. Two baths. And a small balcony with a sliver of the sound poking through the skyscrapers."

"He set up his office in this second bedroom," Meg pointed out. "If anything's here to give us a clue, it would be in here."

"It doesn't look like it's even been lived in. Do you think the cleaning service came this week?"

Meg nodded. "Maybe. No dishes out at all. Not even coffee cups. This looks like a model apartment, not one that's been lived in. Let's check out the den before someone comes and kicks us out."

"Big Brother is watching," Dalton teased. It didn't make Meg feel better.

She sat at Lee's desk and, as Mrs. Anderson had predicted, his laptop wasn't there. She opened the drawers and flipped through his planner. She took a picture of his last week. "Look. He made a note about meeting me at the writers' group. Then a note about our dinner the next night. A star is on Saturday."

"A star? Nothing else?" Dalton paused his review of the bookshelves and looked over her shoulder.

"No, but the next Monday has a note about starting the review for the Local Crab." Meg flipped through the previous calendar pages. "He wrote a column every two weeks. Same setup. He ate the meal on a Wednesday, a star on Saturday. Then the writing started the next Monday. That's weird. I wonder if he went back to the restaurant a second time. The following Saturday?"

"Sounds possible. His bookshelves are typically male. Lots of Connelly and Clancy. Some old stuff that could be first editions." Dalton turned to her. "Okay, what's weird?"

"There's nothing about a second job. Like you said, if you want something to fit into your life, you need to plan it. There's no blocked-off time. Nothing." She turned and looked at Dalton. "I wonder how much he was getting paid from the newspaper."

"I have a friend who works at that same newspaper who says she's in the mid-fifties, and she's been there ten years." Dalton picked up a book and checked the copyright page. "Not enough to pay for a condo here. She lives in Bellevue with her techy husband. He's the one making good money. I called her when we decided to make the trip to see the condo. She says Anderson might have been making the same as she is, but she doubted it. Hard news gets the higher pay."

"So if he had a ghostwriting gig, he didn't work on it. Or hadn't in the last six months." Meg put the planner away and opened the final drawer. It was filled with pictures. One was still in the frame. She took it out and sucked in a breath. "I think I know who Anderson's mystery girlfriend was."

She turned the frame so Dalton could see it. The picture was professionally done and showed the engagement ring front and center. Lee Anderson and Rachel Midler grinned at the camera. "He was dating Romain's new fiancée."

Since they still had time before Meg needed to get to work, they stopped at an Asian fusion restaurant on the way back to the ferry terminal. Meg picked at her spring roll plate as she thought about Rachel Midler. "I guess I'm going to have to buck up and scroll through her Instagram pictures. I tried to go through her Facebook posts last night, but it made me crazy to see her in Italy on my honeymoon."

"Maybe your real honeymoon will be even better," Dalton said as he dug into some version of Kung Pao Chicken. "So, Anderson and Rachel. Do you think that's what he meant about you saving him? You saved him from a life with Rachel by giving Romain to her?"

"One, I didn't give Romain to her. But I guess I introduced them. I don't remember her talking about a boyfriend or the ring. We all went out one night and she said she was in an on-and-off relationship. And right then, it was off." Meg had never even questioned Rachel's loyalty to her. Sure, she might have flirted with all the guys at school, whether or not they had girlfriends, but that was just Rachel. She'd flirt with any guy, no matter the age or status. Had she flirted with Romain that night? Meg couldn't remember. She knew he was in a bad mood when they got home, but she chalked it up to the bar where they'd all met. He hated the local bars. He said they were too loud.

Had Meg missed the opening volley that ended her relationship?

"Meg? Earth to Meg?" Dalton snapped his fingers in front of her face. "Are you okay?"

"Just trying to figure out when my Seattle life came crashing down. I think it was the first time I introduced them." Meg pushed her half-eaten plate away. "I'm clueless."

"You don't expect to be betrayed because you'd never do that to a friend." He took her last spring roll. "You're a nice person."

She sipped her tea. "I got out of a relationship that was going to fail anyway. At least Romain had the decency to call it off before we got married. If he was going to be a cheater, I didn't want him anyway."

"Are you sure he didn't cheat before Rachel?" He must have seen something in Meg's face. "Hey, don't kill the messenger. It's just that Rachel doesn't look like someone who'd be satisfied with being a side piece. And if he'd cheat once . . ."

Meg finished his thought. "He'd cheat again. Thanks for pointing out my entire relationship might have been a lie. Are you done or do you want another order since you finished your lunch and what was left of my spring rolls?"

He grinned and wiped his hands on a napkin. "I can grab a hot dog on the ferry if I'm still hungry. Let's go before you decide to dump me for someone who doesn't point out the obvious."

"Whatever," she said as she stood. Maybe the off-and-on

part of Rachel and Lee's relationship had been because of Rachel's inability to commit. If so, Rachel and Romain deserved each other. She wondered which one had called it off. She bet it had been Rachel when she found a better target.

Meg was quiet on the ferry ride home. "I'll drop the keys off at the Steakhouse on my way into work. I don't think there's anything else for me to see at the apartment. At least nothing that would lead us to Lee's killer."

Dalton finished his hot dog and wiped his face with a napkin before throwing away the packaging. "I still don't understand why Mrs. Anderson would give you the keys to her son's apartment. I mean, you're sweet and everything, but that's a huge jump in trust for someone you just met."

Dalton's words haunted her all afternoon. Long after she'd dropped the keys off to the hostess at the Steakhouse, who assured her that they would return them to Mrs. Anderson as soon as possible.

The bookstore was empty at the end of Meg's shift. She'd finished her tasks and was scrolling through Rachel's Instagram when the answer came to her.

Mrs. Anderson had to have known who Meg was. She had known about Rachel—not only that she'd been engaged to Lee, but that she'd probably dumped him once she had Romain on the line. Maybe Rachel had called Lee to dump him just before Romain had called her at the airport. More like probably than maybe. Rachel took what she wanted. She always had.

Mrs. Anderson hadn't just been a trusting soul when she dropped those keys into Meg's hand. She wanted Meg to know that Lee had been hurt by the same person that had devastated Meg's wedding. That's why she'd given her the keys. So she wouldn't have to be the one to explain to Meg why Rachel Midler had been at Lee's funeral.

Did Mrs. Anderson suspect that Rachel or Romain had

killed Lee? Or did she just want Meg to know what a viper the woman was?

The reason didn't matter. Meg did what Mrs. Anderson had expected she would do after finding out. She texted her uncle and told him about the connection. Rachel would be getting a visit from law enforcement asking where she was the night Lee was killed. Maybe Romain would too. It didn't matter. For Meg, it wasn't spite. Just another suspect to be cleared before they could find Lee's real killer.

Chapter 22

Beware of free information. It might not be worth what you pay for it.

Sunday morning Meg almost rolled over and begged off attending church, but she wanted to be there for her mom. The looks Irene and her mother had given the new couple the last time Meg was there had to be hard to deal with, especially since Meg's mom had done nothing wrong. Besides, maybe some churchgoers would gossip about Lee Anderson's death.

Now that she'd found out why he'd bought her a bracelet and wanted to talk to her, she took all of that out of the picture. Lee didn't kill himself over Rachel. The coroner's report had proved that, otherwise Uncle Troy would have closed the case. Besides, his note expressed that he was thankful for Meg taking the hit and giving Romain to Rachel. That he had dodged a bullet. Unfortunately, a real bullet had found him just a few days later.

Meg needed to take her mind off of Lee Anderson's murder, and a morning of worship and family might do just that. She had the whole day available after church since Glory was taking the Sunday shift.

Meg got dressed and grabbed her crossover purse. It had a small notebook and pen inside, just in case she had a thought while listening to the service.

She wondered if her uncle used his quiet time to think through the investigation. She knew he'd probably schedule interviews with Romain and Rachel next week. Even though she was ninety-five percent sure they didn't kill Anderson, she was glad they had to discuss their relationship with her uncle. Romain would squirm. Rachel thought everything revolved around her, so she'd just be annoyed at having to adjust her day to deal with the interview.

How could Meg have ever thought that Rachel was a friend? Maybe the sermon today would teach how to deal with the emotional backlash of betrayal. She could use some guidance, still. And maybe it would help Derby's ex-wife and daughter as well.

She wasn't happy about how Mrs. Anderson had used her to break the news about Lee and Rachel. She wished she'd just told her face-to-face, but not everyone was as direct as she was. At least she had proved to herself that she was a good investigator. She'd not only found the evidence but also figured out that she was being used to get Rachel's name in front of her uncle.

Lesson learned, she thought. Perhaps "Beware of Free Information" should be one of her chapter headings.

She would write when she got home and then see if Dalton and Natasha were doing anything today. With that plan in place, she slipped on her dress walking shoes and headed to the church.

Irene ignored her when she came into the young adult classroom. Meg made a point of sitting next to her anyway. "How's it going?"

"Mark still isn't talking to me. I tried calling yesterday and he wouldn't even pick up his phone." Irene folded her arms. "Tell Natasha she won."

"I don't know if Natasha is even interested in talking to Mark. Look, she didn't know you and Mark were anything, so don't blame her. This is all on him." Pastor Sage came in the room, so Meg shrugged and tried to end the conversation. "You just need to get over it."

"Right. You have Dalton. You even had a boyfriend before you moved here. Easy for you to say. People like you." Irene grabbed a tissue and wiped tears off her face.

"I didn't have a boyfriend. I had a fiancé who basically left me at the altar. You're not the only one who has had boy troubles. Besides, Mark said you weren't even dating," I muttered as Pastor Sage stood and held up the devotional they'd been studying.

Irene started to say something, but Pastor Sage started talking about the reading. Thankfully, she kept the discussion away from relationships and men and respecting each other for the entire hour. Meg could feel Irene steaming next to her. When the class was over, Irene quickly stood and said, "He was too dating me."

Then she stomped off. The other women in the class shook their heads. One woman next to Meg leaned in and said, "Typical Irene. If a man even looks at her, she's planning the wedding. I take it you're on the receiving end of her spite?"

"No, my friend is, but I stuck my nose in the problem. I should learn not to do that. I'm Meg Gates, by the way." Meg held her hand out to greet the new member of the "Irene's an idiot" club.

"Nice to meet you. I've seen you in class and around town. I'm Sally Tanner. I work with Brooke Hastings at Bay Bistro. She said you are her new Pickleball partner. Thanks for taking the bullet there. She's been after me for months to join their league."

"I like it. And the time frame fits my schedule." Everyone else had left the room, so they stood and pushed their chairs away. "What do you do for exercise?"

"I'm afraid I went down the CrossFit craze. I hit the gym

after work three times a week, then do group runs on Saturday here on the island. You should join us." She walked with Meg out to the foyer where people were coming in for the service. "We meet at the ferry parking lot and then run the entire island. It's a great workout. A lot of people bring their dogs too. It's a good place to meet people."

"I'm not much of a runner," Meg admitted. "And my dog's a cocker and would never make it that far."

"If you change your mind, we meet at eight. Rain or shine." She nodded to an older woman. "That's my mom. I'd better go join her. She has anxiety, so this is her primary social event of the week. After my dad died, she didn't want to do anything."

Meg said her goodbyes and told Sally she'd consider the running group. She totally wouldn't. But maybe Dalton or Natasha would like to join. She'd mention it when she saw them.

Mom and Derby were standing in the lobby waiting for her. Moving home as an adult was hard. But at least she had an excuse most days to not have to deal with Mom's love life or the devastation it was causing. She put on a smile and headed over to greet them, ignoring Irene's stare burning a hole in her back.

After church, she texted Dalton and Natasha to see what they were doing. Dalton texted back first. He was at work but would be free for dinner. Natasha followed up with an offer for lunch if Meg could meet her at the bakery. She asked if they could go somewhere she could bring Watson. They agreed on the Waterfront Dock, which had a nice deck that welcomed dogs.

Meg went to the apartment to change and get Watson. She would write when she got back from lunch. She knew the day was getting away from her, but it was Sunday, and at worst, Dalton wouldn't let her go to dinner until she did.

Just like Sally and her running group. Sally probably went because people expected her to be there. It was an accountability group. Meg had those people in her life too. She went to church not only because she enjoyed the feeling it gave her but also to be with her mom. Her work with Lilly and the bookstore held her accountable. And now, she had Brooke and Pickleball, too. She had missed out on the social part of life when she was in Seattle. Once she stopped working, the only person she saw regularly was Romain, and sometimes her mom to plan the wedding.

She needed people. At least a little.

When she got to the bakery, Natasha waved and gestured for five more minutes. Mark Thomason was in the dining area, talking to her.

Meg nodded and went outside to the bench to sit and wait. It was a beautiful day, and she could smell the lilacs as she sat outside the bakery.

"Hey, fancy seeing you again." Sally from church stopped and knelt to greet Watson. "And who are you, gorgeous?"

Meg introduced Watson and he sat pretty, accepting all the adoration from his new best friend. "What are you doing this afternoon?"

"I'm meeting some friends down at the diner." Sally glanced up into the bakery. "You waiting for someone? Not him, right?"

"No. My friend Natasha and I are going to lunch. Do you know Mark?" Meg turned to verify that Mark was the only guy in the bakery. He was still talking to Natasha.

"Is that his name? He hits on every girl in the bar when he comes in. I saw him there a couple of Fridays ago. He's always buying drinks with strings. But most of us know to steer clear of him. He's always in the ferry parking lot when we get ready to run on Saturdays. At first, I thought maybe he was a runner, but he just went and sat in a car with another guy. They watched us. At least they watched the girls in the group. It was creepy."

"Do you know the other guy?" Meg's senses were telling her that this was important, but she didn't know why.

"No one I knew. I've seen him around, but I don't know his

name." Sally paused, tapping her fingers on her chin as she thought. "I haven't seen either guy the last couple of weeks. And they were always there. I wonder if the ferry security guys ran them off."

"Maybe." Meg paused while Mark left the bakery, shooting her a dirty look.

"You're in luck. He doesn't like you." Sally stood and checked her watch. "I need to get going. My friends are going to think I stood them up. It was nice seeing you again."

Sally left and Meg stayed where she was, waiting for Natasha with Watson. She wondered why Mark Thomason was in the parking lot and with who. If Lee had been killed on a Saturday, it would put Mark in the suspect pool. Now, he just looked like a stalker.

"You look deep in thought. Please tell me that Mark didn't say something to you." Natasha stood by the bench, watching her.

"No, but he looked mad. Did you send him packing?" Meg stood and hugged her friend.

Natasha sighed. "I probably should have, but he talked me into another date. We're going out tonight."

"You need to be careful," Meg said, and then she told her what Sally had said. "I don't want to be a Debby Downer on the guy, but no one seems to have a good story about him. Well, except for Irene, but she was just dreaming."

"You know I love a good project guy," Natasha said, then she laughed. "I'm just kidding. You should see the look on your face."

"Not funny. Let's go get lunch before they stop making Bloody Marys. I need something after being nice for two hours at church. My mother is driving me crazy." Meg stood and Watson ambled out from under the bench where he'd been staying out of the sun. "Now that she has a guy, she wants me to push Dalton into setting a date. He hasn't even proposed."

"Yet," Natasha added. "We all see where this is going."

"Maybe." Meg shook her head. "But I don't want to talk about that. So, what did Mark say that made you agree to another date?"

"He said that Irene misinterpreted his friendship for more. But now that Sally's saying he's pushing the one-night stands with other women, maybe I'll call and cancel. I don't need someone playing games with me." Natasha looked over at Meg as they crossed the street. "You've talked to him. What do you think?"

Meg thought if there was smoke, there was fire. But instead of saying that, she tried to be fair. "He said he cares for you. Maybe he was just waiting for the one. Just be careful. Take it slow. If he doesn't like it, then you'll know."

"You have such good advice. Too bad you didn't listen to yourself with Romain." Natasha's eyes sparkled with humor.

"I wanted the dream more than the man." Meg shrugged as they arrived at the hostess stand for the restaurant. "Besides, if he hadn't sent me home with my tail between my legs, I wouldn't be here now and so happy. Things work out the way they're supposed to."

After lunch, Meg left Natasha at her bakery and then walked the long way home. She needed to write and finish up a couple of things for Lilly as well as check her notes for class on Monday, but she didn't want to go inside too soon. The sky was a deep blue and the sun felt great on her face.

By the time Dalton arrived for dinner, she'd done everything on her to-do list—even her laundry. When he came inside, she was curled up with Watson watching television. "Sure, I work all day and you play couch potato."

"I've finished everything on today's list and got ready for next week, too. I do need to run to the grocery store, but I can do that Monday after class when I have the car out anyway." She stood to greet him. Watson had already jumped off the couch and was in Dalton's arms, licking his face.

"Well, look at you. How did church go?"

Meg knew he was talking about Mom and Derby more than the actual service. "It was less weird than last week? And I met someone. Sally Tanner."

"Sally's a good kid. She came to a few of the bonfires but didn't like the drinking. She's more of a health nut."

"She invited me to run with her group every Saturday morning." Meg kissed him.

"She obviously doesn't know you well. Have you ever gone running?" Dalton set Watson down, then pulled out a chair and sat.

"Yes," she said, then added, "in track at school."

"I'm not sure that counts. But you do you." He glanced at the clock. "What do you think about tacos for dinner? Full disclosure, Junior called me a few minutes ago, and he and Anne are at Marina Taco Tavern and asked if we'd join them. I said I'd ask, but I didn't promise. Just in case you wanted a romantic dinner with just me."

"The last time we had a romantic dinner I found out my mom was dating Derby. At least this time, I know Junior and Anne will be there. I'll be prepared. Besides, I'd like to get to know Anne a little better. Have you met her?"

"No, but it looks like I'm going to tonight." He smiled. "Are you ready? Does Watson need to be walked?"

"Probably. I'll get changed, and you can deal with him. I'll be ready in a jiffy." Meg headed to the bedroom, listening to Dalton talk to Watson as they left the apartment. She looked forward to having dinner with her brother. As long as it didn't turn into a fight like the one with Dad earlier that month. Maybe with Anne there, Junior would be on his best behavior.

One could only hope.

At the restaurant, they found Anne and Junior at the bar waiting for them.

"What can I get you to drink?" Anne asked as she saw them walk in. "Please tell me you'll get a margarita. I don't want to be the only one drinking. Steve is being a good designated driver tonight."

"I drove in to the ferry terminal and parked near there since Anne lives in Bellevue," Junior added as he shook Dalton's hand and hugged Meg.

"You can always stay over at my house," Dalton said as he caught the bartender's attention. "Two margaritas. One strawberry with salt and one lime, both on the rocks."

"I've got to work in the morning." Junior shook his head. "Anne? Are you ready for a second?"

"No, I've got to work in the morning, too." She patted the chair next to her. "We're still waiting for a table, but let the bartender know we're all here now."

"I'm so glad you invited us tonight," Meg said as she sat next to Anne. "And that you came to meet me at the bookstore."

"Wait, you two have met before?" Junior raised his eyebrows. "What did you talk about? Please tell me you didn't tell her any horror stories about me."

"Don't mind him. He knows I stopped at the bookstore this week. He didn't like that I had taken the reins on finally meeting more of his family. Your dad told me where I could find you. Now I have to get up the courage to meet your mom." Anne sipped her drink. "I'm freaking out a little."

"Mom's cool." Meg smiled as the bartender brought their drinks. She mentioned that their party was all here and waiting for a table. Then she turned back to Anne. "She's a little scatterbrained since she started dating again. And she's involved in a Pickleball league. So that's new."

"Did you see Mom today?" Junior asked, not looking at Meg.

"At church. You should come some week. She and Derby have officially announced their relationship to the community. They even sit in a different pew than either of them had sat in before." Meg laughed at Anne's questioning face. "It's symbolic. Derby does a lot of symbolic things, so I think our holidays are going to be different if he's still around."

"Mom better not get a fake tree. Those don't even look like Christmas." Junior sighed, resigned to the changes in his future.

"Let's stop worrying about what might happen in the future and talk about what's happening now." Anne rubbed Junior's arm and then turned to Meg. "Steve told me that you like amateur sleuths. Are you into those mystery game nights? We all should go sometime. It would be really fun."

Dalton snorted and Meg gently slapped his arm. "Actually, I'm more interested in true crime and cold cases. I think I'd like to become a cold case expert, looking at a crime from a different perspective than law enforcement."

"Yeah, Meg sticks her nose into ongoing investigations. Like the murder that happened this month by the ferry terminal. I'm sure she has a theory on who killed Lee Anderson by now." Junior sipped his soda. "You know Uncle Troy's going to kick you out of that apartment if you don't stay out of his cases."

"You're working on an actual murder case?" Anne's eyes widened. "I read all of Lee Anderson's columns. I think some of them were wrong, but food's subjective, right? Some places he loved and I thought they were horrible. And he didn't love that little bakery here on the island, A Taste of Magic? I love that place."

CHAPTER 23

Sometimes the answer is right in front of your face.

Anne's discussion about Lee's columns stuck in Meg's head all night. Lee had given bad reviews on places that Meg knew served good food. Like Natasha's bakery. And the Steakhouse. At first, she'd thought it was due to his connection to Bainbridge Island. But what if he had another reason?

As they got ready to leave, Meg found Natasha in the restroom. "Hey, I didn't know you were here. We just finished dinner with Junior and Anne. Come join us in the bar and you can meet her. She loves your bakery."

Natasha was fixing her makeup in the mirror. "I'm not going into that bar again. Mark is there and he's been horrible all night. He keeps asking me if I paid Lee money for that review. Like a bad review is something I'd pay someone for? What is he, crazy?"

"Sometimes bad press is as worthwhile as good press. But I thought he was trying to convince you he was dating material. Why is he so focused on your business marketing?"

"Good question. But I'm done with it and him. I'm going out the back door and home. I'll text you when I get there, just in case." She tossed her purse over her shoulder and wobbled, a little unsteady on her feet. "I'm really not feeling well. Oh, I left my leather jacket on my chair. Would you go grab it for me? You can give it to me later. I'd leave it, but I spent a lot of money on that jacket."

"I'll go get it and tell Mark that you left. Should I tell him you had a headache or that he was a headache?" Meg asked, concern filling her voice as she met her friend's gaze. "Are you sure you're all right to walk home?"

"I just need some air. I only had a glass of wine, so I must be getting sick. I'll send him a cease-and-desist email. Just tell him I wasn't feeling well." She laughed as she left the bathroom, holding on to the wall for support. "I'll tell him he made me sick, later."

Meg checked her hair and added a little lipstick. Anne looked like she'd stepped out of a fashion magazine. If she was going to hang out with her brother's new girlfriend, she might have to step up her game a little.

Dalton was waiting for her in the hallway near the restrooms. "Are you ready to go? Junior and Anne just left to catch the next ferry. She said she'd call you soon for a girls' night."

"Almost ready. I need to grab Natasha's jacket. She left it at a table in the bar and didn't want to go back to get it." She smiled at Dalton. "Come be my bodyguard?"

"What? Who was she on a date with? A biker?" He turned her toward the bar. "Go ahead. I'm right behind you."

Mark Thomason was sitting alone studying a sheet of paper. It seemed like he hadn't even noticed that Natasha was still gone. Meg walked up and grabbed her friend's jacket. He still didn't look up. She thought about just leaving, but she couldn't do that, not even to Mark. "Natasha went home. She had a headache."

Mark looked up and then around, like he'd just realized Natasha wasn't there. "Oh, well, I hope she feels better."

He dropped his gaze back to the paper.

Meg felt the anger sizzle in her. "You're a real jerk, you know that, right?"

As she stepped away from the table, Dalton took her arm and tucked away his phone.

After they were outside, she looked at him. "What? Were you filming in case he got violent?"

"No, I was taking pictures of that sheet he was working on. It had a list of restaurants with numbers listed after them. The Local Crab had a question mark, as did A Taste of Magic. I think we need to look at it closer." He turned back to make sure Mark wasn't following them. "What made Natasha so mad that she left him at the bar?"

"She said he was asking all these questions about what she paid Lee for his review. She told him she didn't pay him anything. Why would she pay for a meh review?" Meg slowed down as she thought about the night. "Why would Mark even care?"

"I think we need to see if there's a link between Mark and Lee," Dalton said as they walked back to Meg's apartment.

"Sally said she saw Mark at the ferry terminal on Saturdays when the group met. She thinks he was creeping on the girls. But she said something else. That he always met another guy. Do you think that was Lee?"

"Maybe. We still don't know anything about Lee's second job, except that he didn't actually do any work or spend time on it." He turned to her. "Didn't you look at his planner?"

"Yes, and I took pictures of it. If Mark and Lee were working together, maybe that's the second job. Conning restaurants out of money to get a good review from Lee." She started to open her purse, then realized she'd left her phone at home. "We can look when we get back. Maybe Mrs. Anderson knows Mark. She owes me a favor."

"Looks like we have some sleuthing to do when we get back.

You make coffee and I'll take Watson out." Dalton smiled at her. "The Mystery Crew rides again."

"Except I don't think Natasha's up for a midnight skull session. She didn't look good when she left." Meg looked down the street toward Natasha's bakery and apartment.

Dalton paused at the road where they'd turn to go up to Meg's. "Should we stop by and check on her? You can drop off her jacket."

Meg thought about how Natasha looked as she left the bar. "Yeah, I think that would be a good idea. Maybe she's coming down with something."

When they got to A Taste of Magic, lights were on at the apartment above.

An angry voice and then a crash of glass made them both jump.

"Stay here and call 911. I don't think our friend took kindly at being left at the bar." He shoved his phone into her hand and then bolted up the stairs to the apartment.

Meg dialed for help. When the dispatcher answered, she told them what was going on. "Please hurry."

"We've already had a report from a neighbor of a disturbance. A police car should arrive any minute." The dispatcher asked her to stay on the line, then started asking Meg questions. Probably to keep her distracted.

Sirens and lights caught her attention, and she told the dispatcher the police were here.

"Good. Your uncle will be on-site soon as well. Meg, just stay on the line with me until he gets there."

Meg should have realized that the dispatcher would recognize her name. As she pointed the officers to the stairs, Uncle Troy's truck pulled up and parked next to the police car. She ran to him, and he took Dalton's phone. "Carla, I've got her. Thanks."

"Natasha was at Marina Taco Tavern with Mark Thomason, but when I found her in the restroom, she said she wasn't feeling well and that Mark was being a jerk. We came by to drop off her jacket, but, Uncle Troy, I've got a bad feeling about Mark. I have pieces of it, but not proof. I think he might have killed Lee Anderson." Meg hugged Natasha's jacket to her chest. Why hadn't she followed her home? Or told her to wait for her and Dalton?

"Let me see what's going on and we'll go from there." He pulled Meg into a hug. "The guys must have him in custody now, and they haven't called for an ambulance, so that's a good sign. Just stay here."

"Dalton's up there too." Meg didn't want to stay here. She wanted to follow her uncle up the stairs, but she was afraid of what she'd find.

"Of course he is. You guys are always getting in the way." He squeezed her, letting her know that he was kidding, then hurried up to the apartment.

For a few minutes, Meg didn't hear anything. Uncle Troy had ended the conversation with Carla, the dispatcher, and gave her Dalton's phone back as they talked.

Soon, she saw movement, and one of the officers walked Mark down the stairs in cuffs. Then Dalton brought Natasha out.

She ran to them as soon as they were off the stairs. Mark was mumbling about being robbed of his fair share as the officer directed him into the back of the car.

Natasha let Meg pull her into a hug. "Are you all right?"

"Still dizzy, but okay." Natasha felt limp against Meg's body.

"Your uncle thinks she's been drugged, so we need to take her to the hospital ER. He told me to take his truck." Dalton held up the keys and then remote-opened the door.

They bundled Natasha into the back seat of the truck and put a seat belt around her. Meg slid in next to her. "I'll sit back here with her."

Someone, probably Dalton, had grabbed the quilt that Natasha always draped over the couch. She was always cold, so Meg made sure she was covered as he drove them toward the closest emergency room north on the island.

The hospital had been notified, probably by Carla, so as soon as they got there, a team rushed out, put Natasha on a gurney, and wheeled her inside. Meg followed, a pit forming in her stomach. Natasha's parents had moved away from the island. All she had was Meg and Dalton here. And all of Meg's contacts were in her phone. At home.

When Dalton came in after parking, Meg was pacing in the waiting room. She hadn't been allowed back in the treatment area. Instead, she was given a clipboard full of papers. She'd started filling them out but didn't know the answers to most of the questions.

She fell into Dalton's arms, and he led her to a chair, where he took over the paperwork. He shrugged as he went down the list. "They're going to have to get this from Natasha when she comes to."

"If she comes to," Meg said, correcting his sentence.

He pulled her close. "No, honey. It's when. She's going to be fine. She was still reacting to whatever he'd given her at the bar. He was trying to get her to talk about something."

"He's worse than a jerk. He's dangerous. I hope Uncle Troy throws the book at him." Meg leaned back as Dalton took the clipboard to the desk and explained the problem. The receptionist nodded and took the incomplete papers back. When he returned to Meg, she reached a hand out to him and he sat next to her.

"I need to send a message." Meg took Dalton's phone out of her pocket and texted her aunt to let Watson out. Then she gave the phone back to him. "So much for a quiet evening at home playing our own version of Clue."

He snorted and put his arm around her, pulling her close. "She's going to be fine."

What seemed like hours later, a doctor came out and approached them. Since they were the only ones in the waiting room, he pulled up a chair and sat across from them. "Miss Jones is sleeping. She had a nasty cut on her forehead that we stitched up. We pumped her stomach and sent the results to the lab, but we're thinking he used a date rape drug on her. She needs to stay overnight for observation, but unless there are complications tonight or when she wakes up, she's going to be fine. You two should go home. I suspect we'll release her in the morning."

Meg slumped against the bench. "She's good? Can I see her?"

"Not until the morning, sorry." He patted her knee. "I promise, she's fine. Come by in the morning with fresh clothes for her and you can take her home."

Dalton pulled her up to standing. "Let's go, Sleeping Beauty. I'm sure your uncle would like his truck back. Besides, Watson's waiting for you."

The next morning, Meg woke to the smell of coffee and bacon. Someone was in her kitchen cooking and Watson wasn't on her bed, so he must be out there with them. She washed her face, hoping Natasha was doing better.

When she finally made her way out to the kitchen, Aunt Melody and Dalton were sitting at the table, talking. "Hey, you should have woken me for the party."

She aimed toward the coffee but her aunt waved her into a chair and stood to get it for her.

Aunt Melody set the cup in front of her. "Troy's already heard from the hospital and Natasha's fine. She'll be ready to go about nine. And he's already had one of his officers pick up fresh clothes for her. And her purse. They're on your desk."

"She's okay?" Meg felt her shoulders relax. "He didn't hurt her?"

"She told the nurse she fell when she tried to stand and get him to leave. She doesn't remember anything after that. He was asking her questions about how much she paid Lee Anderson."

"She said he was pushing her at the bar about that too. Why would she pay Lee Anderson?"

"Your uncle thinks they were scamming people together. Offering good reviews for a payout. For whatever reason, Lee wouldn't shake down the Bainbridge restaurants, unbeknownst to Mark. Lee gave them bad reviews and lied to Mark instead, insisting the Bainbridge chefs refused to pay in order to cover his tracks. His review of Natasha's bakery wasn't bad, but Mark never received any money from it, so he thought Lee was skimming money," Dalton clarified. "I sent him the photo I took of the paper Mark was writing on at the restaurant. He found it in Mark's pocket when they arrested him. And I told him about what Sally said about the parking lot on Saturday mornings."

"You've been busy." Meg smiled and looked at the pillows and folded blanket on her couch. "You slept here?"

He nodded. "Just in case we needed to run to the hospital again. I figured we'd use your car."

Meg walked over and picked up her phone from her desk. "I need to talk to someone, then I think we can put this all together."

Uncle Troy met them at the hospital where they were waiting for Natasha to be released. She was finishing up the admissions paperwork as she sat on the bed, an IV still in her arm. He smiled at Meg. "Thanks for the information this morning. I just got back from Mrs. Anderson's house, and she told me that Mark Thomason was an old friend of Lee's and that Lee had told her about their partnership. She still thought he was ghostwriting for someone. Not blackmailing restaurants. She said Mark must be lying."

"I don't think she wants to think badly of her son, especially after all he gave her. Will she have to give the money back?"

"None of the chefs so far are admitting to the blackmail.

They all have one pat line: 'It was a marketing expense.'" He shook his head. "They'd rather be ripped off than admit they were blackmailed for a good review. So, I don't have any evidence on the blackmail, but I do have ferry parking lot surveillance cameras showing Mark Thomason walking to the car and shooting him. We've had the film for a while but didn't have a suspect since we only saw his back. Now, we have Mark's gun purchase paperwork and the sweatshirt he wore with Lee's blood. If he'd just stayed away from Bainbridge, we'd probably never have found him." Uncle Troy's phone rang. "Anyway, I've got to go. I just wanted to make sure our Natasha was up and about. I'll see you all later."

After Uncle Troy left, Meg sighed. "I should have figured this out sooner. Before he attacked you."

"You had a feeling," Natasha said as she put the clipboard aside. "You told me to be careful, but I wanted to give him another chance. I can't believe he slipped something in my drink. He had already ordered my wine before I got there. Lesson learned."

"At least we got to you before anything bad happened." Dalton gave Natasha a light hug. "When are you getting that thing out of your arm?"

"Right now." A cheery nurse came into the room and took the clipboard. "You got these done, great. Now, we just have to go over your discharge papers and get this IV out and you'll be free."

Chapter 24

It takes a village to raise a child and to solve a murder.

On Wednesday night, Meg called a mandatory meeting of the Mystery Crew at the bookstore. Watson lay on Natasha's leg. He'd been next to her ever since she'd stayed at Meg's place when she was released from the hospital. Tonight, she'd moved home after Aunt Melody and Dalton had made sure the apartment was clean and free from all signs of the attack.

If Meg knew her aunt, the refrigerator was filled and a chock-full cookie jar sat on the counter. Aunt Melody never did anything halfway. "Are you sure you don't want to stay with me a few more nights?"

"Meg, I love you and Watson, but I miss my place. I'll call if I start to freak out, and you can come over for a sleepover. Besides, your uncle assures me that Mark Thomason will be behind bars for a while. You guys found the clues that proved he killed Lee. It was all about the money."

"Money's a powerful motive. In Mark's case, he thought Lee was screwing him out of his cut of the payoffs from Natasha's review. Instead, Lee was just being sentimental. He didn't blackmail the restaurants on the island he considered part of his home. I think Lee changed his mind when Rachel dumped him. He started to work on being a better man, and he remembered where he came from." Meg picked up the container of shrimp fried rice and took more, sliding it onto her plate, nearly emptying the container. She offered it to Dalton and Natasha, who both shook their heads, so she dumped the rest on her plate. "I think he was trying to do a real review of the Local Crab after I walked out on him. Then he tried to end his deal with Mark, which was the straw that broke the camel's back of Mark's suspicions."

"It's hard to step out of a life of crime," Dalton said as he added more broccoli and beef to his plate. When both women looked at him, he shrugged. "That's what I hear, at least. And all the novels I read confirm my statement."

"Well, in this case, you're right. I can't believe all the restaurants in Seattle denied they had been blackmailed. When Uncle Troy asked to see their financials, they asked for a warrant. He decided not to push it since Mark had already partially confessed to killing Lee, and since the gun and physical evidence were already in custody. The district attorney thinks the trial will be a slam dunk. Especially if Natasha testifies."

"Oh, don't you worry about that. No one drugs me and gets away with it. And I'd just given the creep a second chance. Thank goodness you guys stopped in to see if I was okay. Who knows what would have happened?" Natasha set her plate down but tapped Watson on the nose. "Chinese food isn't good for dogs. And I know you ate your dinner because I fed you."

Meg smiled at her friend and her dog. "Maybe you should get a dog. For company."

Natasha rubbed Watson's ears and smiled. "I'm actually thinking of going down to the shelter next weekend. Do you want to go with me?"

"My friend has some German Shepherd pups," Dalton said as he stood to get more sodas from the back. "Do you want to go see them?"

"I really want to save a pup from the shelter if one bonds

with me. But I'll keep your friend's pups in mind. I think I want a smaller dog, like Watson. He's just enough to cuddle."

"A Shepherd can bring down an intruder and keep them still until help comes," Dalton said as he came back with drinks.

"I'm getting a security system for that. The dog just needs to be a cuddle bumpkin like my Watson. And maybe like to run. I think I need to up my workout plan. I feel out of shape for just hanging around Meg's apartment for a few days."

"Watson doesn't run," Meg said as she finished her dinner. "Anyway, I wanted to thank you both for your help with the investigation and my book. I think I have a rough draft now and I'll run it through a few rounds of edits. Who wants to be a beta reader for me once that's done?"

They both raised their hands.

"I specifically want to make sure that I'm not used as the example of a too-stupid-to-live character." Natasha grinned as she opened her soda.

"I would never," Meg said, deciding not to mention what she had written about accepting a drink from a stranger. But Mark hadn't been a stranger. He'd been a date. Someone who had fooled Meg with his declaration that he wasn't a player. He'd been a player all along. The only reason he had dated Natasha or Irene was to gather information about the island. Meg wasn't sure which one was worse—playing with people's hearts for fun or money.

The bell over the door rang and Irene came inside. She stopped a few feet in. "Oh, I didn't realize you all were here having dinner."

"Grab a plate and join us. We're celebrating the arrest of Lee's killer." Meg listed off the sodas they had in the back. "What would you like?"

"Are you sure? I mean, I wasn't very helpful with the whole Mark thing. I kind of brought him in." Irene's face turned beet red. "Not to mention the thing with our parents."

"Neither you nor I can do anything about who our parents date. Mark was using you just as much as he was using Natasha. And me." Meg rolled her eyes. "I believed him. I thought he was a jerk, but I believed his cover story. So, what kind of soda?"

Irene told her and took the plate that Dalton handed her.

"Meg's devoured all the shrimp fried rice, but there's still lots of food here." He showed her the available dishes and then said, "If it's cold, we can nuke it in the back."

Irene smiled as she sat with a full plate. "It's fine. Thank you for inviting me. I promise I won't try to sell you a cruise plan tonight. Tomorrow? Who knows, but I'll be just Irene tonight. My dad says I can be a little pushy."

"A little?" Meg teased as she handed her a can of soda. "How are you feeling about the whole Mark thing?"

As Irene talked, Meg thought about how many times she'd heard the same story. He seemed nice. We seemed to click. And things were great, until they weren't.

The good news was that they were all safe. This investigation had gotten a little too close for comfort for Meg's liking. She didn't want to face down killers. But Mark had seemed normal at first. She thought about the book on Ted Bundy from the woman who had known him through work. The author hadn't had a clue.

People hide the worst of themselves. So many times, the people around them don't see the evil inside. She'd had a bad feeling about Mark. Sally had thought he was a creeper. But Irene had seen a possible future. As had Natasha.

Who knew everything about the people they let into their circle? Who they let into their beds?

There was something here. Not another guide to investigating, but maybe a book about the ones who hide in plain sight.

"Meg? Earth to Meg? What are you thinking?" Dalton snapped his fingers near her face. "You've been daydreaming."

She laughed as she shook her head. "Not daydreaming. Thinking about another book. Lilly told me this would happen, that I'd finish the first one and then come up with another book idea. I told her she was bonkers. Yet here I am. I think I'm crazy."

"At least you have us to help." Natasha smiled at Irene. "All of us."

As the evening progressed, Meg thought Natasha was right. The Mystery Crew had gained another member. Maybe Irene wouldn't stay or even like hanging out with them. But for now, it was okay.

And sometimes, okay was all you got out of life. Unless you saw the glass as half full. Tonight, all their glasses were half full and, bonus, they were even wearing rose-colored glasses on their faces. The world was back to normal in their little piece of paradise.

Until it wasn't.

Crime Scene Chicken

The scariest question is the one that my husband asks me every morning. What are we having for dinner? I modified this recipe for Crock Pot Chicken BBQ, making it so that it is not only tangy from the addition of green chilis but also an easy answer to the question, since the resulting chicken can be used for sandwiches, frozen for lunches, or added on top of salads. I hope you enjoy the recipe. Warning, it will make your house smell amazing as soon as it starts cooking. And slow cookers have different settings, so watch that you don't overcook if you have it on high.

Lynn

Crime Scene Chicken

- 3 lbs (about 5–6 count) boneless, skinless chicken breasts, trimmed of fat
- 1½ cups BBQ Sauce (I like Sweet Baby Ray's)
- 4 oz. can chopped green chilis
- ½ medium onion, grated (with juice)
- 1 tbsp olive oil
- 1 tbsp Worcestershire sauce
- 2 tbsp brown sugar

Stir together all sauce ingredients in a slow cooker (everything but the chicken).

Add chicken and turn to coat. Cover and cook on high for 2–3 hours or for 6–7 hours on low. Check on the chicken earlier.

Chicken is done when cooked through to an internal temperature of 165°F and is easy to shred.

Remove chicken to a cutting board and shred each breast using two forks. Place shredded chicken back in the crock pot and stir to coat with the yummy sauce.

Serve over hamburger buns.

Acknowledgments

As I finish writing this book, we've had our second large disaster in the United States in the last six months. Or at least disasters that have seeped into my everyday life. Hurricane Helene's aftermath stranded me and mine for three days until the water receded. We took off with the pups and hung out at Kentucky Lake for a week until life returned to a new normal.

Now we're watching the hills and homes in California burn. I don't have people in the fires' reach, but I've driven the 405 from the airport to the little town where my sister lived. I've visited the Getty Museum and wish now I'd visited it more often during my trips. My heart goes out all who have been affected.

I'm always thankful for the grace and support my publisher, Kensington, gives me as I'm writing these books. Especially my editor, Michaela, and her assistant, Cassidy. And the head of the cozy marketing department, Larissa Ackerman. It's great to work with people who you'd be friends with anyway. As always, I'm deeply thankful for the support and knowledge of my agent, Jill Marsal.

I'm writing at home as my husband, Jim, is off dealing with the crowds and doing our shopping before the snow comes that may or may not block us in. The pups are here, keeping me company and barking at the squirrels or other imaginary things they see as threats outside our front window. I'm well protected and I appreciate them all.

Are you over the moon for Lynn Cahoon?

Turn the page to enjoy the first chapter of *Tips and Tricks of an Amateur Sleuth*, the next Bainbridge Island mystery coming soon from Kensington Publishing Corp.

CHAPTER 1

Always have a cover story.

The ferry ride to Seattle from Bainbridge Island always took Meg Gates's breath away. Even on cold days, she'd start out sitting outside on the deck, a cup of coffee or hot cocoa in her hands, and watch as the city came closer and closer in view.

The thirty minutes gave her time to think about her life. She'd come a long way in three years. The ride back and forth no longer made her crave her Seattle life. Instead, she saw it as a period of growth. Where she'd found out how strong she really was and what she wanted to do with at least part of her life.

She was back in school and enjoying the mix between an English and a business degree. She was settling in with managing her two jobs. And her book was done and coming back from the editor that Aunt Melody had helped her hire sometime this week.

The world of Meg Gates was good, even if she wasn't one of those Gates.

Today was her last class for the week. And, better, this was the last week of the semester. She didn't like wishing her time away, but her Wednesday class seemed to bring out the negative in her. And, to be honest, she was looking forward to a few weeks with just her two jobs and a social life. She hadn't seen her boyfriend, Dalton Hamilton, in over a week, and Natasha

Jones, her best friend, had been busy with emergencies at the bakery she owned. Irene Olsen, the newly added fourth to the mystery group, had taken off for a month in San Diego to find herself.

Meg wondered if the process included finding a new job since the rumor mill on the island said that Irene had been fired for not meeting her sales quota. Meg figured she'd run out of friends, her parents' friends, and random people on the street to corner to sign up for the cruise life. Whatever the reason, Meg wasn't missing the weekly push Irene gave when she came to the bookstore for dinner for them all to purchase one or more cruise packages.

Maybe she'd move and start selling Mexican resorts to her new, unsuspecting friends and neighbors.

A man came out of the main compartment of the passenger deck and kicked her shoe as he walked by. He looked back and said, "Sorry, ma'am."

As he walked away, still on his phone, Meg tried to process what just happened. It wasn't upsetting her that he'd kicked her. That had been an accident. But he'd called her ma'am. She was only twenty-eight. This guy in jeans and a Seahawks jersey wearing his cap backward was older than she was. She saw him look back at her as he typed on his phone. Then he stood up and went back inside. *Wimp*. Not everyone liked the brisk air.

Her phone rang. "Hi Aunt Melody. What's going on?"

"I popped up to chat with you but forgot you have class. Jordan just called and said he loves the book. He plans to have the manuscript back to you today. He's got a few tweaks, but I know you can clean those up in no time." Aunt Melody exuded cheerfulness and optimism. No wonder she had been a top-level agent back in the day. "So let me know if you have questions. I know dealing with an editorial letter for the first time can be a bit overwhelming. Just remember, he loved the book."

Meg wondered how overwhelming it could be if he said he

loved the book, but she decided to leave that question alone. Until she read the suggestions. But the fact that her aunt had mentioned how much the editor loved the book was concerning. "I've got a short break between winter and summer sessions. I'm planning on focusing on the book then."

"I know you'll get it done. I've been amazed at all the work you've done for both your mom and Lilly and that's with your classes. You're a rock star, kid."

Meg thanked her for calling, then studied the skyline again. It, like her real life, was coming closer and closer. What would it look like when she finally reached the side that welcomed her into adulthood?

Maybe that was why the ma'am comment had hit so hard. She still felt like a kid. And her life looked that way. She was piecing together a work life that still gave her time to learn how to write. Lilly said the process was like walking. One step after another. This editing letter, it was just another step. How hard could it be?

When did someone hit middle age? She still had to finish college, get married, have a few kids, and a sheepdog. Okay, maybe a sheepdog and Watson. She didn't want to wish away her cocker spaniel's lifespan. She was about to look it up on her phone when she heard the announcement. They were almost at the terminal. She'd freak out about her looks later.

Sometimes when you want to be somewhere else, anywhere else, you can feel your soul dying, minute by minute.

As the bells rang, indicating the end of the period, Meg closed her textbook and tucked it away into her backpack. This had been her next-to-last session of Genre Literature History and Trends. The fact she was counting down the class sessions had less to do with the subject matter and more to do with the instructor. Okay, the professor. He was a stickler for class members to address him correctly. She stood and then

Professor Lawrence Richter waved her up to the front of the class. "Miss Gates, a word please?"

She tried not to groan as she made her way to the front and the waiting man dressed in jeans and a white dress shirt. He wore a tweed jacket with leather patches on the elbows and never a tie. He wore glasses, but Meg thought they were more of an accessory for the college professor image. She knew what this impromptu meeting was about. The professor was having a signing for his debut mystery next week and he had a list of ideas for the bookstore. Meg had tried to hand sell the book last week and hadn't had much luck. The so-called mystery was a mishmash of ideas. Set in London and New York, it was almost a thriller, but not quite. It was almost a buddy story, but the brother to the main character gets killed in the first chapter. The only positive was her grade was a solid A, so if the signing didn't go well, he wouldn't be able to take it out on her grade point average.

Craig Cane, the professor's teaching assistant, met her gaze and rolled his eyes as she walked down the aisle against the flow of students escaping. She wanted to be one of them. Meg tried not to react to his antics. Instead, she hurried to the front, hoping this wouldn't make her miss the ferry back to Bainbridge.

"Professor Richter, what can I help you with?" Meg adjusted her backpack and checked her watch. She was working at her mother's bookstore, Island Books on Bainbridge Island, at three and she still had the Link train and the ferry ride to go. Next semester, she needed to either change her hours or not take classes around her bookstore shifts. Especially since the ferry could be a little unpredictable. Although she had just committed to her summer and fall class schedules. She needed to talk to her mom. She shook her future worries away and focused on the professor, who had just latched closed his leather bookbag.

"Just checking in on Saturday's signing. Have you ordered enough books?" His eyes gleamed in anticipation behind the glasses. "I have to tell you, I'm excited to visit Bainbridge Island. I haven't been there in years."

"Well then, welcome back. I think we ordered enough books. My mother handles the details for the author events." Meg saw his smile dim a little, so she added, "But I've seen several people sign up for the event. And of course, I hand sell the book on every shift."

"I've talked to everyone in the department and I'm sure they'll all be attending if possible." He nodded his head, convinced that his first book release was going to be a wild success.

"It will be fun, that's all that matters, right?" Meg paused before she left. "Oh, be sure to invite your friends and family. It's nice to celebrate something like this with those closest to you."

"Don't worry about that. I've talked to everyone I know. My mother is bringing her church group for the signing, then they're going out to dinner." He glanced at his watch. "I've got another class starting. I better get going. You students have no concept of time. See you at the event."

Meg watched as her professor hurried out the door. As soon as he was out of earshot she mumbled, "You asked to speak with me, remember?"

The empty classroom didn't answer her back. Craig had taken advantage of her distracting the professor to leave with the last of the students. She headed out the door and to the Link station. It was crowded with students. Days like this made her wish she'd driven her ancient but dependable Honda Civic. The car was on its last legs, but she just needed it to hold on for another year or so. Then she'd buy something new.

Meg had arrived at campus early enough to finish registering for summer session and next fall's classes. The good news for her pocketbook was she only had to pay for summer classes today. She'd see what her financial aid package brought for next year. Hopefully, with her grades, she'd be considered for a scholarship, even though she wasn't taking a full load.

Lilly Aster, a local mystery author and her other boss, had offered her a no-interest loan to finish up her education. If it came down to it, her mother or father would give her tuition money. But Meg had paid for all her classes and books since she'd returned to school, and she wanted to keep it that way. She was an adult. Her mom's bookstore was doing well, but Mom needed to save for retirement. And her father's new wife, Elaine, had pointedly talked about the new house they were building during her last dinner with them. Her folks didn't need to be shelling out money for Meg's schooling.

If she had to take out a student loan, maybe considering Lilly's informal loan program would be the best choice since the repayments would come out of her weekly paychecks.

While on the Link, she checked her email. The letter from Mick Jordan had arrived. And like her aunt had predicted, he said he loved the book. There were just some things that they needed to clean up. She opened the attached Word document on her phone and gasped. It was pages and pages long. Maybe that was just because she was looking at it on the phone.

She zoomed in and started reading.

> *Page one, the opening sentence needs to be stronger. Along with the entire first paragraph. This is a prime decision-making area for potential readers. Promise the moon here. Make sure you tell them why they can't put this book down. Your writing is too passive. For example, take out all the I think wordings and just say it. I think you'll find this chapter challenging. Change to—You'll find this chapter challenging. See the difference?*

Meg closed the document and closed her eyes. The editing letter was a nightmare. She wasn't sure how he could have loved the book when he wanted to change every line.

She wondered if two weeks would even make a dent in what Mick wanted done. She was beginning to not like her aunt's friend. Not at all.

She called Natasha, her best friend, and hoped she'd reach her at a slow minute at the bakery she owned on Bainbridge Island, A Taste of Magic.

"Can't talk, the ferry crowd just arrived. See you tonight at the bookstore?" Natasha rattled off the order for a customer she was helping.

"Sure, sorry to bother you. I'm just depressed." Meg wondered if she just had too much going on. Natasha was always upbeat, so she could put this day in perspective.

"Why? Did you fail a class?" She told her customer the balance and then came back on the line. "Sorry, we'll have to talk later. Tootles."

Maybe Dalton was available to talk. He knew her best. He'd been instrumental in pushing her to finish the nonfiction guidebook that Aunt Melody was going to be trying to sell.

Well, her aunt would be trying to sell it after Meg got through all the edits that Mick wanted. She needed to read through it again when she was done to see if any of her original ideas were still there. She hadn't thought the saying *It takes a village* applied to writing a book.

Aunt Melody trusted this editor, so Meg decided to stick with her plan. She would carve out an hour every morning to work on what he suggested. Just as soon as she got the manuscript back with his editorial letter. She'd be done in no time. Dalton talked about his habits a lot, including putting the most important things first. He had a plan for his life. Something Meg had just recently started to implement.

Meg dialed his number and got his voice mail. When the beep sounded, she left a message. "Hey, haven't seen you in a few days. I'm just checking in. Natasha's bringing Chinese to the bookstore tonight if you're not working. Oh, and I got called a ma'am on the ferry today. Now I feel . . ."

The beep cut her off before she could say "old," and she leaned back in her seat to wait for her stop. She turned up the music as she thought about her schedule for the rest of the day. Pick up Watson at Aunt Melody's. Avoid talking about how much she hated Jordan. Work at the bookstore from three to nine. Dinner with Natasha and maybe Dalton at seven. Maybe she should call him back and tell him seven, even though they always ate at that time.

Dalton had been MIA for over a week. No Tuesday date night. No stopping by for coffee and donuts in the morning. No late-night chats at the bookstore. He'd said he was working some extra overtime the last time she saw him, but lately she hadn't even talked to him on the phone.

Was something wrong? Since her first engagement had gone up in flames with Romain taking her bridesmaid off on their Italian honeymoon and leaving Meg at the altar, she could be a little wary in what Dalton said and how she reacted at times.

But Dalton wasn't Romain. Not by a long shot. She walked on the ferry and went upstairs to get some hot chocolate from the food stand. She'd sit outside and enjoy the ride and not worry about paying for college or her future or even Dalton. At least for a few minutes.

She'd read a book on meditation a few months ago, and after finishing it, she tried to spend a little time each day working on the practice. Usually, she did it first thing in the morning, but she hadn't had time today before she hurried out of the apartment.

She cleared her mind and closed her eyes. *Breathe in, hold for four counts, out for six, start over. Breathe in . . .* A woman's voice broke into her breathing session.

"Puget Sound is just as beau-ti-ful as I remember. And the skyline. I don't know why I ever left here in the first place. I'm heading over to Bainbridge Island to talk to him now." The excited voice came from a few benches away, closer to the front of the ferry. "Of course, I couldn't find a job back then. I guess that tells you something, right? Anyway, how's everything in Dallas? I'm sure it's crazy hot at the bar. No one's been asking about me, have they?"

Meg lost control of her meditation and opened her eyes to see who was talking. A woman in her late forties, early fifties in a pair of skintight jeans, boots, and an oversized leather jacket talked on her cell phone. Her face was turned away from Meg, but her hair was long and blonde and blowing in the wind. If her hair was higher and controlled with more hairspray, Meg would have dubbed her a Rocker Dolly Parton look-alike.

"Hold on a sec, Tami, I need to go inside. My hair keeps getting in my mouth." The woman stood and Meg saw the rest of the look. What looked like twenty rows of beads hung around her neck and the T-shirt under the jacket looked like an old rock concert tee. Meg smiled as she walked by, thinking no one would ever call this woman a ma'am, even though she was probably Mom's age.

Where Mom shopped at J.Crew and Bloomingdale's when she found a sale, this woman was clearly hitting the hip, young Forever 21 type of clothing stores. Or Forever 21 before it closed. Meg didn't blame her. If she had the body and the confidence to wear stuff like that, more power to her.

Meg refocused on the meditation, and when the announcement for Bainbridge came over the speakers, she had already thrown away her empty cup and was waiting to disembark. She'd let the day roll as it would. The encounter with the woman from the ferry had brightened her day, even though they hadn't spoken. Everyone had their own journey. Meg had a plan for her life. It wasn't set in stone, but it was progressing. And that was all she could hope for.

* * *

The bookstore was swamped when Meg and Watson, her tan cocker spaniel rescue, arrived right at three o'clock to relieve her mother. She moved slowly through the line, and Watson went straight to his bed behind the counter as soon as she took him off the leash. He hated crowds. Especially inside. Meg shoved her tote under the counter and smiled at the customer Mom was helping, Meg tucking her books into a bag as Mom handed her a charge receipt and a pen. "Those are great choices. I really love the return to fantasy that's happening lately."

The woman signed and moved the paper and the receipt back to Meg's mother. "I know. And honey, when you add in the romance, those dragon riders can come knocking on my door any day of the week."

The next customer came up and Mom took the woman's books from her. "Why don't you see if anyone needs assistance finding something and I'll deal with the line?"

"I live to serve the noble house of Gates." Meg curtseyed and then dodged her mom's friendly swipe. She turned to the crowded store and called out, "Can I help anyone find something?"

A woman near the romance shelves raised her hand, as did a couple of others. Meg made eye contact, then waved them over to the couch. "Hang out here and I'll be right with you."

Then she started with the woman looking for romance. Or at least a book boyfriend. Sometimes that was all you could count on.

By the time the bookstore was empty, it was three thirty. Meg straightened out the pile of Professor Richter's books with the sign announcing his appearance Saturday at two. She held a book up at her mother, who was finishing up a few tasks. "Professor Richter says he's bringing his family and friends to the signing."

"I think we'll still have room here in the store to host the event. I don't seem to be selling a lot of his books." She pointed to the interest sheet. Mom wore a pair of cotton candy pink pants and a flowered shirt that flowed around her trouble spot, as she called her midlife tummy. Her hair was up on her head in a quickly styled updo that she tended to tighten during the day. Compared with the woman on the ferry, she looked like she didn't wear makeup, even though Meg knew that her mother wore moisturizer, foundation, an eye cream, mascara, and an eyeliner. Her lipstick was actually a tinted lip balm. She upped the day look with real lipstick and sometimes eye shadow on date nights, but typically, this was her. Even after she'd started dating Derby Olsen last year. Mom was who she was, and she didn't care for fashion. "Did you tell him we only have five people signed up?"

"I want to keep a good grade in his class, so no, I didn't mention that fact. I'll ask Natasha and Dalton to come. Maybe they can bring a friend or two." Meg filled Watson's water dish as they talked. "I have my summer and fall session class schedule. Do you want a copy?"

Her mom nodded. "Put a copy on my desk and update the store calendar. That way I know when you'll be off the island. I'm so proud of you for finishing your education."

"I'm not done yet," Meg said as she pulled out the paper she'd tucked into her tote. "I might be going for an advanced degree. I'm already used to being broke. I might as well get something out of it."

"You know I'd give you money for school if you need it. I'm sure your dad would as well." Her mom turned and watched as Meg headed back to her office.

"You need to up your retirement savings if you have extra money," Meg reminded her as she came back into the main shop with a cup of coffee. "Besides, Dad and Elaine are building a new house. You both have spent enough money on me."

"I could chip in, if you need college money, Meg," Derby

Olsen, Mom's boyfriend, came into the bookstore and the conversation. "We thought Irene would go for an advanced degree. Maybe law, but she seems settled to just have the bachelor's."

The thought of Irene Olsen being a lawyer, in any world, made Meg's head spin. Derby's daughter was ditzy and direct to the point of mean. But maybe she would have been a killer in corporate law. Meg kept the grin off her face as she politely refused the offer and changed the subject. "That's lovely of you, but I'm good. Where are you two heading tonight?"

"A lecture on the history of Pickleball. I have my league flyers ready to give to people as they leave. The museum isn't going to build itself." Derby patted his jacket pocket.

"We're going to dinner after that," Meg's mother added. "It's not all about the Pickleball Museum. Derby's just excited to get started."

"Did I tell you that we had a house donated for the museum last month?" Derby's eyes brightened as he talked about the new plans.

He had, a few times, but if there was one thing Derby was passionate about, it was Pickleball. And maybe Meg's mother. It was sweet.

They left before she could tell her mother about the woman on the ferry. Or being called "ma'am" by that jerk. But she lived three blocks away and Meg worked the next day. They had plenty of time. One of the reasons she loved being back and living on Bainbridge. Time with the family.

Just before seven Natasha arrived, Chinese food in hand. Meg looked at the door, but Dalton didn't follow her friend inside, his usual habit. He would leave his bike or truck at Meg's apartment, then walk down and get Natasha and walk with her to the bookstore. Then they'd either order the food for delivery or pick it up on the way.

Natasha didn't meet her gaze as she got out the containers. Two large ones and two with rice. "Dalton called and said he wouldn't be here for dinner. But he said he'd try to get here to walk you home."

Meg wasn't trying to read anything into this. But as she went to grab sodas for them from the back fridge, she checked her phone. No calls or messages from Dalton. He'd called Natasha but not her. This distance between them was starting to feel personal.

Meg waited until they were on the couch with Watson between them on the floor and they started eating. She took a bite, then set her fork down. The elephant in the room was crowding her. "Did I do something that's got Dalton mad at me? At least that you know?"

"Meg, this is between you and Dalton. You need to talk to him." Natasha didn't meet her gaze.

"I would, but he doesn't pick up my calls. He doesn't call me. And now, he's relaying messages through you. Seriously, what did I do?" Meg felt the tears start but she swallowed hard. She would not cry over something she didn't even understand.

Natasha rubbed her back. "Honey, it's not you. It's Dalton. He's going through some things right now. He knows you're busy and he doesn't want to burden you."

"But he's talked to you." Meg watched Natasha's face as the red came up from her collar. It was her tell when she wasn't being totally honest. "Natasha, what?"

"Like I said, he's dealing with some things. I can't tell you anything more than that, but it's not about you and him."

Meg leaned back with her carton of honey shrimp. "It is about me and him if he's avoiding talking to me. But you're right, you shouldn't be in the middle. I hope you tell him the same thing."

"I will, I promise. Now tell me what happened at school. You seemed upset when you called me." Natasha quickly changed the subject, and their conversation started to flow again.

But after Natasha left, Meg still felt upset about Dalton. She texted him, knowing she shouldn't, but if their almost two-year relationship was going down in flames, she needed to know why. It was quick and to the point. **Missed you at dinner.**

She set her phone down and cleaned up the mess from their meal. It was almost time to close and leave for home and she hadn't heard from him yet. She rubbed Watson's head as her dog watched the door, probably wondering the same thing.

When the bell rang, just before she closed up, hope sprang into her mind, but she quickly tamped it down. She would not be that girl.

Dalton walked into the store and Watson went wild. He'd missed him too. Meg watched as she finished packing her tote. Then she went and locked the back door. When she came to the front, Watson was on his leash and they were waiting for her. Dalton met her gaze. "Anything you need help with?"

"No, I'm ready to go. Are you walking me home?" She heard the snipe in her voice and wished she hadn't said anything.

He ignored the tension, putting his arm gently around her waist. They paused outside so she could lock the door, then, side by side, headed to Meg's apartment. It was walkable, being just up the hill and several blocks. And the path took them away from the main drag and the crush of tourists out for a Friday night's entertainment.

They were a block away from her Aunt Melody's garage and Meg's apartment over it when he stopped in the middle of the sidewalk. "I need to tell you something."

"Okay," she said. She mentally ran through all the things that could be wrong as she waited for him to speak.

Feeling the tug on his leash, Watson sat down between them, watching from one to the other.

Dalton took a deep breath. "My mother is visiting the island and wants to talk with me."

"Your mother? The woman who left you at age ten?" Meg

grabbed his arm, staring up into his face. She could barely see his features in the dim light. "Are you okay? How did she find you?"

"I don't think she ever lost me." Dalton leaned his head down on her shoulder. "How can I still feel like I'm that abandoned ten-year-old, riding the ferry for hours again the day she left, after all these years?"

VENGEANCE IN VENICE

Books by Erica Ruth Neubauer

MURDER AT THE MENA HOUSE

MURDER AT WEDGEFIELD MANOR

DANGER ON THE ATLANTIC

INTRIGUE IN ISTANBUL

SECRETS OF A SCOTTISH ISLE

HOMICIDE IN THE INDIAN HILLS

VENGEANCE IN VENICE

Novellas

MURDER UNDER THE MISTLETOE

Published by Kensington Publishing Corp.

VENGEANCE IN VENICE

ERICA RUTH NEUBAUER

kensingtonbooks.com

KENSINGTON BOOKS are published by

Kensington Publishing Corp.
900 Third Ave.
New York, NY 10022

All Kensington titles, imprints, and distributed lines are available at special quantity discounts for bulk purchases for sales promotion, premiums, fund-raising, educational, or institutional use. Special book excerpts or customized printings can also be created to fit specific needs. For details, write or phone the office of the Kensington Special Sales Manager: Attn. Special Sales Department, Kensington Publishing Corp., 900 Third Ave., New York, NY 10022. Phone: 1-800-221-2647.

KENSINGTON and the K with book logo Reg. US Pat. & TM Off.

Library of Congress Control Number: On file

ISBN: 978-1-4967-5788-3
First Kensington Hardcover Edition: April 2026

ISBN: 978-1-4967-5789-0 (ebook)

10 9 8 7 6 5 4 3 2 1

Printed in the United States of America

The authorized representative in the EU for product safety and compliance is eucomply OU, Parnu mnt 139b-14, Apt 123
Tallinn, Berlin 11317, hello@eucompliancepartner.com

For Tasha and Andrew.
Love you madly.

Chapter One

September 1927

With a salt breeze ruffling my bobbed hair and a gondolier crooning in a language I didn't understand as he piloted us toward a piazza where Redvers and I were about to have a quiet, romantic dinner, I was in heaven. I closed my eyes briefly, savoring the feeling.

"Is the singing too much?" Redvers whispered in my ear.

"No, I'm enjoying it," I replied.

"Truly? Are you feeling quite well? Perhaps we should go back to the hotel so you can lie down."

I gave him a little pinch on the leg, and he chuckled. I was relieved to hear the sound. After his near-death experience in India, my husband had been rather reserved. Instead of haring off on a new adventure, we'd spent the remaining spring and all of summer in a rented London flat recovering from the trip. Redvers had gone into an office every day and done some sort of desk work—pertaining to what, I had no idea. He didn't talk about it, but after the first few weeks I did get the sense that he was bored. I busied myself with daily walks to discover new parts of London, and when that no longer held my interest, I started visiting the British Museum, wandering the halls and pestering the staff.

I was out of new things to discover there as well.

It had been a long summer. We hadn't said as much out loud, but I suspected both of us were relieved to be out of London, even for a brief trip. Well, honeymoon, actually. We hadn't taken a real honeymoon after our sudden wedding in Scotland, and we were making up for lost time now. My heart felt lighter than it had in some time. Perhaps when we returned to England, it would be time to pack our trunks and find a new adventure.

Our gondola came to a stop, and the boatman stopped his singing to announce that we had arrived. I'd rather been expecting one of the larger piazzas, but we seemed to be disembarking into nothing more than a tight alleyway, although I could see that the passage widened out slightly up ahead. Redvers paid the man, who tucked the money into his pocket, then indicated a small restaurant farther down the cobblestone alley. The sun had nearly disappeared behind the buildings, and the ancient passage looked deserted except for the brightly lit window our guide was pointing to. Redvers thanked him, and with a mutual shrug, we headed that way. We'd asked for a dining suggestion, and this was it.

As I was discovering about many things in Venice, from the outside the restaurant looked impossibly small, but once inside, we could see that the space was larger, if not taller—the ceiling was characteristically low, with thick wooden beams overhead. The restaurant was run by a local family, and the owner greeted us as though we were close relations when we stepped through the door. There were a handful of tables dotting the space, and we were ushered to one near the window and holding glasses of the house wine before we even knew what hit us. Redvers looked bemused, but I was utterly charmed and let the burly owner choose my dinner without reservation.

Redvers was more cautious, ordering a plate of linguine

with scallops. He held his tongue until the owner bustled off. "You're playing roulette with your dinner?" he asked. "You know they serve things—parts—that even I wouldn't touch, don't you?"

"That man clearly eats well," I whispered quietly over the table. "I trust he knows what to feed me." I paused. "Besides, you know I like to try the local cuisine, whatever that might entail." Of course, even saying this, I was mentally crossing my fingers that my dinner wouldn't entail a tongue or a liver. But Venice was known for its seafood, and I was hopeful that that was what I would get.

Redvers shook his head in mock horror. I acknowledged that I was taking a bit of a gamble, but I was also excited to see what was going to be brought to me. I was absolutely delighted with my choice when the proprietor set a plate with gorgeously cooked scallops on a bed of risotto in front of me. Redvers gave a grudging nod to the wisdom of my gamble and snuck a bite from my plate when he thought I wasn't looking.

It was much later than we'd intended when we finally tore ourselves away from the trattoria, and the only reason we were allowed to leave was because we promised Pietro Sartori that we would return the following night. Stomachs full of wine and rich food and some panna cotta for dessert, not to mention the after-dinner limoncello, we waddled back into the alley.

I groaned and patted my stomach. "How will we get back to our hotel?"

Redvers had a hand on his own full stomach. "I think we should walk it off."

I nodded. This was an excellent suggestion.

Venice was a magical city, floating on top of the very sea itself. There were no cars on the streets, since there were very few streets—only canals, winding between the stone houses built on top of a series of low-lying marshes and islands. The entire city felt precarious, not to mention nearly impossible to navigate in order to find our hotel—the gondola had taken so many twists and turns to get us to where we were, I didn't have any faith we'd be able to find our way back.

But I trusted my husband. He had an unerring sense of direction, and while mine was good, his was better. Walking hand in hand, he led us over little bridges and through tiny winding alleyways until we were once more in front of our hotel.

"Lovely," I said on a sigh. I'd enjoyed the walk, not only because I'd had the chance to work off some of the heavy meal but because I'd been able to take in more of the city. We'd only arrived that morning, and I wanted to soak up as much of Venice as I could before we returned to London the following week. Around nearly every corner it seemed there was yet another beautiful view, another enchanting surprise.

The hotel Redvers had chosen for us was itself romantic, designed and decorated in an oriental fashion, although the architectural flourishes very much reminded me of the Mena House hotel in Egypt, where we first met. The hotel was located in a fifteenth-century Venetian palazzo that had been converted into a hotel, overlooking the *Canale della Sensa*. It was a rather residential area otherwise, quiet and tucked back from the more bustling parts of the city, and an ideal spot to enjoy a honeymoon.

We were heading up the marble stairs to our room when the booming voice of a disgruntled vacationer echoed up to us from the lobby, where the front desk was located.

"This hotel is impossible to get to. It's the third one we've stopped at this evening trying to get here. I don't know why you don't give better directions to patrons when they book a room with you." The owner of the strident voice sniffed in a way that was all too familiar.

I stopped dead in my tracks on the landing between flights of stairs. "No," I said quietly. Redvers turned and looked at me curiously. He clearly hadn't been paying attention, or he would share my concern. "No, it can't be."

The voice continued, louder than before, if that were possible. "I have half a mind to try to book a room somewhere better, the Ritz perhaps, but it's late and I'm exhausted, and I simply want to retire to my room."

"There isn't a Ritz in Venezia, madam."

As though in a dream—or perhaps more accurately, a nightmare—I headed back down the stairs, turning at the bottom landing toward the lobby. The owner of the voice had continued her list of complaints, but I'd already tuned them out. I came around the corner and stopped in my tracks.

Sure enough, the owner of the voice was none other than Aunt Millie.

Chapter Two

Redvers joined me, and I socked his arm. "Did you tell her where we were?" Millie hadn't noticed us yet, and I was already considering whether we could escape upstairs before we were noticed.

He shook his head, clearly handling this news better than I was, the corners of his mouth tipping up slightly. I wasn't sure if that was due to my distress at finding my aunt intruding on our honeymoon or just general amusement at the situation.

My aunt's husband, Lord Hughes, caught sight of us and gave a little wave. I sighed—we'd been spotted. We returned his gesture and moved forward, my hopes for disappearing up the stairs, and possibly absconding from the city altogether, completely dashed.

"Jane, why didn't you choose a larger hotel? One with better service?" Millie asked as soon as she turned her head and spotted us.

"Because this hotel is perfectly lovely, as are the staff." I gave the desk clerk a sympathetic look and made a mental note to send Redvers down later with a generous tip for the young man's trouble.

Or perhaps I should say, for Millie's trouble.

Redvers gave my aunt a winning smile. "It's much quieter here at night than at the hotels on the Grand Canal. Less boat traffic at night, not to mention the revelers."

Millie narrowed her eyes at my husband but after a beat gave a stiff nod. She had a key in hand, and after a few more mutterings, she finally stepped away from the desk and the poor clerk behind it.

"How did you find us?" I asked, trying to keep my voice mild.

"Your aunts mentioned where you were traveling to." Millie addressed this to Redvers, then turned her sharp eyes on me. "Marie and Carolyn, you remember them, Jane. They didn't know what hotel you were staying at, however. I had to learn *that* information from your father." Millie's voice was as accusing as her glare, but Redvers' pleasant demeanor never changed, not even when her glare was turned back to him at the mention of his father. I never understood how he managed it under her formidable mien.

I closed my eyes briefly. "Did they also mention that we are on our honeymoon?" I asked, doing my best to keep my voice level. This time I was the one who got a sympathetic look from Lord Hughes.

"Nonsense," Millie said. "You've been gallivanting around the world since your wedding. Which you failed to invite us to, I might remind you."

The wedding had been Redvers' idea, and onc I was beginning to believe we would never live down. Nearly seven months later, and we were still being scolded for having a quiet ceremony in Scotland instead of the big to-do that Millie had been planning for us.

Millie's diatribe continued, but I had already tuned out. She finally stopped and huffed. "I'm tired, so we will retire. But I'll come to your room in the morning to give you your costumes."

I did a double take. "I'm sorry, what costumes? And what are they for?"

Millie huffed again, this time with exaggerated annoyance. "For the party we will all be attending tomorrow night. I swear, Jane, I sometimes wonder about your hearing. Or your memory. Before you know it, you'll be just like your father."

"Mmm," I said, deciding to let that go by without comment. "Well, I suppose we will see you in the morning, then."

Since it appeared we didn't have any other choice.

True to her word, Aunt Millie was knocking on our door while we were still enjoying breakfast on our tiny patio overlooking the canal.

"At least you're dressed," Millie said to me when I opened the door. She had two hangers covered by garment bags draped over her arm. I was a little afraid to see what was inside them.

"Who is throwing this party we are attending?" I asked as she swept past me into the small sitting room. I had gone back and forth about whether to argue with my aunt about even attending said party, but in the end Redvers and I had decided it was best to simply give in, especially since she'd come prepared with costumes for the two of us. I would already be hearing about our wedding until I was in the grave—there was no sense in giving Millie something else to harangue us about.

Besides, we'd made a pact the night before to show up to the party for only an hour and then make our escape. With any luck there would be enough people in attendance that Millie wouldn't notice our sudden absence.

"She's an American heiress," Millie replied. "Sole heir to

the largest salt company in the United States, and possibly the world."

I waited for a beat while Millie draped the costumes over the back of a chair, but no other information seemed to be forthcoming. "What's her name? Why is she here?"

"I can't believe you haven't heard of her, Jane," Millie scolded. "She's Clara Ann Morton, heir to her family's extensive fortune. Salt is a big business, you know."

I didn't know, but I kept that to myself. Redvers had stood up from his chair on the balcony and was now leaning casually in the doorway sipping his coffee. His dark eyes looked entirely amused.

"And why is she here?" I asked. "How do you know her?" My aunt was well-off, but she was far from the lofty status of heiress, even now that she'd married Lord Hughes, who was quite wealthy in his own right. I had no earthly idea how this salt baroness and my aunt might have met. It was even more incredible to me that the two had hit it off, since it seemed unlikely that Clara would have invited Millie and her entourage to a party if they hadn't.

"I explained all this in my letter," Millie said with no small amount of aggravation. "As well as explaining that I would be bringing the costumes."

I hadn't received such a letter. Helpless, I looked to Redvers, who suddenly looked rather sheepish. I raised an eyebrow and he gave a small shrug. With a sigh, I turned back to Millie.

"I guess I'm just forgetful these days." There was no sense in blaming my husband. She would only find a way to turn it around on me anyhow.

She eyed me up and down. "You aren't pregnant, are you? At your age, it would be quite a risk. I wouldn't advise it, although it is a shame for your father's sake."

I needed to shut down this area of discussion. Fast. "No,

I'm certainly not. Thank you for inquiring. What will we be going as this evening? I'm sure your own costume will be quite spectacular."

Redvers was now covering his mouth with one hand, clearly trying not to laugh. It was sometimes maddening how much he was able to get away with—if I so much as giggled, Millie would catch me and demand to know what was so funny.

Millie huffed, but my distraction worked, since she pulled up one of the plastic bags to reveal a Renaissance dress in thick burgundy elaborately embroidered with silver thread. I made appropriately appreciative noises, and she showed us the other costume as well. "This one is for you, Redvers."

Millie lifted the sheath to show us what appeared to be a naval captain's outfit. I was quite curious about the type of party we would be attending, but it seemed that was all I was going to learn before we arrived, because Millie was suddenly ready to leave. "I must dash. James has a gondola waiting for me. Be ready at eight this evening. Eight *sharp*, Jane. I mean it."

She was gone before I had the chance to argue with her that I was actually quite punctual as a habit.

"You're a great deal of help," I said to Redvers, although my tone was teasing. I pushed past him to the balcony where I resettled myself in my seat and took a long sip of coffee. Italians loved espresso, but Redvers had managed to wrangle a pot of American-style coffee for me, and I was going to enjoy it down to the very last drop, even though it had gone cold.

"I am, actually." Redvers took his own seat, eyes dancing. "And what shall we do with ourselves today before eight this evening? Eight *sharp*."

I threw a napkin at him, which was unfortunately caught in a salty breeze and danced past my husband and into the murky canal below us. I gazed down at it and sighed. “It looks as though I’ll have to keep projectiles to myself.”

Redvers chuckled. “Things really are working in my favor here in Venice.”

We could not have known that wouldn’t be the case for the rest of our trip.

Chapter Three

After breakfast we spent a lovely morning wandering around Venice at a leisurely pace, taking in the popular sights and stopping now and again to pop into the various shops tucked around every corner. Our first stop was St. Mark's Basilica or, as the Italians called it, *Basilica San Marco*. The large piazza that the basilica was located on was dominated by both the church itself and the former Doge's Palace that stretched out in a long colonnade to the side and end of it. With similar buildings holding up the other side, the piazza felt like it was sitting inside a beautifully decorated rectangle with the basilica at the head of it. It was quite a large palazzo, considering how the city was essentially built on top of wooden logs, and I marveled at what must have gone into the construction of these hulking buildings. The front of the basilica was fascinating to me, decorated in various colors and shades of marble. It looked to be a hodgepodge of materials and carvings, and I enjoyed the overall effect, as well as the numerous onion domes on top. It meant that the building was a little unusual in addition to being stunning, as was the interior, which we meandered through, enjoying the intensely gilded gold ceilings.

"That's quite a lot of gold," I whispered to my husband,

staring up at a religious mosaic nearly lost in the sea of shimmering gold.

"I cannot disagree," Redvers said quietly.

Once finished inside, we went back out, and decided to climb the St. Mark's Bell Tower, the *Campanile di San Marco*.

As we puffed up the numerous stairs leading to the top, my husband shared his bit of knowledge about the building. "It has been struck by lightning numerous times," he said, pausing on a landing for a quick breath. "It was recently rebuilt in about 1910 or so, and is the tallest building in Venice."

"I'm glad for that," I managed to mutter. "I'm not going up another one." We were nearly at the top, and I was rethinking my choice to climb the thing in the first place, but once we reached the final set of stairs, I was glad we'd made the effort. The city with its terracotta red roofs and serpentine waterways stretched out around us, the skyline dotted with other church towers. When I glanced down, the people looked like a colony of ants on the piazza below us, hustling about. From our lofty position, it was quite obvious just how large the Doge's Palace below us was, with its row of columns stretching its arms wide across the façade. Turning my attention back to the horizon, I could see a few nearby islands dotting the landscape with buildings of their own, and the intermittent boat traffic cruising between them and Venice. Redvers and I stayed there for a while, enjoying the views of the city from every side of the tower before making our way back down, spilling back into the piazza and the bustle of the city, ready to move on to the next attraction.

Before I knew it, it was time to head back to our hotel. I was disappointed we didn't have time to have another dinner at Pietro's restaurant, but I acknowledged that Redvers was correct—if we went there for dinner, there was zero chance we would be back to our hotel in time to meet my aunt and Lord Hughes. Pietro's enthusiasm for food was infectious, and dining at his place would require several hours. Hours we didn't have tonight. Instead, we would have some light snacks sent up from the hotel kitchen while we got dressed in our respective costumes. But I mentally promised myself—and Pietro—that we would dine there the following night.

I slid into my Renaissance dress, holding the front of the costume to my chest while Redvers tightened the laces at my back, not so tightly that I couldn't breathe, but enough that it would stay put. The dress fit well, and I had to admit that my aunt had done a good job choosing for us. Redvers looked wonderful in his black suit with the matching tricorn hat and cape—he cut quite the dashing figure.

Lord Hughes and Millie were resplendent in their costumes, similar to my own Renaissance-themed costumes. Millie bustled us to the pier outside our hotel where a gondolier was already waiting for us. He held a lantern so that we could see while stepping into the boat—it was already quite dark, the moon playing peekaboo with heavy clouds and a light fog rolling in from the sea.

I had no idea how this boatman was expected to navigate the canals with such little visibility. But he was obviously quite experienced, swinging his heavy wooden oar with ease through the dark water, expertly ushering our gondola through the maze of narrow canals until we reached the Grand Canal. Here we joined a wide sea of crafts like our own, the gondoliers in their black-and-white striped tops occasionally calling to one another in Italian. The Grand Canal seemed to serve as a kind of Main Street, the primary thoroughfare through the city where gondolas dodged both each other and the larger boats that served as taxis, ferrying people from one stop to the next.

We continued on toward the edge of the city, where even the Grand Canal traffic began to thin out. I was tempted to ask where we were going, but I would only be scolded for my lack of patience. And it turned out to be unnecessary, since we got in line with a handful of other gondolas waiting to pull up to a decrepit building, its white marble face nearly lost in a sea of vines and ivy. Instead of matching the towering height of the neighboring buildings, this was hunkered low on the water, perhaps only two stories, if that. A series of arched windows, peeking from beneath their ivy curtain, along with carved marble lions marching along the foundation were the defining points of interest for the place.

Redvers and I exchanged a look, and I noticed that even Millie looked startled by the appearance of the palazzo. When it was our turn to disembark, the gondolier eased us close to the entrance, grabbing the marble railing to pull the boat up tight. There was no pier here, so instead we stepped from the boat onto a wide marble platform. I disembarked first, then watched as everyone else safely stepped onto the platform to ensure we all made it safely out of the gondola. Lord Hughes was the last one to get out, and he paid the boatman before joining us on the landing.

For once, Millie looked uncertain, and I was tempted to ask her once again how she'd been invited to this soiree but held my tongue. I was intrigued by both the structure and by my aunt's discomfort.

The wide marble platform had a small set of stairs that led through an iron gated doorway, the gate itself already swung open to admit guests. The gate stretched the length of the platform and was elaborately wrought but showing the ravages of the sea air, rusting at the edges. The gate ended in crumbling stone at either end.

We passed up another set of marble stairs and into the building itself, where we now stood in a long hallway that stretched out on either side of us. The interior was at least better kept than the outside; here we found black and white marble floors with elaborate black and gold walls. I was busy taking in the décor when I felt a tug at my costume. Glancing at my husband, I saw him nodding, and I stepped to the left to gaze around my aunt and her husband.

There was our hostess, standing in a flowing white, barely-there gown with an enormous snake winding around her shoulders, flicking its tongue as it slid along her bared skin—and Clara was nearly all bared skin. She wore a sculpted metal headdress made of snakes as well, clearly in the guise of Medusa, but at least these snakes were not the real thing. As we stepped forward, my aunt set about reintroducing herself and the rest of our party, while Clara introduced her pet snake, stroking it while she did so. I took a small step forward when my name was mentioned, but my husband kept as much distance as was polite between himself and Clara's pet. I was too focused on Clara to take in much of what she said, although I did register that Clara and my aunt had met at some other party in England during the past two years.

Clara was barefoot, and I realized that she must be nearly six feet tall even without shoes on, and as thin as a lamp post. Our hostess's intense eyes were lined with black kohl. They highlighted that fact that they were quite a startling shade of green, even in the flickering lamplight, and were the main feature of her otherwise narrow face. Her hair was also wild, dark half curls gone frizzy in the sea air. Altogether she looked quite mad, although I had to assume this was for dramatic effect.

"Enjoy the show," Clara said with a theatrical sweep of her arm out to both sides. Millie and Lord Hughes thanked her, Redvers and I nodding to the woman as we passed her, hesitating for only a moment before we followed our companions to the left of the central entrance.

"The show?" I asked Redvers in a low voice. He shrugged, but his expression seemed caught somewhere between fascination and fear.

Just past where we'd spoken with our hostess, we found ourselves in an expansive room further decorated in the black and gold design of the brief foyer. The other guests were also wearing costumes, although the staff, moving through the crowd with platters of drinks, were dressed simply in all black. Glancing around, I saw that there appeared to be stations set up for various different types of entertainment, and I assumed the other side of the palazzo would have more of the same. A tarot card reader was seated upon large pillows with a low table before her in one corner. I was only able to catch a glimpse of the woman and her elaborately styled outfit through the thick crowd gathered around her. The other entertainments seemed along the lines of a carnival or circus with the sparkling costumes to match. A pair of women in dazzling leotards stood on a large pedestal and contorted their bodies in ways that seemed impossible. Perhaps the most amazing sight was on the right side of the building where a man was performing daring tricks on a bar suspended from the high ceiling, like a trapeze act with only one bar to work with. In another corner, a man stood stoically while holding the leash of a playful cheetah chewing on his pant legs—Redvers and I would be giving *that* a wide berth, regardless of whether the surrounding partygoers cleared up or not.

"What is this?" Redvers murmured to me, eyes fixed on a slender man swallowing a sword, and I could only shake my head in response. I had no earthly idea what we had walked into. Glancing at my aunt, I was gratified to see that she also seemed startled about what she'd brought us to, her eyes wide and darting about the room. Lord Hughes, on the other hand, seemed perfectly delighted by the various acts, pointing each of them out to my aunt with enthusiasm.

Within moments he'd taken her hand and dragged her off for a "better view" of something he'd spotted through the crowd.

Redvers snagged a pair of drinks from a nearby member of the waitstaff and passed one over to me. I took a sip, enjoying the sparkling bubbles on my tongue. "Champagne," I said appreciatively. "And a rather good one." I turned back toward the foyer, which was now deserted. Our hostess was no longer at her post, and in fact, I didn't see her anywhere, surprising since she *was* rather difficult to miss. I had mixed feelings about this—I knew Redvers was terrified of snakes and wouldn't be keen on getting close to Clara again so long as she was carrying that large serpent around. But I was intrigued by the woman and hopeful that before the night was over, I would have a chance to talk with her, perhaps get a sense of who she was. Not to mention why she would throw this strange and elaborate party.

If I'd known how the evening would play out, I would have sought Clara out much sooner.

We wandered the palazzo for close to an hour, watching each of the performers for a time and admiring their skill before finding a quiet spot toward the back of the party that was relatively uninhabited. Instead of mingling with the other guests, we watched them instead, sipping champagne and commenting on the other costumes.

"How long do you suppose we need to stay here before we can politely escape?" Redvers asked.

I sighed. "I've been wondering the same thing. We promised ourselves only an hour, and we're definitely past that." I glanced around but couldn't see my aunt or Lord Hughes from our vantage point. "This is fascinating, but there are far more interesting things we could be doing on our honeymoon."

Redvers' eyes lit up, and a slow grin began making its way across his lips. He seemed about to say something when there was a piercing scream from a doorway at the center of the building. Clara was the one screaming, hands clasped to her face. She was easy to spot, standing nearly a head above everyone around her. Instead of rushing to her aid, everyone in her vicinity took several steps back even as her screaming continued. Redvers and I exchanged a quick look and then pushed our way through the crowd toward the woman.

"What's happened?" Redvers asked when he reached Clara's side.

She pointed to another ironwork gate, the one she'd been standing in front of when she greeted us. Peering through it, I realized that it appeared to lead to an outdoor space.

"Out there," was all she managed. Tears were streaking down her face, but at least she'd stopped screaming. I glanced at the rest of the partygoers, and they'd put even more space between themselves and Clara, which I found to be very odd. Would no one come to this woman's aid when she was so obviously distressed? I saw my Aunt Millie and Lord Hughes pushing their way to the front, but otherwise the crowd appeared fascinated but disengaged, as though they were merely here to enjoy the spectacle, and not at all interested in the well-being of their host.

It left a sour taste in my mouth.

Redvers moved quickly past Clara and through the iron gated door, and I waited with Clara until my aunt could take my place before following behind him. Stepping through the doorway, I could see that the outdoor space was an overgrown garden. Ivy and vines had taken over not only the front of the palazzo but this area as well. The brick walls, encompassing the garden but also appearing at random throughout the space, appeared to be crumbling beneath the onslaught of vegetation, and the lack of moon made it difficult to navigate the cobbled ground. I was grateful for the scattered lanterns casting what little light they did. "Redvers?" I called tentatively, unable to make out where exactly he might be. I looked at the sky, hoping the moon would reveal itself within the next few moments. But luck wasn't with me.

"Over here," he replied.

I followed the sound of his voice and found him off to the right, standing beside what appeared to be a circular marble gazebo. He'd clearly grabbed one of the lanterns from its stake—I kicked myself for not having done the same instead of tripping over dead foliage and broken stone.

Redvers was kneeling next to the gazebo and I went to his side, bending down toward the light. It became clear that he was kneeling next to a man who was not moving.

"Is he . . . ?"

Redvers nodded, glancing up at me. "He's dead."

"But who is he?" I asked. "And what did he die from?"

"I don't know how he died, but I can tell you who he is," Clara's voice floated to us from where she stood at the top of the marble staircase, tearful but strong. "He was my husband," she said.

Chapter Four

"Are you quite certain he's dead? Should I see if there is a doctor here? Perhaps we can still do something," Clara's voice was getting closer, and Redvers stood. I put a hand on his arm, then moved across the courtyard in the direction of the woman's voice in order to keep her from returning to the body. I stumbled once before coming to where she now stood beneath a dimly glowing lantern at the bottom of the stairs.

"I don't think a doctor will be able to do any good at this point," I said gently but firmly. "He's definitely dead. I'm very sorry for your loss."

"Oh, well, we were no longer married. I should really have said that he was my ex-husband."

I cocked my head at this odd announcement. She was upset at the man's discovery, but she related this information in a very matter-of-fact tone. "What was his name?" I asked. She took a seat on a low brick wall off to the left, and I stepped closer to her. I hoped she wasn't terribly attached to the costume she was wearing because it couldn't possibly survive the beating it was taking from being perched on that crumbling brick.

"Christopher D'Annuzzio." Clara's voice was sad again. "He was a poet, with the most volatile temperament."

Each of her statements was more confusing than the last. Why would she be upset at his loss if he was such a volatile man? Did it mean she had something to do with his death? I sought a more appropriate question to ask, finally landing on, "Did he have any medical issues? Anything that might have killed him?" I chose my words carefully.

Clara looked at me, and I thought I could see surprise on her face in the dim light. "Oh, no, he was killed by someone here. I know that for certain."

I paused. "How do you know that?" I hadn't seen any blood on the man but kept this to myself, since it was an inappropriate bit of trivia to mention to someone who had just lost a loved one—ex-husband or not. I also couldn't say for certain D'Annuzzio was without any visible blood at all since it was impossible to inspect the body properly in the darkness. Even with a lantern shining directly on the man I hadn't been able to discern much except that there didn't seem to be any gunshots or stabbing wounds, either of which would have bled enough to be seen, even in the dim light.

"The tarot reader told me only today that I would lose someone quite close to me," Clara said. "And that his demise would be carried out by someone I loved."

Before I could ask further questions, Redvers joined us and broke in. "We need to contact the police."

Clara fluttered a hand. "Is that absolutely necessary? I would hate to end the party." Both Redvers and I looked at her, mouths agape, at a loss for words. "Why ruin everyone's good time?" Clara asked. "Well, everyone else's. I suppose Christopher isn't having a good time."

Neither of us knew what to say to that, and there was a long moment of silence. Even though I couldn't quite make out his face in the darkness, I already knew what Redvers was going to request next. "I'll be right back," I told them, moving cautiously through our area of the garden, up the stairs, and into the foyer where I could see again. Millie and Lord Hughes were at either side of the foyer, keeping guests firmly corralled in the party rooms. "Lord Hughes," I called quietly.

He turned his head and quickly joined me. I glanced at my aunt, surprised she wasn't kicking up a fuss at not being summoned as well, but she lit into a guest that was trying to sneak past her, verbally abusing the woman up one side and down the other. It appeared Millie was enjoying her role and wasn't willing to give it up quite yet, body or no body. That was actually an asset at the moment, since keeping nosy partygoers out of the garden was precisely what we needed.

"Can you summon the police? And make sure that no one leaves the party until we're able to figure out exactly who is present. I'm sure the police will want to speak with everyone at some point."

Hughes nodded and set off, pushing through the crowd. I fully trusted the man's ability to get things done, and with Aunt Millie holding the line, I returned to Clara and Redvers in the garden.

Redvers and his lantern had joined Clara near the wall. When I returned, she stood, smoothing the front of her nearly transparent costume. "You've called for the *Polizia di Stato*, haven't you?" She sighed. "I should have known you would. I suppose I should go and make some sort of announcement to the guests." With that she swept past me, her height dwarfing me as she passed. It was rare that I felt short—I was actually quite tall, ordinarily towering over the women around me. It was a strange sensation to feel so small next to another woman.

"I do not know what to make of any of this," Redvers said once Clara had left us.

"I'm afraid I don't either," I agreed. I looked up at the thick cloud cover. "I do wish the moon would come out."

I could feel Redvers' grin in the darkness. "So you can get a look at the body?"

I stifled an answering grin. "It was a long summer," I said instead. And it had been. I'd struggled to keep both my mind and body occupied, and I suspected Redvers had found the same.

I would never admit to being pleased at stumbling across another murder—that was entirely too gruesome, and I was truly sorry someone had perished. But I wasn't going to back down from another investigation either. Not when there was a rush of blood in my veins and my mind was already making fast calculations and notes.

"I doubt the Italian *polizia* will let us butt in," Redvers mused.

Especially when we didn't have a reason to. Not yet, anyway.

Chapter Five

Redvers had been correct—once the *Polizia di Stato* arrived and took down our names and the hotel where we were staying, we were sent back to the party with the other attendees. I wasn't surprised, but I did find that I was disappointed, not that I would admit as much out loud. It looked as though we would go back to having a normal, run-of-the-mill honeymoon after all, and that wasn't the worst thing in the world, was it?

Well, it would be a normal honeymoon as long as we could get private time apart from Aunt Millie. That would be a feat unto itself.

The costumed party crowd was being allowed to leave as they also gave their names to the *polizia*, a stream of gondolas waiting to whisk their passengers away from the scene of a tragic death. I was already mentally considering it a murder, especially after Clara's strange statements, but I wasn't quite certain whether D'Annuzzio's death was actually a murder or not.

"Do *you* think he was murdered? Or do you think it was simply a medical emergency?" I asked Redvers.

"Impossible to say without getting a better look at the body." He sighed, and I suspected he was having similarly mixed feelings about being booted from a potential new investigation. I was about to ask him about it when we were interrupted by my aunt.

"Well," Millie said with a huff, sipping the champagne she'd snatched from a final passing tray. It appeared the staff were hustling to leave this place as well, and I wondered whether they had been hired only for the evening. "Just when things were getting interesting, we're being kicked out."

It was, in fact, what I'd been thinking, but I was still shocked to hear it said out loud. I kept my surprise to myself, however. There was no good reason to poke the hornet's nest masquerading as my aunt.

Millie took another sip and then regarded me. "Did you happen to see your friend?"

Now I frowned. "What friend?" I hadn't seen a single soul that I recognized, let alone a friend in this crowd.

"Oh, what was her name. Deedee? Doris? Something like that."

I was still frowning and looked to my husband for help. He gave me a helpless shrug and I shook my head at his lack of help and turned back to my aunt. "I don't know who that might be. Where do I know her from?"

Millie glanced around, her eyes falling upon the now empty nest of cushions where the tarot card reader had been sitting when we first arrived at the party. The deck of cards, once resting on the tabletop, had apparently disappeared with their reader; there was nothing to be seen but the pillows and the low table, which was now liberally covered with both empty and half-drunk glasses of champagne. "Well, I don't know, Jane. I don't keep track of your friends."

I couldn't imagine any acquaintance of mine showing up in Venice, and the circle of friends I'd once known had disappeared during my first marriage, largely due to my abusive husband and the tight control he'd held over my life.

They'd given up on me, one by one, never to resurface, even once I'd been widowed and reclaimed my freedom. All this to say, I could only imagine that whoever my aunt had seen wasn't someone that was actually known to me.

Instead of continuing to search the crowd for a stranger, I turned my attention back to my husband. "Should we return to our hotel now?" I asked, eyeing the fleeing crowd. "Or should we wait a few more minutes?"

Millie's jaw dropped. "You truly mean to leave? During a murder investigation? When any person in this room could be the killer?"

I shrugged. "We don't have a reason to get involved, especially since we don't even know that it was a murder. He might have simply had an attack of some sort. I'm sure the *polizia* have it well in hand."

Aunt Millie looked aghast, but it was true that neither Redvers nor I had any reason to get involved. Before she could argue further, Lord Hughes gently urged her toward the exit. "Let's head back, darling. We can always get a nightcap at the hotel."

"I would at least like to say goodnight to our hostess," Millie said, heels digging in quite literally, as though her husband might bodily drag her to the exit. It was a spectacle that I couldn't imagine happening, not with the even temperament Lord Hughes always demonstrated, but it was one that I would privately enjoy seeing.

Instead, our three heads swiveled in an attempt to locate Clara. It shouldn't have been a difficult task, tall as she was, with a rapidly thinning crowd, but the woman was nowhere to be found. "Is she with the *polizia*, do you think?" I asked Redvers beneath my breath.

"Most likely," he replied, eyes still sweeping. "Since she was once married to the victim."

"Oh," Millie piped up. "Was it Christopher D'Annuzzio that was found dead?"

"Do you know him?" I asked, my attention turning back to my aunt.

"I only know *of* him. He's quite the scandal, even beyond the absolutely *obscene* poetry he writes. It's shocking that anyone is willing to publish such rubbish."

I had a few further questions about the dead man, but movement in the corner of my eye distracted me. I turned my head to see the tarot card reader moving rapidly in our direction, and I squinted, trying to place her face. She did seem familiar, but I didn't recognize the thick black braid of hair bouncing against her shoulder with every step. Her costume was less sparkling than the other performers—subdued and flowing, rather than skimpy and sequined.

"Jane," the woman said breathlessly when she reached our little group. She took a quick glance behind her, then at the people I was standing with before turning her attention back to me. "It's me."

I felt in my gut that I somehow knew this woman, but how? My brief pause was enough to frustrate her, so she spoke again, quickly, her words nearly running together in her haste. "Deanna Parks. We met in Egypt." She glanced behind her again. "Jane, I think they're going to arrest me for murder."

My cheeks heated with embarrassment that I hadn't immediately recognized Deanna—of course, I knew who she was. "Your hair," I said, trying not to sound as though I was making excuses, but likely failing. "It's so dark in here, and I remember you being blonde."

Deanna clearly didn't feel she had time to make me feel better about my brief lapse in memory. "I darkened it for this party. Look, can you help me?"

I switched to the issue at hand. "Why do you think they're going to arrest you?" I nearly asked whether she had killed him, but I bit my tongue and managed to keep that question to myself.

She sighed. "I have a sneaking suspicion that Clara is going to make me the scapegoat."

My eyebrows knit together. "Why would she do that?"

"Honestly, that guy was a louse, and when he tried to put his hands on me earlier today, I nailed him right in the family jewels with my knee. He ratted me out to Clara, and she almost fired me, but kept me on because it was too close to the party and she 'wouldn't have time to find someone else.'" The last part Deanna must have been quoting from our hostess directly, since she flicked her fingers angrily as quotation marks while she said it.

"I don't think they'll arrest you on that charge. We don't know how he died yet, but I doubt that was the cause."

"Of course, it wasn't. Don't be ridiculous. It sure hurts, usually takes a man right to the ground, but it won't kill him." Deanna's eyes sparkled. "I know from experience."

I grinned in response. But then her expression returned to worry. "But that doesn't mean Clara won't blame me, let me take the fall for this," Deanna said, hands fisting in the flowing blue fabric of her dress. "I heard the coppers talking, and they don't think it was natural causes."

I wondered how they'd come to that conclusion. With more light, had they seen something suspicious? I cocked my head and asked the next question on my mind. "Do you think Clara did it?"

I'd been ignoring the rest of our entourage but was reminded of their presence when Millie gasped at my question. "How can you even think that?" my aunt asked, clearly scandalized.

It took a great deal of effort not to roll my eyes, since I knew that if I did, I would never hear the end of it for the remainder of my days on this earth. So I briefly closed them instead, then did my best to keep my voice level. "Because if they were married, Clara might have any number of reasons to want the man dead."

"They were divorced," Millie said.

"Even still. She may have motive." I turned back to Deanna. "Speaking of husbands, is Charlie with you?" I'd very much enjoyed spending time with the couple in Egypt and hoped they were still together. It had been about a year since I'd met the two, and they were newlyweds at the time.

"He's here with me," Deanna said, and I let out the breath I'd been holding. "Not at this party, but here in Venice." She shook her head. "He's trying to get hired as a gondolier, which I told him is nuts. You gotta be a local, and speak Italian." Deanna looked around again. "But we can talk about that later. For now, I gotta get out of here."

Deanna was about to leave, but just then the overhead lights came on, nearly blinding us all for a second. We all blinked, our eyes having become accustomed to the shadowy lantern light of the cavernous room, lit specifically for the mood of the party.

Then Clara strode into the room, her diaphanous white dress blowing behind her, truly leaving nothing beneath to the imagination, especially here in the suddenly brightly lit room. She was followed by several *polizia*, one of whom was dressed in a pinstripe suit—likely the local detective assigned to the investigation. Clara pointed a dramatic finger in the direction of our huddled group. "She's right there, officers. Arrest her."

Chapter Six

I moved to stand in front of my friend, blocking her from the officers' view, fully knowing it was a futile gesture. If they wanted to arrest her, they could easily do so.

The *polizia* and Clara joined us, the lead officer—detective?—pausing to take a long look around the room before sauntering over. There wasn't much left to see. Most of the guests had escaped the palazzo, as well as the evening's entertainers and hired staff.

"Once the lights come on, everyone scatters like vermin," the detective drawled, one hand in the pocket of his dark wool suit. "It is always this way, but here we find your suspect. Now, Mrs. Morton, do you have *proof* this woman killed your husband?" He gave a flippant wave of his other hand toward Deanna, who had stepped out from behind me and was now just to my right.

"Ex-husband," Clara said, her expression never changing.

The detective didn't acknowledge Clara's correction, keeping his dark eyes fixed on Deanna.

While this played out, I breathed a little sigh of relief that the man seemed reasonable; perhaps he wouldn't arrest Deanna on the spot. But I could tell by Deanna's breathing—fast and shallow—that she wasn't equally as convinced.

"She assaulted him earlier today." Clara's arms crossed

over her chest, and she radiated haughtiness. It was at odds with her earlier manner—in fact, she'd seemed like a different person nearly every time I'd encountered her thus far. I couldn't figure Clara Morton out; she was the definition of an enigma. At least she was no longer wearing the huge snake. I hoped for Redvers' sake that she had secured it somewhere and the creature wouldn't make a surprise appearance at our feet. My husband might launch himself into the canal simply to avoid the thing, "pet" or not.

The detective's eyebrows rose at Clara's announcement, his question implicit, and Deanna shrugged. "He touched me first. I simply let him know his advances were not welcome." Her attitude was one of casual disdain, but I could feel the anxiety radiating off her body—Deanna was scared. This defiant response was nothing more than a show, and I wondered if the detective was buying it. Or anyone else for that matter.

Redvers stepped in. "Have you examined the body, *ispettore*? Do you have any idea what killed him?"

The *ispettore*—not called "detective," then—stepped forward. "And you are?"

"I'm Redvers, and this is my wife, Jane Wunderly," he tipped his head toward me, then paused, clearly deciding how much to reveal. "I work for the British government."

The *ispettore*'s eyes narrowed, studying Redvers for a moment longer. "Ispettore Fizzoli," he finally said.

Ordinarily I would have felt anxious for my husband and myself at this close inspection, but for once, we weren't personally invested in either the murder victim or his former wife. I would do all I could to help Deanna, of course, but for the first time I felt confident that I would not be accused of this crime, nor would Redvers. It was a rather novel feeling.

"Please leave your names with the *polizia* on your way out. Except you, Mrs. Parks. You need to come with me."

Deanna stood stock-still for a long moment before stepping forward. "We'll do what we can to help you," I whispered to her as she passed me, my hand on her arm.

She stopped, her eyes searching mine. "Charlie is at the Silva Ariel hotel, near the Jewish quarter. Please go find him and tell him where I am."

"Of course," I said as she slowly moved away and joined the officers, two of whom parted from the small group to flank her on either side. My stomach dropped at the sight—this did not bode well. It also hadn't escaped my notice that the *ispettore* had avoided answering Redvers' question about whether anything had been found on D'Annuzzio's body indicating how he'd died.

The little group left the room, Clara Morton trailing behind, and I turned to Redvers, my face creased with worry. I didn't even need to say anything before he reached out a hand to grasp mine. "We'll find Charlie. And I will send a telegram to the office, see if we have contacts here that we can use to get information." He shook his head. "I should have asked before we left, but I assumed we would be on our honeymoon, acting as tourists."

I smiled ruefully. "The best intentions, my dear." I paused, then quietly asked what an *ispettore* was.

"It's about the equivalent to what a police detective or inspector would be at home," Redvers explained. I nodded, filing the information away.

My aunt was uncharacteristically quiet, and I expected her to interject that we should mind our own business, leave Deanna to her own devices. I was pleasantly surprised when she did speak. "Is there anything we can do?" Millie asked.

Redvers blinked, clearly as surprised as I was, then nodded. "I'll let you know if we think of anything." He glanced around at the nearly emptied room. "For now, let's grab a gondola and see if we can find Charlie Parks."

* * *

Aunt Millie and Lord Hughes went back to the hotel, leaving us to find Charlie Parks on our own. It was actually a relief. Four of us converging on Charlie would have been overwhelming, and there wasn't anything either of them could do at the moment anyway. Not to mention the fact that neither of them knew Charlie or Deanna well.

The gondolier dropped us off at the nearest dock, only one canal over from our own hotel, as it happened, and we walked in near darkness along the cobblestone street. The buildings were quiet, only an occasional light shining from an upper-floor window; the city seeming to otherwise have gone to sleep.

Our first turn led us down a narrow alley that dead-ended where several of the surrounding buildings connected. There was an unpleasant odor here, one I couldn't put my finger on the source of, but we retraced our steps quickly all the same. On our second try we found the hotel, the name above the door blessedly lit; it was so small we might have missed it otherwise. The alleyway and the hotel seemed abandoned, but when we stepped into the lobby, we found a clerk behind the counter, feet on the check-in desk, sound asleep. Redvers and I exchanged a look before he tiptoed carefully behind the man to search the desk. Soft snores were escaping the rather large nose perched above a bushy moustache, and they stuttered briefly, then stopped when Redvers found the beat-up sign-in register, causing my husband to freeze. But the snores resumed after only a few beats, and Redvers was able to flip through the pages, running his finger down the list of names until he stopped, nodded, and rejoined me on the other side of the desk.

We headed to the stairs, the snores trailing behind us, growing more distant the higher we climbed. We came to the third floor and stepped into a tiny corridor, a shared bathroom at one end and a series of numbered doors along either side. I followed Redvers to door number nine and stood beside him as he knocked. The door opened immediately—Charlie had clearly been waiting for his wife to return.

"Did you forget your key again?" Charlie was saying as he swung the door open, then stopped abruptly when he saw Redvers. His face creased in confusion, clearing only slightly when he saw me as well.

"I know you from somewhere," Charlie squinted at me then cocked his head. "Jane?"

I nodded. It only took a moment for him to take in our costumes and realize where we must be coming from. "Were you at the party? Where's Deanna?" His brow furrowed in concern.

Redvers glanced up and down the hall. "Let's go inside," he suggested gently. Charlie moved into the room, leaving me and Redvers to follow and close the door behind us.

"Where's Deanna?" Charlie asked again as soon as the door was closed. I barely had time to take in the tiny room, furnished with only a bed and a dresser, a threadbare rug tossed over the equally worn carpeting. A small shuttered window let in a little breeze through the slats—I assumed the view was nothing to speak of, tucked as this place was between buildings. If I had to guess, they had a lovely view of the cramped alley below. Charlie took a seat on the bed, and Redvers and I stood awkwardly against the wall, trying not to bump into the sea painting hanging crookedly there.

"Deanna is speaking with the police. Someone died at the party, and she's being questioned," Redvers said.

Charlie said some colorful words, stringing them together in a uniquely American way. "I told her she shouldn't accept that job. That woman—Clara what's-her-name—is just too odd. Something about her isn't right."

"Why are you both here in Venice?" I asked. "You didn't go back to the States after your honeymoon in Egypt?"

Charlie shook his head. "We decided to come to Europe, see if we could find work here." His expressive face looked rueful. "I'm sorry to say we haven't been too successful and we've had to move around a lot. Then we ran out of cash, so we couldn't afford to get the boat ride home."

When I'd met the two, they were newlyweds, having met on the vaudeville circuit in America. Deanna worked as a snake charmer, among other things, and Charlie had been quite artful with cards—a little too artful, truthfully. He'd nearly been caught cheating at the gaming tables in Egypt, and the couple had beat a hasty escape from the hotel. It wouldn't surprise me if his card tricks had been the cause of them being forced to move around.

As though he could read my mind, Charlie gave a rueful chuckle. "I can see what you're thinking, Jane, and you're right. But I've been trying to find more honest work than cheating at cards."

"Deanna mentioned you were trying to get work as a gondolier," I said.

Charlie gave a small shake of the head. "That or tending bar. The trouble is that I don't speak Italian beyond a few basic words, and that seems to be a requirement around here."

I didn't even have to look at Redvers to know he was thinking that Charlie wasn't the sharpest—or most honest—person we'd encountered. But I genuinely liked the couple. I'd intended to keep in touch with them after meeting them in Egypt, but my whirlwind travels, not to mention their own, had kept that from happening.

"We are hopeful that the police will release Deanna after they speak with her, but perhaps you should be prepared in case they don't." Redvers said, steering our conversation toward the purpose of our visit and exchanging a quick glance with me. It was a difficult line to walk—wanting Charlie to be prepared for what might happen but also not wanting to cause him unnecessary panic. It was entirely possible that the *polizia* would release Deanna, but it was equally as possible that they wouldn't.

Charlie seemed to pick up the unspoken thread, his long fingers plucked at the quilt on the bed. "Do you think we'll need a lawyer?"

I knew he was worried about what that would cost. "I don't think so. And if it comes down to that, we'll figure something out." Either Redvers and I or my aunt would foot the bill for a good lawyer.

Charlie looked uncomfortable with my assurances but didn't say anything.

"I think all we can do now is wait and see what happens with the police. We don't know how the man died yet, so it might not even be murder." I said this with conviction, even though I was privately convinced that it *was* murder. If D'Annuzzio had died of natural causes, there would have been no reason to pull Deanna aside and interrogate her.

No, I thought, *Clara was right, and someone at the party killed the man.*

Chapter Seven

We did some further planning before leaving Charlie to wait for his wife's return. There was little else we could do that night, so we left Charlie to fret on his own. Staying wouldn't help him feel any better—not until he saw Deanna, anyway—and I rather felt like we were doing an impression of three sardines in a can, so we bid him good-night and promised to speak with them the next day.

It was less than a ten-minute walk back to our own hotel, so instead of looking for a water taxi or a gondola, we walked the cobblestone path, out of the alley and to a larger path, making our way over the little footbridge crossing the first waterway.

"I'm glad the moon is out, but I do wish these foot-bridges had taller railings," I muttered as we crossed the first one. It had nothing more than a low brick wall between us and the water below. The moon had finally decided to make an appearance, so we were better able to navigate without fear of missing a step and winding up in the canal, but it still made me a little uneasy.

Redvers looked amused. "You sound like your aunt."

I gasped in mock outrage. "How dare you! I can't believe you would say such a thing to your own wife."

Redvers chuckled. "You aren't going to like what I suggest next, then."

My eyes narrowed of their own accord and I made a guess. "You want to walk quite a bit farther than our hotel."

Redvers' answering grin told me I'd been correct, and I sighed. "Lead on."

"You don't even want to know why or where we're going?"

I shook my head. "I imagine it has to do with the events of the evening. And to be fair, walking doesn't sound so bad." I didn't mention that it would carry us away from the bar where my aunt was drinking. I wasn't ready to discuss the evening with her and Lord Hughes just yet, and fortunately, the gown I was wearing was comfortable enough to walk for a while.

Redvers grew serious. "Speaking of wives, I'm concerned for your friend Deanna."

I sighed. "I am, too. We need to find out more about Clara Morton as well as her ex-husband D'Annuzzio."

"Not to mention we need to learn the cause of death." Redvers was leading us along, and I was grateful that he had such an unerring sense of direction, although at times it seemed he wasn't quite sure of our destination. We were crossing numerous footbridges, walking through even more small alleys—some of which we both had to duck a little to pass through, since there were buildings stretching low overhead—and more than once he stopped and looked about before setting off in a slightly altered direction.

"That goes without saying," I said. "And should be our first priority, really. It seems foolish to do much else until we accomplish that."

Redvers stopped once again, and I glanced up, taking in our surroundings. "Are you certain you know where you're taking us?" I thought I recognized the large building on our left. And there was the *campanile* that we'd climbed. "Are we back to St. Mark's Square?"

"We are, actually, but my gamble paid off," he said, nodding toward the piazza we were about to enter. I followed his gesture, and in the moonlight, I could see Clara Morton ambling across the open space, with what appeared to be the cheetah on a leash pacing along beside her. She was followed by a member of what I could only assume was her staff, dressed in the black uniform that all the staff had been wearing. Clara was still wearing the costume from her disastrous party.

Redvers cast a wary eye at the cheetah. We'd had a near-death run-in with a tiger in India, and neither he nor I were keen on the idea of making the acquaintance of another large cat. We'd given the beast a wide berth at the party, but it was now apparent that it hadn't been hired merely as entertainment. I had to assume that this was yet another one of Clara's unusual pets.

But we couldn't turn down the chance to speak with Clara privately. The perfect symmetry of needing to speak with the woman and coming upon her was too good an opportunity to let pass by. Unless Redvers had somehow known she would be here?

"You didn't know she'd be out, did you? Is that why you brought us here?" I murmured as we walked briskly toward the woman, hoping to catch her before she disappeared down an alley or over a bridge. Once she did, it would be nearly impossible to find her—Venice was a series of winding canals and narrow alleyways, punctuated by dead ends. It would be all too easy to lose someone here, something I made a mental note of.

Redvers didn't answer, but he did stifle a smile. I could only assume he'd somehow learned that Clara would be out for an evening stroll.

"Mrs. Morton," Redvers called out once we were in earshot. The woman paused, glancing around, her servant stopping several feet behind her. I wondered if he was required to keep a certain distance from his employer.

To my surprise, Clara waited, but only after staring at us for a long moment with her eyes half shut in a squint, clearly trying to place us even though we'd interacted with her extensively only hours before. Truthfully, I fully expected her to continue walking—even if she'd recognized us immediately, she had no good reason to speak with us, especially after it had become clear in the aftermath of the party that we were friendly with the woman Clara had accused of murdering her ex-husband. I was grateful we weren't going to have to chase Clara down, though, whatever her rationale for waiting. I was certain I would end up falling face-first on the uneven stone if I were forced to run.

While she waited, her cheetah took the opportunity to lie down on the ground, licking a paw before rolling onto its back, apparently quite uninterested in our approach. I was relieved, since it would be less quick to pounce on us from its reclined position.

I could tell my husband was keeping one eye on the animal as well. "Carmine is quite harmless," Clara said when we stopped a respectable distance from her. "Do you want to pet him?"

Both of us shook our heads emphatically, and Clara gave a casual shrug, then passed the leash back to her servant and came to us instead, seeming to understand our reluctance to come near her pet.

"Mrs. Morton," Redvers started to say.

"Please call me Clara. I hate the sound of 'Mrs.' It's so awful, isn't it? And besides I'm quite divorced." She looked us over again. "Who are you, exactly? I assume by your dress that you were at my party."

We reintroduced ourselves, although I had serious doubts about whether the woman would remember our names even for the duration of this conversation. Something told me that Clara's attention was difficult to keep hold of.

"Such a shame that the party had to end." Clara's eyes darted about, like a dragonfly looking for somewhere to land.

Redvers and I made polite noises but didn't comment on that. It was an odd thing to say since the party had ended due to a death—the death of her former husband—and it wasn't the first time she'd mentioned it. I practically bit my tongue in order to keep from commenting on it. I was also very curious why the woman was out this late at night, walking a cheetah of all things, but we needed answers about her dead ex-husband, not her pet cat, so I held my tongue there too.

Holding my tongue was becoming quite the circus act in itself.

"Did the police say anything to you about how D'Annuzzio died?" Redvers asked.

Clara shook her head. "No, they were taking his body somewhere to examine it properly." She paused. "I did hear the *ispettore* say there were some red marks on his neck, though."

I was tempted to ask whether Clara had known that before or after she accused Deanna of murder, since Deanna had sent a knee to the man's groin, not put her hands around his neck, but Redvers continued his own line of questioning. It was just as well, since he was doing a fine job of asking questions without insulting the woman. I wasn't sure I'd be able to do the same.

"Do you have any idea who might have wanted him dead?" Redvers asked.

Clara waved a dismissive hand. "Any number of people."

Redvers raised an eyebrow, and I blinked at the woman several times. "Did *you* have any reason?" Redvers spoke slowly.

"Certainly. That's why I pointed them in the direction of that girl."

My blood quickly heated to boiling at the woman's casual cruelty toward someone she employed. My hands clenched into fists at my side. I wouldn't have thrown a punch or acted out in violence, but Clara noticed my reaction and took a step back.

"Do calm down, Mrs. Wunderly," Clara said, tone dismissive despite her initial reaction. "Nothing bad will happen to her, and I fully intend to pay for a lawyer on her behalf. I simply needed the distraction."

My anger wasn't necessarily assuaged, but this did set me back on my heels. I was completely baffled by Clara Morton. Why would Clara blame another woman, a woman less fortunate than herself? I'd never understood women who didn't support and protect one another, especially as someone who had very much needed support in the past and hadn't received it.

But why would Clara go to the trouble of blaming Deanna for the murder only to hire a lawyer for her? Why throw Deanna to the wolves only to help her later? Would she go through with that promise or simply forget about it once Deanna was out of her sight?

Who on earth *was* this woman?

Chapter Eight

Redvers and I both stared at Clara for a long moment, not saying anything. She glanced between the two of us, then gave an easy shrug. "In any case, the *polizia* have already released that girl." Clara's eyes flitted about the square again before returning to us. "I don't remember her name."

"What reason did *you* have to kill your ex-husband?" Redvers asked, trying to get back on task. I was impressed with his focus, finding my own difficult to recover in the presence of Clara Morton.

"A hundred reasons. His fooling around with other women. Numerous other women, really. The lying, the manipulation, the casual threats." Clara's voice was conversational, as though we were discussing the weather. It was disorienting. "Not to mention the money he was stealing from me." She realized from our faces that what she was saying was unusual at the very least, and more than a little damning. "But there were other people there who had excellent reasons as well." For the first time her tone was defensive.

"Such as?" Redvers pressed.

"Katherine Conrad, Orsola Chini, Ignacio Catral . . .

who else?" Clara ticked the first three off on her fingers, then paused. "Oh yes, Isabella Fontana and her brother, Alonzo." She held up five fingers when she was done.

"That's quite a list," I said.

Clara nodded. "Everyone but Alonzo was at the party."

"And why was D'Annuzzio there if you were divorced?" I asked.

"We're still friends," she said. "And lovers, of course. I simply couldn't have him stealing money from me any longer, and it was far too easy for him to do that while we were married. I also thought it might teach him a lesson, stop his philandering."

I knew my mouth had fallen open, and I closed it slowly, blinking several times as well.

Clara laughed, a deep throaty sound. "You should see your face. You'll likely be shocked to know that we were both sleeping with all of the people on that list, on occasion. Although some of the affairs happened many years ago, and not since. That I know of, anyway."

Behind Clara there was rustling, and we all turned to see that her servant was trying to keep hold of the cheetah's leash while avoiding the animal's sharp claws as it rolled toward him and swatted at his pant leg.

"Carmine is restless. He needs a nightly walk to burn off energy," Clara said. "I'm done here. Feel free to come by the palazzo tomorrow for a drink, though. You amuse me."

With that, she turned, her diaphanous costume twirling in the moonlight, once again revealing everything beneath. She took her cheetah's leash from the beleaguered servant—his face could not have looked more relieved if he'd tried. Then the three of them left, quickly disappearing over a footbridge and out of sight.

Redvers and I simply looked at one another, speechless, until the moon ducked behind another scudding cloud.

"Let's get back to our hotel. We have a lot to talk about," Redvers said.

"That is quite the understatement, my dear."

We were both exhausted by the time we got back to the hotel, both from the evening's events and the late hour, so we saved any conversation until the next morning, dropping into our bed instead. I was dead asleep as soon as my head hit the pillow, not even remembering whether or not I dreamt when I awoke the next morning. It was quite late when I did finally wake up, my eyes puffy in the bathroom mirror. I wandered through the little sitting room to find my husband on our balcony, enjoying a cup of tea.

I dropped into the chair opposite him, tucking my robe a little tighter against the chill rolling in from the sea, although the sun was quickly burning the nebulous mist off the canal below. I reached for the pot that I instinctively knew held coffee—my husband wouldn't dare order breakfast without it, he knew me too well for that—and poured myself a cup. "Was Millie here already?"

"She was. And had quite a few things to say about the hour you were sleeping until."

I hadn't heard a sound, thankfully, I'd been that sound asleep. "That's no surprise. I suppose she wanted to know what we learned." I took a sip of the dark coffee and nearly purred in pleasure. Or perhaps I actually did purr, judging by Redvers' amused look.

"Do you want some time alone with your coffee?" he asked.

I smiled at him over my cup. "No, you can stay. For now, anyway."

"As long as I'm not interrupting anything." He gave his head a fond shake, then returned to the subject of my aunt. "I'm still baffled as to how Millie knows Clara Morton. They seem . . . unlikely friends."

"Another understatement. I haven't the faintest idea how Millie came to know her and why she would pursue a friendship with Clara, given the outrageous outfits, equally outrageous parties, and the scandalous affairs with heavens knows how many people." My aunt had a few of her own secrets, but I was certain that they paled in comparison to Clara Morton's. Millie was also entirely buttoned-up and so allergic to scandal that I was mystified by her attraction to an acquaintance who was her diametric opposite. If anything, I would have expected Mille to deny even knowing Clara Morton.

Both women were something of a mystery, although Clara certainly received top billing.

There was a knock at the door, and Redvers and I exchanged a glance. "The Parks, I would assume," Redvers said. "I'll let them in if you want to get dressed."

I looked into my coffee cup mournfully, and Redvers laughed. "Or you can stay dressed as you are so the love of your life doesn't get cold."

He went to the door before I could assure him that *he* was the love of my life, even if coffee was a very close second.

I grabbed the pot and my cup and settled myself into a small upholstered chair in the sitting room just as Charlie and Deanna came in. Neither so much as blinked at the fact that I was wearing a robe and pajamas, not yet dressed for the day.

"Good for you," Deanna said without preamble. "I wish I'd been able to get as much sleep." She rubbed her eyes, and I gave her a sympathetic smile.

"What time did they finally release you?" I asked.

"Four in the morning, I think?"

Charlie nodded. "It must have been about then. You got home about thirty minutes after that."

"Did you learn anything from the *polizia*?" Redvers asked. He settled himself into the small chair next to mine, and the

Parks squeezed together on the little love seat. Our sitting room was at least larger than their bedroom—it would have been impossible for the four of us to comfortably have a meeting in their hotel quarters. It had been hard enough the night before with only the three of us.

"I learned zilch. All they did was ask me the same questions over and over." Deanna sighed heavily. "I'm relieved they let me go, but Fizzoli said I wasn't to leave the city."

"That's fairly standard," Redvers said. I could tell he was trying to reassure her, but I also knew that she was not out of the woods, not by a long shot. The *polizia* could come for her again at any time, and in fact, I thought it likely that they would.

"That may be so," Deanna said. "But I'm not holding my breath. My guess is they'll arrest me." Her tone was unhappy, but she wasn't panicking, not yet anyway. I'd always liked her practical nature—she was fun-loving and a bit whimsical, but at heart she was a very pragmatic woman.

"I sent a message to my employers this morning. I'm hoping they can put us in touch with someone that can fill us in on both the murder and what the *polizia* are up to," Redvers said.

Charlie looked confused, but Deanna looked amused. "At the bank you purported to work for?"

Redvers gave a rueful grin. "Ah, yes. I'd nearly forgotten about my job at the bank."

When I first met Redvers in Egypt, a desk job at a bank had been his cover story, and he'd stuck to it for the entirety of his time there. I'd smelled a rat immediately, but it looked as though Charlie had swallowed my husband's story wholesale. "You don't work for a bank?" Charlie asked.

Redvers shook his head. "That was just a cover, I'm afraid. I work for the British government."

Truthfully, I was surprised he admitted to even that much. My husband liked to keep his cards very close to his chest, and that included the nature of his employment. It was lucky for me that I was very good at prying those cards loose.

"That's great and all," Charlie said after a beat. "But we're American. How is the British government going to help us in Italy?"

"They won't," I cut in. "But we will."

Chapter Nine

Redvers nodded his agreement at my assurance of help. "Hopefully my employer can get us some inside information, but beyond that, it is up to Jane and me to investigate and figure out who actually killed D'Annuzzio."

Deanna blinked her eyes rapidly, wiping a finger quickly at one corner. "I'm sorry, I never cry, I'm just so tired. And I'm so relieved that you're both here."

"I'm glad too," I said kindly, then got down to business. "What do you know about Clara Morton, and how did you get a job with her?"

Deanna sat up in her seat, sharpening her focus. "I met Clara at a festival, either the Festival of the Redeemer or the Venice Biennale, I can't quite remember which. In any case, we were both Americans and she was so . . . well, *different* than anyone I'd met before. We talked for a while, and when she found out what I did for work, she hired me for her parties."

"This isn't the first party of Clara's that you've worked at, then."

Deanna shook her head. "No, not by a long shot." She squinted her eyes. "This might be the fourth or fifth? I mostly read tarot cards at her events, but sometimes she has me do other things, often involving her pet boa constrictor Anoraxas."

Redvers' lips twisted into a grimace, and he shifted uncomfortably in his seat. Deanna noticed and nodded. "Snakes aren't for everyone, but I'm very good with them."

This is what I remembered about her from the first time we met. "What type of snake does Clara have?"

"She has several. Anoraxas is the boa constrictor, but she also has a viper and an asp."

"All deadly," I said.

Deanna nodded. "To varying degrees."

"Do you think one of them could have killed D'Annuzzio?" I asked.

"That occurred to me as well," Deanna said. "It's certainly possible. Although it's unlikely to have been Anoraxas. He'd just eaten a rabbit earlier in the day, and boas don't have a lot of reason to kill a human unless they're hungry."

Even I shuddered at that, and I didn't have the debilitating fear of snakes that my husband did.

Speaking of, Redvers had gone stock-still. I could tell he was attempting to hide his reaction to Deanna's casual statement about the snakes, so I didn't look at him, since I didn't want to draw attention to him, but I did sneak my hand into his and gave it a squeeze.

He would need a moment to gather himself, so I continued asking the questions. "Besides Anoraxas, were any of the other . . . animals at the party?" Perhaps if I referred to the snakes as something less threatening, Redvers would be able to breathe more easily.

Deanna shook her head. "The rest were all secured downstairs. There's a whole second level, sort of like a basement, where the bedrooms are. She uses one of those for the snakes. Then there's her cheetah and the monkey, which have entirely different rooms because they don't get along."

I hadn't even known about the monkey. "That's . . . a lot."

"I've never met anyone like her." Deanna paused and glanced at Charlie. "I suppose I'm not surprised that she blamed me for the murder. She was awfully sore when I kicked her ex-husband that morning, which honestly shocked me since they're divorced and he's a louse."

I'd nearly forgotten that Deanna had assaulted the man. "Was D'Annuzzio staying at the palazzo? He's Italian, isn't he? And Clara is American?" I wanted to make sure I was remembering everything correctly.

"Nah, D'Annuzzio wasn't staying there. He *is* Italian like you said, from Rome, I think? Anyway, he has his own place in town. And yes, Clara is American."

Redvers seemed to reanimate. "Was D'Annuzzio there often, do you know?"

Deanna shrugged. "I was only at the palazzo on the days that she threw parties. She paid well enough that we were able to mostly get by on that." She glanced at Charlie again and smiled. "Which is good, cause Charlie's Italian is awful." It was said in a teasing tone, clearly meant as fun, but Charlie smiled tightly. His arms were crossed and pulled tight against his chest. The man was clearly unhappy, not at all the jovial and easygoing man I'd met before, but it was hard to say exactly what was bothering him. I would have loved to say he was simply worried about his wife being arrested for murder, but my gut told me it was something more than that.

I also knew we'd have to get Charlie alone to pry it out of him.

Deanna frowned a little at Charlie, then turned back to us and continued on. "D'Annuzzio was there every time I was. He was a really jealous man. More than once I've seen him scream and yell about who Clara was spending time with." The emphasized way that Deanna said the last part made me believe this was a euphemism for having an affair.

The new Jane, the one so happy with her marriage to her current husband, couldn't understand how or why a woman would put up with such behavior from a man. Especially a man who was her ex-husband. The old Jane, the one that had been trapped in an abusive marriage, had a better inkling of how that might happen. But Clara Morton was wealthy and could escape at any time—I hadn't been so lucky. The only reason I'd been freed from my prison was because of the Great War and my husband's death.

I pushed the unpleasant thoughts from my mind. I hated reliving that part of my life.

"Did he ever touch you before?" I asked.

Deanna shook her head. "I always steered clear of him—gave him a real wide berth. But he cornered me in Anoraxas' room when I was getting him out of his cage. Clara must have been right outside the door, since she saw it all." Deanna frowned, considering. "Actually, I wouldn't be surprised if that rat knew Clara was there and did it just to make her jealous."

My friend and I looked at each other, and I wondered for just a heartbeat whether Deanna had in fact killed D'Annuzzio. But only for a moment.

"We saw Clara last night," I said. "She said that her tarot card reader informed her that her husband would be killed by someone close to her." Deanna frowned, and I pressed on. "You didn't say this to her?"

"No, what a strange thing for her to claim. I read her cards that night, just once, and it was about being careful with money." Deanna shook her head. "Why would she make that up?"

I looked at my friend and murmured some agreement. But I couldn't help but wonder which woman was lying.

Chapter Ten

Deanna answered a few more questions, then she and Charlie took their leave. They both looked exhausted, and I hoped that they would be able to go back to their hotel room and get some rest. They would need it—I suspected that the police were far from done with Deanna Parks.

Once they were gone, I tucked into my breakfast. I'd quickly learned that the Italians normally eschewed a large breakfast, instead contenting themselves with tiny cups of espresso and a pastry, sometimes eaten standing up at a café counter. This suited me fine, since their pastries were delicious, and Redvers had ordered several. I bit into the simple buttery croissant that I'd left on my plate, washing it down with my now-lukewarm American coffee. The flaky layers were perfection, and I immediately began eyeing up one of the others. The pistachio-filled croissant looked especially appealing this morning, and since we'd done so much walking the night before, I didn't think a second pastry would hurt.

Redvers sank into the chair across from me. "Do you think she could have done it?"

I sighed, sliding the pistachio croissant onto my plate and tearing a piece off. I popped it into my mouth and chewed while I considered his question. It did take some doing to focus on the case and not the heavenly pastry I was enjoying, but I managed it. "It crossed my mind for a brief second. But I truly don't think that she did." Redvers looked skeptical, and I shook my head. "Do I think she's capable of it? Certainly. But she didn't have enough motive. Certainly not as much as some of the other people that Clara mentioned."

"A reasonable conclusion," Redvers said. "And one I came to myself."

I pulled a face at him. "Then why challenge me on it?"

Redvers grinned. "I just wanted to make certain we were thinking along the same lines."

I rolled my eyes, then dropped it. "I'm loath to admit it, but this is exciting. I was a bit bored back in London." Redvers' eyebrows went up, and I shrugged. "It's true."

"Why didn't you say something?" he asked.

"Because we truly did need some rest after our exploits in India. But then time started to drag on."

Redvers chuckled. "I felt the same."

I playfully tossed my napkin at him, and without a breeze this time, it made contact. "Why didn't *you* say something?"

This time he gave a casual shrug. "For the exact same reason."

We regarded each other for a long moment, both of us clearly amused at ourselves. "We need to do a better job of not tiptoeing around one another," I said.

"Agreed," Redvers said. He tipped his head to the side. "Is this the kind of excitement you've been missing? A murder investigation?"

I thought about that. "I hate to admit that it might be." I hurried to add, "Not that I want anyone to die or be murdered. Nor have a friend accused of it."

"Of course not," Redvers reassured me.

That was as much as I was willing to admit, even to myself. It was too morbid to continue examining the idea that I might enjoy investigating murders. I asked a question instead. "Do you have any inkling about which of the two women is lying?"

Redvers looked grim. "I suspect it's Clara. Deanna looked genuinely confused. But I wouldn't bet real money on my being correct."

I sighed. I wouldn't bet money on it either. "What should our next steps be?"

I was relieved that Redvers let the personal matters drop. "It's likely to be at least several hours before I hear back from my employers. In the meantime, I think we should start interviewing the list of partygoers that Clara mentioned. The ones with the strongest connections to D'Annuzzio," Redvers said.

"That's quite a list," I said. I wasn't optimistic that a single one of them would tell us the truth and said as much.

"They won't, but it will give us a starting point for picking apart the lies."

I nodded. "Who should we start with? And how will we find them?"

Redvers didn't have a chance to answer before a pounding on our door interrupted us.

We exchanged a look, and I sighed again. I already knew who it was, without so much as opening that door. Redvers stood, crossed the sitting room, and let Aunt Millie and Lord Hughes in.

"Good morning, Aunt Millie, Lord Hughes," I said.

Millie didn't bother responding. "Have we learned anything since we last spoke?" She took a seat in the love seat that the Parks had just vacated. Lord Hughes gave us both an apologetic look before joining her. "You're still not dressed yet, Jane," Millie said, lips pursed.

I ignored the jab, looking sadly at the other half of the

croissant. There was little chance I'd be able to finish it now until after my aunt was gone. "How much did Redvers share with you this morning?"

Millie gave my husband a dark look. "He said we should come back once you were up so that we could discuss it together. I wasn't sure whether we should just come back this afternoon at that rate."

I nearly smirked, since normally Millie focused solely on my own foibles, but this time she was sending some ire my husband's way as well. A glance his way, however, told me he was completely unbothered. I wished I could maintain such equanimity around my opinionated aunt.

"We ran into Clara last night, walking her pet cheetah quite late at night," I said, focusing on the task at hand—discussing what we knew so far about the murder. "She gave us a list of . . . friends that might have a motive to kill D'Annuzzio." I decided not to scandalize my aunt by sharing the true nature of Clara's relationship with the people on that list. I myself was a little shocked by how open Clara had been about her affairs and with whom she'd had them, and I considered myself a modern woman. My aunt might keel right over if we told her.

While I was explaining this, I hoped Redvers was devising a plan to dissuade my aunt from trying to "help" us investigate this murder. Millie meant well and was even quite useful at times, but she was mostly like a bull with a red flag waved before it. She had a tendency to charge in without thought, and that wasn't always useful for getting people to cough up their secrets.

Millie nodded, as though this was not new information. I cocked my head, realizing that she'd never actually explained in detail how she met Clara—her explanations had been vague at best. "How *did* you and Clara meet? And how were you invited to her party in Venice?"

My aunt pursed her lips as though she was going to admonish me instead of answering, but a gentle poke in the side from Lord Hughes' elbow, and with a sigh, she launched into an explanation instead. I shot Hughes a smile to thank him, and he winked in return.

"We first met when Clara was very young, back in Boston," Millie said. "Her father and my husband knew each other through something—I can't remember what, exactly. In any case, Clara was an unusual girl, even then. She had an extraordinary sense of dress and was quite socially awkward." Millie paused, remembering. "Several years passed, and I didn't see her again until about a year ago in England. James and I went to a ball, held by . . ." Millie paused, perhaps noticing that my eyes had begun to glaze over in anticipation of hearing every last detail about a long-past ball. "Very well, Jane. I'll get to the point. We saw each other again, and Clara said she remembered my kindness from those earlier years, and that I should come see her in Venice. She has a renowned reputation for throwing the most fantastical parties."

That much I could attest to, having been to one.

"When we received an invitation in the mail a few weeks ago, we decided to come. It worked out neatly since you two were already here." She looked at Redvers. "It's such a shame your aunts couldn't join us."

Redvers' eyes widened in alarm, and I hid a smile. I adored his aunts Carolyn and Marie, but all three aunts together would have made this investigation challenging indeed. All three of them had an unmatched interest in assisting with our inquiries.

Perhaps "meddling" would be a better word.

"Now," Millie barreled on. "What can we do to help? I assume we need to speak with this list of Clara's friends," Aunt Millie said. "To divide and conquer is probably best."

"It would be most helpful if you could help us learn where they're all staying. We haven't been able to figure that out yet," Redvers said.

I slid him a sideways glance. We hadn't even started to look into that, yet he made it sound as if we were failing at the job.

"And we will also need to find the best lawyer in Venice for Deanna."

Aunt Millie nodded. "She'll need a good one." Millie stood, and Lord Hughes followed suit. "We'll work on that, as well as where these so-called friends of Clara are staying. We will let you know what we learn."

I was impressed that Millie hadn't argued about either of these tasks. And equally impressed with my husband for so quickly coming up with a direction to push her in that wouldn't interfere with our own inquiries.

"Thank you, Millie," Redvers said. "It's a relief to know we can count on you."

My aunt and Lord Hughes left, full of purpose. Once the door had closed behind them, I raised an eyebrow. "Do you think you might have been overdoing it?"

Redvers grinned. "Perhaps. But she's happy and out of our hair."

And we could get down to business.

Chapter Eleven

I quickly dressed in a forest green day dress with a silky cream tie at my chest and matching band at the bottom. I dithered for a moment about my shoes, finally deciding on the most practical pair that were both comfortable for walking and could withstand a little water if they happened to get wet.

Venice was quite damp—both because of the time of year and because the entire city was at or below sea level. Who knew when a canal might overflow? The gondolas and water taxis also made me a little nervous. I hadn't asked, but I did wonder if they ever tipped passengers into the murky, and likely quite frigid, water.

We reached the side of the canal, but instead of setting off to where we might hail a water taxi or a gondola, my husband casually stepped into a small motorized boat that was tied up only a short distance from our hotel.

"Are we stealing boats now?" I asked. "I do think the owners will object."

Redvers grinned, then reached a hand up to help me into the small craft. It was made of wood, with reasonably comfortable seats considering they were nothing more than wooden benches, and room for not much more than three people. "I thought it would be more convenient while we are here to have our own means of transportation," Redvers said. "Especially since we have an investigation to attend to."

"That's true," I replied, settling my skirt around my legs and tucking it in against the wind. "But that doesn't answer who this belongs to."

"A local," Redvers said as he unwrapped the mooring rope from the wooden pole standing sentry next to the side of the canal and went to the back, starting the engine and settling into the seat next to the motor.

I wrinkled my nose at him. "That isn't an answer, and you well know it."

Redvers chuckled as he piloted the little boat down the canal, careful not to use too much speed. There were strict rules about boating on the canals and how fast a boat was allowed to go. "I'm not trying to be difficult, I promise, darling. I simply don't know the fellow's full name—I only know he was willing to give up his boat's use for a decent price."

I gave him a mock shake of the head and settled into my seat to enjoy the ride. Once we were far enough from the hotel that I felt safe Aunt Millie wouldn't be within earshot, I followed up with another question. "Where exactly are we going? Have you learned where someone is staying?"

Redvers shook his head. "I wasn't up *that* early. I simply figured that the crowd Clara Morton is running with would be staying at some of Venice's finer hotels. We're headed to the most expensive one now."

It was a sensible plan, and I told my husband as much. I spent the next several minutes enjoying the view—it was a very different experience of the city from the water itself instead of walking the paths and footbridges. We were passing between buildings I would never have seen otherwise, the front entrances leading directly to the water. I assumed many of the private entrances I was seeing held boats on the other side, since that was the primary means of transportation here. The buildings' foundations were crusted green and black where the water lapped, and I idly wondered if some of what I saw were barnacles, like might be found on the hull of a ship.

Redvers turned our little boat cautiously into the Grand Canal, and I found myself gripping my bench seat, even though I fully trusted my husband's ability to navigate nearly any situation. There was a lot more traffic on the water here, though, and our little craft rocked with the wakes left by other boats as he zipped us into our lane of travel. After only a minute or two more, he turned down a side canal, slowed to a stop, and tied us off at a wooden pole, then stepped from the boat and reached out a hand to help me step out as well.

"Excellent piloting, my dear," I said, brushing my skirt out to remove any wrinkles from the ride.

Redvers winked in reply.

We made our way along the waterfront, turning left before the intersection with the Grand Canal—there was no walkway along that waterway, so we would approach the hotel from the pedestrian entrance. We strolled through the doors and into the lobby of the hotel, doing our best to look as though we belonged, which meant I had to keep myself from gawking at the opulent décor. The ceilings were still characteristically low—as all ceilings were in Venice—but the rich wood, marble, and gilding made quite an impact.

Redvers was skilled at charming strangers, so I let him take the lead. He asked the clerk behind the desk whether our friends had checked in yet, using his snootiest "I belong here" voice, while still seeming warm and friendly—it was a difficult balance to strike, but he pulled it off with aplomb. Yet despite this, we struck out; none of the individuals on Clara's list were staying here.

We made our way to the next up-scale hotel, and the next

one after that, and one by one the clerk checked the register and told us that our "friends" had not arrived or at least were not staying at this particular hotel. It took some doing, but we finally hit pay dirt—Ignacio Catral was registered at the fourth hotel we inquired at. The clerk wouldn't give us Ignacio's room number, but he did call up to the room to see if the man wanted to see us. Redvers looked completely unbothered, but I was holding my breath. Would Catral reveal that we were not, in fact, dear friends of his and get us ejected from the hotel? I supposed it didn't matter all that much, since we'd already learned the others weren't staying here, but even still, I would not enjoy the embarrassment, so I did my best to maintain a neutral expression.

But my worry was all for nothing, yet again. The clerk hung up the phone, and smiled at Redvers. "Mr. Catral says you may come up. He is in room sixteen."

We thanked the man, then crossed the lobby to step into a diminutive elevator. The operator closed the ornate metal accordion door and asked us what floor we wanted. I was impressed that there even was a working elevator—it was quite the luxury in Venice, from what I'd seen. Every other building I'd stepped inside had only stairs leading up, which made sense to me. The city's buildings were stacked on wooden pylons that were driven down into the sea floor; it hardly seemed a stable base to begin with. And everything had to be brought to the city by boat, so both building materials and regular supplies were likely difficult to transport into the city. I didn't imagine that the makings for an elevator—shaft, car, and all—were commonly floated in.

We were dropped off on the fourth floor and knocked on the door to room sixteen. After a few beats, during which Redvers raised his hand to knock again, the door was swung open by a woman in a simple maid's uniform. She gave us a long look with her dark eyes, then tipped her head, gesturing for us to follow her.

The sitting room we stepped into was far larger and grander than ours, although it was still smaller than what one might find on the mainland. Even still, it was elaborately appointed, with rich velvet drapery and dark flocked wallpaper. Ignacio Catral sat—or rather sprawled—on the upholstered couch, a finely carved wooden guitar propped beside him.

He looked us up and down, then dismissed the maid. We all stared at each other in silence until she'd left the room, which she did slowly and dramatically, clearly peeved to have been told to leave.

"I thought perhaps you were the *polizia*. But no, you are strangers. *Interesante*."

I opened my mouth to ask Catral why he'd let us in if he thought we were the police, but Redvers beat me to it. "Why would you invite the *polizia* up?" Redvers asked, taking a seat in a chair opposite Catral's love seat. I sat down in the chair next to my husband, watching Catral curiously.

At Redvers' question he spread his arms. "I have nothing to hide from the *polizia*. If they want to speak with me, I speak."

It was the type of answer that sounded impressive but didn't actually have any substance to it. Redvers nodded, then pivoted. "Why are you willing to speak with us, then? Since we aren't the *polizia*?"

Ignacio gave a small shrug. "I am curious about what you want. Any friends to Clara are friends to me as well." He picked up his guitar and picked at the strings, sounding a few notes. I wondered if this was nerves or simply how he operated.

"Are you a musician?" I asked. Stroking an ego was an easy way to warm a person up before asking tougher questions. "You seem to be very good with a guitar."

"*Si*," Ignacio nearly crowed, then narrowed his dark eyes

at me with a smile. "You are wise, *senorita,* to understand so quickly a true musician."

I didn't speak Spanish, but I knew Catral was addressing me as though I was not married to the man sitting beside me. A glance at Redvers told me that he was registering this as well and was quite unamused by it.

But if my instincts were correct, Ignacio was more likely to spill information to me, rather than another man, especially if I stroked his ego. "You must play something for me," I said, leaning forward. "I would love to hear it."

The words were barely out of my mouth before Catral began strumming in earnest, singing along in Spanish to whatever song or ballad it was that he was playing. I didn't know much about music, but from what I could tell, the man was reasonably good at what he was doing. I bobbed my head along, not actually paying much attention to the song but doing my best to look as though I were enjoying it immensely. Out of the corner of my eye I could see that Redvers was doing his best not to roll his eyes at this display, but Ignacio only had eyes on me, so he missed the irritation on my husband's face.

When Catral finished his song with a flourish, I clapped boisterously. "That was the most beautiful thing I've ever heard," I told him. Was it sincere? Hardly. Did the man know that? Absolutely not, because he beamed at my praise.

"Has Clara Morton heard you play so beautifully?" I asked.

He sighed sadly. "Clara does not have the same *apreciación* that you do." He wrinkled his nose. "She only cares for paintings, bah." Ignacio waved a hand, as though he were wafting away a bad smell.

"She is missing out," I said. Next to me Redvers stifled a laugh, so I hurried on. "How long have you known Clara?"

Ignacio's face twisted into petulance. "Ah, so this is why you are here. It is not to hear my playing, it is to know about Clara." He set the guitar down at his feet and crossed his arms over his chest, clearly pouting like a child. He was wearing a pair of dark trousers with suspenders over nothing more than a white undershirt, which strained at the biceps now that his arms were crossed. Ignacio Catral was a handsome man, slender but muscular, with thick, wavy black hair and a jawline to rival Redvers. I imagined that he would have no trouble finding women to fawn over him, although I wondered how many were willing to put up with this type of childish display.

Would Clara put up with it, find it charming? Perhaps he had a different persona for her, since it had to be difficult to find women as wealthy as Clara Morton. And judging by the room where Ignacio was staying and his stated profession as a musician, I doubted he was the one paying for this room. No, I would wager my own money that Clara Morton was footing this bill.

I expected him to ignore my question after his little display, but his face soon cleared and he answered anyway. "In truth, I have known Clara's husband, D'Annuzzio, much longer than I have known Clara. D'Annuzzio wrote such beautiful words, and when he asked me to write music for one of his poems after hearing me play, it filled my heart. That was how we came to know each other."

Redvers and I both shifted in our seats, and I kept my eye on Ignacio's hands. Catral was a fine musician, but we had a list of people to speak with today, and I was hoping that he wouldn't pick up his guitar to demonstrate more of his musical skill for us. One song was about all I was willing to sit through. I breathed a small sigh of relief when he left his instrument where it was and kept talking instead.

"Christopher paid me well for my music, and we have

worked together many times since then." Ignacio cocked his head. "I refused to go to bed with him, though. Despite his persistence."

I didn't know how to respond to this entirely unexpected and unsolicited information, opening and closing my mouth twice before Redvers took over. "Clara seemed to think that you had."

Ignacio sat up taller, indignant. "That woman, she thinks she knows everything, but she lives in a fantasy." He paused, considering. "Or perhaps Christopher told her that lie."

"Did Christopher lie often?" I asked.

Ignacio gave a slight shrug of his shoulders. "They both did."

I hated liars and couldn't imagine continuing a relationship of any kind with someone that lied so casually, even a friendship. But perhaps it was different when your livelihood was tied up with that person. Or perhaps it had to do with the fact that the people under discussion had a great deal of money. Was there anything money couldn't buy, including friendship?

"Do you know who may have wanted him dead?" Redvers asked.

"Anyone who knew him, I think," Ignacio said. "Except me, of course. He was generous with me, paid for this room." A grimace. "I suppose I will have to move now that he is dead, since Clara will not be so generous." Seeming to realize how this sounded, he made a noise and changed course. "But more important, of course, I will no longer have the pleasure of writing music to match Christopher's words. It is sad, a very sad thing that has happened."

We asked a few more questions and then excused ourselves, waiting until we were out on the cobblestone street before discussing anything. There was a small square only a short distance from the doors we'd exited, and we walked to it, standing dead center and glancing around. At one corner there was a small café, and I took Redvers' hand and led him in that direction.

"Haven't you had enough coffee this morning?" He shook his head, then muttered. "I don't even know why I'm asking that."

"Honestly, dear. What a silly question," I said with a laugh.

There was a small iron table with chairs on the sidewalk outside and I planted myself in one of them. Redvers glanced around the piazza, then sat in the opposite chair. A waiter came and took my order for an espresso with a side of cream, while Redvers opted to order nothing for himself but a glass of water. Once the waiter left with our requests, we jumped in.

"Ignacio Catral is . . . quite the character," Redvers said.

"That's a polite way of putting it," I replied with a chuckle. "I'm not sure we learned anything useful, except that he doesn't seem to have a motive." At Redvers' look, I waved a hand and continued on. "Motive that we know of *yet*. The most interesting part, to me anyway, was D'Annuzzio paying for Catral's hotel room."

"So he says."

I nodded, acknowledging his point, then cocked my head. "Interesting that Catral called both D'Annuzzio and Clara liars, though. Of course, everything we're told by any one of these people could be a lie and should be treated like one. Which will make uncovering the murderer all the more difficult." The waiter brought my coffee and I added a hefty dollop of the cream, then took a careful sip, not wanting to burn my tongue. I actually enjoyed the taste of espresso, although in a much less concentrated amount than the locals.

Redvers looked a bit wistful as he watched me over the top of his water glass. "I do wish we'd get word that D'Annuzzio died of natural causes," he said with a sigh once the waiter retreated again. "We could go back to having a normal honeymoon."

"It would be nice, darling, but I think it's unlikely. Men of D'Annuzzio's age don't typically drop dead at a party. He couldn't have been more than, what, forty years old? And there are also the marks around his neck. I've never known someone to choke themselves."

Redvers cocked a sardonic eyebrow, then gave his head a little shake, obviously deciding to leave my brilliant observation alone. "We should swing past our hotel and see if we have any messages," he said. "I'd like to have a more definitive cause of death to work with."

"After that who should we try and speak with?" I asked.

Redvers glanced at his watch. "I think by then it will be time for lunch, and after *that* we should swing by Clara Morton's place for that cocktail she mentioned."

I frowned. "That's awfully early for a cocktail, don't you think?"

A teasing light lit Redvers' eyes. "Can't you go straight from coffee to cocktail?"

I laughed and agreed to his plan. He already knew the answer to that.

Chapter Twelve

The stop at our hotel desk proved fruitful since there was a telegram waiting for Redvers. He tore it open and passed his eyes over it quickly while I tapped my foot. I thought about reading it over his shoulder, but I'd seen enough to know it was a short missive—he'd be done before I could even scoot around behind him and leverage myself for a view.

He let the paper drop to his side and cocked his head. "Well?" I asked, then spoke again when the pause went on a beat too long. "You're clearly thinking, and I recommend you let me do it with you."

"Or what?" he asked, clearly amused. He passed the paper to me and I read it quickly without giving him a response.

It was my turn to let the paper drop. "Interesting."

"Very," Redvers agreed. "D'Annuzzio was poisoned, but they are not sure with what."

"How can they know he was poisoned but not the method used?"

"I'll telegram and find out, but it's likely a study of the tissue during the autopsy showed some necrosis or abnormality."

I didn't need to think any harder about that. "Do you think we'll find out the type of poison once they're finished with the tests?" There was such a wide range of things that a person could be poisoned with that I hated to even speculate. I knew what my fear was, though.

"We won't learn from the police, obviously. But yes, there is someone here that we can get information from, according to that." He gestured to the telegram in my hand.

I nodded, still worried about what the poison might be. "I'm worried," I started to say, then paused, trying to parse out the best way to explain my feelings. Redvers put a hand on my shoulder and nodded.

"You're concerned that it was done with a snake?" Redvers asked. It was precisely what I'd been thinking, and I nodded. "I am as well," he said. "It would not bode well for your friend Deanna."

I bit my lip, then frowned. "The marks on his neck are strange, though. A snake with poisonous venom would bite, not strangle."

"Unless he . . . enjoyed that type of thing and the marks aren't snake related."

My eyes got very wide. "I had not considered that."

"There's no reason you should have." Redvers glanced around the lobby. It was deserted, except for the clerk. "Let's find lunch and then talk to Clara. We have plenty of things we can ask her about before we talk to the others on her list."

I nodded. "And maybe we'll get some truthful answers." Although we both knew how unlikely that was.

We left our boat moored where it was for the moment and walked to an area one canal over where there was a collection of small restaurants along the water. We opted to sit inside, since the sun had disappeared behind a cloud bank and without it beating down on us the day felt downright cold. Redvers ordered the *risotto al nero di seppia*—risotto with cuttlefish ink, and I opted for the tamer sounding *polenta e schie*, which consisted of small shrimp on a bed of polenta. Both were delicious—I dared a taste of Redvers' inky black meal—and we were wiping our plates clean with crusty bread before long at all. We refused the suggestion of dessert, although I did pause at the mention of espresso, regretfully shaking my head in the end and opting to get back to work instead.

We got back into the boat and headed off to Clara's, opting to moor at the same landing we'd used during our first visit to the palazzo rather than on a side canal. The entrance in the light of day was more run-down and less mysterious than it had seemed in the dark. The ivy clinging to the front of the building appeared to be chewing through the brick and marble, and the landing area needed some serious restoration work as well. Redvers used the cast-iron door knocker on the heavy wooden door, and it was answered moments later by the servant we'd seen walking with Clara the night before, again dressed entirely in black. He nodded, seeming to recognize us.

"Madam Clara is sitting for a portrait at the moment." He gestured for us to follow him down the short hall and into the cavernous room the party had been held in, our footsteps echoing a bit on the black and white marble tile beneath us. "If you could wait here," he gestured to where we stood before trekking across the large room and disappearing through a doorway.

While he was gone, I took the opportunity to take a good look around, although I didn't wander much farther than where the man had left us. In the daylight I could see that this room had clearly been restored, unlike the canal-side façade and the garden at the back. In fact, the room may have been completely redone, not just restored, judging by the uniformity of the gorgeous—and modern—tile work. But why Clara would choose to fix up only select parts of the palazzo instead of the entire building was beyond me. Unless she liked the run-down façade as it was?

The servant returned moments later. "Follow me," he said.

I very quickly guessed that we were being led out to the garden. Sure enough, we followed the servant directly across from where we stood, through a door, down a set of stairs and into the garden, where we found Clara lounging in the nude on a low crumbling wall. A woman was standing at an easel, painting the figure before her—she didn't so much as look at us when we appeared.

"I vaguely remember you two," Clara said after flicking a glance our way. "Why are you here?"

"You invited us," Redvers said wryly.

"Did I? Well in that case, welcome." This was all delivered from the exact same position. I shouldn't have been surprised that Clara was entirely unembarrassed by her nudity—she had, after all, been wearing a completely see-through costume at her party the night before, which she then wore while striding boldly through the city, flaunting her assets. The woman obviously didn't care who saw her, or how much of her they saw.

A small part of me envied this about Clara, although I would never do the same even if I found myself in her shoes. I could wish for a bit of her confidence, though.

Glancing around, it suddenly struck me that this was where D'Annuzzio was found dead the night before, and I couldn't stop my face from telegraphing my shock. I tried to rearrange it before Clara noticed, but I wasn't quick enough.

"You are easily shocked," Clara said casually. "I don't know your name, what is it?"

Redvers and I both reintroduced ourselves for what was

probably the third time. Clara frowned, appearing to search for a connection but coming up short. "How do I know you?"

"You appear to know my Aunt Millie."

"Oh, Millie!" Clara crowed. "I do so *love* that woman."

I'd never before in my life met a person who had this reaction to my aunt. I was still mystified as to why Lord Hughes had married her—and actually seemed happy for having done so. "Uh, she's quite fond of you as well," I stuttered. I didn't know how else to respond.

I looked at my husband, whose eyes were darting around the garden. I immediately knew what he was looking for. "Clara, are your snakes out and about?" I asked.

"Oh no, they're in their cages upstairs. Why do you ask?"

Redvers visibly relaxed, although he still avoided looking directly at our hostess. I appreciated his discretion, although I doubted our hostess even noticed.

"Just curious," I said. I stepped forward, craning my neck to look at the painting the artist was doing. It was a stunning portrait, artfully done. I may have been uncomfortable with Clara's flagrant nudity, but I could tell that this woman was a gifted artist—she had captured both Clara and the setting very well.

For the first time, she turned to look at me, flicking her eyes up and down once. "You wouldn't be a bad subject."

I blushed, avoiding her loaded statement. "We haven't been introduced."

Katherine held out her hand, giving mine a firm shake. "Katherine Conrad, but call me Kate, everyone does."

"You're American," I said in surprise.

Her right eyebrow lifted in amusement. "So are you."

Redvers took this opportunity to excuse himself. "If you'll excuse me, I'll leave you ladies to it. I have some business to attend to." He gave a little bow, then strolled from the garden, doing a good job of hiding just how quickly he wanted to be gone from this scene. I had no idea what he was up to, but I was sure he had a plan of some sort. A plan that likely involved searching this palazzo and trying to uncover some of Clara Morton's secrets.

Which meant I needed to keep these ladies occupied for as long as possible.

Chapter Thirteen

Clara was watching Redvers' exit with amusement. "He certainly seems eager to leave. Where is he going?"

I thought fast, deciding it was unlikely either of the women would find out how we'd arrived here. "We kept our gondolier waiting. My husband said he wanted to do a quick errand—a surprise for me—while I spent time here." Every word of this was a lie, but Clara seemed to accept my story. I couldn't tell what Kate was thinking—she'd gone back to work on the portrait.

The question at the top of my mind was why these two would choose to paint Clara's portrait in the same place where D'Annuzzio had just been killed. Or at least, where his body had been found—I realized that I couldn't stop glancing to the other side of the garden where the gazebo stood sentry over the spot where D'Annuzzio had died. Since he'd been poisoned, it was possible the poisoning had been done elsewhere in the building, and he merely died out here. But even still, it seemed a particularly morbid choice, one I was searching for a way to ask about.

Luckily, Clara took care of that for me.

"I know you're shocked that this is where we're painting my portrait, but Christopher would have wanted it this way," Clara said. "Besides, we'd already started. Kate just needs to add final details."

Clara missed the look that Kate gave me, which included an eye roll and a shake of the head. I suspected Kate was telling me—without so many words—what I already suspected: Clara was more than a little dramatic as well as self-involved. She would spin a story to suit her, and what suited her at the moment was being painted out here, at the site of her ex-husband's death.

Or perhaps I was writing my own interpretations of Clara's behavior. Which made sense since my mind could find no easy way to categorize the woman.

"I'm getting bored, lying on this stone. Are you finished, Kate?" Clara didn't wait for a response before she stood and stretched her long, sinewy body, then took a few steps over to where she'd tossed a red silk robe. She pulled it on, and for once it covered most of her anatomy, the exotic birds and dragons, beautifully embroidered in gold thread, glinting in the sun that was now peeking through the breaking cloud cover.

She may have been bored, but I needed to keep the women here in the garden so Redvers could finish his "business."

"It's such a beautiful day. I can see why you would want to be painted here, where the light is so good," I said, gesturing vaguely at the garden.

Clara retook her seat on the low wall, and I breathed a little easier. For the moment, anyway, since Clara seemed happy to stay put—for the time being. Kate ignored the both of us and continued what she was doing, dabbing paint here and there between her palette and the canvas. From her reaction to Clara a moment before, I had to wonder why she was even here at the palazzo and whether Clara's claims of an affair were correct.

"Have you known each other long?" I asked.

Apparently, this was the right thing to ask, because Clara beamed. "We have. It's been, what, five years now? Many of those I spent pursuing Kate, though, trying to convince her that she should paint me." Clara sat a little taller. "This is our third portrait now. Of myself, of course."

My next question was pure curiosity. "What do you do with them? Sell them to museums?"

Clara laughed, a loud, raspy sound, like a door on rusted hinges desperately needing to be oiled. "No, that's silly. I hang them in my gallery downstairs. Come, I'll show you."

"In a minute," I said quickly. "I would dearly like to see them, but I'd like to watch a little more of Kate's work. I've never seen an artist paint before."

Clara frowned, and I lobbed another quick question to distract her. "Have the police been by to speak with you again?"

This time, Kate paused what she was doing for a long moment before starting up again. I suspected she knew exactly what I was up to, but she didn't comment on it.

Clara flapped her hands. I hadn't noticed before, but they were quite large, in keeping with the woman's height, but they were also quite thick, almost mannish. In the portrait, they were long and elegant—I made a note to myself to ask Kate about the choice later, then focused on what Clara was saying.

"Not yet," Clara lamented, "although I expect that *ispettore* will be back any time now. Which I certainly would expect, since I'm the widow and the death happened on my property. Of course, I would like to know what he's learned about poor Christopher's death. And during one of my parties, too. The nerve of that man, to ruin such an exquisite soiree. Though really, it was just like him to make it about himself."

There was a lot to unpack in that sentence, all of it seeming to revolve around Clara's warped view of how the world worked. What I was most disturbed by was her seeming lack of grief over D'Annuzzio's death. She claimed to love him, but it appeared she had no feelings about his death except that it had inconvenienced her and her party.

I'd kept my face neutral and hadn't voiced my thoughts, but Clara seemed to read my mind. "I can see that you think I'm quite calloused, but we had a volatile relationship, and I will grieve him in my own time."

I murmured something appropriate, then went ahead and asked the next thing I was wondering. "We spoke with Ignacio Catral this morning. He said D'Annuzzio was paying for his hotel room."

Clara laughed again, the rusty sound filling the garden. "He might think that. Christopher probably even told him that. But I've been footing the bill for most all of Christopher's entertainments, including that young man. He's quite handsome, isn't he? Christopher was so angry that he couldn't get him into bed. It's part of the reason I kept paying Ignacio to stick around." She stood, apparently finished with this conversation. "I need a cocktail," Clara said, moving to Kate's side and kissing her soundly before breezing past me. "Do you want one, Kate?" This was thrown over her shoulder.

"No, I'm still working," Kate volleyed back, not even turning to look at Clara disappearing down the hall. I prayed that Redvers was done searching the place or he might be answering to Ispettore Fizzoli as well.

I stood for a moment, staring off into the shambles of a garden and trying to figure out Clara Morton. Every time she opened her mouth, it completely shattered what I thought I'd figured out about her.

Kate chuckled, and I glanced over to see that she'd put

down her paintbrush and was watching me. "You'll never figure her out. I've known her for five years, and I still haven't been able to do it." She gave a casual shrug. "It keeps me coming back, though, the not knowing."

"Is she actually sad about Christopher's death, do you think?"

Kate considered that before nodding slowly. "I do think so, in her own way. And before you ask, no, I don't think she had anything to do with his death."

"What makes you say that?" I asked, genuinely curious. She'd sounded quite certain.

Kate reached for the paintbrushes sitting on the ledge of her easel, gathering the bunch up in her hand. I assumed she was going to wash them out somewhere, but I could tell that she was operating automatically, thinking about how to answer me. "I think they were terrible together, they fought like wild animals, but I believe they genuinely cared about one another." Kate frowned, then gave her head a little shake and cleared the crease between her brows. "Clara has plenty of money. She didn't need anything from Christopher. I really can't think of a reason to kill him, or even have someone else kill him."

"Can you think of who did have a reason to kill him?" I asked.

"Well, I did," Kate said casually.

Chapter Fourteen

My mouth dropped open, and she chuckled. "You weren't expecting that, were you?" I shook my head as I closed my mouth, and she moved toward the building, paintbrushes in hand, gesturing with her head for me to follow her. "I was supposed to have an exhibit of my paintings, one of the biggest of my career. I think this was about two years ago? Maybe three? It's hard to say—time is like taffy sometimes."

Instead of going up the stairs into the main floor of the palazzo, we headed down a very small set of stairs leading down to a small wooden door. Kate twisted the knob and pushed it open, and I followed closely behind. This was clearly a shortcut to the "basement" level Deanna had referred to—the little green door had opened to a hallway with a series of closed doors on either side. I stayed close on Kate's heels, interested to see where both this story and ourselves were going.

"It was to be held in Florence at the Academia. It would have been an incredible honor. But Christopher spoke to the directors and got it shut down. I couldn't get a single other place in town to host my exhibit."

"Why would he do that?" I asked the question even though I was pretty certain that I knew the answer.

"Because he was jealous of my relationship with Clara," Kate said on a sigh. "They were still married at the time, although neither of them was faithful, and that was part of their understanding with one another. He really had no right to be so angry, but he was a very jealous man. Not to mention a volatile one."

I found it interesting that those were the two words used to describe D'Annuzzio, over and over, from everyone we'd spoken to that had known him. "Jealous" and "volatile." Neither was an attractive quality.

We'd entered the first room at the end of the hallway, with a trunk full of clothing at the end of the bed and an attached bathroom. It took only a few steps inside for me to realize this was her bedroom. Kate stepped into the bathroom with her brushes, and although I was curious to see what she did with them, I stayed where I was near the doorway. For a room on a lower level, there was a surprising amount of light. I made a note to look for the windows of this room when we left.

"He ruined your chances for an exhibit," I called into the bathroom, trying to prompt her to continue her story.

"I can't hear you. You can come in, you know."

I stepped farther into the room, repeating the question. Now I was standing over the trunk, peering into the confusion of clothes piled inside, looking for something interesting. Of course, without actually poking through her things, I thought it was unlikely that I would see anything useful, and I wasn't going to touch anything with her in the next room.

Kate came back into the room, now brushless, and looked amused at finding me peering into her trunk. "Need a change of clothes?"

I smiled. "I do love a good pair of trousers. But yours are covered in paint."

"Hazard of the job," she said. "Yes, that man ruined my

chances. And has done so several times since then. I've considered going back to America, where his reach wouldn't extend, but Clara keeps insisting that I do one more painting of her. And then one more. And one more after that."

"She seems a bit . . . possessive."

Kate nodded grimly. "She is. But I love her, so here I am."

I didn't understand how someone could give up their chances at fame or even recognition as an artist for someone as disconcerting and enigmatic as Clara Morton. Especially if fidelity wasn't on the table, which certainly seemed to be the case.

"I noticed that you made her hands in the painting more . . ." I was searching for a polite way to comment on the changes she'd made.

"More feminine? More attractive?" Kate gave a low chuckle, as though she were afraid of being heard by Clara. Her speaking voice dropped as well. "She's quite sensitive about them. I made the mistake of painting them accurately the first time, and she had a complete meltdown. I haven't made the same mistake since."

At first, I was surprised, since Clara seemed more self-possessed and unbothered than that, but on second examination, I decided it wasn't actually all that shocking. Everyone was entitled to their insecurities. I changed course. "Clara is also American, isn't she? How did she come to be married to an Italian man?"

"She took to gallivanting about Europe both before and after the war. She claimed that the art was better here, and it was the only place she could possibly live." Kate shrugged. "She's not exactly wrong. Nearly all of the masters are from some part of Europe."

"And D'Annuzzio? Where did he come into the picture?"

"Oh, yes. They started up years before the war. Perhaps when she was still married to her first husband? I don't know the timeline exactly."

I hadn't realized that Clara was married before. I must have looked confused because she continued on.

"Once she met Christopher, she divorced George," Kate explained. "I think Clara thrives on chaos."

That agreed with what I'd been thinking about the woman.

Kate had some questions of her own, though. "Why are you here asking so many questions?"

I smiled. "Because I'm a very curious person and Clara is so interesting." Kate narrowed her eyes at me and I sighed. Kate Conrad was too clever to be easily fooled—I would have to give her a real explanation, or at least something bordering on real. "My friend Deanna is being scapegoated for D'Annuzzio's death. I want to find the real killer so the police have no reason to arrest her."

Kate gazed at me for a few beats, then seemed to accept this as a reasonable answer. "You're a good friend," she said.

"I try to be."

"Do you really think he was murdered, though?" Kate asked. "He didn't just die of natural causes? He wasn't the healthiest man, you know."

I didn't have the chance to ask what she meant by this because voices drifted down the stairs from the cavernous room above, faint but unmistakable.

Kate and I looked at one another and, by silent agreement, headed up to see what was happening.

Clara was still wearing her robe but now had a cocktail in one hand and was gesticulating rather wildly with her free hand while explaining something to Ispettore Fizzoli. I wasn't surprised to see the *ispettore*, but I *was* surprised to see my husband standing next to him. Where had Redvers come from? And how had he emerged from wherever he was without getting caught?

I went to stand next to Redvers, relieved that he was

here—I felt on more solid ground with him beside me. Talking to Clara was like having a rug pulled out from under you, a bit at a time, and you weren't sure if you were going to wind up on the ground with each tug. I liked having Redvers there to keep me from tumbling.

It took me a moment to catch up, but I finally pieced together what Clara was upset about—her snakes. It sounded like the *ispettore* wanted to have them examined to see if they were the source of the poison that killed D'Annuzzio.

"They don't even have venom; they've been defanged. I will not have you subjecting them to torture," Clara nearly shouted. "And they cannot go out in this weather, they'll catch their death. They must not leave the palazzo, not this time of year."

"Not even to solve this murder? The murder of your former husband?" Ispettore Fizzoli asked. His manner remained calm, despite Clara's raging. Looking at him, I thought he probably remained calm regardless of what he was faced with—he radiated that type of temperament.

Clara opened her mouth, and the *ispettore* held up a hand to stop the onslaught that was surely coming. "Very well, we can leave that matter. For now," he said sternly. I was frankly surprised he was leaving it even that long. I soon found out why.

"I've already arrested the suspect, Mrs. Parks, and she will eventually talk. She will tell me where she got the poison from, so perhaps we do not need to touch the animals." Ispettore Fizzoli looked confident in his assessment that his suspect would crack under interrogation.

My stomach churned, and I did my best to clamp down the nausea. He'd already arrested Deanna.

"Excellent," Clara said with a smile. "That's settled then. Perhaps we should open a bottle of champagne."

"No, thank you," was the reply that went around our circle. Fizzoli was frowning at the suggestion, and everyone else looked similarly put off.

"James!" Clara shouted. Her servant appeared in a doorway at the other side of the room. "Open a bottle, and bring glasses."

He disappeared, presumably to follow Clara's orders, which were given despite the fact that the *ispettore* and everyone else had expressly said they didn't care for a drink. I was both shocked that Clara would feel compelled to celebrate Deanna's arrest and that she had already forgotten her promise to find Deanna a lawyer. It appeared that it had been less a promise and more an offhand remark immediately forgotten, probably tossed out simply to mollify me.

I may not be able to figure Clara Morton out, but one thing was certain—I did not like the woman. And she was currently at the top of my list for the real killer.

Redvers silently reached out and gave my hand a reassuring squeeze. I quietly took a deep breath to slow my pounding heart. We'd already sent Millie to find a lawyer, so that was being taken care of; Millie was many things, but she was very reliable, so it would be done and done well. I just hated the idea of Deanna being subjected to hours of interrogation for something I was certain she hadn't done.

"Can we visit Mrs. Parks?" I asked. Hopefully with her lawyer in tow, whoever Millie had been able to retain.

The *ispettore* narrowed his eyes at me. "You are friends with the snake woman?"

I nodded. Fizzoli looked between myself and Redvers several times before answering. "Perhaps. When I am finished with her."

My stomach roiled again. That sounded quite ominous for Deanna. Redvers squeezed my hand again, and I squeezed back, but I didn't dare look at him, keeping my eyes squarely on the *ispettore*, as he was the threat in the room. I bit my tongue to keep from demanding why the man had arrested Deanna instead of any of the other people in D'Annuzzio's circle who had plenty of motive to kill the man, certainly much more than Deanna.

James appeared a beat later, carrying a silver tray with five glasses and a chilled bottle of champagne. It had already been opened, in what I presumed was the kitchen, although I had no idea where that was located. None of us spoke as James poured the glasses, neatly, without spilling a drop. He then passed them out to each of us. Clara put her empty cocktail glass on the tray James held, then raised her champagne flute in a toast. The rest of us held our own in front of us, not responding in kind, nor taking a drink. The last thing I could do right now was take a sip of alcohol—I felt sick at Deanna's predicament, which was largely due to the woman celebrating in front of me. I was more tempted to toss my drink in her face.

Clara took a long sip, then coughed. "This tastes funny," she complained. "Perhaps it's the year." She took another small sip and made a face at her glass.

I glanced around for somewhere to dump mine, but that turned out to be unnecessary. Ispettore Fizzoli took the champagne flute from Clara's hand and sniffed it, frowning. He sniffed his own glass and shook his head.

"No one drink this." His voice was commanding even though no one in our group had any intention of drinking it—we were all clearly uninterested in the drinks in our hands. "I will take it to be tested. It may have been poisoned."

Clara gasped. "Do you think someone is trying to kill me, too?" One hand went to her heart and the other went to her forehead. I did my best not to roll my eyes at the dramatics. Frankly I wouldn't have been surprised if there were nothing wrong with the champagne at all—it was entirely likely that Clara was setting this stage herself. Nor would I have been surprised to learn that she'd poisoned the bottle herself. I bit back the urge to mention this out loud to the *ispettore*.

Fizzoli didn't answer Clara's question but began gathering our glasses, carefully pouring each back into the bottle. "I will take this with me. Do you have the cork?" This was addressed to James, who walked briskly back in the direction of the kitchen.

"Could it have been my own servant?" Clara asked even before James had left the room. "I'll send him with you, *ispettore*. You must take him away in handcuffs."

Fizzoli looked bemused. "That won't be necessary. We are not yet sure if poison is the case or if the champagne is simply bad. I am simply exercising caution, since your former husband was killed in this palazzo."

Clara shook her head, voice raising. "No, I insist. I cannot have James here any longer. I will find new help, perhaps an Italian this time, someone who does not know me and will not wish me dead."

This last was uttered while James was returning to the room with the wine cork, and it was obvious that he'd overheard his employer. I searched his face, wondering if this sudden dismissal would be devastating, but he appeared relieved.

It said quite a lot that the possibility of a jail cell was better than working for Clara Morton.

Chapter Fifteen

We left the palazzo at the same time as Ispettore Fizzoli and James, and watched as James and the *ispettore* loaded themselves into the *polizia* boat next to ours at the dock. We followed at a distance, noticing that as soon as they were on the other side of the canal, the *ispettore* had the boatman—not dressed in the usual black and white striped shirt but in a *polizia* uniform—drop James off at the nearest pier. We waited until the *ispettore* had pulled away before sidling up next to James and offering him a ride.

James looked surprised at our sudden arrival and didn't immediately agree. I couldn't blame him—I would have been suspicious as well.

"Can we buy you a drink? Or a meal?" Redvers asked.

The man tipped his head, considering the offer. Redvers upped it. "We'll put you up for a night at our hotel so you have some time to get yourself situated."

This time James gave a little shrug, nodded, and passed his small bag to Redvers before stepping down into our boat. He'd packed his things in a very short amount of time once Clara had insisted on dismissing him, so either he'd never had many things there to begin with or had already been packed and ready to leave. We used the ride back to our hotel to acquaint ourselves with the man who was formerly employed by Clara Morton.

"Did the *ispettore* say anything when he dropped you off?" I asked.

James gave a brief laugh. "Just not to leave the city and to leave word at the *polizia* station where I will be staying. I was shocked he didn't take me to jail, honestly."

"Where are you from?" I asked.

"England," James said with a glance at Redvers. "Not as posh as you, though, mate." James' voice had slipped from its previously polished tones into something you would hear from the working class in London.

"Why did you come here with her instead of staying in London?" I struggled to understand this question about everyone in Clara's circle—how had they wound up here, in Clara's apparent thrall?

James shrugged. "She offered me a pot of money. More than I could ever make back home, especially with skin as dark as this, and working the docks is backbreaking."

"I haven't seen any other staff," I said. "I assume there were others." I couldn't imagine she would fire the only person who worked for her. Clara was not the type of person to do things for herself.

James waved a hand. "Nah, there are a handful of others, working out of sight. She just made me her personal butler. I was paid the same as the others, though." He frowned. "It's strange—I'm not sure she knows how much she's paying for anything. I can't even count how many times she's been swindled by shopkeepers—charged much more than the items are worth. I mentioned this to her once, and she waved her hand." James demonstrated Clara waving her hand and I nearly laughed—it was quite a good impression. "'It does not matter. Let them have their pittance,' is what she would say." He shook his head. "She's an odd one a'right. For a while she wanted me to say I was from Africa, but I can't do that kind of accent. I tried for about a day, but no one bought it."

The idea that she might hire a black man simply for the novelty of it and insist he playact as though he were from somewhere else wasn't surprising to me, although I did find it incredibly tasteless. If it weren't for the fact that a friend was being blamed for murder, I would have left this investigation and Clara Morton far behind without a second glance.

The three of us were quiet for a moment. "I'm glad I'll never have to walk that damned cat again," James muttered, then breathed an audible sigh of relief.

I couldn't blame the man.

We left our boat moored near to our hotel and strolled into the lobby. I should have braced myself for the inevitable encounter with Aunt Millie, but I was caught unprepared, busy thinking about what James had just told me and trying to figure out how the information might be useful to our investigation. I nearly walked right past her, but a sharp call of my name stopped me in my tracks. Millie was waiting for us in one of the upholstered chairs near the front desk and didn't look pleased about it, despite having a cocktail in her hand.

"Where have you been?" she demanded.

Redvers wisely took James to the front desk to get him checked in and left me to contend with my aunt. I didn't blame him, but I could silently curse him for throwing me to this snarling wolf.

"We went to speak with Clara," I started to explain.

"And you didn't think to take me with you? Honestly, Jane, that woman and I are well acquainted and it's foolish for you to hare off and see her without me."

I nodded my head. "I realize that, and I do apologize. We would have learned much more with you there," I said, hoping this would mollify her, even slightly. She gave a little sniff, and my shoulders relaxed back down ever so slightly. "We did learn that Deanna has been arrested, though, and I'm hoping you were able to secure a lawyer for her."

"Yes, we already sent him to where she's being held." She sniffed again, clearly pleased to know something before I did. "I am sorry for your friend." Millie paused, sounding sincere, and I smiled in return, genuinely thankful for her help. "You're quite certain she wasn't responsible?" Millie asked.

Exasperation quickly replaced my gratitude. Luckily Redvers and James joined us before I could say something foolish.

"And who is this now?" She asked with a finger pointed at James.

"That is Clara's servant. She fired him this afternoon."

"Why? Is *he* responsible for that man's death?" Millie asked. She took a sip of her cocktail—a neat whiskey from the looks of it, and I nearly asked why the alcohol hadn't made her less combative.

I valued my life, though, so I kept that to myself.

It did, however, make me want a cocktail of my own. This whole day, in fact, made me thirsty for a drink. "Where is the bar?" I asked, instead of answering any of her rapid-fire questions.

"It's through there." Millie nodded her head past the front desk. "My husband is getting me another drink."

This, despite the fact she still had a half-full glass in her hand. I shook my head and headed for the bar. Redvers turned his head and caught my eye, his own sparkling. He knew exactly what he'd left me to contend with.

The bar was small, with four tables for customers and its own door leading out to the tables next to the canal. It had the same oriental theme as the rest of the hotel, and I went to stand at the curved bar top standing beneath a matching wood ornamentation at the ceiling with carved arabesque details marching along the front of both. Lord Hughes was chatting with the bartender, Millie's second glass on a coaster beside his own cocktail. I greeted him wearily and asked the bartender for an aperol spritz. It seemed to be the cocktail of choice in Italy, and though it was slightly too sweet for me, I'd found that I did enjoy it.

"You're not having a gin rickey?" Millie asked, having followed behind me. "They do have gin here."

"Well, as they say, when in Rome," I replied.

"We're not in Rome. We're in Venice."

I closed my eyes and waited for my drink, which was mercifully quick, and took a long sip, keeping my fingers crossed that the alcohol would start working quickly. Lord Hughes stepped in to save me before Millie could start back up with her interrogation, and I was deeply grateful.

"We sent the lawyer to the *polizia* station. From what I understand, the man is quite good," Hughes said.

"Thank you," I said with genuine gratitude. "I'm very grateful you were able to find someone reputable and send him to her." I hoped it would help Deanna feel even a little bit better, knowing that we were doing everything we could to help her.

"Our pleasure," Lord Hughes said. Both of us ignored Millie's snort.

Redvers entered the bar, followed closely by Charlie Parks. I was a little surprised that it wasn't James with him, but I was pleased to see Charlie. Although I did hope he already knew about Deanna's arrest so that I didn't have to be the one to tell him.

Millie had turned to greet Redvers, but whatever she'd been about to say died on her lips. She blinked a few times then announced, "I know you." She was looking right at Charlie, finger pointed. "You were skulking around Clara's party."

Chapter Sixteen

I was about to contradict my aunt and assure her that Charlie hadn't been at the party, but I saw the flush of red creeping up Charlie's neck and into his cheeks. I made a noise of exasperation. "You were there, weren't you, Charlie?"

Charlie gave a guilty shrug. I sighed before going over to the corner of the bar to pull some chairs together and dropping into one. Lord Hughes and Millie promptly joined me, and we waited for Redvers and Charlie to get drinks of their own before joining us.

"Spill," I said to Charlie. The tone of my voice was stern, almost school matronly, and I caught a gleam in Redvers' eye.

I decided to ignore my handsome husband for the moment and kept my attention focused on Charlie. I half expected him to pretend to spill his drink, since he was ordinarily a bit of a prankster with a smart mouth. But for once, Charlie was quite serious. "It's true, I snuck into the party. I rented a costume from one of those tourist shops and made sure it had a mask so no one would recognize me." He grimaced. "But it hurt my nose so I took it off once I was sure that Dee couldn't see me."

"Why were you there, young man?" Millie demanded. She was now working on the drink Lord Hughes had ordered for her. I hadn't even seen her finish the first one.

"I just wanted to make sure that Deanna was okay," Charlie said. It was a lame excuse, and every single person seated there knew it.

I pursed my lips and locked eyes with him. He was only able to maintain eye contact for a few seconds before he ducked his head and fiddled with the drink in his hand. "Okay fine, I was worried she was stepping out on me."

"What?" I asked, genuinely shocked. "Why would you think that?"

Charlie puffed out a sound of frustration and glanced around the room, as though looking for some type of salvation from this conversation. He wasn't going to find any. "Things have been sort of . . . strained between us lately. I think she's frustrated at how much money I've been losing and that we keep having to move around. But if I could just . . ."

I stopped him right there with a hand held up. "That is your trouble right there, the 'if I could just.' You have to stop making those excuses and thinking you can turn your luck around."

Charlie looked like he wanted to argue, but I shook my head vehemently while Millie glared at him. "Is playing cards more important than your marriage to Deanna?" I asked.

He didn't even have to think for a second about the answer. "No."

"Then pull yourself together. Find a new profession." My tone was stern. We didn't have time for such male foolishness, not while Deanna was being interrogated by the Italian police for a murder she hadn't committed. Of course, even without that piece of the puzzle, I would have given him a talking-to.

There was an uncomfortable quiet, then Redvers stepped in. "Did anyone else notice you?"

"I'm not sure," Charlie said with a frown. "I didn't talk to anyone, so maybe not?"

"Did you do anything while you were there?" I asked. "Besides walk around the party?"

"I did go upstairs to the snake room."

My mouth dropped open. This was not good news for either him or Deanna. "Why did you do that?"

"Deanna had talked about them so much, I just wanted to get a peek at them."

I groaned and covered my face with my hands. "Did anyone see you up there?"

"Just the one servant. I don't think anyone else did," Charlie said.

I dropped my hands and did some fast thinking. It was probably James he was referring to. But if one person saw him, it was likely that someone else had as well. Likely more than one someone else.

"Did you touch anything?" Redvers asked.

Charlie shook his head. "I'm not stupid enough to let those things loose. Deanna might love them, but I sure don't."

That was at least a little bit of good news, although it was possible he'd touched something without remembering or even realizing that he had. Now that the *polizia* knew D'Annuzzio's death was a murder, they would be taking fingerprints at the palazzo, and especially in the snake room, since it had been death by poisoning. We could only hope Charlie's fingerprints wouldn't be found in there as well as his wife's.

Redvers and I also needed to speak with James and find out whether he remembered seeing Charlie. If we were lucky, James would know if other servants had seen Charlie as well, although I knew that was a long shot.

"What's the panic, anyway?" Charlie asked.

I pursed my lips before answering. "Your being there and

trying to cover it up points the finger at either you or Deanna being the killer. Especially since the murder was done with poison, poison that likely came from a snake in that room." I wasn't sure about the last part, but I was so incensed by his nonchalance that I exaggerated a bit for effect. And it *could* actually turn out to be true.

Charlie's eyes went wide—it was obvious this hadn't occurred to him. Or maybe it *had* occurred to him and that was why he'd been covering up his sneaking around the party.

"This really didn't occur to you?" I asked.

He shook his head. "I just didn't want Deanna to be sore at me."

My stomach churned again, and I took a sip of my aperol spritz in an attempt to calm it. Deanna was going to be a lot more than sore if we didn't prove someone else killed D'Annuzzio.

I turned to Redvers. "Where did James go?"

"He took his bag up to his room." Redvers frowned. "He did say he was coming back down, but perhaps he changed his mind."

"Would you go check on him?" I asked.

Redvers nodded and quickly left, leaving his drink on the table. I was sure James' absence was nothing suspicious, but we did have pressing questions for him.

While Redvers was gone, everyone sat in silence, lost in their own thoughts. I sipped at my drink and wondered whether Charlie was being truthful this time. I nearly sighed out loud when I realized that he likely wasn't. Parts of his story were probably true, but there was a very good chance—a certainty, even—that there was a lot more he wasn't sharing with us. I wasn't sure he would come clean even if we were alone, without my aunt and Lord Hughes present. A glance in his direction didn't tell me anything either—Charlie was staring blankly at the wall opposite him, so there was nothing I could read from his face about what we'd just discussed.

Redvers soon returned, holding two envelopes. He handed one to Aunt Millie before retaking his seat and handing me the other envelope. I looked at the front, curious.

"These were just delivered to the front desk."

I was about to pull a card from the inside of the envelope, but I paused to ask about James first. "Is he coming down?"

Redvers shook his head. "He wasn't in his room, and he's not in the lobby."

I frowned. Where could the man have taken off to? Millie was already reading the contents of her envelope, so I hurried to pull the thick paper from my own. It was an invitation, printed on gorgeous cream-colored paper stock. I ran my eyes over the words, and my eyebrows rose further with each sentence I read.

Millie and I looked at one another. "It looks as though we're invited to a funeral," she said.

I nodded. "So it would seem."

Gold-leaf invitations were an unusual way to invite guests to a funeral, but since they came from Clara Morton, I wasn't surprised. What *was* surprising was that my aunt seemed to take it all in stride without a single comment about the odd nature of the affair.

Millie set her invitation on the table and finished off the last sips of her drink. She handed the empty glass to Lord Hughes. "One more, darling, if you please." She turned her attention to me. "Do you have something appropriate to wear? I brought a very suitable black dress and matching jacket. It's always smart to be prepared for this type of occasion, but I'm going to hazard a guess that you didn't think to do the same. And since this funeral is tomorrow, you don't have much time to purchase something."

I thought quickly, mentally reviewing what I'd packed. She was correct. I didn't have anything funereal in my luggage, but neither did I want to waste valuable time shopping for something "suitable" either. We still needed to speak with Alonzo and Isabella Fontana. Despite the fact that no one on Clara's list was bothering with the truth, we still needed to speak with all of them, if only to paint a fuller picture of each person and their relationship with D'Annuzzio.

Thankfully Redvers was a step ahead of me with this one. "Millie, perhaps you could do us the honor of picking something out. Jane and I would greatly appreciate it, and neither of us could do as fine a job as yourself anyway."

"Well, that much is true." Millie sniffed. "But what will you be doing that's so important that I need to do the dress shopping for you?"

Redvers nodded gravely while I worked on stifling a snort of my own. "I would see it as a personal favor," he said. "Jane and I need to interrogate the other three people on the list."

My aunt narrowed her eyes at him and I leaned back in my seat, enjoying the show since I wasn't the target of her barbed remarks for once. "And you don't think that Lord Hughes and I are up to that errand?"

We all looked at Redvers, awaiting his reply to her volley. He and I both knew that he needed to tread very carefully or he would find himself in the nearest dress shop with me. "There is no one that I would trust more," Redvers said, choosing his words carefully. "But my employers, you know. They're quite particular in how I go about things. I'm afraid they would insist that I do the questioning myself."

Millie narrowed her eyes, then sat back in her seat looking slightly mollified, although I sensed she was about to ask how his employer was involved with this death. A death far from England and with no apparent connection to the British government.

"I really would be so grateful, Aunt Millie. You've always had such a good eye for fine clothing. And I wouldn't even know where to start in a foreign city," I said.

Millie turned her attention to me, eyeing me up suspiciously. "That is also obvious." Lord Hughes returned with the drink Millie had requested. He looked quite amused, which meant he'd overheard everything from his position at the bar. Not surprising—Millie had a voice that carried far and wide.

"Very well, Jane. I'll find you something appropriate to wear tomorrow. I wouldn't want to be embarrassed by my own niece." She waved a hand toward Redvers. "I'm not worried about you. I'm certain you have an appropriate suit."

Neither of us responded to this, instead thanking her before standing to excuse ourselves. Charlie shot out of his chair and nearly stumbled over it in his haste to do the same. Despite everything, I almost laughed at how quickly he'd decided that it was time for him to depart as well.

I wouldn't want to be left alone at the mercy of my aunt's tongue either.

We parted ways with Charlie once we stepped outside. "I need to go to where they're holding Deanna and see if they'll let me see her," he said.

I reached out a hand and touched his arm. "If you see her, please tell her we are working on getting her free."

He nodded and hailed the nearest water taxi, disappearing down the canal.

I looked at my husband. "Do you suppose he was telling the truth?"

"I think it's likely that some of that was the truth. But not all. He is holding something back," Redvers said.

I had wanted to be wrong about this, but as per usual my husband and I were in agreement. Charlie Parks was hiding something. Something more than having attended Clara's party in order to check up on his wife.

Redvers began strolling toward where we'd moored our rented boat.

"Time to interrogate the Fontana siblings?" I asked. "We have one more person to track down after that, as well." I'd nearly forgotten about the fifth person on Clara's list.

"Yes, to the Fontanas, but I think before we track down Orsola Chini, we should do a thorough search of D'Annuzzio's lodgings."

A small smile crept across my lips. I did love a good search.

Chapter Seventeen

We alighted from our boat just off the Grand Canal and walked the short distance to our first stop, where Alonzo and Isabella had taken up residence. The exterior of the building was rather nondescript—just another pale stucco building in a row of them, with a large wooden entrance facing this smaller waterway. Redvers used the heavy door knocker to announce our presence, and within a minute the door was answered by a man wearing a dark suit whose expression did not change in the slightest when he saw us. Redvers told him we were there to see the Fontanas, and he nodded once then told us to follow him.

We stepped into the foyer and went up a flight of stairs. Once on the first floor, I found myself gaping at the interior. Gone were the low ceilings I'd come to expect, and had in fact seen in every other building I'd been inside in this city. Instead, the ceilings soared, with carved detailing running around the edges, setting off the elegant gold and green wallpaper. The floor was marble, with thick rugs covering anywhere that the siblings might be expected to walk.

We followed the butler into what appeared to be a sitting room, where Alonzo and Isabella appeared to be lounging about. The room was bright, since one whole wall was dominated by oversized windows, nearly floor to ceiling, that I imagined swung open so one could conveniently walk out onto the small terrace overlooking the Grand Canal. The windows—or were they considered doors?—were draped artfully with heavy gold curtains along the top and sides, and a series of lighter-weight beige curtains gathered across the center. The top half of the room was done with more tasteful wallpaper, but the bottom half was marble—grey marble blocks swirled with cream, set off by more cream marble. Alonzo was sitting at a heavy wooden desk with a pen in his hand but staring at a blank space on the wall, and his sister Isabella was draped across a low velvet fainting couch and staring at the ceiling. It certainly didn't look as though we were interrupting anything.

I did a fast scan to ensure that they didn't have any unusual pets themselves, but there was nothing out of the ordinary, and I breathed a small sigh of relief.

When Alonzo finally spotted us, he jumped up and said something in rapid Italian. Redvers shook his head slightly and responded in English. "We're sorry to bother you, but we have a few questions for you," he said.

"Ahh, you are English," Alonzo said. He walked over to where his sister was sitting and pushed her legs out of his way to sit on the couch with her. This didn't faze Isabella in the slightest, she simply put her legs back where they had been but now draped over Alonzo's lap. This way she could still recline against the back of the couch.

Looking between one and the other, I didn't see much family resemblance, if any, which I had anticipated since they were brother and sister. But Isabella was fair-haired with a light complexion, while Alonzo had thick black hair with matching eyebrows, and his complexion was darker, with more of an olive cast to it. They seemed a mismatched pair.

"What brings you here?" Isabella asked. "We are pleased to have someone visit us at all. We've been dreadfully bored."

Her voice had a lovely musical sound to it, but she lacked the thick Italian accent her brother spoke with. She did have some kind of accent, but I couldn't quite place where it originated from. I'd have bet money it wasn't Italian, though.

I found myself unexpectedly intrigued by these two, although certainly not charmed.

"We attended Clara Morton's party the other night," Redvers said. This clearly wasn't enough information, since the brother and sister stared back at him blankly. "It was just two nights ago." Still nothing. "The party where Christopher D'Annuzzio died." Redvers' voice had just a hint of exasperation by the end, although I doubted these two noticed.

"Oh, yes! *That* party," Alonzo said. "I wasn't at that party, you see."

"Yes, why is that?" I asked.

"Well," Alonzo said confidentially. "I'm studying to become a writer." He looked expectantly at the two of us for long enough that I felt it was necessary to nod at him encouragingly. This was apparently what he needed.

"You understand. Anyway, I had just really hit my stride with the words, with writing the words, and I simply could not leave for the party. I had to follow the words while they flowed."

I hoped his writing was less repetitive than his speech. "I see," I said slowly. "And you were here all night? At home?"

Alonzo nodded seriously. "This is true, what you say. I was here with the words."

A glance at Isabella told me that she was clearly annoyed with her brother. "And I had to go to the party alone. I nearly stayed home as well, but I was deathly bored. Deadly bored?" She made a little hmm-ing noise. "Either one, I think."

I was about to ask Isabella what she remembered about

the party when someone else walked into the room from a doorway at the back. "I heard voices," she said. The newcomer was tall, about the same height as myself, with bouncing curls cut into a fashionable bob. It was done reasonably well, although her curls were so tightly wound that it gave her hair something of a pyramid shape. She reached a hand up and smoothed one side, apparently well aware of this fact.

Isabella looked at her and back at us, then waved a seemingly dismissive hand at the other woman. "This is Orsola Chini. She is Italian."

This was a pleasant surprise since it meant we wouldn't have to track the woman down, although I did find it strange that Isabella felt the need to announce her friend's nationality.

Orsola elegantly dropped into an armchair next to the siblings. "*Allora*. I could not stay at Christopher's after he died. It was too, too morbid." She gave a dramatic shudder. "I come here."

That was another question answered as well. Perhaps if we just stood here quietly, the trio would continue to spill information without us even having to ask for it.

But that was too much to hope for. Once Orsola had taken her seat, the three of them stared at us, clearly waiting for something to happen. These three were either very odd or very young. Orsola appeared to be a few years older than the siblings. I frowned, trying to work out how much older D'Annuzzio would have been than this young woman.

Oblivious to my mental calculations, Redvers broke the awkward silence. "May we sit down?" Redvers pointed to a couch opposite Orsola.

There was silence for a beat, and then Alonzo spoke up. "Certainly, please. Can we offer you something to drink as well?" The two women nodded as though suddenly realizing this was the appropriate thing to do with guests.

"No thank you," Redvers said politely. "We will only take a few moments of your time."

Again, the three young people stared at him with open curiosity but didn't say anything. "How did you know Clara Morton and Christopher D'Annuzzio?" Redvers asked after a beat.

All three of them started speaking at once, but by virtue of being the loudest, Alonzo was allowed the floor. He started over, which was good since I hadn't understood anything over the cacophony the three of them had created. "I met Christopher in Rome. I wrote many letters to him pleading to study at his feet. He is Italy's greatest poet, you know." Alonzo looked at us, clearly expecting us to agree with this sentiment. Redvers and I nodded and, satisfied, Alonzo continued. "He agreed to take me under his wing, as you say. I have studied under the great man ever since." Alonzo's eyes filled with tears. "Until now, of course. I do not know how I will continue without him."

Isabella reached out a hand and stroked Alonzo's arm. Orsola watched the movement with narrowed eyes before appearing to remember herself and smoothing her face into a neutral expression.

Interesting. Was Orsola jealous of Isabella, perhaps wanting Alonzo for herself? Or was it something else?

Alonzo was still sniffling, so Redvers posed the same question to the two women. They exchanged a glance, then Isabella spoke first. "I met D'Annuzzio through Alonzo, of course. But he was such a, how do you say? Magnetic man?" She cocked her head in thought, then continued. "Yes, magnetic. And through him we met his wife, Clara." Isabella's expression visibly soured when she mentioned Clara.

"You don't care for Clara?" I asked.

Isabella glanced at the other two before answering, and I was sorry that we hadn't spoken with each of them individually, despite how time-consuming the task would have been. This was more efficient, but I suspected a lot less truthful, especially since they seemed to need permission from one another to speak. Redvers shifted in his seat next to me and I sensed he was thinking the same thing.

"She is very . . . generous," Isabella said slowly. The other two nodded. "Both with her money and . . . in the bedroom."

I did my very best not to appear shocked at this casual statement, forcing my head to nod as if this was the most natural thing in the world, something I heard regularly. I couldn't stop my overactive imagination from starting to wonder how many of these young people were in Clara's bed at a time, though. With some effort, I brought that line of curiosity to a screeching halt. It wasn't my business who had an affair with whom, at least as long as it wasn't directly related to murder.

That said, I watched as Alonzo nodded again, then reached over and threaded his fingers through Isabella's, their palms clasped together. I didn't have siblings, so I couldn't say for certain, but this seemed odd and overly intimate. Orsola frowned again, quickly catching herself and smoothing her face once more, but not before I caught her look of what seemed like disgust. Perhaps she wasn't in fact jealous but also found their relationship odd. Either way, I knew we'd have to get her alone to find out.

Redvers cleared his throat. "I sense you have something else to say about Mrs. Morton."

This time Orsola spoke up without looking to the others. "I don't care for her, regardless of how much money she throws at me." She sounded defiant, and I thought I heard a small gasp from one of the siblings.

"Why is that?" I asked.

Orsola shrugged. "I simply don't. I think she is strange

and should go back to her own country instead of staying here."

"Ors, you know she cannot go back," Alonzo said.

Finally, here was something interesting. "Clara can't go back to the United States?" Redvers asked.

Alonzo shook his head. "No, she cannot. Because she killed her first husband and can never return."

Chapter Eighteen

My mouth dropped open slightly, only to slam shut a beat later when Isabella rolled her eyes and contradicted her brother. "Alonzo, you fool. That isn't true. Her first husband isn't dead."

Alonzo sputtered. "But that's what Christopher told me! He wrote a whole poem about it."

"And you believed him?" Isabella disengaged her hand from her brother's and pulled her legs from his lap, then stood and began pacing the room. "Clara's husband was at the party with his daughter. He is alive and well."

My mouth had unfortunately dropped open again at her announcement that Clara's first husband had been present at the party. That and the shocking news that Clara had a daughter—a first husband or a daughter hadn't been mentioned to us or, as far as I knew, anyone else. Such as the *polizia*.

"How do you know it was her former husband and child?" I asked Isabella.

"Because she introduced them to me as such," Isabella said, finally alighting on the arm of Orsola's chair, causing Orsola to edge over slightly in her seat, away from the other woman. Isabella didn't appear to notice, but I sensed tension radiating from the other woman at her space being invaded.

I didn't recall seeing any young children at the party, and I turned to look at Redvers. For once, he looked as shocked as I did, but the wheels of his sharp mind were already turning, quickly incorporating the new information and spitting out new questions. "What is the daughter's name? And is she still a child, or an adult herself?"

"It was Helen, I believe," Isabella said. "She was not attractive, but then neither is Clara, so this is not a surprise."

I thought that was a rather harsh assessment of Clara Morton. She wasn't conventionally attractive, especially with her height and elongated limbs, but her features were striking and she played them up well, especially her large green eyes, which nearly dwarfed her narrow face. I noticed that Isabella hadn't answered Redvers' second question and was about to ask again, but I was interrupted.

"Are you certain they weren't actors that she hired?" Orsola looked skeptical. "She's done that in the past."

Isabella shook her head. "No, I've seen the photographs in her bedroom, and they were the same. Her daughter at least, was the same as in the photographs." Isabella's hands moved dramatically as she spoke, lending credence to her story.

"I'm beginning to regret missing the party," Alonzo muttered.

Isabella speared him with a look. "You should be. The old husband and Christopher had an argument in the garden. It was getting heated, so I went back into the house, but then I saw Helen walk out to where they were."

"Was D'Annuzzio already in the garden?" I asked. "Did it seem like Clara's first husband sought him out? Or the other way around?"

Isabella shrugged. "How would I know? I do not keep track of Christopher, not like Alonzo does." The siblings glared at each other for a moment, and I lobbed another question before they could begin what I sensed was a brewing argument.

"How old is Helen, do you think?" I asked.

Isabella cocked her head and looked at me. "Not many years younger than myself. So perhaps, nineteen?"

It made sense then, why we hadn't seen a small child at Clara's party. Her daughter was a young woman. A young woman who might have spoken with Christopher D'Annuzzio in the garden before he died.

We left not long after Isabella dropped that explosive information. We said our goodbyes and left the Fontanas' apartment, returning to our little boat. Redvers and I were quiet for the first few minutes, each lost in our own thoughts. He suddenly pulled the boat up next to a canal wall, letting it idle for a moment. "Are you hungry?" he asked.

My stomach answered for me, and his lips curved into a grin.

It took some navigating and a few wrong turns before we found Pietro's restaurant—even though we'd been delivered by gondola once before, it was different when we were doing the navigating ourselves in a city built like a maze. We both sighed in relief when we saw that Pietro's was open and still had a few tables available. The place was so small that it filled to capacity quite easily, and the day had gotten away from us, so it was now rather late. Pietro was delighted to see us and seated us at a table for two in the back of the restaurant. After a lively discussion with the restaurateur, we settled into our seats and sipped the house red wine he'd delivered.

"Well," I said.

"Well indeed," Redvers replied. "What are your initial thoughts?"

"That everyone we've spoken to is absolutely screwy."

Redvers chuckled. "I can't disagree with that."

"Should we find Clara's first husband and daughter next?" I asked.

He shook his head. "Let's stick to our original plan. I'm quite certain they'll be at D'Annuzzio's funeral tomorrow, and we can speak with them then."

I nodded, relieved. We'd already spoken to so many people that day that I needed some time to process everything we'd heard. I wasn't sure I'd be able to pick apart what—if anything—was the truth, so searching D'Annuzzio's residence was much more appealing than speaking with yet another person.

"Do you suppose anything we heard today was the truth?" I asked, even as my stomach rumbled again. The smells wafting from the kitchen were more than enticing, so I took a piece of crusty bread from the basket and dipped it into the olive oil I poured on my plate, taking a bite and humming happily.

Redvers gave his head a little shake, although whether in response to my noises or the question, I couldn't say. "It's nearly impossible to tell," he said. "Are you enjoying that bread?" His chin was now propped in his palm and he looked amused.

"How on earth are we going to figure out who did it?" I asked, ignoring his question and taking another bite. It was obviously delicious; I didn't need to tell him that.

We were interrupted by Pietro bustling out from the kitchen carrying two steaming plates of pasta. "*Allora*, here you are. You choose well," Pietro said as he placed our dinners before us. I had ordered *bigoli in salsa*, which were long, thick pasta noodles in an anchovy, onion, and white wine sauce. Redvers had ordered *spaghetti alle vongole*, which was spaghetti noodles served with clams.

We tucked into our meal, which sent my tastebuds into further raptures. Despite the fact that dinner here would take much longer than elsewhere, I was pleased we'd sought Pietro's out—it was a lovely respite after the long day of asking questions and untangling lies. I declined the offer of another carafe of wine, but I couldn't say no to the dessert and limoncello that Pietro brought once we'd both wiped our plates clean. I was absolutely stuffed full of pasta and crusty bread, but I still managed to find room for some delicious tiramisu. The limoncello was a small serving, and a lovely way to cleanse the palate after a heavy meal.

I leaned back in my chair. "Perhaps instead of taking the boat, we should walk."

Redvers chuckled. "That's not a bad idea. We could use a walk after all this."

By the time we managed to leave Pietro's restaurant it was quite late, and we were only able to leave by assuring Pietro that we would once again be back the next day. This would be an easy promise to keep since the place already felt like home, except with divine Italian food.

We left our boat where it was moored and started our walk through the city, following the winding walkways running along and sometimes over the canals. The city was quiet now, and I found myself grateful that the moon was out tonight, illuminating our steps and bouncing off the water. A light fog had rolled in off the sea, but it only added a little mystique to the evening instead of obscuring our view as it had done on evenings prior.

"Do you think we could get a look at D'Annuzzio's body?" I asked.

"What made you think of that?" Redvers asked. I could hear the amusement in his voice. "The moon," I said simply. "It wasn't out the night of the party, so you couldn't have gotten a very good look at him, even with the aid of a lantern."

Redvers nodded. "It was one of the things I asked about in my telegram. It will be very difficult to get to the body, and even more so tomorrow. He'll be transported to the San Michele cemetery first thing in the morning—and the cemetery is on a small island between Venice and Murano."

I gave a defeated sigh.

"But never fear, my dear. A copy of the coroner's report will be delivered to us."

This put a little pep back into my step. "Excellent," I said. I was happy enough with the report—I didn't actually want to take an up-close look at a dead body.

Redvers slowed to a stop, looking up at the building before us. It was several floors tall, with numerous arched windows in the reddish-orange stucco. I noticed that the stucco had broken away in quite a few places, revealing the similarly colored brick below. We were standing before a heavy wooden door that was itself carved into a series of squares, although the wood at the bottom was showing signs of age and wear.

"This is it," he said. "D'Annuzzio's residence."

Chapter Nineteen

"Huh," I said curiously, looking up at the place. It was not at all what I had anticipated for the residence of a proclaimed nationally renowned poet. But perhaps the interior was grander, like the Fontanas' apartment or even Clara's palazzo—from the outside Clara's place looked to be crumbling into the canal, but the interior had been largely restored and was fairly modern.

There were no police guarding the place, and there was no one else on the street at this time of night. Redvers went to work on the sturdy wooden door with his lockpicks, and before my nerves could rattle me enough that I felt compelled to urge him to hurry, we were slipping inside.

"Nicely done," I told him quietly as I shut the door behind me.

"You seem surprised."

I smiled in the dim light of the foyer. "Not surprised, dear. I'm merely impressed," I whispered.

"Isn't that the same thing?" he asked softly, scanning the area. I presumed he was looking for a bank of mailboxes or something that would tell us which apartment D'Annuzzio had stayed in.

"Don't you know which apartment it is?"

"I do," Redvers reassured me, heading toward the staircase. "I was just hopeful there would be some unclaimed mail."

I followed him up several flights of stairs until we came to a landing with another wooden door, much less heavy and ornate than the one leading outside. It took my husband only a matter of seconds to unlock this door, and we were inside the apartment with the door closed without hearing so much as a whisper from anyone else in the building.

It was pitch dark inside, and I stood stock-still with my back to the door while Redvers searched the wall for a light switch, finally locating one and flipping it on. The cramped hall where we stood was now dimly illuminated.

"Should we have brought some flashlights along?" I asked, still whispering. The overhead lighting was dim, but I thought there was little chance that the lights coming on wouldn't be noticed by someone passing by outside.

"It's getting close to midnight. I think we're safe, as long as we're quick."

We stepped into the main living area, where Redvers flicked on a lamp. I glanced around, shocked at how small and spare this apartment was. D'Annuzzio was a celebrated poet, so I had anticipated a lavish apartment, more in line with where the Fontana siblings were staying, but here the ceilings were once again low with thick wooden timbers running overhead. The terrazzo floor was worn, as were the rugs tossed on top of it. Given D'Annuzzio's profession, I had also anticipated books and papers and things to write with, perhaps even a cluttered desk that he might work from. But there was none of that. There was not a single book or piece of paper in sight. Nor was there any art on the walls or any indication of the type of person who stayed here.

The sparse furnishings meant that the space was easy to

search—there was little to look at in the sitting room, and we quickly dispatched the tiny kitchen and bathroom as well. That left us with only the bedroom. Redvers entered and I stood in the doorway, hands on my hips. This room was just as sparse as the rest of the apartment, with a simple bed, dresser, and wardrobe filling the space, but nothing else.

"Are we certain this is where D'Annuzzio was staying?" If I'd been told that one of the gondoliers or a restaurant worker was living here, I would have easily believed it. But a rich and famous poet? I was beginning to wonder if we had the wrong address.

"I was assured that this is the address," Redvers said. It was muffled since he had his head in the wardrobe that stood against the wall. I heard the gentle shuffling of clothing. "And these look to be his suits."

I stepped forward and moved the door to the side so that I could see what Redvers was referring to. He pulled one suit from the row and held it out. I ran my fingers down the arm and nodded. The fabric was very fine quality, the only thing that made sense in this apartment so far.

I turned my attention to the bed, lifting the corner near the foot and finding nothing. I repeated this action all the way around the mattress until I finally struck gold. Here, at last, was an envelope addressed to D'Annuzzio. I sat on the bed and studied the envelope before I slipped the letter out.

"This at least is addressed to the right man," I said, giving the letter a little wave.

Redvers had been searching each piece of clothing in the wardrobe with no result. He glanced my way, then quickly finished what he was doing before joining me on the bed.

I waited for him so we could read the letter together. Unfortunately, it was short, and entirely less interesting than I had hoped, nothing more than a request for D'Annuzzio to pay his tailor. The amount quoted was quite a hefty sum.

"It looks as though D'Annuzzio didn't pay for those suits. I wonder if he expected Clara to take care of that for him."

I glanced at Redvers who had a speculative look on his face. "I wonder," he said.

He was quiet for long enough that I prompted him to finish his thought. "You wonder what?"

"A lot of things, but right now, I'm wondering whether D'Annuzzio had some kind of hiding spot in the building. A place to stash important documents."

The floors throughout the apartment were marble terrazzo flooring, a speckled sort of marble instead of slabs, which meant that nothing could have been hidden beneath them. We swept through the entire apartment again, tapping on walls and checking the baseboards, with no luck. Redvers even stepped back outside and scanned the outside of the building, but there was no watery garage beneath and no access to the foundation. He came back inside and glanced at his watch.

"Perhaps there's nothing here," he said.

I walked through one more time, stopping in the living room. We'd looked up inside the small fireplace and even checked the hearth, but what about the mantel? It was a long marble piece, and I ran my fingers over it but found nothing except cool, smooth stone. Frustrated, I dropped my hands and was about to agree with Redvers that we should leave when I had another idea.

I moved into the tiny kitchen and pressed the terra-cotta tiles on the wall above the stove. Here, one of them gave slightly. I wanted to crow in triumph, but I also didn't want to attract attention—we'd already been in the apartment for far longer than I was comfortable with.

"Excellent job, my love," Redvers said, moving to my side to help me pull the piece from the wall. "What made you think of the stove?"

"There were marks in the fireplace—it was obviously used, and likely recently. But the kitchen looked as though it hadn't once been used to cook something."

"Making it an ideal hiding place," Redvers said as he leaned over the small stove and put his hand into the crevice we'd created by removing the tile. It took only the span of a few heartbeats before he was pulling out a small leather case, tied closed with matching leather ties. He placed it on the small table, the only furniture in the kitchen, and flipped it open. There were a handful of papers, all in Italian, which limited my ability to understand what we were looking at. Redvers rifled through them quickly while I watched, growing increasingly more uncomfortable with our presence in the apartment.

"Shouldn't we go? We can look at those back at our hotel," I finally said. Without the distraction of scanning the papers myself, I was getting nervous.

"Yes," Redvers said. "We can look at the rest of these later. Because for now, we have this," he held up one particular piece, passing it over to me.

I couldn't read any of the Italian, but I could read the name printed on it. "This says Giovanni Marchesi."

Redvers nodded. "The man who was killed isn't Christopher D'Annuzzio."

Chapter Twenty

I gasped, then quickly covered my mouth with my hand because just then there was a knock at the door to the apartment. I silently passed the paper back to Redvers who bundled it in with the others and slid the leather folder into his jacket pocket.

"Christopher?" We heard a man call at the door. He then asked something in Italian. Redvers and I stood stock-still, not daring to make a noise. The man called out something else and rattled the knob, which made my heart stop dead in my chest before it began fluttering again, much faster than before. I began looking about for an escape route, but there didn't seem to be one available other than the door where this late-night visitor stood.

Redvers moved silently to the kitchen window and looked down, then shook his head. I wasn't surprised that it wasn't a viable escape route—we were backed up to a canal, and I wasn't interested in an evening swim. I hadn't seen fire escapes on the buildings here either; something else I would have normally considered as a way out.

We would just have to wait the man out and hope that he didn't have a key to let himself in. I was grateful that Redvers had thought to lock the door behind ourselves.

There was some more muttering, then the noise stopped altogether. I didn't hear retreating footsteps, but we were also far enough from the door that we might not have heard them. We waited in silence for another ten minutes before we attempted to open the apartment door; a quick scan of the hallway outside told us it was empty, so we bolted from the place, although Redvers took the time to lock the door behind us. Once we were safely back on the street and had put a few blocks of distance between ourselves and the apartment, I asked him why he'd bothered.

"It would be more suspicious if he came back and could suddenly get in. I don't want it reported to the police that someone was in Marchesi's apartment—especially once that man, whoever he was, finds out that Marchesi is dead."

It was a fair argument, even though the extra time it had taken him to get the door locked had raised my heart rate even higher.

We were exhausted by the time we made it back to our hotel and fell into bed, especially since we had to go and retrieve our little boat from where we'd moored it earlier that night. With every step we took, I was fully aware that we were only going to get a scant few hours' sleep since we needed to be up quite early for D'Annuzzio's funeral.

Or rather, Giovanni Marchesi's.

I was in the middle of a strange dream involving circus performers and gondolas when Redvers gently shook me awake. "What time is it?" I croaked.

"Very early. But I wanted to make sure you had time to drink coffee before we need to leave the hotel."

"You're a thoughtful husband," I mumbled, eyes still sealed shut. I was grateful for the man, despite the fact that I was struggling to wake up. I pushed myself into a sitting position on the bed and sat there for a minute or so, trying to pry my eyes open. A few hours' sleep wasn't nearly enough for me—I didn't understand how Redvers managed it on a near daily basis.

The smell of coffee wafting from the sitting room finally propelled me out of bed. I slipped on my silk robe, bracing myself for Millie to come barreling through the door. I wasn't sure my aunt ever slept either, and with the funeral that morning, it was only a matter of time before she appeared.

It took a full cup and a half of coffee before my eyes were fully open. I had set into eating the breakfast pastries Redvers had ordered as well when there was a brisk knock at the door. I closed my eyes briefly, then nodded at Redvers to let Aunt Millie in. I was as ready as I would ever be.

"I found this for you, and I think it will do quite nicely for the occasion," Millie announced as she entered. She was gesturing to the bag-covered dress that was currently draped over Lord Hughes' arm.

"I'm certain it will be exactly right," I said. "You've always had wonderful taste." This wasn't necessarily true, but I knew it was what she needed to hear.

She beamed, then became serious as she took a seat in the chair across from me. Redvers picked up his teacup from where he'd set it on the table beside her and leaned casually against the fireplace mantel. He knew better than to point out that my aunt had commandeered his seat.

"What did you find out?" Millie asked.

I thought about being coy, but it was too early to play games, especially with my aunt. "Redvers, did you get a better look at that paper? Is it what we thought it was?"

He nodded and went to retrieve the leather folder we'd found from the bedroom. I had no doubt he'd stashed it away in a secure location, so it would take a moment to dig up. He returned with it a minute later, during which time my aunt's foot maintained a pounding rhythm on the floor.

"We found this hidden in D'Annuzzio's apartment."

Redvers pulled the incriminating paper from the stack. "It would appear from this birth certificate"—he paused for effect before continuing—"that he wasn't Christopher D'Annuzzio at all."

Millie gasped, and I took a sip of coffee, enjoying the theatrics. Redvers gave me a quick wink while my aunt and Lord Hughes studied the paper he'd brandished, and I smiled behind my cup.

"So where is the real Christopher D'Annuzzio?" Millie asked. "Surely there is one. And how did this man get away with such a deception? Clara even *married* this man."

These were actually some of the same things I'd been wondering since we'd found the document.

"All excellent questions, especially since Christopher D'Annuzzio is in fact a real person and a reasonably famous poet here in Italy." Redvers gave a little shake of his head before picking up his teacup once again. "It's quite impressive, actually, imitating a renowned poet in the very country where that man lives. I think the first thing we need to do is find out whether any of our suspects know what the real D'Annuzzio looks like."

Aunt Millie frowned. "Without telling them that this man is a fraud?"

Redvers nodded. "I think we need to proceed as before, pretending that Marchesi is D'Annuzzio."

"Why is that?" Lord Hughes asked.

"Because it might help us smoke out who the killer is," Redvers said.

Lord Hughes nodded his understanding of the plan, but Millie frowned. "How will it do that?"

"Every person we've spoken to so far has lied about one thing or another. Each of them has motive to want D'Annuzzio—or rather Marchesi—dead." We hadn't exactly figured out what the Fontana siblings or Orsola's motives might be, but it was easy to assume they each had one.

"Not to mention Clara's first husband and their child. They were at the party as well," I said.

Aunt Millie gasped. "I didn't know Clara had a child."

Redvers paused for a beat to let Millie and Hughes absorb that, then continued. "I think it's possible the killer knew that this man wasn't actually Christopher D'Annuzzio. If we hold back this revelation, we might be able to use it to figure out exactly who the killer is."

"Unless they all knew," Millie said.

"That's true. Which makes this a gamble that might not pay off. But it's the best one we have right now," Redvers said.

"James is just next door," I said thoughtfully. "Perhaps we should talk to him first. See what he knows about D'Annuzzio."

"Excellent point. I'll rouse him while you get dressed."

I excused myself and went to the bedroom, taking the dress that Millie had purchased along with me. It was a simple black wool dress with clean lines, and I found myself surprised at how well it fit—my aunt really had done a wonderful job.

I reentered the sitting room just as Redvers rushed back in. "Call the front desk and ask for a doctor. Or an ambulance." He was breathless and already leaving the room again, calling one more thing over his shoulder. "James has been stabbed."

Chapter Twenty-one

I grabbed the phone and dialed the front desk, asking for both a doctor and an ambulance in English. I was relieved that the clerk seemed to understand both my request and the urgency. I rushed next door and found Lord Hughes and Redvers kneeling over James, pressing a towel into what I could only assume was a wound at his shoulder, based on the blood.

"Is he . . ." I started to ask.

"He's still alive, but barely. His pulse is weak, and he's lost quite a bit of blood," Redvers said.

That was apparent from the amount of blood my husband was kneeling in. Luckily, he was wearing a black pair of trousers, but the knees would still be sticky with it. "Someone should be here soon," I said, mentally crossing my fingers that this was actually true. I was relieved when moments later I could hear the distant sound of sirens. I went to the window and peered out—a medium-sized watercraft was pulling up to the dock, the word *ambulanza* written on the side.

Knowing the room was about to become cramped with the addition of the medics, I ushered Lord Hughes and my aunt back into my own sitting room. "Aunt Millie, I think the two of you should go to the funeral. Pretend that everything is fine, and nothing has happened." I looked at her. Her face was still pale from the shock of seeing James bleeding so profusely. "Can you do that?"

Millie straightened her spine. "Of course, Jane. Honestly."

I almost smiled, but kept my composure. "Excellent. We'll meet you there as soon as possible. I'm hopeful we'll get there while the funeral is still in progress."

"Is there anyone in particular we should speak to?" Lord Hughes asked.

I thought that over. "I'm most curious about Clara's first husband and daughter."

They both nodded, then I shooed them on their way before returning next door. The men from the ambulance were already preparing to move James, and I stood out of the way while they carried him on a stretcher down the hall. Redvers joined me.

"Should we follow them?" I asked.

Redvers shook his head. "He won't be awake for some time, I don't think. I learned what hospital he'll be taken to. It's not far from here, and we can head there directly after the funeral to check on him. In the meantime, I think we should see if any of the staff or other guests on this floor saw anything."

"How long ago do you think he was stabbed?" I asked.

"I would say within the hour, or he might not have survived at all," Redvers said. "He was bleeding pretty badly."

My stomach turned over at the thought, but I steeled myself. We had work to do.

Nearly an hour later, we didn't have a whole lot to show for our efforts. After speaking to the other hotel guests on our floor, the staff in the lobby and even the surrounding merchants on the street outside our hotel, all we had was two vague descriptions of a person with long black hair—likely a wig—an oversized dark coat, and a large, floppy sun hat. It was impossible for any of the witnesses to say with certainty whether the person they had seen leaving the hotel was a man or a woman, and no one had seen any blood.

"It feels like that was a waste of time," I said. My frustration had slowly but surely built with every person we spoke to.

Redvers shrugged, checking his watch. "Not necessarily. We know that whoever did this was well prepared with a disguise. Which means it was a planned attack. James clearly knows something that the killer doesn't want getting out."

"What makes you so sure it was the killer?"

"My gut," Redvers replied easily. "Now, I think if we hurry, we can catch the tail end of the funeral."

I looked down at his crusty, blood-soaked trousers. "You'll need to change those first."

Redvers was fast, a quality I always admired about my husband. While he changed his trousers, I paced the sitting room and sent up some fervent hopes that James would be alright. Once my husband was ready, we hurried to our little boat, which I was relieved we'd had the foresight to retrieve the night before.

It was a clear, crisp morning, and the sun was already burning the last of the sea mist off the water. Our hotel was close to the northern edge of the island, so it was short work to navigate us through the canals and out onto the open water between Venice and the island of San Michele. The cemetery sprawled across the small island, which was neatly fenced with red brick walls surrounding the entire island. It was greener than I'd anticipated, especially having become accustomed to Venice, where there was no grass or trees to be seen; but here on San Michele there were Mediterranean pines and shrubs throughout, not to mention plenty of grass to be found.

We moored our boat at the landing and stepped through the entry gate. San Michele, much like Venice, appeared to be something of a maze, although this was a maze of small mausoleums and long walls with markers for burials within. "I suppose it's difficult to bury them in the ground here, with the water table so high," I murmured as we passed yet another wall covered liberally with names and dates of births and deaths.

"There are a few," Redvers said. "But yes, these types of internments are more popular."

It took a few turns before we came upon the wall where Christopher D'Annuzzio was being interred. I would have expected this type of ceremony to be reserved for family only, but having met Clara Morton, I was unsurprised to see a crushing crowd gathered. I had the uncharitable thought that she might have just gathered strangers off the streets, but I squashed it quickly.

I was glad to see that Aunt Millie and Lord Hughes had found their way to the front of the crowd, sandwiched in right beside Clara. I could only imagine how many people were elbowed by Millie to get to that position. On Clara's other side was a young woman wearing a brown tweed wool coat over a red dress. The bright color stood out against the sea of black—it was an interesting choice for funeral attire.

Redvers and I sidled around the side of the gathered mourners spread in a wide fan along the wall and moved to the back of the crowd. The officiant was droning on, and since I had no idea when the ceremony would be completed, I contented myself with studying the people around us and trying to decide whether I'd seen them before.

It felt like an eternity later when Redvers gave me a little elbow in the side, and the crowd in front of us began shuffling their feet, either leaving altogether or joining the press of mourners moving forward to offer Clara their condolences. I couldn't help but wonder how many people here knew that Clara and D'Annuzzio were divorced. I also wondered whether anyone here knew that D'Annuzzio was really Giovanni Marchesi.

I gave Redvers a return elbow in the side and tipped my head toward the break in the brick wall behind us. There was a green space with a few trees on the other side. I was restless and needed to walk off a little of my nervous energy by taking a stroll rather than wait for the crowd ahead of us to disperse. I was roiling with anxiety for my friend Deanna, as well as worried about James Robinson and whether he would recover from the stabbing.

About half an hour later, we could see that the majority of the crowd had left, leaving a clearer path for us to approach Clara and her inner circle. Alonzo and Isabella stood nearby, as did Kate Conrad. The only two missing were Ignacio Catral and Orsola Chini, but a quick scan of the funeral crowd heading to the dock revealed those two were leaving, and it appeared they were doing so together.

"Interesting," I muttered, before turning my attention back to Clara. She was wearing a tight black sheath dress and a matching pill hat with a dramatic heavy veil stretching over her face and falling nearly to her waist. I was pleased that she hadn't brought any of her menagerie with her—from what I knew of the woman, I wouldn't have been surprised if she had. Her snake, in particular, seemed as though it would have made a dramatic statement draped across her ensemble, but perhaps she really did have the welfare of her animals at heart.

Now that we were closer, I noted the fresh carving on the stone, located at about eye level in the wall before us. "Christopher D'Annuzzio," was what it read, leading me to believe that Clara didn't in fact know her second husband had been a fraud.

Aunt Millie was attempting to make conversation with

Helen, Clara's daughter, and it didn't appear to be going well. Now that I was standing beside them, I could hear Helen's one-word responses to my aunt's questions and chuckled to myself at Millie's increasing frustration with the young woman. Millie finally gave a dramatic roll of her eyes and stepped away from Helen, then muttered something to Lord Hughes, who nodded agreeably at whatever grousing my aunt was doing. I took her departure as my cue to take over.

"Nice dress," I said to the young woman. "A bold choice for a funeral, but I like it."

Helen looked at me with narrowed eyes, then shrugged. "I hated him, so why should I go to the trouble of wearing black? I'm glad he's dead."

I couldn't stop my eyebrows from disappearing into my hairline.

Helen smirked at my reaction, but I was gratified that she bothered to give me an explanation. "Clara left my father, went gallivanting around Europe, and married this man." She waved a hand dismissively at the wall. "I always thought there was something . . . not right about him. I don't know." Her brows pulled together, and I could tell she was giving this real thought, not the flippancy of the moment before. Clearly Helen was very perceptive, especially for someone so young, since there *had* been something wrong with D'Annuzzio.

While she thought, I studied her. Her brows were heavy, like her mother's. In fact, Helen bore a striking resemblance to her mother in everything but height. The girl was a few inches shorter than Clara's towering stature.

Helen focused on me again, and rather than address the multitude of issues surrounding D'Annuzzio, I changed the subject. "Is your father here?"

She looked at my left hand, the one wearing my engagement ring and wedding band. "Aren't you married already? He doesn't have any money," she said.

I just looked at the young woman steadily, awaiting a real response.

Helen huffed, then tipped her head down the path to our left. "He's over there."

I glanced in that direction to see a short, stocky man in a dark suit walking along that section of the cemetery, hands clasped behind his back as he examined the carvings on the wall there. I was surprised at the man's stature—I'd anticipated someone with Clara's height—but I supposed that was where Helen got her own height, or lack thereof.

But I wasn't finished with this young woman, not quite yet. "And why are you and your father here in Venice?"

"Why are *you* here in Venice?" Helen countered instead.

"I'm on my honeymoon," I said calmly.

Helen made a noise, somewhere between a grunt and a question. "Well, we're here to see if we can get some money out of Mother." She said the word "mother" with enough disdain that it may as well have been poison itself.

I nodded as though this made perfect sense and didn't give both Helen and her father a motive for murder. Which of course it did. It was as plain as the ski-slope nose on Helen's face that D'Annuzzio might have been viewed as what was standing between them and Clara's money.

Chapter Twenty-two

I was actually relieved when Clara joined us. I had plenty of things that I wanted to know, although I couldn't think of a way to ask them that wouldn't be confrontational or accusatory.

"Helen, that jacket does nothing for that dress. How many times have I told you that if you're going to be avant-garde in your dress, you have to go all the way," Clara said.

"It's the only coat I brought with me," Helen said, then tossed her head in defiance. "I don't have money to buy a new one."

"Well, you shouldn't run through your allowance so quickly." Clara's eyes darted around the stragglers milling around us. "Where's your father?"

"Why don't you ask him yourself?" Helen tossed back, then huffed and stomped away. It wasn't a winning riposte, and I suspected she knew it.

Clara watched her go and shook her head. "Children. I've never understood them, honestly. They're a mystery to me, especially that one." Her gaze zeroed in on me. "Do you have children?"

I shook my head. "No, we . . ."

"Good for you," she interrupted.

It took me a second to regain my footing. "I'm very sorry about Mr. D'Annuzzio."

"Yes, you and everyone else here," Clara said dismissively. "I'm glad your aunt was here, though. She's a comfort to me."

I blinked, then let that pass. "How did you and Mr. D'Annuzzio meet?"

"At a salon in Rome, I think it was." She sighed. "We were so taken with one another. I doubt I'll find that type of obsession again."

Obsession was an odd way to describe a relationship and sounded far from healthy. "Will you stay in Venice?" What I really wanted to know was whether Clara was aware of D'Annuzzio's real identity, but Redvers and I needed to do some poking around in both their pasts before coming directly out with a question like that.

"Most likely," Clara said. Her eyes flicked around again, and I could tell that she was finished with this conversation. "If you'll excuse me, I want to find my first husband." Her eyes snagged on him, still wandering near the tombs. "And I'd like to do it without Helen around. I'll avoid her for as long as possible." This last was muttered as she walked off.

Redvers joined me as soon as Clara was gone. "Learn anything interesting?"

For now, I could only shake my head. This family was nothing but troubled, and I didn't envy a single one of them.

We were quiet on the way back to Venice. Or rather, Redvers, Lord Hughes, and I were quiet. Aunt Millie had plenty to say about everyone and everything that had happened so far that morning.

"Clara's dress was a bit tight, but the veil was in good taste. I suppose it was odd for her to be considered the widow since they were divorced, but perhaps there's a reason for that. Her daughter's dress was shocking, though. Can you *imagine* showing up at a funeral wearing red, of all things?"

I thought about offering the information that some cultures wore red for a variety of reasons, but I kept it to myself.

"Very disrespectful, if you ask me. Not to mention that girl has no manners besides," Millie continued on. She was clearly wound up, as though she were on some kind of high from the morning's events, and I thought it was best to let her wear herself out. I was paying attention, though, since the moment I allowed myself to drift off I would be called on for an actual response. It never failed.

"What did you think of Clara's first husband, Jane? George Kelley, I think his name is," Aunt Millie said, turning slightly on her wooden bench seat to look at me.

I'd been right. Good thing I'd been paying attention. "I didn't get a chance to speak with him."

Aunt Millie nodded as though she'd already known the answer to her own question. "He wandered off directly after the service, which I didn't actually find odd. I thought it was odd that he was there in the first place. Why would your first husband come to the funeral of your second husband? Especially when she'd left you for him."

I shook my head, unable to answer even though the question had occurred to me, too. Millie was also on her second husband, but asking if she knew the answer to her own question would bring me nothing but trouble. I glanced at Lord Hughes, who looked incredibly amused—although it was impossible to say if it was because of his wife or the question itself.

"Everyone was at the funeral when we arrived, we were a bit late," Millie announced. "Because of the *incident*. But I looked around, and I didn't see blood on anyone's clothes. So it must not have been someone who was there."

I frowned. I hadn't seen blood on anyone's clothes either, but then again, I hadn't expected to. Perhaps the more important question was whether the attacker had time to change and get to the island. I thought that it would have been cutting things close, but whoever had stabbed James might have had enough time to change into funeral attire and catch a water taxi to the funeral if they'd been prepared.

"I can't believe you've hired this boat and didn't think to tell us," Millie continued, oblivious to my internal calculations. "It would have been most convenient for all the running about we've had to do, although I suppose you've been doing your own running about." Redvers looked relieved when he pulled our boat up outside the hotel and watched Lord Hughes help my aunt out onto the walkway, although Millie kept up her running commentary until we reached the lobby.

"If you'll excuse me," Redvers murmured, then stole off to ask at the front desk if there were any messages for him. The clerk passed over a telegram, and I perked up, anxious to know what it might be.

"I think we should get a drink," Millie said, already heading toward the bar.

"It's not even noon yet," I protested. My words fell on deaf ears—Aunt Millie was already gone and fully expecting us to join her. But I went to stand next to my husband, anxiously waiting for him to finish reading the telegram.

"What does it say?" I asked as he handed it to me. My impatience outweighed my ability to concentrate on reading the thing.

"It's a summary of the coroner's report," Redvers said in a low voice.

"And?" I flapped the telegram. I'd glanced down at it and seen a lot of jargon that I didn't want to wade through, not when my husband could summarize it for me much more quickly.

"There were no snake bites on D'Annuzzio's body, although he *was* poisoned with snake venom."

I felt a zing of triumph that what I'd told Charlie Parks had been correct, but then I frowned. "Then how was the venom administered?"

"That's the mystery, my dear."

Chapter Twenty-three

That wasn't a nearly satisfying enough explanation, so I pressed him further. "My guess is either he was stabbed with a needle somewhere very discreet—there's no mention of a needle mark either—or it was slipped into his drink," Redvers said.

My money was on the latter. "Was there a glass next to the body?" I didn't recall seeing one.

Redvers shook his head. "Whoever did this was likely careful to remove it."

"I suppose this lets Clara's snakes off the hook," I said, and Redvers shuddered. "Does it say what kind of venom?" I halfheartedly scanned the telegram I was still holding but gave up again rather quickly.

Redvers shook his head. "There were a few guesses, but nothing concrete. They'll do some more testing. It did say that he ultimately died of internal hemorrhaging and cardiac arrest caused by the poison. Which means it wasn't a snake that is native to Italy."

This time I was the one who shuddered. It sounded like an awful way to go. "Why not a native snake venom?" I asked.

Redvers looked deeply uncomfortable with the topic, but he answered my question. "Vipers are most common here, and quite a lot of venom would have to be used. Not to mention, blood vessels in the eyes and the kidneys would be affected by venom from a viper, but neither was found."

I nodded. But I hadn't forgotten about the marks on D'Annuzzio's throat and was about to mention them when Lord Hughes stepped out from the bar. "Your aunt is waiting for you, I'm afraid." He gave me a wink, and I read the unspoken subtext—my aunt was demanding our presence.

I tucked the telegram into Redvers' coat pocket before we followed after Lord Hughes. Redvers and I stopped at the bar on our way to the table where Millie was awaiting us, and I briefly considered a cocktail but ultimately ordered a cup of coffee. It was too early in the day to start imbibing alcohol, for me at least, but it was never too early for Aunt Millie. Redvers ordered a hot tea, which I supposed was a near equivalent to my coffee, although I would never be fond of the stuff. I thought it was nothing more than weakly colored water that had been heated up, and I couldn't see the point of that.

"What are our next steps?" Aunt Millie demanded when Redvers and I sat down. I decided to let Redvers field this one.

"Well," Redvers said slowly. "We need to check in on James Robinson at the hospital. And we also need to see if Deanna Parks is still in custody. I'm hopeful that the solicitor you sent over will have arranged for her release."

Aunt Millie pursed her lips. I could tell neither of these assignments were exciting enough for her. Redvers appeared to be drawing a blank as to what else we might ask my aunt to do.

"We do need to reinterview the individuals who had the best motives for wanting D'Annuzzio dead," I said slowly.

"Why is that? You've already spoken with them," Aunt Millie demanded. "And you saw most of them at the funeral. You could have asked your questions then."

I glanced at Redvers, then back at my aunt. "Because D'Annuzzio was likely a fraud," I said. "I decided the funeral wasn't the best place to bring that up, since the wrong name was on the tombstone. It felt . . . disrespectful."

Millie huffed. "You already told us he was a fraud. I was hoping you'd learned something new and interesting." But she sat up in her seat and looked at Lord Hughes. "I think we could manage asking the suspects about the fraudulent name, though, don't you, darling?" Lord Hughes nodded amiably, and Millie set to work draining the two fingers of whiskey she had left in her glass. The only person who seemed shocked by this was the bartender, who had arrived with my coffee and Redvers' tea.

"Bring us a piece of paper and a pen," Aunt Millie barked at the bartender.

He scurried away, returned with the items she'd requested, and left again just as quickly. I couldn't blame him and made a mental note to tip the poor man well.

Aunt Millie instructed Redvers to make a comprehensive list of our suspects, complete with the addresses where they could be found. Once she had that in hand, she and Lord Hughes left. I breathed a guilty sigh of relief once they'd gone—I felt bad for wanting Millie occupied away from us, but I was able to think more clearly with her gone.

"Nicely done, my love," Redvers said once they'd gone, sipping cautiously at his hot tea.

"Thank you." I paused. "Although heaven knows how well she'll do. We probably should have done it ourselves."

Redvers seemed remarkably unconcerned. "Hughes was in the war. I trust that he knows how to conduct an interrogation without tipping his hand entirely."

I wasn't worried about Hughes—it was my aunt that was likely to give too much away to our suspects. The slightest frustration would set her mouth to spilling everything. But something else had occurred to me. "We're assuming what we found is Marchesi's real birth certificate. Is there a way to confirm that?"

Redvers took a fuller sip of tea. "I'm having Marchesi's background and the real D'Annuzzio's background investigated. We won't have access to enough records here in Venice, since D'Annuzzio was reportedly from Rome. Hopefully someone will get back to us soon."

I thought about that. "Do we know where Clara and this fake D'Annuzzio were married?"

"What are you thinking?" Redvers asked.

"If it was here in Venice, we might be able to get a look at their marriage license. I'm curious about what name the groom used."

Redvers nodded. "Excellent idea."

Other than that, I trusted that his fellow employees of the British Crown would get us the other information we needed. In the meantime, though the tasks didn't appeal to Millie, we would speak with James Robinson and Deanna and see what information they might have for us. Worry for Deanna was never far from my mind—and my stomach—and I hoped that seeing her would assuage some of my anxiety.

Although it was entirely likely that seeing my friend in a jail cell might have the completely opposite effect. All I could really hope was that the lawyer Millie had hired was a good one, and that in the meantime we were able to find the real killer.

We decided to head to the hospital and see if James was awake. With luck, he'd be able to identify the person who had stabbed him. And at the very least, he might know where Clara and the fake D'Annuzzio were married, given that he'd worked for her for some time. Not since the wedding itself, but it seemed like something that would have come up at least once during his employment.

On our way, I filled Redvers in on what I'd learned about Clara's first husband and daughter.

He frowned. "That gives both of them a motive, although Helen seems a bit young to poison someone with snake venom."

"Never underestimate the rage of a young woman," I said airily.

"I defer to your greater knowledge."

"You should," I said, looking up at the building we'd arrived at. "Are you certain this is a hospital?" I was only half joking—from the outside this looked more like a church, with its white marble façade and carved statues dotting the series of half-moons running along the top.

Redvers stepped from our boat, tugging at the rope to make certain it was secure before joining me in looking up at the building. "I see what you're getting at, but I can assure you it's a hospital."

He led me toward the elegant building, breaking toward the right, to the smaller entrance located there. Once inside, I again had to question whether this was a hospital. Beautiful white marble pillars scattered about the cavernous room stretched from the dark timbered ceiling down to the grey and orange patterned marble floor. We traipsed to the other end of the room, where it finally felt as though we were in a medical facility, although the gorgeous marble was still present throughout. We easily spotted a nurse, and Redvers asked her in smooth Italian where we might find James Robinson; she pointed us toward the back of the hospital. We asked twice more before we were able to locate James' room, since it was tucked away, smaller than the other rooms we'd seen, and I suspected this was largely due to the color of his skin. The upside was that it made him more difficult to find if his attacker decided to try again.

James appeared to be dozing, and we waited quietly at

his bedside for several minutes. A nurse came in to check on the patient and frowned at us but didn't ask us to leave. She did, however, wake James up by checking his pulse, and he was surprised to see us.

"How are you feeling?" Redvers asked.

"Grateful that you found me when you did," James said.

Redvers nodded, then got down to business. "Do you remember who attacked you?"

James shook his head. "I've been racking my mind, but I can't remember anything."

I tried to hide the disappointment from my face, but I wasn't terribly successful.

James noticed and sighed. "I know, I wish I could say who it was. I'll keep trying, though. Maybe once I'm feeling better it will come back to me."

I didn't have a lot of faith that that was likely to happen, so I changed the topic. "Did they have to do surgery?" I asked.

His hand drifted to the white bandage on his shoulder, the edges of which were visible at the edges of his hospital gown. "No, they were able to stitch me up and then pump some blood into me." He gave a half smile that looked more like a grimace. "Good as new, I guess."

If they hadn't had to do major surgery, the knife must have missed the most important parts. I wondered if this was because the attacker was bad at stabbing someone, or whether James had managed to avoid worse damage by defending himself as he had. I supposed we wouldn't know the answer unless James managed to remember what happened.

"Do you have any idea why you were attacked?" I asked.

James shook his head. "I've been wondering that since I woke up. Maybe someone thought I had some money? But I didn't take anything from Mrs. Morton's place."

I would never have accused the man of that, and I was sorry it was the first thing he assumed someone might think.

Redvers interrupted. "Is there anything you might have learned about Clara? Or about her husband, Christopher D'Annuzzio?"

James looked confused. "Like what?"

Redvers and I looked at one another, not wanting to come out and ask about D'Annuzzio's real identity but lacking a good answer otherwise. "I don't know," Redvers admitted. "I'm just wondering if there is something you might have learned about them or even someone else, something that your attacker doesn't want anyone to learn. It might be something strange, not necessarily a secret." Redvers' brow wrinkled when he finished—I could tell he wasn't happy with his convoluted answer.

But James considered that for a long moment, then shook his head. "I can't think of anything. Of course, with all the goings on at that place, it's hard to say what might stick out to someone. But I'll keep thinking about it."

He made an excellent point. With such an eccentric employer, it was probably quite difficult to say what was considered strange.

"Do you happen to know where Clara Morton and Mr. D'Annuzzio were married?" I asked.

James's eyebrows pulled together. "I wasn't working for her then, but let me think." He closed his eyes, and after some time, I started to grow concerned that he'd fallen back asleep. But then he opened them again, caught the concern on my face, and grinned. "I'm still with you. And I do remember hearing her mention that they were married here in Venice. But not at the big church."

"St. Mark's Basilica?" Redvers asked.

James cocked his head, then winced. "Shouldn't do that. Yes, St. Mark's. She was very angry that they wouldn't let her get married at that one." He squinted his eyes nearly shut, clearly trying to remember the name. "Um, I think it was something about miracles."

"Thank you," Redvers said. "We can figure it out from that."

James' face relaxed again, then winced in pain when he adjusted in his bed.

"Are they keeping you overnight?" I asked. I didn't want to scare the man, but I was concerned for him staying here, unprotected. At night it would be much easier to track him down with quieter halls and sleeping patients, and though he was clearly in pain, I thought it might be better for him to recover outside of the hospital.

"It seems so, but I'm going to do my best to get out. I want to find somewhere to hide out, maybe outside of the city. I'm not interested in acquiring another scar," James said, his tone light, even playful.

I smiled. I was relieved that he was aware of the danger he might still be in, and even had a sense of humor about it.

I couldn't help but think Clara was a fool for firing this man.

Chapter Twenty-four

Back outside we briefly considered splitting up, one of us to identify the church and the other to the jail to speak with Deanna, but ultimately we decided to do them together. We worked well as a team, not to mention the limiting fact that I didn't speak any Italian beyond *buon giorno* and *grazie*.

I really needed to start studying foreign languages.

We headed to the police station first, winding our way along the canals until we had nearly reached the westernmost edge of the city and came upon a long, red brick building, clearly newly built and several stories tall, and by far one of the least attractive in the city. *Polizia Municipale* was carved on a metal plaque next to the wooden entrance door, which Redvers pushed inside as I followed close behind. The typical low ceilings and terrazzo floors were present, marking it as a typical Venetian building. A *polizia di stato*, and a very young one by my estimation, stood behind the long wooden desk where visitors were expected to register when they entered. Redvers asked to speak with Ispettore Fizzoli, and we were told to wait while the young officer looked to see whether the man was in.

At least that's what Redvers told me the young man said.

He could have told us to jump into the canal for all I understood.

But Fizzoli himself was standing before us only moments later, hands on hips, eyes narrowed as he looked us over. Redvers said something in rapid Italian, while I gave my most winning smile. Fizzoli looked from Redvers to me and back again before giving his head a little shake and motioning for us to follow him.

We stepped past the desk and through a doorway, then down a hall past numerous doors leading to I could only guess where, since they were mostly unlabeled. We followed the *ispettore* into what appeared to be his office, a small, cramped space with one window and nothing more than a wooden desk and a filing cabinet, with absolutely nowhere for visitors to sit. I was unbothered by this since I didn't want to spend any more time here than absolutely necessary; I wanted to check on my friend Deanna and then get back to uncovering a killer so that we could get Deanna out of here.

It looked as though Fizzoli had the same idea, at least the part about us leaving as quickly as possible.

"I hope you are not making a nuisance of yourselves around the city," Fizzoli said in accented but beautiful English.

"We're simply trying to figure out what happened to Christopher D'Annuzzio." Redvers left out the fact that we were trying to discover exactly who D'Annuzzio *was* as well. "And what happened to James Robinson, who was stabbed at our hotel this morning."

"Yes," Fizzoli said. "I heard there was some trouble. Not likely to be related, though. Is that all? I have much work and many cases I need to attend to."

That didn't bode well—if he had "many cases" it was unlikely that he was concentrating on finding D'Annuzzio's real killer. I hated the idea that the *ispettore* thought he'd already sewn this case up by arresting Deanna.

Redvers was clearly thinking along the same lines. "Are you certain you have the right person? That there isn't someone else out there you haven't considered? D'Annuzzio wasn't well liked—there were plenty of people within his own circle with a motive."

Fizzoli's face was annoyed, and I wondered if we'd made a misstep by pressing the question. "D'Annuzzio was killed by snake venom, we have the snake woman."

Redvers looked at the *ispettore*, then pulled the leather folder from his pocket. "What if that man wasn't truly Christopher D'Annuzzio?"

It was nothing more than a distraction, but a good one since the *ispettore* now looked worried rather than annoyed, even more so when Redvers passed the birth certificate over to him. "Where did you find this?" Fizzoli demanded.

"In D'Annuzzio's apartment."

"My men went over that apartment and found nothing," Fizzoli muttered.

"It was well hidden," Redvers offered.

Fizzoli dropped the certificate on his immaculate desk. "I will have to look into this." He rubbed a hand down his face. "If it is true, it is not good news. I have already spoken with the newspapers about D'Annuzzio's death and given an official statement. He is a beloved poet here in *Italia*. How could someone be impersonating him?"

This was the *ispettore's* real worry then—he'd spoken to the papers and would look incredibly foolish if the real D'Annuzzio stepped forward and proved himself to be alive. Especially given the poet's apparent popularity. I was hopeful that this was good news for us—it might spur the *ispettore* to do a more thorough job, although I was now concerned that he might simply snap someone else up in order to save face. Someone like Charlie Parks, whose fingerprints could be anywhere in the palazzo, including the snake room.

"I have some experience with these types of investigations and would be happy to assist you. Or at least tell you everything we learn," Redvers said cautiously.

Fizzoli narrowed his eyes slightly at Redvers. "I did some checking about you. It is true that you work for the British, but how can I trust your information? Perhaps you have some other motive."

Redvers regarded him steadily. "I have no other motive than finding who killed this man and helping our friend go free. I do not believe Deanna Parks was responsible."

"And so you will make sure someone else was responsible," Fizzoli said.

I could sense Redvers' frustration, although he showed no outward signs beyond a slight tightening of his shoulders. He shook his head adamantly. "I only search for the truth. Even if that means I am wrong about the identity of the killer, I will be honest about that."

Fizzoli searched my husband's face, then finally gave a brisk nod. "Very well. And I suppose you want to speak with your *friend*."

I didn't care for the way he said "friend," but I kept my face and body perfectly still. We were about to get what we'd come for, and I knew better than to anger the man and throw away our opportunity to see Deanna.

"We would like to see her, actually, but I have another question for you first," Redvers said.

I tensed even further, if that were possible. I had no idea what he meant to ask, but I was concerned we had just wasted our chance to see Deanna.

The *ispettore* cocked his head at Redvers, who continued with his question. "Was Clara Morton's drink actually poisoned? The champagne?"

I was worried that this delay would cause Fizzoli to change his mind about letting us see Deanna, but I *was* curious about the answer.

Fizzoli gave a casual flip of his hand. "It was not," he said. "Merely a bad bottle. It was tested, and nothing could be found." He narrowed his eyes. "Is *that* all?" Redvers nodded, and Fizzoli shouted something in Italian, causing me to jump, but another young *polizia* quickly appeared in the doorway. The *ispettore* told us to follow the young man, and with that, we were dismissed.

We traversed the rest of the hallway, then turned through a doorway and walked past an open space with other desks, then down a different poorly lit hallway and through a thick door that closed with a final-sounding thud behind us. Here it appeared we were in the jail portion of the building, with a row of heavily barred cells on either side. We walked to the end of the row, passing women who were passed out or shouting things in Italian at the officer we were with. A glance at Redvers' face assured me that whatever was being yelled was crude at the very least.

Deanna looked awful, her long hair frizzing out from its braid and dark circles under her eyes. The small cot in her room did not look comfortable, although that was surely intentional, since the rest of the cell looked modern. Her large eyes pooled with tears at the sight of us, and she rushed forward to the iron bars. I gripped her hands—we were not allowed inside the cell, so I couldn't offer her a proper hug.

Redvers said something to the *polizia*, but the young man shook his head. This was as good as we were going to get. I supposed we should feel grateful we were being allowed to speak to her at all.

"How are you holding up?" I asked her.

Deanna simply shook her head, a few tears spilling onto

her cheeks, which she hastily wiped away after releasing my hands.

"Has the solicitor been here to see you?" Redvers asked.

Deanna took a deep breath and nodded. "He seems quite good. He said he would file paperwork to get me released. He doesn't think they have enough to hold me, so he is hoping to speak with a judge to get me released, even if I can't leave the city."

I hoped that would come to fruition. She'd already been incarcerated for far too long, and it had only been two nights. From the looks of it, it had been two nights with very little sleep, which made sense given where she was. I was at least grateful she seemed to be in a women-only portion of the building.

"Are they feeding you at least?" I asked.

She gave a sad chuckle. "Pasta, and better than you can get at home. At least the food in here is decent."

"We're doing everything we can to get you out, and that means finding the real killer," I said. "Do you know anything that could help us?" I didn't think it was likely since she'd told us everything she knew already. But it was always worth asking.

Deanna dropped her voice to a whisper. "Charlie was at that party."

I nodded. "He told us."

Her eyes searched mine, pleading. "I think he might have killed that man."

Chapter Twenty-Five

This was certainly an unexpected accusation. "Surely you don't mean that," I said. "Charlie wouldn't do something so stupid." I could acknowledge that Charlie seemed inclined to do stupid things—quite a few of them, honestly. But I didn't think he was capable of murder.

Deanna looked scared for the first time—up until this moment she'd merely looked tired or even defeated by her situation, but not scared. "I don't know for sure, but he's been acting strange for a few weeks now. And every time I brought up D'Annuzzio's name he would get angry. I've never seen him like that before."

I was still frowning. "Do you think Charlie was simply jealous?" Jealousy was something I could see, especially since it was the reason Charlie had given for being at the party in the first place. But was it possible that Charlie thought Deanna was having an affair with D'Annuzzio and decided to eliminate the competition for his wife's affection? Even as I thought it, I shook my head. I knew there was no way Deanna would have trifled with D'Annuzzio. He'd touched her once and she'd sent him to the ground—even during her recounting of that event, she'd been so delighted at the outcome that there was no way she would have had an affair with the man.

But would Charlie have come to that same conclusion?

Deanna sighed, her expression easing into worry instead of fear. "Charlie does have a jealous streak." Deanna made a face, nose wrinkled. "But D'Annuzzio? I don't know why Charlie would be jealous of that man. He was so *oily*, I hated to be in a room with him. And Charlie knew that, or at least he should have, as many times as I've complained about him."

This was in line with what I thought. "Did D'Annuzzio ever touch you before?"

Deanna shook her head. "No, just the one time. And I don't regret how I reacted." This was said with more than a little defiance, and I gave a small smile.

But my smile quickly faded. It looked like Deanna and Charlie were both in hot water, especially if Fizzoli learned that Charlie had been at the party as well. The couple would likely find themselves in adjoining cells. "I don't think Charlie had anything to do with it," I told her. I pushed confidence into my voice despite the doubts that had begun to creep in. "But I do think you should talk to him about it, tell him your concerns." It wouldn't be good for their marriage to let any kind of secret simmer, and I would truly hate to see them torn apart, especially at a time like this when they needed each other more than ever.

Deanna pursed her lips but nodded. Redvers and I said our goodbyes, giving her our best assurances, before we were escorted out. I hated the sound of the heavy door closing behind us—it sounded so final, with my friend trapped on the other side of it.

I vowed once again to find the truth and set her free.

We waited until we were outside and well away from the police station before we spoke, and it was Redvers who went first. "None of this bodes well for either of the Parks," he said.

"I know," I replied, reaching for his hand. He gave me a

reassuring squeeze. "I'm worried about both of them, as well as their marriage."

"One problem at a time," Redvers said reasonably, but he gave my hand another squeeze.

I nodded and took a deep breath, filling my lungs with sea air. "What next?"

"Let's see if we can figure out where the church of miracles is," he said.

We took our little boat back to our hotel, mooring it nearby and heading to the front desk, both to ask about messages and to inquire about the church we were looking for. There were no messages for either of us, but the clerk behind the counter was very helpful when we inquired whether there was a church of miracles in the city.

"A church of miracles? Do you mean the Santa Maria dei Miracoli? It means St. Mary of Miracles."

Redvers and I both flashed him big smiles. "I'll bet that is exactly what we're looking for," I said. "Do you know where it is?"

He shrugged. "Certainly, it is not far."

I wasn't convinced it would be close either, since "not far" could mean almost anything, but he assured us it was only a twenty-minute walk, so we opted to go by foot instead of by water.

We strolled hand in hand over cobblestones and stone footpaths, seeming for all the world like a pair of newlyweds instead of what we truly were—an agent of the British Crown and his murder-focused wife. For the moment, anyway. I was hopeful that we could solve this particular murder quickly and get back to enjoying our honeymoon.

The clerk was correct, and it was twenty minutes later that we arrived in front of the Church of St. Mary of Miracles. It wasn't as large or striking as St. Mark's Basilica, but it was still a gorgeous building, with a marble façade of varying colors beneath an arching half-moon at the top, flanked and topped by carved statues. The half-moon itself had a series of circular windows in varying sizes, most of which looked to be made of stained glass.

The inside was no less stunning, done entirely in marble of varying shades and colors. Wooden pews made two rows on either side leading to the front, where a long series of marble stairs led up to the altar. The ceiling was also something to behold, intricately carved with painted scenes in geometric shapes, the carvings themselves painted in gold. Redvers let me gaze around, soaking in the gleaming beauty for a lingering moment before we got down to business. He knocked on a wooden door off to the left, just before the marble stairs, and found a young priest. Redvers asked him a question in Italian, and the young man gave a detailed reply, complete with elaborate hand gestures.

I hoped the priest was giving us directions. This wish was granted when Redvers began leading me in the direction that the priest had indicated. "There's an office next door," he said. "We should be able to ask there."

We left the same way we'd come in and went to the rather reserved-looking building next door. Redvers knocked on the large wooden door, and we waited for a moment before it was opened by a woman in a habit. Redvers spoke to her in Italian, and she nodded, then gestured for us to follow her. We stepped inside and followed the nun down a long hallway, until she paused and directed us through an open door.

Here we found a woman—not a nun—with wire-framed glasses and grey hair pulled into a severe bun at a desk in the front part of the office, poking at keys on a typewriter. She looked at us over the top of her glasses, and Redvers made our request in Italian once again. Cocking her head, she replied, looking at me curiously. Redvers spoke again, this time to explain that I did not speak Italian, or so I assumed.

"Is no problem, we speak English," she said with a kind smile pointed my way that I immediately returned. I was surprised that a woman her age spoke such good English since it had seemed to be a much younger Italian crowd that was conversant in it. "You need to see wedding certificate? You are already married, no?"

Redvers agreed with her that we were already married. "No, we need to see the marriage certificate of Clara Morton and Christopher D'Annuzzio."

"You are not them," she said. Her voice was pleasant—she seemed merely curious.

"We are not," I said. "They were married here, and Mr. D'Annuzzio was killed. We are trying to learn what happened."

The woman gasped, her hand going to her chest. "No, not Mr. D'Annuzzio! This is tragedy."

I was taken aback by her reaction, before remembering that the man was meant to be a famous national poet. I soberly nodded my head in agreement. "You can see why we need help."

"Yes, yes," she said. "But we do not have the certificate here." My heart dropped—this was a wasted trip, then. But the woman stood, her black dress swishing as she moved to a large bank of wooden cabinets. "We only have register."

Redvers and I looked at one another and he shrugged. A series of leather-bound books were stacked on top of the cabinets, and she began pulling them down. Redvers quickly moved to help her, and soon the three of us were paging through books, propped open on a table that she cleared off for us to do exactly this. We had an idea of when the two were married, but we didn't know exactly when, which meant reading about the births, deaths, and marriages of an overwhelming number of local Italians. I was beginning to despair that we would be here until we went blind when I finally heard music to my ears.

"Here," Redvers said. The woman—whose name turned out to be Maria—and I hurried to his side. Maria frowned as she read the names Redvers was pointing to.

"But this says Giovanni Marchesi," Maria's voice was scandalized. "What does this mean?" It was clear that Maria's affront was very real. I wasn't sure if it was on behalf of the church or the real D'Annuzzio, but either way, I hoped Redvers had an answer that would appease her.

"Perhaps she did not know she was marrying the wrong man. Could this Marchesi have hidden his name while signing this?" Redvers asked.

Maria thought this through. "No," she finally said. "Both this Clara and Giovanni would sign at the same time. I do not see how he could hide this lie." She continued muttering. "In front of God and the church." She made the sign of the cross.

We thanked Maria, then helped her return the heavy registers to where we'd pulled them from before taking our leave, making sure we thanked her again for her help. She seemed a little more disgruntled than when we'd arrived, but that couldn't be helped.

Back on the street outside, I insisted we find a café. I needed a coffee and a bite to eat, not to mention a moment to think everything through before we decided on our next steps. For once Redvers agreed without giving me a hard time about my coffee intake. I took this to mean he was deep in thought.

The sky was overcast and chilly, a brisk breeze rolling off the surrounding sea, so we opted for a small table indoors at the first café we came upon. I ordered an espresso and a large slice of tiramisu.

"Are you willing to share that, or should I ask for my own?" Redvers asked with a sparkle in his eyes.

"I *suppose* I can let you have some of mine," I replied. "But if you eat too much of it, I will order a second piece that will be only for myself."

Redvers smiled, although the waiter looked less amused at our repartee and left to get our drinks and dessert. "He didn't find us charming," I said.

"It's his loss," Redvers said. He then put his chin in his palm, balanced on the small table. "What are you thinking?"

"I'm thinking that Clara Morton had to know she was marrying an imposter."

Redvers bobbed his head in agreement against his propped hand. It was slightly ridiculous, but he was still so handsome that I was compelled to smile at him, setting aside my worry and frustration for just a moment to enjoy my husband. We were meant to be on our honeymoon, after all.

The waiter returned with my coffee, Redvers' tea, and our slice of tiramisu. I took a bite of the spongy dessert and sighed with pleasure. It was delicious and just a little decadent, smacking of espresso and cream.

We enjoyed a few moments of silence while we savored the dessert, and then turned back to the topic at hand. "We should speak with Clara again," Redvers said.

I pressed my lips together but couldn't argue the point. "I do wish there was a way around that. It's impossible to tell whether that woman is telling the truth or telling stories."

He dipped his head in acknowledgement, then paused. "You appear . . . I can't quite think of the right term. More invested? More determined?" He cocked an eyebrow. "Either works, I suppose. Anyway, more determined than usual, with this case. Which is saying something, really."

I sipped at my espresso. It was thick and dark and, once I added a splash of cream, absolute perfection. "I know that Deanna and Charlie are really nothing more than acquaintances—we didn't keep in touch after Egypt, even if I meant to. But I still feel a real . . . duty, I suppose, to ensure she's released. She had nothing to do with D'Annuzzio's death, I know that in my gut." I paused, deciding how best to explain my feelings. "During my first marriage I thought I had a number of friends, but one by one they disappeared. There was no one to help me, not really. I never want to see that happen to someone else, especially someone accused of murder."

Redvers' liquid brown eyes held mine, and he nodded solemnly. "We'll sort this out and make sure she goes free."

I smiled at him. It was yet another lovely reminder that I'd made the right choice in marrying this man. Then I sobered. "I'm disturbed that Deanna thinks Charlie might have killed D'Annuzzio. Do you think it's possible? Have we incorrectly been ignoring Charlie Parks as a suspect?"

Redvers considered, then cocked his head, but when he opened his mouth, he did not give me the answer I expected, or even hoped for.

"Anything is possible," he said.

Chapter Twenty-six

I stared at him, agog, until he explained further. "Perhaps I should say, I think it's possible, but unlikely." I breathed out a sigh of relief. "Whoever poisoned D'Annuzzio had to either bring in the snake venom or import it, since it's not native to Italy. I think Deanna would have noticed a vial of poisonous venom in her husband's things, and I can't imagine something like that is easy to obtain on short notice," Redvers said.

I thought over the prospect of Charlie Parks importing poison. I couldn't imagine the man having enough foresight to bring such a thing along with them on their travels across Europe, nor did I think he'd be effective at hiding it from his wife, not in the long term. Or even in the short term, for that matter. Charlie's sleight of hand was excellent, but Deanna was likely to see right through it, since she was no slouch herself in that department. They'd both spent a lot of time on the vaudeville circuit before going to Egypt and then coming to Europe—I imagined they'd both seen all the tricks of the trade.

"Who would have imported such a thing?" I mused.

"Any one of them," Redvers said. "Any of the rest of them, that is."

"I wonder if Aunt Millie has gotten anywhere with our

suspects." I was mostly being flippant, but a small part of me was holding out hope that Millie would be able to extort some useful information from our list of suspects.

"If anyone can, it's Millie," Redvers said with a smile. "Shall we?"

I sighed and drained the very last drops of my espresso. It was time to visit Clara Morton again.

We got into our little rented boat and wound our way through the side canals, coming out onto the Grand Canal nearly across from Clara's palazzo, so we only had to make a small leap across the busiest waterway. We alighted onto the marble platform and walked up the stairs to the front gate. Redvers used the knocker, and we waited only a few beats before it was opened.

By Charlie Parks.

My mouth fell open, and Charlie's eyebrow popped up before he gave his head a small shake. "Who might I say is calling?" he asked loudly.

Redvers was doing a much better job of taking this unexpected development in stride. "Mr. and Mrs. Wunderly," Redvers said. "Here to see Mrs. Morton."

Charlie nodded and had us stand just inside the front door. Redvers and I exchanged a look. "He's being reckless," I muttered.

"Or he may learn something," Redvers replied, equally as quiet.

Charlie returned and led us to a sitting room downstairs. We hadn't been in the room before, and I gazed around at the gallery of paintings and photographs hung on the walls, all of Clara in various states of dress. My eyes finally fell on Clara, lounging on a fainting couch upholstered in black velvet and positioned beneath the room's largest window along the top of the low ceiling. She was wearing the elaborately embroidered silk robe again with nothing underneath, and I wondered if this was because she'd just finished being painted or because it was more comfortable for her. Either way, I decided I was pleased she was wearing anything at all.

Charlie was still standing in the doorway, wearing a black suit identical to the one James had worn while working for Clara. I wondered if she had a collection of them at the ready, for servants that might come and go based on her whims.

"That will be all, Robert," Clara said. Charlie gave a little bow and took his leave, his employer Clara frowning after him. "He's new, and not a bad replacement, although he still has quite a bit to learn."

I nodded politely, doing my best to mask how horrified I was at Charlie's subterfuge. I didn't think it could last long before he was found out by either Clara or the police—I hoped he could work fast to learn something useful and make this dangerous game he was playing worthwhile.

"I was just speaking with Millie," Clara said, refocusing her gaze on me. "She suggested that I have a dinner party, and I think it's a grand idea. In fact, I'm planning one for tomorrow night. You're both welcome to join us, of course."

So far, our visit was nothing but a series of shocks, and it was a struggle each time to keep my face neutral. I was horrified that Clara would have a dinner party so soon after someone was murdered in her palazzo, and equally horrified that my aunt would suggest such a thing. Luckily, Redvers stepped in to save me from saying anything inappropriate. "We'd be delighted to join you," he said. "What time should we arrive?"

"Seven in the evening. We'll begin dining at eight," Clara said.

I would be sure to have a snack before we arrived or I would be famished by the time we were actually eating. "Who else is joining us?" I asked.

"Ignacio, Alonzo and Isabella, your aunt and her husband." Clara cocked her head, her eyes now focused on a painting of herself, windswept and nude on the edge of the ocean. "My first husband and Helen, my ungrateful daughter. And Kate, of course."

Nearly every person on our suspect list, then. I wondered if instead of speaking with each person, Millie had simply convinced Clara to throw this dinner party and arrange for everyone to be in one place. It certainly sounded like something my aunt would cook up. I also wondered if we were being invited as an afterthought or if Millie had bothered to include us from the beginning of her scheme. It didn't truly matter either way, it was simply bemusing.

"Where is Kate?" I asked. The last time we'd met, I had genuinely enjoyed the woman's company as well as her wit.

Clara refocused on me, lips pursed. "Since Helen decided to take up residence here, Kate has been making herself absent. It's quite annoying, and I'm thinking about having Helen go back to stay with her father, maybe return to America altogether. It's interfering with my *pleasure*."

I didn't need her to explain what that meant—my imagination could do quite well on its own without any further information. "Kate doesn't care for your daughter, then?" I asked. I moved to one of the upholstered chairs clustered near Clara's fainting couch and took a seat without being invited. I'd realized it was the only way I was going to get off my feet.

Clara watched me without any sort of reaction, answering my question instead. "Well, who does? She's always been such a difficult child."

"According to you," said a voice from the doorway.

I whipped my head around to see Helen standing stiffly and quite still, as though trying to make up her mind about something. She finally took a few lurching steps into the room, then settled into a more natural gait and finished crossing the room before dropping into the seat next to mine. I glanced at Redvers, who decided to walk to the nearest window and lean against the wall beneath it rather than try to find alternative seating.

Clara had merely shrugged at the announcement, watching her child cross the room and join us. "Well, it's true, Helen. I think even your father would agree."

"I very much doubt that," Helen countered. "And we haven't agreed to join your dinner party."

"See what I'm saying?" Clara said with an exaggerated sigh.

This was going nowhere, and I needed to find a way to redirect the conversation toward what we'd come here to learn. I glanced at Helen, wondering if we should mention D'Annuzzio in front of the girl, then decided she would hear about it later anyway. I also decided that it was best to use what we'd already learned in a direct way with Clara—perhaps it would compel her to tell the truth as well. "Clara, it seems you were fully aware that Christopher D'Annuzzio wasn't your husband's real name."

Clara's face didn't change, although Helen's eyes went wide. "My ex-husband, but yes, of course I knew that. Couldn't very well marry a stranger, could I?"

"Why was he pretending to be D'Annuzzio the poet?" I asked. Out of the corner of my eye I saw Helen's mouth drop open.

Clara shrugged. "The real D'Annuzzio is a hermit. They're related . . . second cousins, I think? Or maybe third. Either way, they're relations of a sort, and D'Annuzzio was content to have someone else play the public role of the great poet. And of course, Giovanni couldn't write worth a damn, so it worked out for the both of them."

We'd seen the inside of Giovanni's sparse apartment, so it

was hard to say that the ruse had "worked out" for the man, especially since he'd been murdered. "Where is the real D'Annuzzio?" I asked

Now Clara looked amused. "Rome, I think. Do you want to speak with him, see if I'm telling the truth?" I didn't answer, and she shrugged again. "You can try, but he doesn't have a telephone and refuses to answer the door. There is a local woman who brings him food, cleans the place up a bit, it's a real hovel, but that's all the interaction he's interested in."

I glanced at Redvers, who was frowning. I suspect he thought what I did—that this was all very convenient, a man who refused to speak to outsiders. It made it difficult to figure out whether she was telling the truth or not.

"And you know this firsthand?" Redvers asked.

"Of course not," Clara said. "How would I speak to him? D'Annuzzio doesn't speak to outsiders." She said this last part slowly and loudly, as though Redvers was either stupid or hard of hearing and that was why he hadn't understood her.

But this admission meant that everything Clara knew about D'Annuzzio came from Giovanni, which meant it could be entirely invented. There was no real way to know for certain without speaking with the hermit directly, although perhaps it didn't matter? We knew that Clara was fully aware of her second husband's deception, which was what we'd come to find out.

I was curious about something else, though. "The Catholic church won't marry someone who is divorced. How did you convince them to let you have the ceremony at St. Mary's?"

Clara seemed unfazed by how much we'd learned about her. "You offer someone enough money and they'll look the other way. Works every time. Even with the Catholic church, although I still can't believe they wouldn't let me use St. Mark's

Basilica." Clara frowned. "Even with the sum I offered, the best the cardinal said he could do was St. Mary of Miracles. In the end, I decided it was fitting, since it was a miracle I was getting married again, so it all worked out."

Helen had been tracking our entire conversation with wide eyes, but her face darkened like an impending storm at the mention of money. I wasn't surprised—this seemed to be a major point of contention between Helen and her mother. I was, however, surprised that Clara noticed her daughter's reaction. The woman seemed oblivious to quite a lot.

Clara waved a hand dismissively at her child. "Your father signed paperwork before we were married, Helen. It clearly stated that he wouldn't get any of my money if we divorced. That's his own fault, darling. And besides, he has had plenty of opportunity to make his own fortune."

This did nothing to appease Helen, who opened her mouth to reply but was interrupted by Redvers. I was grateful—I didn't need or want to witness more arguing between these two.

"How did you come to hire the new butler?" Redvers asked.

Clara didn't even pause, completely unfazed by the sudden change in conversation. "He just showed up, looking for work," Clara said. "And I obviously needed a new butler, since I had to let James go. After he tried to *poison* me."

It wasn't worth arguing this with her, even though I knew the champagne hadn't actually been poisoned. In fact, I thought it likely that Clara knew this as well—which was a good reminder that anything Clara said or did was either exaggerated or a lie told for effect. "Do you know what became of James?" I asked.

Clara actually looked confused by the question. "How would I know? He probably went back to his own people, in Africa or wherever I found him."

I could not stop my lip from curling this time. I was beyond disgusted by her calloused attitude and casual dismissal of a loyal employee, but nothing would be accomplished by pointing out that James was a human being with a life and family of his own. Nor did I mention that he'd been stabbed, likely because of something he'd learned while working for Clara, since it was unlikely to elicit any sympathy from her and might only make things dangerous for James, having that information put into society. With any luck, the attacker thought James was dead and wouldn't make a second attempt.

Although I no longer wondered if Clara had been his attacker, since she seemed genuinely unaware of what had happened to her former employee. She played the part of a dramatic actress, but she wasn't necessarily a good one.

But something *did* occur to me that hadn't until I was sitting directly across from Clara Morton. James Robinson was likely attacked because of something he knew, something he'd learned while living in this house. Did that mean Clara could be the next target?

Chapter Twenty-Seven

Redvers and I excused ourselves. I was still mulling over what might have precipitated both D'Annuzzio's death and James' attack and whether Clara was also in trouble. Despite what Ispettore Fizzoli had said, I couldn't believe the events were simply coincidence—they had to be connected. But I also knew there wasn't any good reason to bring this up to Clara since she would either turn it into dramatics or dismiss the possibility entirely, and neither would bring positive results.

Charlie showed us to the door, and once it was opened, I grabbed his sleeve and pulled him outside with us, after first ensuring that no one else was watching. Redvers closed the door behind us for privacy, but we kept our voices low all the same.

"What the hell do you think you're doing?" I hissed at him, fully aware that the windows at the top of the room where Clara was lounging were right below us.

"I'm gathering information. The killer has to be someone either in this palazzo or in her little circle of friends that comes to this palazzo, and I intend to find out who that is." Charlie's voice was quiet but threaded with urgency. "I need to get my wife out of jail. I need Deanna safe."

"We're working on that," I countered. "And if the police find you here, you're likely to end up in a cell next to her."

"I'm willing to take that chance," Charlie said, his face set stubbornly.

I could tell there would be no changing his mind—he truly thought this was the best way to help his wife, and while I thought it was foolhardy, even suicidal, perhaps he *could* learn something useful. Charlie was lucky neither Ispettore Fizzoli nor the *polizia* had learned about him sneaking into the party yet, although I worried it was only a matter of time before the *ispettore* found out.

Redvers had held his tongue until now. "Keep an eye on Clara, too. I'm not convinced that someone isn't trying to harm her as well."

Charlie nodded. "I'll let you know what I find out." He shot a quick glance at the door behind him. "I don't know when that will be, but I'll do my best. I have to get back inside—she'll wonder where I went."

We nodded and watched him disappear back inside the palazzo, the door closing with finality behind him. "I don't like this," I muttered, eyes fixed on the heavy iron gate.

"I'm not crazy about it either," Redvers said. "But clearly the man isn't going to be dissuaded."

Redvers stepped lightly down the marble stairs and pulled the rope from the mooring post after stepping into the little boat. He then helped me step in and take my seat before firing up the motor. I held the rest of our conversation until we were safely in the craft and headed down the Grand Canal, well away from Clara Morton.

Mentally I was still bemoaning Charlie's risky choice, but it wouldn't do any good to worry about him as well; I was worried enough about Deanna in her jail cell. "Do you think the *ispettore* will find Charlie out?"

Redvers thought about that. "It's hard to say. I think the

ispettore was truly bothered by the possibility that he'd already announced to the newspapers that a fake D'Annuzzio was dead, and even more bothered by the possibility that the real D'Annuzzio may come forward and make Fizzoli look like a fool. I suspect he's currently focused on tracking the real poet down, which is one less task for us to focus on."

I frowned. "Do you think he'll tell us what he learns? I *do* want to know whether the story Clara gave us is true." It wouldn't help us in any way, not really, but I still wanted to know.

Redvers gave a casual shrug, but he had a gleam in his eye. "If not, we'll simply find a way ourselves."

That gleam meant trouble, likely breaking into the police station and Fizzoli's office to rifle through the man's reports. For once, I hoped it wouldn't come to that. I loved a good break-in, but not one in an active police station.

I changed the subject. "It occurred to me that Clara might be in danger as well. Do you think we should have warned her?"

Redvers shook his head. "She either wouldn't believe us, or she'd decide to use that to dramatic effect."

It was exactly what I'd been thinking. "In other words, fake another attempt on her life."

"Exactly," Redvers said.

I knew we were correct. If Clara thought she might be in danger, she'd make a performance out of it, and that wouldn't be beneficial to her or us. Hopefully Charlie would be able to keep an eye on things and keep his new employer out of trouble. But would he be effective at keeping Clara safe if someone was out to get her?

This left me feeling a little conflicted, and Redvers must have seen it in my face. "The many faces of Jane. What does this particular one mean?"

I could feel my mouth quirk on one side, then did my best

to relax my entire face of whatever strange contortion it was doing. "I don't want anything bad to happen to Clara, I really don't."

"But," Redvers prompted.

"But I'm more concerned about freeing Deanna. And keeping Charlie out of jail as well. That's all." I wasn't ready to admit aloud that if it came to a choice between freeing my friends and harm befalling Clara, I would choose my friends. It was difficult to even *like* Clara, let alone sacrifice someone else to keep that woman safe.

Redvers seemed to understand what I was saying without even having to say it. "With any luck, we'll be able to figure out who the killer is without anything bad happening to anyone else at all."

I could only hope that would be the case.

There was little to do now except wait until the dinner party the following evening. Redvers sent some telegrams back to London, hoping we could gain some more information on a variety of topics, but the distance meant we had to wait for a reply, and that would take longer than a few hours. We checked back at the hospital, but James had disappeared, leaving no information about where he'd gone to. I couldn't blame the man—I would have done the exact same thing in his position.

We finally checked in with Aunt Millie, who was rather defensive about having orchestrated a dinner party with all the suspects present. "The first two individuals we spoke to were most unhelpful," she told us. "I decided the best way to learn what we needed to learn was to get them all in one place. Like bees."

I waited a beat, but that was all the explanation she appeared interested in giving. "Bees?" I asked.

Millie huffed in frustration. "Yes, Jane. If you put bees in a jar and shake them up, you'll see them attack one another."

I disliked this metaphor and didn't want to see any of the suspects actually attack one another, but I supposed I could see what she was getting at. In a roundabout way.

Lord Hughes and Millie had their own plans for the rest of the day, which they quickly hared off on, without so much as a backward glance. I was relieved we weren't expected to be a part of their scheme, but it also meant there was little else for us to do but more sightseeing. We'd already seen most of Venice, so I suggested we take a ride out to one of the nearby islands—Murano or perhaps Burano. The first was known for glassblowing, while the second was known for its exquisite lace-making. Neither would be able to fully take my mind off of things, but they might at least provide an interesting distraction. Redvers agreed only so long as we put a moratorium on discussing the murder until after we'd returned. I felt guilty for putting aside Deanna's troubles for even a few hours but eventually agreed to his terms.

We stopped at the edge of the island to fill our little boat with gas, then joined the line of boats leaving Venice, the lanes to and from marked clearly with more of the wooden logs that were so commonly seen throughout the canals, although these were a series of tripods, lashed together and spaced out to create something like driving lanes.

The first island, Murano, was just on the other side of San Michele, and I couldn't help but think about the funeral we'd only just attended as we passed the cemetery island. But we were soon on the other side and finding a place in one of the narrow canals of Murano to moor our boat. The island was full of small shops and factories where men stood at hot furnaces holding long poles that they used to blow air into the molten hot glass at the end. We stopped to view a demonstration, since both Redvers and I found the process fascinating, and watched a man shape a ball of what looked to be orange lava into a gorgeous red bird, using nothing but air, a few metal tools, and a consistent rocking motion of the pole. It was astounding to see.

The island of Burano was much farther north than I anticipated, but once we arrived, I was pleased that we'd decided to take the time to travel up that way—the island was entirely charming and very different than its neighbors, since the houses were elaborately painted in bright, cheerful colors. The entire city seemed to be a profusion of color, pinks and reds and blues and greens and yellow, all jumbled together in the most delightful way. We spent some time walking along their canals and taking in the views, not to mention admiring some of the lacework handicrafts that were for sale in the shops—on impulse, I bought a few lace handkerchiefs to take home as gifts. My father could always use a new handkerchief, since he was consistently losing them, and I got one for Redvers' father as well, although I doubted he ever lost a thing.

It was a long ride back to our hotel, and by the time we arrived, my stomach was grumbling, announcing that it was time for supper. We headed back to Pietro's, who was, as always, entirely delighted to see us. It was the most welcome I'd ever felt at a restaurant, so it was little wonder that we kept returning. That, and for the delicious food he prepared every evening. Redvers and I both decided to let Pietro surprise us with whatever he felt like serving—we both trusted Pietro's taste.

"Today almost felt like a real honeymoon," I mused.

Redvers cocked an eyebrow. "It still *is* a honeymoon, technically speaking."

"I suppose what I meant is that it was nice to just enjoy the city and each other without discussing murder. For a few hours anyway." I glanced around before I said this—I didn't want to alarm our host or any other diners. But no one was within earshot of our small table. Pietro had taken to seating us at the same little table in the back near the kitchen, away from the others but close to the wafting smells.

"It does seem to be an anomaly, doesn't it?"

"It does. But I'm glad I agreed to it."

"It didn't stop you from ruminating on things, I'm sure," Redvers said cheerfully. "But I hope you were able to enjoy yourself at least a little bit."

I cocked my head. "You know, I did, despite myself."

Pietro brought us our dinners, and soon we were absorbed with enjoying his kitchen's magic. Not long later, and then quite full, we sipped our after-dinner limoncello in silence, each of us lost in thought. I suspected Redvers' mind was racing along similar lines to my own—our murder investigation. I'd taken a few hours off, but my mind quickly reattacked the issues at hand, energized by the short break. We would have an opportunity to learn things at the dinner party the following night, and I was now considering how we would extract the information we needed from the assembled players.

"Something I'm still curious about," I started to say slowly. It had just occurred to me, and I was working out the details as I spoke. "Is the relationship between Alonzo and his sister Isabella. I don't have siblings, of course, but they seemed . . . unnaturally close." It was a polite way to state what I was really thinking about the interaction we'd seen.

Redvers nodded. "I did find their relationship to be more than a little unusual. It might be unrelated to our investigation . . ." Here Redvers trailed off.

"But then again, it might not." I thought back to our interview with the siblings and their unexpected guest. "I got the sense that Orsola found them odd as well."

Redvers nodded. "I didn't pick up on that, but I trust

your judgment. Which, of course, begs the question of why she would stay with Alonzo and Isabella, if that's the case." He paused, glancing into his near-empty glass before setting it on the table. "Why bring this up now?"

I finished my own drink. "I'm mentally cataloguing all the things I would like to poke into tomorrow night. I think this is one of them—my gut tells me there's something there."

"Consider it added," Redvers said. "As long as it isn't simply your dinner talking."

My lips quirked into a smile, even as I rested one hand on my very full stomach. "Why can't it be both?"

He chuckled. "Touché."

"What were *you* thinking about?" I asked.

Redvers' grin was wolfish. "How long it will take us to get back to our room."

I blushed, but a grin crept across my face in return. Perhaps we *could* take the rest of the evening and simply enjoy our honeymoon.

Chapter Twenty-eight

I awoke late the next morning, having gone to bed rather late and subsequently taken the opportunity to catch up on some much-needed sleep. I was surprised to see that Redvers was still in bed as well—he was ordinarily up well before me, dressed and having accomplished several tasks before I even opened my eyes. I blinked at his still form before I felt a rush of panic and gave him a hard shake. "Redvers? Redvers?"

"Wha . . . what's happening?" he said sleepily.

I let out a puff of relief. "Nothing, I was just worried," I said. "Go back to sleep."

Now it was his turn to roll over and blink at me. "There's little chance of that now," he said, then rubbed his eyes. "Did you think I'd been poisoned in my sleep?"

I got up and grabbed my robe, tying the belt around my waist. "Well, you're always up so early. I honestly don't know how you operate on so little sleep." I walked back and gave him an apologetic kiss. "I am quite sorry to have woken you, though."

Redvers simply returned my kiss, then pushed up and out of bed himself. He put on his own robe before strolling to the phone to call down for breakfast to be brought up. I felt a bit foolish now, seeing him up and about, but that moment of panic had been real. I suspected, but would never admit out loud, that it had to do with how close a brush with death we'd had back in India. Once I acknowledged that, I reminded myself that this time we weren't the ones in danger. I felt some guilt that we'd spent the previous day—and night—enjoying ourselves while Deanna was languishing in jail, but there had been little else for us to do. We'd spoken to everyone, including Ispettore Fizzoli, sent telegrams requesting more information, and searched D'Annuzzio's lodgings. What else was there?

Something that had scratched at the back of my mind earlier finally sprang to the forefront. "Redvers," I said. "I think there's another question we need to ask tonight." Alonzo and Isabella's strange relationship had reminded me of something else—the reason Orsola was staying with them as well.

Redvers was now seated in an upholstered chair, waiting for our breakfast to be delivered. He looked at me expectantly, waiting for me to explain.

"There was no sign of another person at D'Annuzzio's." I took the seat across from him, wishing I had a cup of coffee in my hand already.

He caught on immediately. "And Orsola claimed to have been staying with him," he said. "So where are all her things?"

"Exactly. If she were staying with him, there would be some trace of her. Even if she packed up her things, there would be *something* there—a bit of trash in the waste baskets, or in the bathroom. But there was no trace of another person. As it was, there was hardly a trace of D'Annuzzio."

Redvers nodded. "It stands to reason that Orsola wasn't really staying with D'Annuzzio. She lied about that."

"But why? Why lie about staying with him? Was it simply an excuse to move in with the Fontanas?" I frowned. "And given her reaction to the two of them, why would she want to do that?"

"Perhaps your first priority this evening should be getting Orsola alone to ask her that very question."

I was about to agree when there was a knock at the door. I sat up in my seat, hopeful that our breakfast had arrived. Redvers went to answer the door, and both my aunt Millie and Lord Hughes followed him back inside. I felt my shoulders sag until I saw that they were followed by a member of the staff carrying a breakfast tray—some good with the bad, then. I shrugged to myself; as long as I had a hot cup of coffee, I would be fine with whatever my aunt had come to dispense, whether it be information or opinions or unwanted advice.

Per usual it was a bit of everything. "Jane, how did you get yourselves invited to the supper tonight?" Millie asked after settling herself on the love seat. Lord Hughes bid us a pleasant good morning before taking a seat next to her.

Redvers handed me my coffee, and I took a fortifying sip before answering my aunt. "Clara invited us. Were you hoping we wouldn't be there?" This was asked mildly.

"You can do what you like, you always do," Millie said. "I simply thought the two of you might have something better to do. This is supposed to be your honeymoon, after all. And Hughes and I have things well under control."

I was deeply amused by this, especially since it seemed that she'd organized a dinner party rather than talk to the suspects, but knew better than to let it show on my face. "We had a lovely afternoon yesterday, and we have some time yet today to enjoy a bit of our honeymoon. I think it will be nice for us all to work together tonight." I smiled at my aunt over the top of my cup.

She looked at me suspiciously, eyes narrowed, but could find nothing amiss to point out, precisely as I intended. I looked to Lord Hughes while she gathered her steam for another assault. "Do you have plans today? Before the dinner party?" I asked him.

He gave me a wide smile—he knew I'd riled up his wife with my amiability this morning. "Your aunt wanted to do some shopping this morning."

"The glass here is supposed to be quite lovely. And valuable," Millie said, rather grudgingly. "You're welcome to join us, I suppose."

Redvers broke in. "We would love to, but we have an appointment at the jail this morning, and after that I have something planned for Jane and me."

Millie looked as relieved as I felt. For once my aunt and I seemed to be on the same page.

Redvers and I spent the day continuing to explore the nooks of Venice, popping into the occasional shop that caught our fancy or stopping for espresso. The jail visit had merely been an excuse—we'd had no appointment there, and when we did stop by, we were unable to visit Deanna since she was meeting with her lawyer. Or so we were told. It was hard to say whether the *polizia* was being truthful or simply wanted us to leave. So we reluctantly occupied ourselves elsewhere and even had a nice time, although I felt tremendously guilty for pushing Deanna's situation from my mind the day before, so both guilt and worry dogged my steps. When it was time to get ready for the dinner party, I found I was rather relieved to be heading back into the lion's den—or cheetah's den, rather—to continue our attempts to get to the bottom of D'Annuzzio's murder.

We met back up with Lord Hughes and Aunt Millie just before we set off for Clara's palazzo, piling into a gondola that Hughes hailed instead of our little rented boat. I assumed this was because the boat we'd been using wasn't up to the level of comfort that Millie required, but I didn't comment on the choice. The gondola seats were well padded, and it was probably nice for Redvers to have someone else navigate for a night.

I was concerned that Millie would question us about our fake trip to the jail once we met up with them, but once again my worries were unwarranted. She spent the entirety of our ride regaling us with stories about their own day, filling the boat with her observations about the city and its people on our way to Clara's. I barely had time to tell my aunt that Charlie was now working for Clara, only just managing it when we were disembarking at the palazzo, and asked her to pretend that she didn't know him. Millie was disgruntled by the instructions and the information, grumbling about Charlie and his scheme, but she ultimately agreed.

That was a relief since moments later the door was answered by Charlie himself, who I was relieved to see hadn't yet been arrested by the *polizia* or Ispettore Fizzoli. The rest of the invitees had already arrived and were milling around in the large main room off to the right where the party had been held. All except for Ignacio Catral. According to some whispered information from Charlie, Catral had sent word that he would be arriving a little later than anticipated, although he hadn't given a reason why.

"Millie!" Clara exclaimed with delight when we came through the doorway. "I'm so glad you came! And the rest of you as well, I suppose." She gestured for us to join her and the other guests where they sat or stood in the center of the room. "Robert!" she barked. "Get them drinks!"

Charlie came over with a tray of drinks, and we each took one, although I had no intention of drinking it. There had been too many incidents surrounding drinks in this palazzo for my taste. Frankly, I was surprised any of the guests were actually drinking.

Clara grabbed Millie's arm and began chatting animatedly at my aunt. I took the opportunity to tune out and look around at our fellow guests. Kate Conrad was sitting slightly apart from the rest on a wooden bench, dressed in a pair of brown trousers and a cream blouse with suspenders over her shoulders. The masculine outfit was offset by a single rose pinned to her lapel.

Alonzo and Isabella were seated next to one another on a fainting couch, although they weren't piled on top of one another as they had been at their own palazzo. I was frankly surprised at their sudden modesty. Or had they simply been putting on a show for us? They were each sipping at a champagne flute, talking quietly with one another.

Orsola entered the room from the hall leading to the garden, looked around at the others, then strode forward to take a seat next to Kate. The two of them sat quietly, observing but not speaking to one another, which led me to believe they were well acquainted. It would otherwise be awkward to sit in such silence, but they both seemed perfectly at ease. I also couldn't help but wonder if Orsola had been in the garden and what she'd been doing out there.

The other two people in the room were Clara's first husband, George Kelley, and their daughter, Helen. George was already finishing his drink, grabbing another from Charlie and placing the empty flute on the tray. Helen rolled her eyes at this, taking a delicate sip from her own. I couldn't blame George for his discomfort—not only were he and Clara divorced, but her second husband had been killed in the garden here. I imagined I would have been equally as uncomfortable, although I wouldn't have been using alcohol to cover my discomfort. Perhaps the man wasn't aware of what had been used to kill his replacement.

Redvers and I had agreed in advance to split up once we reached the gathering, so I left him with my aunt and Hughes and made my way over to Orsola and Kate. They both greeted me pleasantly, and I returned their greetings, although I stayed standing.

"Any idea why we've all been called here?" Kate asked.

She had a gleam in her eye that told me she probably had more of an idea than she was letting on.

I gave a little shrug and shook my head, doing my best to look innocent.

Orsola narrowed her eyes slightly. "I don't believe that. Not when you were at the Fontanas' palazzo asking questions. So why are you really here?"

I shifted uncomfortably before taking a seat opposite the two of them while both women stared at me. I felt relieved when Kate answered that for me. "She's something of a detective, I think. She was here asking questions as well."

Orsola considered me. "Then I would like to speak with you later," she said. "Alone."

"Certainly," I replied. "Shall we step outside now?"

Orsola shook her head. "After supper."

I agreed, although I found this to be unnecessarily cryptic. Why not tell me now? Unless Orsola was hoping something would happen between now and then? With that possibility in the back of my mind, I changed the subject to Kate's painting of Clara and asked how that was going. While Kate and I chatted, Orsola was watching the rest of the guests, appearing to pay us no mind. Although, shrewd as she was, I doubted she was missing a word.

We were soon all called in to supper. I hadn't seen a dining room, so I was curious about where we were being led. I quickly realized, however, that we were headed out to the garden, where Clara had had a long table set up to accommodate our number.

"I thought we should eat here, since it's a beautiful night," Clara called as we found our seats. "And we can pay tribute to my dearly departed husband as well."

No one pointed out that D'Annuzzio was her ex-husband, or that her first husband was quite present. I caught a fleeting look on George's face—it appeared to be a mixture of disgust and a touch of fear. Both of which seemed like perfectly reasonable reactions.

Redvers and I were seated at the far end of the table from Clara, with my aunt and Lord Hughes seated right beside her. It was an arrangement that worked just fine for me on numerous levels, including the fact that it allowed us more opportunity to speak with the guests at this end.

The chair to my right was empty, since Ignacio Catral hadn't arrived yet, although we were clearly forging ahead without him. Charlie and a young woman in a matching uniform began serving us, bringing bowls of soup and setting them before us. Another member of staff was refilling drinks for anyone who needed a new one, which did not include Redvers and myself. I had simply held on to the glass in my hand, without taking a single sip—Redvers had clearly done the same.

"You're not drinking tonight, Jane?" Orsola asked me from across the table.

"Oh, no. I simply got caught up in my conversation with Kate," I said. I put my glass to my lips and pretended to take a sip. I hoped it was convincing. I was nervous enough about eating, although any poison in the food would affect the whole table, so it was unlikely to be an issue.

We'd moved on to the second course when Ignacio Catral finally made his appearance. He swept into the garden carrying a bottle of wine in one hand and champagne in the other. "I brought reinforcements," he announced, holding the bottles aloft. Alonzo cheered, and a few other faces seemed pleased to see Catral—if not the man, then at least the alcohol. He took his seat beside me, giving a general greeting to everyone at our end of the table.

Charlie arrived with a plate for Ignacio and took the bottles that Ignacio had brought back into the kitchen. "I'll open these for you and bring them back," Charlie said.

"Excellent," Catral said and dug into his wild boar.

We all resumed eating, and between forkfuls Redvers leaned past me to look at Ignacio. "What kept you?" he asked.

Catral chewed for a second, swallowed, and glanced at my husband. "I was working on a new song, a beautiful song to pay tribute to our friend D'Annuzzio." Alonzo and Isabella nodded, clearly familiar with Ignacio's music. "I will play it for you all later."

I hoped we would be able to leave before that portion of the evening began.

Charlie came back with Catral's bottles, setting them in the middle of the table, then hurried back to the kitchen. Orsola reached across and took the bottle of wine, dumping the remnants of champagne in her glass onto the stones behind her. "I much prefer wine, but Clara never seems to have any. She's obsessed with champagne." She poured herself a healthy glass of the red wine, swirling it for a moment before taking a long sip. She coughed, putting the glass down.

I put my fork down, watching as Orsola's face began to contort. I elbowed Redvers. "Something is wrong," I said in a low voice.

Everyone else seemed completely unaware of what was happening until Orsola began clawing at her neck, pushing away from the table. She quickly fell to the ground and convulsed on the stone. Redvers and I rushed around to her, but she'd gone still, and I knew it was already too late.

Orsola was dead.

Chapter Twenty-nine

Everyone else at the table panicked immediately, screaming and pushing their seats away from the table. Several individuals were dumping their beverages into the thick array of plants around us, and I made a grab for the two bottles that Ignacio had brought. Isabella tried to take them away from me, screeching that they would kill me, but Redvers stepped in.

"Everyone stop this instant," he said. His voice was loud and commanding even in this open courtyard. The panic seemed to slow as people paused what they were doing. Even Charlie stood stock-still at the edge of the garden. "Now, one of you will phone the *polizia di stato*." Charlie tentatively raised his hand for the task, although I knew he was frightened to alert the police that he was here. "Good. Go do that now." Charlie disappeared back into the palazzo.

"These bottles will be given to the police." Redvers said this with a sharp look at Isabella, who dropped her hands from my arm. I actually appreciated that she'd been trying to save me, in a manner of speaking, but I breathed a sigh of relief that our game of tug-o'-war was over. I'd been terrified that the wine—and the poison—would splash out of the bottle and onto me.

"We will all go inside in an orderly fashion to wait for Ispettore Fizzoli," Redvers pointed, and one by one people began to slowly take steps in that direction.

"What about poor Orsola?" Clara asked tearfully. It was difficult to say whether she was actually upset about Orsola's death, or whether she was upset that this turn of events had ruined yet another party. I felt a little guilty for having such uncharitable thoughts toward the woman, but she'd been unusually insistent about trying to keep the last party going, even though a man had died. She'd then followed that performance with a lament about how D'Annuzzio's death had ruined the evening, so I was hesitant to give her the benefit of the doubt now.

Redvers responded. "The police will take care of her. And I will stay with her until they arrive."

The group picked up their pace a little, trudging back inside in a straggling line. I was bringing up the rear of the group, behind Clara and Helen.

"My garden is cursed," Clara was muttering. "I will need to tear the whole thing out and start again."

No one bothered to respond to this. Once they were all inside, I turned back to Redvers from the doorway. I was still clutching the two bottles of wine, one of which was likely poisoned, if not both. "Should I leave these here?"

Redvers nodded, coming forward to relieve me of them. "I doubt Catral did this, it would be entirely too obvious," he said.

I agreed. "I'll ask where he got the bottles from. I have a sneaking suspicion they were sent to him."

"I was thinking the same thing," Redvers said, then frowned. "And please see if Charlie actually made the phone call to the *polizia*."

I sighed. It hadn't occurred to me that Charlie wouldn't make the call, but now that Redvers said it aloud, I had the same concern. I hurried from the garden and down the hall, then down the stairs leading to the downstairs kitchen. I stuck my head inside, finding only the woman who had been serving the party alongside Charlie and the cook. Neither spoke English well, so I only received head shakes to my questions about where Charlie was.

I went back up into the main room where everyone was gathered. "Has anyone seen the butler?" I'd already forgotten what name Charlie was going by here. A few people shook their heads, and I hurried past them to the front door. The ironwork gate was slightly ajar. I poked my head outside, and seeing nothing amiss on the landing or the canal, I closed it again and went to find a phone.

Redvers' assumption had been correct, then. Instead of calling the police, it looked like Charlie Parks had taken off instead.

Ispettore Fizzoli arrived not long after I made the call, quickly taking control of the situation. "Another murder," he said, shaking his head. "I will take statements from each of you. And you," he said to Ignacio. "I will take you to the station and question you there."

Catral sputtered for a moment but ultimately went quietly with the *polizia* who escorted him to the police boat. I felt rather bad for the man—I didn't think he had anything to do with the poisoned wine. On the contrary, I thought it likely that he was the intended victim; especially after he confirmed for me that both bottles had been sent to his room without so much as a card to identify the sender. It was dumb luck that Catral had brought them here instead of drinking them at his hotel.

Millie stayed with Clara, occasionally patting her arm to comfort her through this latest crisis. Lord Hughes, Redvers, and I stood off to the side, watching the others as they interacted with Fizzoli.

"They'll ask about that Parks fellow," Hughes said quietly.

Redvers and I agreed. "I'm not sure what's better, telling Fizzoli now who the butler really was, or letting Charlie stay out of jail for the time being," I said. "Charlie's an idiot," I muttered, more to myself than to the others. I was frustrated with the man for disappearing into the night instead of staying to talk with the police. It certainly made him look more guilty than he might have if he'd just stayed behind.

"I have to agree," Redvers said. "And I'm not sure anything will keep Charlie out of jail unless we deliver the real murderer to Fizzoli."

I flapped a hand. "It could be any one of them." I recalled that Orsola had wanted to speak with me. "Before we went in to supper, Orsola said she wanted to tell me something, but she wouldn't say what it was until afterward."

Both Redvers and Lord Hughes frowned. "Do you have any idea what it might have been about?" Redvers asked.

"It was right after she learned that I was investigating," I said. "I would guess that she knew something, although I haven't the foggiest notion why she just wouldn't tell me then." It went without saying that I wished she had. Now we would never know what it was she'd wanted to say. Not to mention what a coincidence her death was—the one person with something to tell me was the one who drank the poison intended for Catral. Could there be a connection?

"Where was she staying?" Hughes asked. "Perhaps a search of her things would prove useful."

I smiled at Lord Hughes. He always proved to be a helpful—and thoughtful—ally, and I was pleased my aunt had married him.

"There was also the fact that she claimed to be staying

with D'Annuzzio, but nothing of hers was in his apartment," Redvers said. "I think we should search her room at the Fontana place, but I wonder if she had lodgings of her own somewhere else."

I didn't disagree with his conjecture, but I was curious as to why she would go to the trouble of maintaining multiple places to stay and hiding that from her so-called friends. "Why go to the trouble?"

Redvers' brow was pulled low. "I don't know, but it's worth looking into."

I was anxious to leave right then in order to search through Orsola's things, but we needed to wait until after we'd spoken with Fizzoli. The *ispettore* still didn't fully trust us, and we didn't want to give him a reason to suspect we weren't being truthful by haring off into the night like Charlie Parks had. Which was the first thing Fizzoli brought up when he finally got around to speaking with us.

"Do you know this butler?" Fizzoli asked. "The one who disappeared instead of calling the police?"

I kept my face neutral and waited for Redvers to answer the question. Redvers shook his head. "I'm not familiar with him." Hughes and I took our cue from him and mumbled similar answers.

"Outrageous," Fizzoli said. "No one here knows who this man was. And he has disappeared, poof, into the night."

"I don't think he had anything to do with it," I offered. "He simply opened the bottles. Catral brought them here, but I also don't think he's the one who poisoned them. They were sent to his hotel anonymously."

Fizzoli bristled. "Yes, yes, that is what he said. I'll make the determination of whether that is true or not."

I wisely kept my mouth shut after that.

The *ispettore* then asked us a series of generic questions, mostly about how we knew the dead woman, all of which we answered honestly. He seemed frustrated that he wasn't getting any useful information from us or from anyone else present, and I honestly couldn't blame him. When Fizzoli seemed to have finished with his interrogation, Redvers asked a question of his own. "How did Clara Morton know Orsola Chini?"

Fizzoli looked at my husband for long enough that I became certain he wouldn't answer, but then the *ispettore* surprised me. "Mrs. Morton claims that Orsola and her former husband met at a party during Carnevale and became . . . intimate. I do not know why she would then be invited here."

I had a number of answers to that, but it wasn't a question and I'd already learned my lesson about speaking out of turn. My face apparently had other plans, however, because Fizzoli sighed. "I can see that you have something to say about that, Mrs. Wunderly. Come out with it."

I pursed my lips, then barreled ahead. He'd told me to, after all. "It sounds like there was a lot of . . . switching of partners within this group." I didn't know how else to explain it. "Everyone seems to have been having an affair with at least one other person, and from what we were told by Mrs. Morton, there wasn't any jealousy about it."

"I doubt that," Fizzoli said dryly. "But thank you for the information. Now, you may leave this palazzo, but do not leave the city."

I wasn't sure which part of my statement he disagreed with, but I wasn't about to ask. The three of us nodded at his instructions to stay in Venice, then Lord Hughes went to join my aunt Millie. Redvers and I started toward the canal-side entrance, but the *ispettore* had one more thing to say to us.

"If I find your friend," Fizzoli said in a dark undertone. "He will end up in a cell next to his wife."

Chapter Thirty

I was still fuming about Charlie when Redvers snagged us a gondola, instructing the driver to take us to our hotel. "Getting himself arrested isn't going to do Deanna any good," I muttered as we disembarked from the gondola. "I told him that working there was foolhardy."

Redvers agreed. "It isn't doing us much good either since Fizzoli obviously knew we were lying about not recognizing the butler."

I frowned. "How did he figure that out? I thought we were better liars than that."

I'd nearly forgotten my aunt and Hughes were with us, until I glanced at my aunt. Her face was reddening and her lips were clamped together. I pinched the bridge of my nose, eyes squeezed shut. "Aunt Millie, you didn't."

I opened my eyes, and she defended herself—loudly. "Well, I didn't know we were hiding the fact that we knew the man from the police."

"Did you say as much in front of Clara?" I asked.

Aunt Millie didn't answer, but the red on her face got a shade darker.

A few curse words sprung to my lips, but I managed to hold them back. What was done was done—we needed to keep moving forward, and it would do no good to start issuing recriminations.

We stopped at the front desk where Redvers collected a telegram. Aunt Millie, quiet and chastened for what might be the first time in her life, had already gone ahead into the bar, followed closely by Lord Hughes. I waited with Redvers, anxious to see if what we'd been sent had any useful information. He skimmed the paper, then handed it to me and waited for me to do the same.

It was less useful than I'd hoped it would be. It confirmed that Giovanni Marchesi and Christopher D'Annuzzio were distantly related and D'Annuzzio was still alive, but it had no further details than that. It was likely that if we wanted to know the real story of how Marchesi had come to take D'Annuzzio's identity, we would either need to go to Rome and interview the Italian poet ourselves, or hope that Fizzoli had learned the truth and was willing to tell us the story.

Either way, it didn't seem crucial to our investigation. I passed the telegram back to my husband with a sigh. "It's frustrating that we can't get more timely information. For instance, right now we need to know where Orsola was actually staying."

Redvers nodded. "And sending another telegram isn't going to help us with that."

I glanced at the bar, then back at my husband. "No, but perhaps we'll find something among her things at the Fontanas' apartment."

"And if we leave now . . ."

Without another word, we quietly disappeared back out of the same door we'd just come in and went to our little boat, moored several spaces down from the front of our hotel.

"Millie is going to be livid that we disappeared on her," I said.

Redvers gave a little shrug. "I think she'll get over it. Especially since she spilled what she knew about Charlie to the *ispettore*."

I gave my head a little shake, bemused. If we were in hot water for our disappearing act, I vowed to make him the scapegoat for once.

We arrived at Alonzo and Isabella's palazzo, moored our boat, and rapped on the front door. The evening was growing late, but given the events of the evening I assumed the brother and sister would still be awake.

I was wrong. The butler answered the door after a second series of knocks, scowling ferociously.

"Are Alonzo and Isabella at home?" Redvers asked.

"They are in bed. As you should be," the man said. He still held the door half closed, but I could see his robe peeking through the slim crack. It looked as though he was about to close the door on us when a voice behind him called, "Antonio, who is it?"

The butler sighed and opened the door the rest of the way, clearly displeased. Redvers and I stepped past him, up the stairs, down the short hallway, and into the sitting room where we'd last met with the siblings as well as Orsola. It was a sobering reminder that the young woman was no longer with us, and was in fact the entire reason for our visit.

Alonzo was the one who'd called out, and we found him dropping into one of the upholstered chairs wearing a silk pajama set but no robe. I thought he must be cold since the fire had already been banked for the night and it was chilly in the room, but he seemed quite at ease. "Ah, you two. What are you doing here?"

Redvers was direct. "We would like to look through Orsola's things."

Alonzo's eyebrows nearly disappeared into his thick hair. "That's quite a request. Especially at this time of night."

"Have the police been here yet?" I asked. In my mind, it was likely that the police had already come and gone. Orsola hadn't seemed to have brought much with her here, so it likely wouldn't take long to search.

Alonzo's eyes darted around the room, and I narrowed my own. "You didn't tell the police that she was staying here, did you?" I said slowly.

After several moments it became clear that Alonzo wasn't going to answer either of my questions, and he looked relieved when his sister Isabella swept into the room. "No, we didn't," Isabella said. "We didn't think it was relevant."

Isabella took a seat across from her brother, and I looked back and forth between the two of them. There was definitely something amiss here, some reason why these two wouldn't want the police searching Orsola's room, which was a very reasonable request given what had happened to the young woman. What were these two hiding?

I mentally prepared myself for a prolonged argument with the siblings, but Redvers had other plans. "We'll search every room in this house if we need to, so you may as well tell us now which room Orsola was staying in." His voice was stern and direct, reverberating with authority. "The sooner you tell us and we finish our search, the sooner we will leave. Without reporting you to the *polizia*."

Both Isabella and Alonzo looked shocked, and Alonzo opened his mouth, likely to argue, but Isabella shot him a quick look and he snapped his mouth shut. "Fine," Isabella said. "Her room was up the stairs and the first door on the right."

I gazed at the pair for a moment, then followed Redvers from the room. There was something they didn't want anyone to find out, which meant I was determined to learn what it was.

* * *

We entered the room where Orsola had been staying and shut the door firmly behind ourselves. "There's something amiss with those two," Redvers muttered.

"I agree. We need to learn what it is, but after we finish searching here first," I added.

Redvers and I looked around the small room. There was not much to see except a four-poster bed and a heavy wardrobe. Redvers started with the bed, and I crossed the room to the wardrobe, flinging open the doors. A few dresses hung at one end, but there wasn't much else to be found. Two pairs of shoes, one sparkling gold with a high heel, and another sensible pair with a low stacked heel and T-strap sat in the bottom of the wardrobe. I picked up each shoe and inspected them individually but found nothing unusual, nothing tucked away in a toe or stuck to the bottom. Setting them back down, I turned to the dresses but heard rustling behind me. I turned and found Redvers pulling a suitcase from beneath the bed.

He placed it on top of the quilt and flipped it open. I was tempted to join him, but I needed to finish my task first. I quickly but thoroughly searched each piece of clothing, making sure I checked all the seams before closing the wardrobe and joining my husband.

"Nothing in there," I said, peering hopefully into the suitcase.

"Nothing in here either," Redvers said.

"Are you sure?" I asked, running my own hands along the bottom and ignoring my husband's amused snort. He'd clearly already done this, but I couldn't stop wishing this battered case would reveal *something*. Defeated, I stepped back and put my hands on my hips. This suitcase clearly wasn't where we were going to find something interesting about Orsola Chini. But where else?

My eyes fell on the small bedside table where two books were stacked haphazardly. I picked the first one up and flipped through it, finding nothing. It was in Italian, so I had no idea whether I was looking at a novel or a book on farming equipment or something else entirely. The book underneath, however, was written by Christopher D'Annuzzio. This was also in Italian but at least looked to be a book of poetry. I flipped through it and nearly missed the small ticket tucked between two pages.

I pulled the ticket out triumphantly. "Aha!" I said, remembering at the last second to keep my voice down. I turned the ticket over, finding a few words printed in Italian. "Looks like a ticket for the train station."

I handed the ticket to Redvers who examined it closely. "I think it's a ticket for the baggage claim."

I was disappointed we hadn't found something more immediate, but it was better than nothing at all. With a little luck, this ticket would lead us to something of interest and wouldn't prove to be simply a wild goose chase across the city.

We finished our thorough search of the room, but the little claim ticket was the only thing we found. It looked as though Orsola hadn't brought much with her to the Fontanas' palazzo, which made sense if she had a place of her own. I wondered once again why she would go to the trouble of taking up residence here, with nothing more than a handful of dresses and shoes, but she must have had a reason. One we might never learn, sadly.

We said our goodbyes to the siblings downstairs and headed out into the night. We hopped back into our little boat and were quickly back on our way, this time to the train station at the northernmost tip of the city.

The baggage claim was closed, and had been for several

hours, but Redvers found the station master and convinced him to open it so that we could retrieve the bag listed on the ticket. In a very short time, we had a leather satchel in hand and were walking quickly to the exit. My heart was pounding from both our rapid pace and excitement—it *finally* felt as though we had something useful in our grasp.

"Couldn't we open it here?" I asked quietly, taking large steps to match my stride to my husband's.

He shook his head. "Too open."

We got back in our boat and headed back to our hotel—hopefully our last trip of the evening. I was sorely tempted to snatch the bag from my husband's hands and rifle through it right there in the boat but sat on my hands instead. Waiting was difficult, but we wouldn't be able to see much in the intermittent moonlight anyway.

Our plan was to hurry through the lobby and get safely to our room to open the satchel, but we were intercepted by my aunt, her voice booming out from the bar's doorway and across the tiny lobby. "Where did you two run off to? And what do you have there?"

For once it was Redvers who closed his eyes, and I nearly hooted with amusement. But I contained myself and hurried over to my aunt to keep her from announcing anything else to the hotel at large. "We're going upstairs and then we'll find out what we have. You're welcome to join us."

I didn't think there was any way we could get around including her, so we waited while she gathered up Lord Hughes and their cocktails and joined us in our trek up the stairs. I was surprised that she didn't insist on taking the elevator, since she complained about the exertion on the way up, but at least it forced her to let go of her numerous questions until we were behind closed doors. We tromped down the hall to our room, waiting like a row of ducklings while Redvers unlocked the door and pushed inside. I was close on his heels, so when he stopped dead in his tracks, I ran right into his solid back, then went up on my toes so I could peer over his shoulder and see what had caused him to stop so abruptly. I blinked at what I found.

Both Charlie Parks and James Robinson were waiting in our sitting room.

Chapter Thirty-one

Behind me, Millie's voice was demanding to know what the holdup was, so we quickly filed into our room. There wasn't really space for all of us, so Lord Hughes and Redvers pressed themselves against the far wall, while James offered Aunt Millie his seat. She took it, although I thought she could have been a bit more gracious about it.

"How did you get in here?" I asked. I was less than thrilled that our room was clearly quite easy to break into. I stood near the little fireplace, wishing there was an actual fire in it—I was a bit chilled from our trips around the city on the moonlit canal.

Charlie had the grace to look embarrassed. "I stole a key from housekeeping. I apologize, but I didn't know where else to go. The police are probably watching the hotel where Deanna and I were staying, so I thought it was best not to go back there."

I looked at James. He looked equally as abashed. "I knocked and this gentleman let me in. He said he recognized me from Mrs. Morton's party the other night." James frowned. "I don't remember seeing him, though."

"When did you get out of the hospital?" I asked.

"Late this afternoon. I considered where I might go and came back here to get my things. I'm still nervous about my attacker finding me, though, so I knocked here first," James said.

I thought this was very reasonable considering what had happened to him. I wasn't sure I would have even returned for my things, although it was likely his passport and any other identification were here—it would be difficult to get back to England without it.

Aunt Millie was surprisingly quiet, and I glanced over at her. She was studying her fingernails, and it took me a second to figure out what her sudden reticence was about. Then I remembered—she'd told the police that the butler was Charlie. Which meant she was the reason his hotel was being staked out. I was strangely glad that she was embarrassed. It was nice to see that my strong-willed aunt might be able to admit when she was wrong.

Well, perhaps "admit" was a strong word.

I turned back to James. "Did you happen to remember who stabbed you?"

James squinted. "It's all still a little fuzzy, but I vaguely remember someone tall with a long coat and long hair, but that was probably a wig. I didn't get a good look at the person's face. Or if I did, I don't remember it."

It was better than nothing, although it didn't narrow things down significantly—or at all, really. Especially when one considered that his memories were likely flawed to begin with. What he recalled as "tall" could actually be someone of merely medium height. I thought the only thing we could probably narrow down was that it wasn't likely to have been someone short. All in all, it wasn't terribly helpful.

Then I turned to Charlie. "What the hell were you thinking?" It did not escape my notice that this was the second time I'd asked him that very question, with about the same amount of exasperation, if not more. Millie's eyes sharpened on Charlie—I wondered if she was hoping for some absolution.

"I had to get out of there," Charlie said defensively. "As soon as the *ispettore* saw me, he would know who I was and arrest me."

"I'm not sure being outside jail is going to do you any good," Redvers said. "You're not exactly walking free with the *polizia di stato* looking for you."

"I didn't really think that through," Charlie admitted. "I just wanted to stay out of jail so I could keep trying to help Deanna."

My frustration with the man was tempered by his genuine desire to help his wife, but only a little. I looked at Redvers, and he met my eyes. We needed to find somewhere to hide these men, but where was the best place?

"You can both stay in James' room," Redvers said.

"Back in the room where I was stabbed?" James asked, horror in his voice.

Redvers nodded. "Your attacker isn't likely to think you'd go back to staying there. And if there are two of you, you should be able to keep an eye out for one another."

The two men looked at each other and then shrugged. "It's as good a plan as any, I suppose," Charlie said. "I've got a deck of cards."

"Don't bet real money," I warned James. "He'll fleece you."

Charlie gave me a wounded look, but I narrowed my eyes in response, earning a grudging nod. As the men left, Redvers advised both of them to stay put and not answer the door unless he gave a specific knock. I hoped they would be able to follow through with their promise to do that.

Once Charlie and James excused themselves, we were left with Lord Hughes and Aunt Millie. I turned my suspicious gaze her way.

"Are you certain you can trust those two men?" Aunt Millie asked quietly.

I frowned. I opened my mouth to answer, but paused and gave the question real consideration. Could I answer that truthfully? Did I fully trust either of the men? I was saved from answering by Redvers.

"We've looked into both men, and their stories ring true. I believe both men are telling the truth and don't have anything to do with either murder," Redvers said.

Millie shuddered. "I'm surprised the *ispettore* didn't arrest that Catral on the spot. He nearly killed all of us."

"I don't think he was trying to kill any of us. I think he was actually the target of the poisoned wine," I said thoughtfully. "He just happened to bring the bottle along with him to the dinner party."

Redvers nodded in agreement. "Precisely. Truthfully, I would be worried if I were Catral. Whoever the killer is may come after him again."

On that note, Aunt Millie and Lord Hughes excused themselves, citing the late hour. We bid them good night, and once the door had closed, I breathed a sigh of relief.

"She must have forgotten about the satchel," I whispered.

Redvers chuckled. "She can't hear you, they're gone."

I gave my head a little shake. "You don't know that for sure. She has ears everywhere."

Redvers was still sporting a small smile, but he moved into the bedroom where he'd stashed the little piece of luggage we'd collected and returned with the bag, then took a seat in the upholstered chair that my aunt had vacated. I sat across from him, nearly leaning across the table, anxious to see what was in the satchel. Redvers began pulling items out and set them neatly on the table while I examined them. There was a day dress, lovely but threadbare in a few places. The kind of thing you might have expected Orsola to discard ages ago, before it began to show so much wear. This was followed by a scarf that appeared to be handknit, and a pair of shoes whose soles were in dire need of being replaced.

I placed the shoes carefully on the table after looking them over carefully. "These items are leading me to believe that Orsola wasn't as posh as she would have had us believe."

"I think you're right about that," Redvers said. The last few items he pulled out were some bits of makeup, a coin purse, and a toothbrush.

"Is that all?" I asked. This was a rather disappointing haul, all told.

"Not quite," Redvers said. He pulled his hand from the bag, and I saw that it was clutching a leather-bound notebook with a matching leather tie. Redvers flipped it open, and I jumped up to come around the back of his chair and look over his shoulder.

It was a journal, written in a feminine hand.

Chapter Thirty-two

It took a great deal of restraint for me not to rip the journal from Redvers' hands. As it was, I was nearly dancing in place as he examined the first page and then flipped to the last. The entry was dated two days after D'Annuzzio's death.

> I still can't decide who might have killed Christopher. I saw Helen walk into the garden with him, and she came back out to join the party, but Christopher didn't. Next thing I knew, Clara was screaming and he was dead.

"Could Helen have had something to do with the man's death?" I asked, scanning the rest of the entry. That was the only interesting part, so I reached over Redvers' shoulder to turn the page back. He chuckled, closed the journal, and handed it to me.

"Why don't you take it and just read me the more interesting parts?" he said.

I smiled sheepishly but only for a second before taking the journal to my own seat and scanning previous entries. But not before I asked the obvious question. "If Orsola was Italian, why are these entries in English?"

"That is an excellent question," Redvers said, leaning back in his seat and watching me with amusement. He didn't seem to have an actual answer, so I went back to reading.

"Here's something," I said a moment later, reading another short paragraph out loud.

> I should have known Christopher wasn't what he claimed to be. Here I thought I was getting involved with someone who had money, but he was just another con artist. His wife is the only one with any real money. I'm not going to be able to get anything out of Christopher. I should have known when he insisted on only coming to my place, never his.

"Interesting," Redvers said. "Sounds as though Orsola was something of a con artist herself."

"That would explain the worn-out clothing in the bag. I wonder if she saved her fancier clothes for playing the part of a wealthy socialite." I tried to recall what she'd worn to the dinner party but could only picture her contorted face as she died. I shuddered.

Redvers watched me, then tipped his head to the journal, drawing my attention back to it. "Anything else of interest?"

I would need to read quite a bit of this—and thoroughly—to make sure we didn't miss anything, but a close reading was something I could do later. At the moment, I was skimming for the most important pieces, paging backward as I skimmed. There were a lot of observations about Italy and even some about the suspects in the case, but nothing worth mentioning or even asking the individuals about. Her observations did make me think Orsola wasn't a native Italian, though. I took a moment's pause to wonder where she might have actually been from, before continuing my hunt.

There was another interesting piece that jumped out at me, and I read it aloud:

I found out that Christopher has been blackmailing A. and I. That fool let the secret slip, but he wouldn't tell me why he was blackmailing them. Now that he's out of the picture, I think I should do the same, but I need to find out what they were being blackmailed for first.

Redvers and I looked at one another. "I'm willing to bet that was why Orsola took up residence with Alonzo and Isabella. She wanted to figure out what they were being blackmailed for so she could do the same," I said.

"It also gives that pair a motive to kill both D'Annuzzio and Orsola," Redvers said.

It was too late to do much more that evening, so we went to bed instead, vowing to speak with the Fontanas in the morning. Redvers slept peacefully, but I tossed and turned for several hours before finally falling into a light sleep. When I stumbled out of bed the next morning, I knew even without a mirror that the bags under my eyes were a testament to my poor night's sleep.

"Did you stay up all night reading that journal?" Redvers asked, sipping his tea, and peering at me over the top of his cup.

I sank into the chair across from him, pouring a cup of coffee for myself before I managed to even acknowledge the question. "No, but it would have been a better use of my time," I muttered between sips.

A small smile was playing at his lips, but he refrained from comment. "I think the first thing we need to do is speak with Helen Morton, and then with the Fontana siblings."

"Not necessarily in that order, right?" I turned to look at the door, fully expecting a knock announcing the arrival of my aunt. I waited a long beat, but there was none.

"No Aunt Millie this morning?" I asked as I turned back and reached for a croissant.

"She sent a note that we are being left to our own devices today," Redvers said.

I raised an eyebrow. "Did it mention what *they* would be up to?"

"Not a word." Redvers shrugged. "Once you're finished, shall we get on with it?"

I eyed his empty plate, nothing but a faint smear of butter left on it. He was always an early riser, which benefited me because it usually meant that breakfast and coffee were waiting for me when I got up. The downside was that I sometimes felt rushed to finish my own meal, like right now.

"Yes, but once I've eaten something as well," I said. I was tempted to forgo breakfast altogether in order to start our interviews, but it was better to start with a full stomach. I did much better thinking when I'd had something to eat, not to mention several cups of coffee to get my tired mind going.

Thirty minutes later we were in our boat, winding toward the Fontanas' palazzo. When we knocked, we were told that they were out and wouldn't be back until the afternoon. I couldn't help my suspicion at hearing this. Had the siblings left town? Would they in fact return? Or had they cleared out, knowing that sooner or later someone would learn the secret they were being blackmailed over?

Since that was currently a dead end, we went to Clara's palazzo next. Here, at least, we learned that Helen Morton was at home. We waited in the downstairs sitting room while a maid fetched the young woman from down the hall. In the meantime, Clara swanned in, wearing a loose caftan with flowing sleeves. "I heard you were here and wanted to speak with my daughter," she said, draping herself across the velvet fainting couch.

"That's right," Redvers said. Then the two of us proceeded to sit quietly and regard her. This was clearly not what she expected, and she huffed.

"Well, what do you want to speak to her about?" Clara demanded.

"If Helen wants you to know, I'm certain she'll tell you. After we're finished speaking with her," Redvers said calmly.

A range of emotions flitted across Clara's face, including surprise and finally outrage, which is where she finally landed. She sputtered a few times, then stood abruptly. "Very well. I'll leave you to it, then." With this she stomped out of the room, pausing at the doorway for a long moment. When we didn't say anything to stop her, she huffed again and left, slamming the door behind her.

Redvers and I looked at each other and shrugged. I was about to comment on Clara's behavior when the door opened again and Helen walked in. She'd been defiant the day of D'Annuzzio's funeral, but today her attitude was different, certainly meeker. She also had her hands clasped behind her back in a way that made her procession across the room seem especially awkward. She took a seat in one of the chairs across from our love seat and here too hid her hands in her skirt.

I forced the frown to clear from my face and greeted the young woman. "Helen, thank you for agreeing to meet with us."

She didn't say anything, simply waiting for whatever it was we had come to say.

"We have a few questions we'd like to ask you," I said, but there was still no response.

I was glad when Redvers stepped in. "Young lady, we want to know what you had to do with this." His voice was stern. "We have plenty of evidence, so you might as well come clean. It's better to talk to us than the *polizia*."

Helen's face switched from haughty to scared in the span

of a heartbeat. "I don't know what you're talking about," she whined, although her face clearly said otherwise.

"I think you do," Redvers said, nodding to her hands, hidden in the folds of her skirt. "Otherwise, why would you be hiding your hands?"

I would have loved to know whether my husband had actually figured something out or whether he was simply guessing, but I kept my eyes trained on Helen. Tears were welling up in her eyes, and for all her attitude, it was a good reminder of how very young she was. It had taken no time at all to get her to crumble. In fact, she was now crying openly.

"I didn't really mean to kill him. I hated him, and my father did too. And we talked about how if he was dead, then Papa could marry Mother again. But I never thought I was strong enough to actually kill him." Helen was sobbing now, hiccupping between nearly garbled sentences. "I'm a killer. And then I stabbed that other man because he saw me leave the garden, and I didn't mean to kill him either but I was so scared that I would be arrested and they would hang me."

I could tell that my eyes had gotten quite wide during the girl's muddled recounting, which tumbled from her like the stream of water pouring from her eyes. "You didn't kill either man, Helen, although what you did is very stupid and there will be consequences."

She hiccupped again. "I didn't?"

Redvers and I both shook our heads. "No. D'Annuzzio was not killed by strangulation and James Robinson is still alive," Redvers said. "He was released from the hospital with stitches. They did not even keep him overnight, although he did lose quite a lot of blood. You're very lucky you didn't do more damage, young lady."

The tears were slowly drying up, and Helen wiped her face with her hands, although she nodded, acknowledging

Redvers' warning. Watching her, I could now see that she had inherited her mother's hands—rather large with long, thick fingers. I suspected they would match the marks that had been found on D'Annuzzio's neck, although as Redvers had said, that wasn't what had killed the man. Had Redvers noticed Helen's hands at the funeral? I would have to ask later how he'd guessed so well about Helen's involvement—I hadn't once suspected the girl, not in any meaningful way.

"You are very lucky that we found James when we did," I told her, figuring it couldn't hurt to emphasize the point. I was curious about something, though. "How did you make it to the funeral on time?"

Helen gave a big sniff. "I threw away the coat I was wearing over the top, it was one of my mother's, and the wig too. I had my dress on underneath the coat—red, so it wouldn't show any blood—and I got lucky at the water taxi stand. One arrived to take me to the island just as I got there."

I nodded. We were actually quite close to the outer edge of the island, where there were regular taxis to San Michele.

I fixed the young woman with a hard look. "We will still have to inform Ispettore Fizzoli of all this."

Clara chose this moment to sweep back into the room. "Is it really necessary to inform the *polizia*?" She came to stand behind her daughter, not exactly comforting her but standing guard behind her. Clara had clearly heard everything, and I wondered if she'd been standing with her ear pressed to the door while Helen made her confession. "I'm more than happy to compensate James for his troubles, so there is no need to involve the *ispettore*," Clara said. "After all, she's just a child and didn't know what she was doing."

Helen stiffened at being called a child, and I fully expected her to argue, but for once she kept her lips firmly clamped shut. Perhaps she felt she'd done enough talking for one day.

Redvers and I regarded the both of them for a moment before Redvers spoke. "I can get in touch with James and see whether he wants to press charges against Helen." He sounded reluctant to make the offer.

Clara considered him. "If I could just talk with him, I think I could convince him that the *polizia* won't be necessary."

I gave a little sigh. It looked as though being rich really could buy you out of anything, including stabbing a man. Or in this case, your wealthy mother could.

Chapter Thirty-Three

Redvers and Clara went to call James to see how he wanted to proceed. I trusted that Redvers would be discreet about where the man was staying. We didn't want another attempt on the poor man's life, even if the young woman who'd done the initial attempt was sitting before me and unlikely to try something so foolish a second time.

In the meantime, I was stuck with Helen. A series of emotions kept playing across her face, and I would have felt sorry for her except for the fact that she'd tried to kill two men, unsuccessful though her attempts had been. But there were a few other things I wanted to know, and there was no time like the present, especially since the girl seemed vulnerable. I wasn't convinced that would last.

"Is Kate Conrad avoiding you?" I asked.

Helen looked surprised, then frowned. "I don't know. I thought we were friends, but lately she's been leaving every time I come into a room. I thought maybe she knew what I'd done and that was why."

From what I knew about Kate, I thought she would have called the *polizia* if she knew what Helen had done. So there had to be another reason the woman was avoiding Clara's daughter. It was unlikely to be jealousy, since Clara wasn't exactly playing the part of doting mother with her daughter. Sure, she was paying someone off to keep the girl out of trouble, but I didn't think Clara's affection would go far beyond that. Or perhaps Clara simply didn't know how to show affection, and throwing money at things was how she showed that she cared. Regardless, "maternal" wasn't a word anyone would use to describe Clara Morton.

Which meant there had to be some other reason that Kate was avoiding Helen. "Did your father know you tried to kill two people?" I asked.

"No, he certainly did not," George Kelley said loudly as he stepped into the room. I hadn't even heard the door open that time, so I was surprised by his entrance.

Upon seeing her father, Helen stood and ran across the room, burying her face in his shoulder. It was a far more touching scene than the one between Helen and Clara, and I felt a pang of sadness for the girl since she was unlikely to ever get real affection from her mother. But at least she had her father, who appeared to be a very loving parent.

"How could you do these things, my dove? Without coming to me?" George chided her, but gently.

"I thought I was helping you," was Helen's muffled reply.

George patted her back, then peeled her off his shoulder and led her back to her chair. "Surprisingly enough, Clara called me," he said to me, taking a seat in the chair next to Helen's. "She's not a good mother, but at least she did that much."

From what I'd seen, I couldn't argue with George's assessment of his former wife. "Why do you want to remarry her?" I asked.

George sighed. "I do love her, in a complicated way. And I was doing well with the mining company I founded. Well," he said reluctantly. "I founded it, but she funded it. Anyway, there were a series of mishaps and the company went under. And I've been . . . somewhat underfunded since then."

This seemed a rather genteel way to explain that George wanted to marry Clara for her money. It allowed me to put some pieces together, though. "And you felt that D'Annuzzio was in the way of your . . . reconciliation."

George nodded. "But I never should have spoken about this to my daughter." He cast a look at her. "These are my troubles to work out, darling, not yours."

The girl still looked miserable, and I was having mixed feelings about what type of punishment she should receive. She clearly was troubled, and little wonder, with the upbringing she was having, not to mention being saddled with Clara Morton as her mother. Although that didn't excuse what she'd done. Stabbing one man and trying to strangle another were rather serious offenses.

"Helen, did D'Annuzzio die while you were strangling him?"

Both George and Helen stared at me in horror. "What an awful question," George said.

I shrugged. It was, but it was also relevant. "Perhaps I should ask why you were convinced that you killed him, instead."

"He started coughing and was bent over, so I took the opportunity to choke him," Helen shuddered, then wrapped her arms around herself, and I was glad to see it. At least she had some feelings about what she'd done. "I stopped after a bit, and he fell to the ground, still choking, and then he stopped."

George looked horrified at his daughter's admission.

"And did you see anyone give him a drink right before this happened?" The venom clearly worked quickly, if Orsola's death was any indication.

Helen thought, cocking her head, then shook it. "No, I don't remember where he got his drink from."

"Do you know where the drink went after you choked him?" I asked.

Helen frowned. “It fell out of his hand, but I didn't see what happened after that.”

So someone else had picked up the glass. I turned to George. “Regardless of what happens next, I think you need to get Helen some help.”

Helen's face twisted as though she wanted to argue, but her father reached over to put his hand on her arm. “I agree, Mrs. Wunderly.” His eyes locked on mine, and we shared what I thought to be a look of mutual understanding. Redvers and Clara returned not long after, with Clara looking quite triumphant. Redvers' face was carefully neutral, and I could make several guesses as to why.

“That went quite satisfactorily,” Clara said, taking a seat next to me on the love seat. Redvers looked bemused and went to stand beneath the window. “James has agreed to take the money and not report this little incident.”

Referring to a stabbing as a “little incident” made my blood boil, but I held my tongue. Lecturing Clara would be like tossing pennies into the canal—each one would simply disappear, leaving nothing but a ripple in their wake. Instead, I inquired after Kate Conrad.

Clara frowned for a second, then answered me. “I believe she's in her room painting,” she said.

I nearly asked why she'd frowned at the mention of Kate, but instead I excused myself—it wasn't worth the verbal game to find out. Not to mention I had doubts that anything further would be learned here, since Helen had confessed to her mad attempts to kill two men. I still couldn't rule out either George or Clara as the culprit behind D'Annuzzio's death, but neither did I think we'd learn anything else useful from them as they fawned over their homicidal child.

Redvers gave me a quick wink as I left, and I gave him a crooked smile in return. Perhaps I was wrong and he would learn something useful from this complicated little family. Luckily, I knew he would report to me anything he found out.

I walked down the hall and knocked on Kate Conrad's door, peeking my head around the wooden door when I heard a voice say "come in."

"Are you busy?" I asked instead of barging in, despite her invitation to enter. The woman was standing near the window, brush in hand, studying a piece of canvas set on the large easel before her.

She looked up when she heard my voice and smiled, wide and genuine. "Jane! Come in, please. I was just finishing up this piece for today. I want it to set a bit before I start on the next layer."

I was tempted to ask for a peek but decided I had more pressing questions to ask. "I'm curious, have you been avoiding Helen?"

Kate's eyebrows went up. "That's an odd question," she said slowly, although she didn't answer it.

"We've just had an enlightening chat with the girl and discovered that she was behind a bit of violence. I thought perhaps that was why you'd been avoiding her."

Kate looked at me, then set her brush down and sighed. "It's true. I knew that she'd gone after D'Annuzzio in the garden. We'd talked about him briefly, and I could see that she hated the man. For good reason, really, he was terrible," Kate said with a dry chuckle. "I suspected that she'd done something stupid, and I didn't want to hear anything that would force me to call the *polizia*."

I nodded, absorbing this. It all seemed quite reasonable, on the surface. But was that all there was to it? Or was I merely being paranoid? Kate was in love with Helen's mother, so it stood to reason that she wouldn't want to turn the girl over to the police, right?

"Thank you for being honest with me," I said.

"Will Helen be arrested?" she asked, brows furrowed in concern.

I shook my head. "Her mother seems to have paid her way out of trouble."

Kate sighed. "That is the way of the rich," she said. "Although I am glad for Helen. I don't think she meant any real harm."

We chatted for a few more moments, then I told her that Redvers was waiting for me. I couldn't shake the feeling that I was missing something, but I couldn't put my finger on what that was.

Chapter Thirty-Four

We left Clara's palazzo, pleased that we'd solved one mystery, although we still had quite a lot of questions that needed answers. On the boat ride over to talk with the Fontanas, we discussed what we'd learned. I went first, sharing what Kate Conrad had told me.

"That's a reasonable reason to avoid the girl," Redvers said slowly.

"I feel like I'm missing something there, but I don't know what it is."

Redvers sighed. "I certainly know that feeling."

"Did you learn anything interesting from Clara or George after I left?" I asked.

He shook his head. "Nothing useful or interesting. They began quarreling, all three of them, about the best way to get Helen some help." He paused for a beat. "I think it's sad really, that poor girl. What she did was terrible, but her upbringing doesn't seem much better."

"I agree. I thought the same thing," I said before we fell into a companionable silence. "We should decide how to approach the Fontanas," I said once their building was in sight.

Redvers gave me a sly grin. "I thought we would simply do what we've been doing. It seems to be working so far."

The direct approach, then. I couldn't argue with him, since he was right about its effectiveness.

Alonzo wasn't at home, but the butler took us in to see Isabella. She was sitting on the settee with her feet tucked up under the layers of her gauzy pink dress. Redvers and I took seats in the chairs opposite her after some brief greetings.

"I imagine you're here about Orsola. What a terrible tragedy," Isabella breathed. "It was terrifying too, that it could have been any one of us who'd drunk the wine. We could be *dead*." Her eyes were wide, hands fluttering in her lap, and I thought that there was genuine fear beneath this little show.

I gave a brisk nod, then got down to it. "Why was D'Annuzzio blackmailing you?"

Isabella's mouth fell open in shock, and she blinked rapidly a few times, then glanced toward the door as though she were hoping her brother would come in and save her. But no one appeared to be coming to her rescue—for once, she was entirely on her own.

"I don't know what you're talking about," she said slowly, but it was obvious that her shoulders had tightened and were now creeping toward her ears.

I gave a small chuckle, not unkindly. "If only that were true. You see, we have proof." Of course, we didn't have any proof besides Orsola's journal, but Isabella didn't need to know that. "We know that D'Annuzzio was blackmailing you because of your relationship with your brother. What I want to know is how he found out." I could feel Redvers quickly glance my way, since this was news to him and not something we'd discussed on the way over. But I kept my eyes on Isabella, watching the obvious distress that was flooding her neck and face. I'd been right, then. There was something amiss with the relationship between the brother and sister.

Her hands were twisting together in her lap, and she was clearly unsure how to answer me. I cocked my head. "Wouldn't it feel better to just come clean and tell us everything?" I hoped this would compel her to do exactly that. If we were very lucky, she would confess to something about D'Annuzzio's murder.

She looked at me, eyes searching my face, then glanced at Redvers and sighed. "You must know that Alonzo and I aren't blood related."

I nodded, not at all surprised since they looked nothing like one another.

"My mother married his father when we were in our teenaged years. Over time we just . . . fell in love with one another."

I did my best to keep my face from showing my disgust at this little announcement. Regardless of whether or not they were blood related, I couldn't help but feel that this was wildly inappropriate.

Now Isabella sounded defiant, sitting up in her chair, as though she knew exactly how she sounded. "I don't care what you think," she said. "I don't care what anyone thinks."

I doubted this was actually true. It was more likely that she didn't *want* to care about anyone else's opinion. "And how did D'Annuzzio learn about this?" I asked.

She sighed. "I don't know how D'Annuzzio found out. Alonzo and I have discussed it over and over, and we can't figure out how he knew." She slumped a little. "He said he had proof, too, and he wanted us to pay him in order to keep it quiet. At first it was just the one payment, and he promised us that would be the end of it. But one payment became two and so on until he was demanding bigger and bigger sums."

"So that's why you killed him," I said.

"No!" Isabella cried. "We didn't kill him, I swear to you on my mother's grave." She swallowed, then continued, glancing desperately back and forth between the two of us. "We talked about it, I'm not proud to admit that, but we couldn't bring ourselves to go through with it."

Redvers chimed in. "How much money did he take from you?"

Isabella shook her head. "A lot. I'm not sure of the amount, but he was draining our funds. We have only so much allowance from Alonzo's father, you know. Once the old man dies, we'll inherit everything and we can go somewhere and marry. Somewhere they've never heard of us, Belgium maybe. Or the Americas even."

It was a lot of work to keep my face neutral. Even if they weren't related by blood, Alonzo and Isabella had been brought up as siblings, and this plan to leave Italy so they could marry one another was shocking.

It also occurred to me that Alonzo's father had best be careful or he'd find himself in an early grave as well, regardless of whether these two had killed D'Annuzzio. They may not have gone through with a plan to kill D'Annuzzio, but that didn't mean they would stop the next time around.

Alonzo chose that moment to return home, sweeping into the room where we sat, but he stopped short at the look on Isabella's face. "What . . . what is happening here?" he asked.

"I've told them everything," Isabella said.

Redvers and I exchanged a quick glance. If that had truly been everything, then these two were not our killers. Which still left us with a dwindling list of suspects.

Alonzo gasped at this and took a seat next to Isabella, grabbing her hand. "Everything? Even how we tried to blackmail D'Annuzzio?"

This raised my eyebrows. "We didn't hear that part."

Isabella grimaced. "I forgot that piece. And we were unsuccessful anyway, he *still* wanted more money, that greedy man."

"We didn't kill him," Alonzo said, his voice loud and insistent. "You must believe that."

I let Redvers field this. "We believe that you're telling the truth," Redvers said slowly.

Both siblings let out a breath, deflating a bit, but Redvers wasn't finished. "What were you trying to blackmail D'Annuzzio about?"

They exchanged a glance, and Isabella shrugged. I was a little sorry that Alonzo had chosen that moment to return home—I suspected we were getting a more complete story from his sister, even if she'd forgotten a few items. "We did quite a lot of research," Alonzo started to say but was cut off by Isabella.

"We followed him," she said. "That's what he's trying to say."

Alonzo gave his sister a dark look, then said something rapidly in Italian. I glanced at Redvers, who narrowed his eyes. I hoped he'd understood all that. Whatever Alonzo had said, Isabella looked displeased, crossing her arms over her chest, causing Alonzo to roll his eyes. "Very well, we followed him. He was having an affair with Orsola, but of course you already know that. She told you that when you were here." Alonzo was frowning, looking as though he was trying to remember everything that had happened. I didn't blame him on this point—a lot had happened within a few short days.

"And that's all you learned about him?" Redvers asked.

Alonzo glanced at his sister, who hissed something in Italian. Alonzo paused, then went ahead. "We learned that he's not truly Christopher D'Annuzzio." He sat up, clearly feeling smug at having this bit of information, but once he realized that we weren't going to react to his news, he looked crestfallen. "You already know this?"

Redvers gave a casual shrug but didn't otherwise answer,

asking another question instead. "How did you learn D'Annuzzio wasn't who he claimed to be?"

Alonzo was pouting now, so Isabella answered instead. "We heard Christopher and Orsola arguing outside a café one night. A café that we followed them to after they left Clara's."

"When was this?" I asked.

"Erm, some weeks before the party." Isabella paused, then continued. "I thought it was strange, because they were in the Jewish quarter. I do not know why either of them would be in that part of town."

I found that interesting, since D'Annuzzio—or Giovanni Marchesi, rather, although it was easier to call him by his assumed name—lived close to that part of town. From what we'd seen of his place, and what I'd learned from Orsola's journal, Orsola hadn't stayed with him at his apartment. It was clear that the siblings weren't familiar with D'Annuzzio's little apartment either, but that made more sense to me. If I had a secret identity, and the paperwork to back it up, I would have a little hideaway all to myself as well. Somewhere that I wouldn't invite anyone to see, something only for myself. That's why it was surprising that Orsola had even been in the neighborhood. Especially since, according to her journal, she'd never been to D'Annuzzio's place.

"Had you ever seen where either Orsola or D'Annuzzio were staying?" I asked.

Isabella and Alonzo were both frowning now, and they exchanged a look. "We don't know where they were staying. Orsola was staying with D'Annuzzio, but he never actually said where he was staying. Do you think he was living in the Jewish quarter?" Alonzo asked, clearly shocked. "With so much money, why stay there?"

I realized that Alonzo was probably accounting for all

the money they were paying D'Annuzzio in blackmail. "What happened when you tried to blackmail him in return?" I asked.

Alonzo wrinkled his nose. "He just laughed and said no one would believe us because we had no proof. But he said that he did have proof about us, so we had to keep paying."

"Did he ever show you proof?"

Now Alonzo looked defiant. "No, we didn't need to ask. He gave us enough details, I knew he had what he said."

Redvers and I exchanged a look. I doubted that D'Annuzzio had actually had real evidence, but this admission gave these two a pretty solid motive for killing D'Annuzzio. And I hadn't heard much so far that would rule them out from having done it.

Isabella seemed to realize this. "We really did not kill him." She held up her hands. "You can see my hands are too small to have made the marks, and Alonzo was here all night. Our staff will attest to that."

I considered them, then looked at my husband. He seemed to be considering them as well.

"We'll look into what you've told us, make sure that everything is the truth," Redvers said, standing. I slowly got to my feet as well. "I hope for both your sakes that it is."

Chapter Thirty-five

Once outside, we stepped back into our boat. "That was a rather ominous warning you gave them," I said.

"Did you like that?" he asked with a cheerful grin. "I thought it might spook them into admitting something else. Or if not that, then at the very least, it might keep them out of trouble. Amateurs, out there following people around. I hope they don't have any more ideas like that."

I chuckled. I did enjoy it when Redvers engaged in some dramatics. And he had a point—with any luck one of the siblings would come forward with some other bit of information they'd been holding back, although it had felt as though they'd given us most of what they had. Before we'd left the house, we'd spoken with the kitchen staff, and they had confirmed that Alonzo had been home "writing" the night of the party. Whether he'd actually been writing anything or simply avoiding the party was irrelevant—he'd been at home all night, and so was unlikely to have administered the venom to D'Annuzzio's drink.

I doubted Isabella's culpability as well. They had a great deal of motive, certainly, but I wasn't sure they were clever enough to obtain the venom and pull the murder off. Besides, Isabella seemed to have no idea snake venom was even involved.

"You're deep in thought," Redvers said as he navigated expertly into the next canal, nodding in a friendly manner at a passing boater.

I nodded, then waited till we were well past the other boat. "They have excellent motive to kill D'Annuzzio, but I don't think they did it," I said in a low voice.

"I don't either," Redvers replied. "We should keep them on the list, of course, but I believe Isabella sincerely thinks D'Annuzzio was strangled. If I'm not mistaken, they both do."

I nodded. "So far, no one knows that he was killed with snake venom."

"No one but the murderer," Redvers said. "And Fizzoli, of course."

Even Aunt Millie and Lord Hughes didn't know about the snake venom. I loved my aunt and her husband, even trusted them to a certain extent, but I was also fully aware that it didn't take much to get my aunt to spout off—like she had about Charlie's role as a butler. And given how close my aunt appeared to be to Clara Morton—well, it was best to keep the real method of murder from Millie as well.

"What next?" I asked.

"I was thinking two things. First, we should see if we can visit Deanna."

"I was thinking that as well. She must be going crazy with worry over Charlie. I'm sure he hasn't been to see her since Orsola died."

Redvers nodded his agreement. "Then I think we should take another crack at that journal. We—or you, rather—didn't get much past the last few pages, and I wonder what other tidbits of information Orsola might have gathered."

It wasn't the most exciting way to spend an evening, reading someone's journal, but my husband was right, the thing needed reading. There might be something else there that would help us narrow down who the true killer was.

* * *

At the *polizia* station we asked to see Ispettore Fizzoli, but were told that he was out. Redvers asked what the *ispettore* was out doing, but the officer just stared at him, offering no explanation.

"Fair enough," Redvers said. "We would like to visit with Deanna Parks."

The officer looked us both over, then called to another officer in Italian. The two of them had a long conversation, then the first officer turned back to us. "You may see her." He raised a finger. "But only for a few minutes."

We both agreed to the restriction, relieved that we were being allowed to see her at all, especially without Fizzoli there to give us permission.

The second officer led us through the hallways and the heavy door blocking off the women's cells. At the sight of us, Deanna began to weep, and tears flooded my eyes as well. She looked even worse than she had before; the dark circles under her eyes were now like bruises, and she looked as though she hadn't bathed or slept since she'd been brought here.

"Where's Charlie?" she asked, clearly desperate. "I've heard nothing from him and I've been going crazy."

I felt terrible, truly terrible that we hadn't come sooner or at least sent word that Charlie was fine, especially since it wasn't safe for him to do so without being discovered. I wrapped my hands around hers where they gripped the metal latticed bars. "He's safe, he's okay."

Deanna let out a guttural noise of relief mixed with tears. "I was so worried that he'd been killed."

I shook my head vehemently. "He wasn't. Now, he's done a few stupid things," I said, and was rewarded with a tearful smile. "But he's okay. He had to go into hiding, which is why he hasn't been to see you. And it wasn't really safe for him to send word to you."

Deanna closed her eyes for a moment in relief. "I should have known he would do something stupid. What was it this time?"

I explained everything that had happened, although I was careful not to reveal where Charlie was staying just in case our conversation was being overheard either by the *polizia* standing at the end of the hall or even another prisoner. When I'd finished speaking, she at least looked a little better, a little less desperate. "Thank you for keeping him safe," Deanna said. "That man." The exasperation was clear, but there was also a small smile on her lips. I knew how much these two loved one another—I just hoped against hope that they could be reunited soon.

We couldn't exactly share with Deanna what we'd learned or what we were doing to prove her innocence—there were too many ears nearby—so we made do with discussing her lawyer and ensuring that she had everything she needed. The short few minutes we were given flew past in the blink of an eye, and we were being escorted back out before I had time to process anything. Back out on the street, Redvers took my hand, gave it a reassuring squeeze, then led me to the nearest café.

"You need some coffee, then a cocktail and something to eat," Redvers said kindly.

I didn't argue because he wasn't wrong. I needed some caffeine and some food in my system if I was going to be any use for the rest of the day. And I knew we had more work to do, although I could also use a moment to simply think about my friend's predicament.

Our waiter came to our table quickly once we were seated to take our drink orders, which were many, and managed to talk me into trying a different kind of cocktail than the aperol my husband had ordered. "This one is too sweet for you, I think. You would like a select spritz better," the young man insisted. I was too overwhelmed to argue with him, so

I easily agreed. As long as he returned with my espresso drinks, I reasoned that anything else was a bonus.

It was a bit of a wait, but he did return with my cappuccino and a side of espresso, as well as the promised cocktail and a glass of water for Redvers. I poured the shot of espresso into the cappuccino and set about downing the cup of caffeine before I even considered a sip of the select spritz, although I was intrigued to see an olive garnish instead of the orange slice. Once my blood was buzzing from the caffeine, I turned to the select spritz, which was a similar color to the aperol. I took a sip and oohed in pleasure. It was much less sweet than the aperol, with a perfect hint of bitterness, yet still refreshing.

"That young man was correct, I think this might be my Venetian drink of choice," I said, taking another healthy swig.

Redvers raised an amused eyebrow, and I turned my attention back to the case.

"Of the people I think we can eliminate as suspects," I began, pausing for a second—a second that Redvers used to effortlessly finish my sentence.

"Alonzo and Isabella are at the top," Redvers said.

I wrinkled my nose at him. "I hate it when you do that, but yes."

He winked, and then did his best to look penitent. "I'll try to let you finish your own thoughts from here on out."

I looked at him suspiciously, then continued with my list. "I think Helen is an unlikely murderer. She did some damage, but she truly thought that she'd killed D'Annuzzio by strangling him. Which means she didn't know about the venom."

"I agree. I think we can safely eliminate Helen. Her mother and father, however, I'm not so certain we can do the same."

I sighed. "I think you're right. Clara is harder to pin down than a squirrel with a nut." Redvers' eyebrows went up, and I stifled a smile. "Very well, it's not my best metaphor, but you know what I mean."

"I do, actually. She's eccentric, but more than that, she's contradictory. It's impossible to say whether she was or wasn't responsible."

I nodded once, then took a sip of my cocktail. The waiter came back with a plate of tomato-topped bruschetta and some cheeses, and I waited until he'd left again to finish my thought. "Clara stays on the list. So does George. I believe that he was shocked by his daughter's actions, but that doesn't mean that he didn't give D'Annuzzio the poison. He had plenty of motive."

Redvers considered that. "I agree, although I think we should keep him toward the bottom of the list."

"Very well, but who do you like better?" I asked, curious.

"Both Ignacio Catral and Kate Conrad," he said without hesitation.

"I can see Catral, since we know little about him and he seemed to have motive. But Conrad openly admitted her motive. Why come clean if you're the killer?"

Redvers' dark eyes were narrowed. "True, but there's still something there that doesn't feel quite right."

I shrugged. I'd spent more time with Kate than he had, so I thought I had a better sense of her, although there *had* been something nagging at me. I just hadn't been able to figure out what it was. "Very well, she stays on the list. But she's at the bottom of mine."

Redvers looked satisfied with that, although neither of us were satisfied in general. "It's still too long of a list," Redvers said.

"Far too long," I agreed. Then I frowned. "Should we

check back at the hotel and see if Millie has returned?" I hadn't had time to think about her disappearance that morning and where she might have gone, but I did want to know that she was okay. And Lord Hughes as well.

"Certainly," Redvers said. "And while we're at it, we should make certain that Charlie is still there as well."

The possibility of Charlie disappearing again hadn't even crossed my mind, but now it was all I could think about.

Chapter Thirty-Six

I was glad we'd had a bite to eat to fortify us until supper, since that was quickly approaching but I didn't want to take the time to have a large meal quite yet. Even if we went to a new restaurant, I knew a meal would take a while—Italians seemed to savor their meals. Which was ordinarily a good lesson to learn, unless you were trying to quickly solve a murder and get your friend out of jail.

"We could stop for some *cicchetti*," Redvers suggested.

"If I knew what that was, I could decide whether I wanted to eat it," I replied.

He smiled. "It's little . . . bar foods, I guess you might say. You go to a place serving drinks, and they have little meat-topped breads or small sandwiches. They were initially for the gondoliers to enjoy fast meals, but they've gained in popularity as an easy meal while you are enjoying a drink."

That did sound rather appealing, but I wasn't sure we had time for even that.

Back at our hotel, we stopped at the front desk to see if there were new messages for Redvers and to call up to Aunt Millie's room. There was no answer, and I felt a spike of nerves. "She's still registered here, isn't she?" I asked the clerk. "She and her husband haven't checked out?"

The clerk smiled. "No, no, they are still here. They are simply not in their room."

"Did you see what time they left?" I asked.

Now the friendly clerk gave his head a quick shake. "No, I only work afternoon through the evening."

I sighed and thanked him for his information, then turned to my husband. "Anything interesting?"

He shook his head. "No, nothing useful. Any word on Millie and Hughes?"

I bit my lip. "No, and I'm starting to get worried. It's not like her to go off without at least telling us where they're going." I started across the lobby and poked my head into the bar, but they weren't there either. I slowly retraced my steps back to Redvers.

"Not there either, eh?"

"No. And now I am definitely worried."

"I know that even if I tell you not to worry about your aunt and Hughes, it won't stop you from doing it," Redvers said, earning a small smile from me. He really did know me well. "Let's see if Charlie is in his room, where he should be, so there is one less thing to worry about."

It was an excellent idea, and we took the tiny elevator up to our floor. I followed Redvers down the hall to the room where the men were staying. My husband gave a distinct knock on the door, followed by a complicated series of raps and pauses. There was a long moment before the door was opened by James.

"Is Charlie here?" Redvers asked. I could tell from my husband's relaxed demeanor that he clearly expected the answer to be yes; he physically startled when he heard James's reluctant "No, he's not."

James stepped back into the room, and we hurriedly followed him inside, shutting the door firmly behind ourselves. "What do you mean no? When did he leave?" I asked. The nagging anxiety I'd felt before now felt like a tidal wave.

"He was gone when I woke up this morning," James said, holding up a hand to stop us from asking the obvious next question. "We were up late playing cards, and I slept quite late to make up for it. I probably didn't get out of bed until well after ten o'clock this morning."

"He didn't leave a note?" I asked hopefully, even though I thought I already knew the answer.

James shook his head, "I'm sorry, he didn't."

I looked around the room. Nothing was disturbed, so it was unlikely that anyone had broken into the room and physically removed Charlie from it. No, the man had likely slipped out himself, although heaven only knew why he would leave the sanctuary of this hotel when he was well aware that the *polizia* were out looking for him. I felt the exact same exasperation that Deanna had earlier. Charlie was eminently likeable, thus my worry, but he was also incredibly frustrating. Especially when he did stupid things like this.

I flopped unceremoniously into an armchair while Redvers asked after James' health. I was at least relieved to hear that he was feeling fine. "Why take Clara's money instead of turning that girl in?" I asked.

James sat down on the love seat across from me. "She's very young and very troubled," James said seriously, but then a small smile crept onto his face. "And I gotta say, that much money, you know what I can do with that?"

I shook my head. I hadn't heard the number that Clara had offered him, and hadn't asked since it ultimately wasn't any of my business.

"It's enough to buy my own cab. I can go back to the neighborhood and become a taxi driver. It's all I ever wanted, really, and I know all the streets like the back of my hand."

James' face had lit up with such enthusiasm that I felt my own smile mirroring his own. I knew James hadn't come from much, and even though this had been an awful attack, it looked as though something truly good was actually going to come of it.

I had one major concern, though, and I looked back and forth between James and Redvers, wishing I didn't need to bring this up and possibly ruin James's enthusiasm. "Will Clara go through with paying it? She's notoriously flighty."

James's grin got even bigger, if that was possible. "It's already in my account."

I breathed a quiet sigh of relief. At least one good thing *had* come of this, then.

We went back to our room after James assured us that he would send Charlie to us when he returned. I was worried that it was more a question of if Charlie returned, but I kept my concerns to myself.

Redvers and I were both hungry now, but there was little chance I'd be able to enjoy dinner at a restaurant, not with so many people I cared about missing. Redvers called down to the front desk and asked for a nearby place to have some dinner sent up, then went into the bedroom and returned a moment later with Orsola's journal.

"While we wait for everyone to return, we might as well see if there's anything else of interest here. How far did you get the other night?" he asked.

I hung my head sheepishly. "Not very far, I'm afraid. Only the last three entries, if I'm honest. I fell asleep."

Redvers looked amused, but he didn't comment. "Do you want to read it?"

"I won't be able to concentrate, so it's best if you do," I said.

"What will you do, then?" he asked.

"Pace."

"Don't wear out the carpet," he said dryly, cracking the journal open and flipping ahead to the end. Then he flipped forward a few pages, and started reading quietly. I nearly asked him to read aloud but decided I wouldn't be able to concentrate on the words, so I meandered around the room, crossing back and forth between the small patio and the sitting area. Every time I heard the sound of a nearby gondola—or rather the sound of a singing gondolier—I scurried onto the balcony and gazed down, hoping I would see my aunt, but each time I was disappointed. And soon it was too dark to see anything at all.

The dinner Redvers had requested was brought up and left on the table in our sitting room. Instead of pasta dishes, we had a tray with different meats and cheeses, even some fruits and vegetables, a basket of sliced, crusty bread and a bowl holding a variety of different types of olives. It was actually quite perfect—nothing too heavy, and easy to snack on as I paced the floor.

I wished I was better able to enjoy it—in fact I hoped we could find the killer soon so that I could put my anxiety and fear aside and spend a few days in Venice actually enjoying the city and the delicious cuisine. I was just wiping my mouth with a napkin when there was a knock at the door.

I nearly knocked Redvers out of his chair in my hurry to open it, and gave a cry of relief when I found Aunt Millie and Lord Hughes on the other side. "You had me worried, Aunt Millie! We didn't know where you'd gone!"

"Jane, don't be silly. We're fine. Honestly, it's not like you to be so hysterical," Millie said as they came into the room and sat down on the love seat. I was so pleased to see them that her greeting didn't even faze me.

"Where did you go?" I asked, reclaiming my own seat.

"Rome," Millie said simply. "I see you decided to dine in this evening." She gestured to the table.

I stared at her agog until she explained further. "We went to find the real Christopher D'Annuzzio."

Quite a number of questions were spinning in my mind, but the first one that popped out was "all in one day?"

Aunt Millie frowned. "It's just the matter of a train ride there and back. We got the address from Clara, of course, and took a taxi from the train station."

Instead of asking *why* she'd gone, I stuck to more useful questions. "Did you learn anything?"

"The question you should be asking is whether he even let us in," Millie admonished. "Which he did, but it took quite a bit of convincing."

I thought bullying was likely a more apt description, possibly even forced entry, but I bit my lip and gestured for my aunt to continue.

Millie looked suspicious at my lack of response, but Redvers smoothly filled the void. "I have no doubt you were quite convincing, Aunt Millie."

She preened. "Thank you, Redvers." She gave me a triumphant look, then finally got down to business. "When Clara told us that the man who was killed was someone called Marchesi, well, I demanded to know exactly what she knew about the man she married."

She gave me a piercing look. "I know you found that birth certificate, but I needed to know whether *Clara* knew anything about it. So I went ahead and asked her. Can you believe that she knew about this all along? She married a man who was lying about his identity. Apparently, Marchesi and the real D'Annuzzio were second cousins or some such relation."

I simply nodded, not bothering to tell my aunt that we'd already discovered all of this. I was pretty sure we'd told her, too, but it had likely either slipped her mind or she hadn't been paying attention. There was of course, a third option—Millie wanted to be the one to do the discovering and would conveniently forget everything else to achieve that.

"Once we got into the place—and what a hovel it was—we got the real D'Annuzzio to answer some questions," Millie said.

I wondered briefly if the man still had all his pieces and parts intact but continued listening attentively.

"D'Annuzzio was absolutely fine with Marchesi's scheme to pretend to be the great poet. D'Annuzzio apparently hates going outside and hates speaking with the public, including his own fans. And I have to say," her voice dropped to a conspiratorial near whisper. "I can see why. The man is quite unattractive."

I murmured something that I hoped was appropriate, sneaking a glance at Redvers. He looked wholly entertained by the entire thing—both my aunt's storytelling and my inner battle to hold my tongue and sit quietly.

"Anyway, as long as the fake D'Annuzzio reported back with information and details about the places he'd gone and the people he'd met, the real poet was happy with this arrangement. He could use that information about the outside world to continue writing his poems without having to leave his house, and Marchesi could take the fame. But not the fortune. The only part of this that didn't benefit Marchesi is that he didn't get any money for this. Not from D'Annuzzio, anyway."

I had to admit that I was impressed with the amount of information Aunt Millie had managed to squeeze out of the hermit.

"We also learned that D'Annuzzio does *not* care for Clara, which I think is a failing of his personality and not hers," Millie announced loftily. Again, Redvers and I simply nodded, which she likely took as agreement but was meant just to keep her talking. There was no way I was going to admit to my aunt what I really thought of her friend. "He didn't care for Ignacio Catral either."

Here, at last, was some novel information.

"Has D'Annuzzio met Catral?" Redvers asked. It was the very question that was on my tongue as well.

"I asked the same thing," Millie said. "As soon as he admitted that he didn't care for the man, but no, he has not. Although it appears that D'Annuzzio heard enough about Catral to form an opinion. Catral was just out for money, which is no real surprise." She snorted. "If only he knew that Marchesi didn't have any."

It wasn't anything terribly earth-shattering after all—I'd already assumed as much about Catral. I was about to change the subject when Millie dropped one last bombshell.

"I also wonder if Catral knows that *Clara* is the one who paid for his trip with Marchesi to Australia."

I sat up straight in my chair. The snake venom that had been used to kill Giovanni Marchesi had come from somewhere outside of Italy—could that somewhere have been Australia?

Chapter Thirty-Seven

"When was this trip to Australia?" Redvers asked, leaning forward in his seat.

"Earlier this year. In the spring, I believe. Catral and Marchesi spent several weeks traveling around Australia, and Clara footed the bill for the entire venture." Millie sniffed. "I'm not surprised that Clara didn't mention it, it would be rather an indelicate matter to bring up, how she chooses to spend her money."

Redvers and I exchanged a quick look, which I immediately regretted. "What is that about? You know something, don't you?" Millie demanded.

My husband and I exchanged another look, but this one was more a battle of who was going to field Millie's displeasure. Redvers finally gave in, and I did my best not to smirk at my small victory.

"We learned that D'Annuzzio—or rather, Marchesi—wasn't strangled. He was poisoned with snake venom," Redvers said.

Aunt Millie's eyebrows leapt up in surprise, but Lord Hughes, who'd been quiet this entire time, merely looked speculative. I made a note of that—I would ask him about it later, privately. He always let Millie take center stage, but he was a shrewd and observant man, picking up far more than anyone gave him credit for because he was so quiet.

"That makes a great deal more sense," Millie said. "Especially given how Orsola died as well. I assume it was the same poison."

This time I looked to Redvers. "Has that been confirmed yet?"

Redvers shook his head. "Not yet, but I think it's a pretty safe assumption."

Now my aunt frowned. "But what does that have to do with a trip to Australia?"

"Well, if the type of snake venom used is native to Australia," Redvers said slowly. "Then Catral is likely the person who picked it up and brought it here."

"And so you think . . . what? Catral picked up the poison in Australia? Brought it home and gave to it to D'Annuzzio here the night of the party?" Aunt Millie asked.

"I'm afraid that's exactly what I think," Redvers said.

We were all quiet for a moment, then Lord Hughes chimed in. "But why wait until they are back in Italy to administer the poison? Why not do it there in Australia? It would be simpler, especially since it was native to the place."

"I was thinking along those very lines," Redvers admitted with a furrowed brow.

"Could someone have asked Catral to pick it up and bring it home?" I asked slowly.

"It's a possibility," Redvers admitted. "Though a risky one."

Risky or not, it looked like Ignacio Catral was the person we needed to speak with next.

Millie was quite proud of the information she'd gathered from D'Annuzzio, so there was zero chance she would stay behind while we went to speak to Catral. This meant that while Redvers and I trudged down the stairs to the lobby, Millie and Lord Hughes rode down in the elevator. We suggested taking our little boat, but Lord Hughes was already hailing a gondola to take us to the hotel where Ignacio was staying.

"This is far nicer than our hotel," Aunt Millie announced when we arrived at the hotel pier. She pursed her lips and elbowed her husband. "Perhaps we should move hotels."

Lord Hughes patted her arm but didn't say anything. I wondered if they would be packing their things before the night was over or if Hughes would be able to convince my aunt that their current accommodations were just fine.

We didn't bother asking for Catral's room at the front desk, which was busy with several customers, and instead took the stairs to the floor where Ignacio was staying, taking a chance that the musician would still be in the same room. Redvers knocked on the sturdy door, which flew open almost immediately, and Ignacio greeted us warmly.

"Come in, come in," he said. I eyed him up suspiciously—he was awfully friendly for someone who'd recently brought poisoned wine to a party. "Have a seat," he said. "Can I offer you anything to drink?"

We all shook our heads, even Aunt Millie. No one in our party was willing to risk it.

"What brings you to see me? Would you like another demonstration of my music? Is that why you brought your mother?" Ignacio asked, glancing between my aunt and myself.

"Her mother, please be serious," Aunt Millie huffed. "I'm not nearly old enough."

Both Ignacio and I gave her a skeptical look, but I quickly reined myself in and answered his question. "No music, thank you, we have some questions about the wine you brought to the party."

"Such a tragedy," Ignacio said mournfully. "It was a lovely vintage, all gone to waste."

I felt my eyes narrow. He was sorry about losing the wine but not Orsola losing her life?

"And that Orsola died, that too was very sad," he said quickly, having caught my look.

"You didn't care for Orsola, did you?" I asked.

Ignacio puffed up slightly. "How could you say such a thing? It was a tragedy, an accident that she drank the wine. I did not know that it was poisoned. It could have been any one of us that died."

"That much is true, but Orsola was having an affair with D'Annuzzio. I think you were jealous," I said.

He shook his head vehemently. "I did not want to have that kind of relationship with that man. No." Catral paused. "It was merely a little . . . frustrating that she occupied so much of his time. When we could have been working instead."

I made a hmm-ing noise but didn't say anything else.

"What about your trip to Australia?" Redvers asked. "Whose idea was that?"

"D'Annuzzio wanted to go there, and I agreed to accompany him so that he would not be lonely."

I doubted that D'Annuzzio was *ever* lonely, not for long anyway.

"And did you pick anything up while you were there?" Redvers asked.

Catral's brows pulled together. "Like what? A pet kangaroo? Clara requested one, but we did not bring one. They grow to be far too large and powerful." He wrinkled his nose. "The muscles, they are unnatural."

Aunt Millie made a little noise of agreement, which drew my attention, but Redvers continued on without skipping a beat. "No, not another pet or an animal. But perhaps a type of poison?" Redvers clarified.

"Why would I pick up poison in Australia? What a crazy

thing to . . ." Ignacio stopped short. "You think this is the poison that killed Orsola? No." He shook his head. "I would not pick up such a thing. And that wine was sent here, to my hotel room, from Clara. There was a note with her name on it."

"Can we see the note?" I asked.

"That *polizia ispettore* has the note. He came and searched my things after Orsola died." He caught my eye again. "So tragic."

I didn't believe for a second that this display was sincere, even though he was doing his best to make me believe that it was after his initial misstep. But I wanted to look at the note and compare it to Clara's handwriting so I could see if it was, in fact, a match. It seemed unlikely that Clara would send a poisoned bottle of wine to Ignacio, but I also couldn't completely ignore the possibility that she had. But since Fizzoli had the note and the bottles, I supposed I could only hope the *ispettore* was looking into things and doing a more thorough job than he appeared willing to do the first time. It was frustrating to investigate a murder without cooperation—and information—from the local police.

We were all quiet for a beat, and it was clear that Ignacio was thinking about his trip to Australia because he began speaking slowly. "You know, there was a morning when I could not sleep, but D'Annuzzio did not want to wake. I was bored, restless, so he sent me to pick something up for him. He did not say what it was, just that I was to pick it up at a local post office in Sydney. It was being held under his name."

Redvers and I looked at each other. Had the poison been sent to D'Annuzzio himself? Had the man poisoned *himself*? There hadn't been any indications at all that the man was depressed or lacking the will to live.

"Did he say what it was?" I asked.

"No, he only said that someone from home had asked him to pick up this package while we were there. He did not say who, although I assumed it was Clara."

Clever, very clever. Whoever poisoned D'Annuzzio had the venom sent to D'Annuzzio himself in Australia and had him bring it home, then used it to kill the man. The only reason we even knew about the plan was because D'Annuzzio wanted to get some extra sleep.

Now it was just a matter of figuring out who had asked D'Annuzzio to pick up the package for them. This was, of course, made difficult by the fact that D'Annuzzio was dead and couldn't tell us who had asked for the "favor." Nor had we seen any type of journal or letters in his house that might have given us an explanation. So while we may have eliminated one more suspect, we still had a list of them.

The four of us were quiet on our way out of the hotel and onto the dock, although Millie started in once we were settled into a gondola. "Why haven't you two spoken to this *ispettore* to see if he'll give you information?"

I closed my eyes, and Redvers squeezed my hand, then answered my aunt. "We have spoken to Fizzoli, but he's not too keen on sharing information with outsiders."

Aunt Millie harrumphed, then continued giving us an inside look at her train of thought. "Clara wouldn't have sent a poisoned bottle of wine, so I, for one, would like to take a look at that note. I'm sure this Fizzoli will be reasonable and show it to me. Then we can prove that Clara isn't the one who sent it."

I fought a smile and once again held my tongue. I mentally wished her luck getting Fizzoli to show her *anything* besides the door.

"Who else could have sent it? Perhaps that butler? The original one, not Mr. Parks," Aunt Millie said. "Though lord knows that Mr. Parks does like to get up to some mischief, doesn't he?"

That caught my attention. "You mean sneaking into the costume party?" I asked. "Or getting hired as Clara's new butler?"

"Yes, all that *plus* sneaking out of town while the police are looking for him," Millie said easily.

I turned in my seat so fast that the gondola rocked, and our gondolier said something rapidly in Italian. I apologized, using the few Italian words I knew, but kept my eyes trained on my aunt. "What do you mean he left town?" Would Charlie really have abandoned his wife and fled?

"He got on the train with us this morning. Not the same class, obviously," Millie said simply.

I slowly turned back around in my seat, gut churning. I'd believed the best of Charlie, or tried to, but if my aunt was right, the man had abandoned his wife without so much as a goodbye. Redvers patted my hand. "There has to be a reason why. He wouldn't just leave her," he murmured.

"I hope you're right," I said. Both for Deanna's sake and for Charlie's.

Chapter Thirty-eight

My mood was somber when we returned to our own hotel. We still had other potential suspects to speak with, but it was late and a good night's sleep before continuing was the most sensible course of action. I hoped I would actually be able to sleep and was considering a nice hot bath before bed when I smacked directly into Lord Hughes' back. I hastily apologized, even though he was the one who'd stopped in his tracks, then peered around him.

Ispettore Fizzoli was standing before our little entourage. My heart did a little stutter-step, and so did my feet, stepping out past Lord Hughes so that I could see more clearly. Only then could I see that Deanna was standing just behind the *ispettore*.

"Deanna," I cried, rushing forward. I ignored Fizzoli and embraced Deanna, giving her a tight hug. I could tell that the days in jail had taken their toll in more ways than one—she'd clearly lost weight and seemed almost fragile in my arms.

"I didn't know where else to go," she said. "We aren't at the old hotel anymore, and the *ispettore* brought me here to your hotel."

"I'm so glad he did," I said, giving the *ispettore* a curious look. Why had he suddenly released Deanna and given her assistance?

Fizzoli had been watching our reunion, and from the glint in his eyes I knew that he was fully aware of what I was thinking. "I have someone who confessed to D'Annuzzio's murder—or Marchesi's, rather—so it was no longer necessary to keep Mrs. Parks in jail," Fizzoli said.

I thanked him, but I could feel that my brow was still furrowed. "Who did you arrest instead?" I asked.

"Clara Morton."

Aunt Millie gasped, and I worried for a moment that she might attack the man, but she simply asked a question instead, although she did step forward aggressively. "On what grounds?"

"On the grounds that she confessed to his murder. I went to her palazzo to ask her to explain why the note attached to the wine sent to Catral matched her handwriting, and she confessed to the murder when she saw it," Fizzoli said with a small shrug.

I looked to my husband, who was also frowning. It looked as though neither of us could understand why Clara had confessed to murder. Was it possible that she'd done it and we'd been ignoring the obvious all along?

That was all the information Fizzoli was willing to share, tonight anyway, although he looked resigned to the fact that Millie would be appearing in his office the following day. She was demanding to see the note and to speak with her friend—I nearly wished the *ispettore* luck.

For now, though, my top concern was getting a comfortable room for Deanna, some food and a bath, not to mention some clothes that she hadn't been wearing for days. I had Redvers speak with the front desk about whether they had another room available while I waited with my friend.

"Where's Charlie?" Deanna asked.

I paused, wondering how much to tell her. She'd already been through so much and needed some rest without further worry, so I did my best to reassure her. "He's not here right now, but he'll be back tomorrow. He said he was following up on a lead, hoping to get you out."

This was a pretty big lie, but Deanna considered it for only a moment before nodding her head and closing her eyes. "Okay," she said. The poor woman was dead on her feet.

I mentally kept my fingers crossed that I was telling the truth and Charlie would return quickly from wherever he'd gone.

An hour later and Redvers and I were back in our room, alone again for the first time in what felt like forever. I'd gotten Deanna settled into a room of her own, loaned her some clothing, and run her a nice warm bath so she could get cleaned up and then get a good night's sleep—something she probably hadn't had in days.

I sighed heavily once our door was firmly closed behind us. "Charlie better come back tomorrow," I said. "I would hate to be made a liar."

"Did Deanna believe you?" Redvers asked.

"I think she was tired enough that she'd believe anything she was told. I figured she should have a good night's sleep first before having to deal with her wayward husband."

"Lord Hughes at least had a good idea of where Charlie went," Redvers said.

"Bless that man," I said. "And where does he think Charlie went?"

"It sounds like Charlie was also headed to Rome. Hughes didn't know why, but he did say that Charlie planned on coming back soon."

I rubbed my eyes. "Well, at least that much of my story was true. I wonder what on earth he thought he would accomplish by heading down to Rome, though."

"I suspect we'll have to wait to hear until he gets back."

I nodded, then switched directions. "Do you think Clara could have done it?"

Redvers cocked his head. "I think she could have, but I don't think that she did."

"Why would she confess, then?"

"Because she believes the killer is someone she loves," Redvers said.

Thinking it over, this was a very likely possibility. "Do you think she'll tell us?"

Redvers had already pulled off his shoes and his coat and was working on removing his tie. "We'll find out tomorrow."

I was actually able to get a decent night's sleep for once, likely because I was already so tired and because Deanna had been released from jail and was in a nice, comfortable bed of her own. Over coffee, I felt a bit guilty that I hadn't been kept from sleep by Clara's current predicament, but it was not only one that she'd brought on herself by confessing but also one she could probably buy her way out of. Or so I told myself.

Even still, we needed to go speak with her and see if she would come clean about why she'd confessed to murder. I didn't like the woman, but I wasn't willing to see an innocent woman hanged for something she hadn't done.

Besides, I already knew that any possibility of letting this investigation go now was out of the question—there was simply no way my aunt Millie would stand for it. No, we had to see this through to the end and make certain that the correct person went to jail for D'Annuzzio's and Orsola's deaths.

The sun was already up, warming the breeze and burning the gentle fog away from the water sluicing along the canals. Once we'd finished eating our breakfast, we dressed, then stopped by Deanna's room to see if she was awake yet. I gave a few gentle raps, but when there was no answer, I slipped a note under the door explaining where we went and that we would come back later to check on her. She clearly needed the sleep, and I was glad that she was finally getting it.

Redvers and I slipped out of the hotel and onto the pier without once discussing the possibility of speaking with Aunt Millie and Lord Hughes. It wasn't until we were safely in the boat that I even ventured to bring it up, as though by mentioning her name she might appear.

"I figured that Millie and Hughes would already be up and pounding on Fizzoli's door," I said.

Redvers chuckled. "Is that what you really think, or were you just hoping to avoid your aunt this morning?"

I smiled sheepishly. I felt badly for avoiding Millie, especially since I'd been so worried about her the day before, but she would be making a really big racket now that a friend of *hers* was the one in jail. "Why do you think she went to Rome, anyway?" I asked.

"Funny you should ask that," Redvers replied. "Hughes told me that while she will never admit it, Millie felt bad about ratting out Charlie Parks to the police. And she was worried about your friend Deanna. She wanted to do something useful."

"Huh," I said. "I do wish she could just be forthcoming about these kinds of things."

"You mean feelings?" Redvers asked with a smile.

I leaned back and bumped my shoulder into his. Both of us were in high spirits that morning, which was a welcome change of pace from the last few days. We would of course keep doing our best to find the murderer, but it was a relief to have the pit of anxiety in my stomach dissipate.

Mostly anyway. There was still the matter of when Charlie Parks would come back and why he'd left in the first place.

We moored our boat at the public pier near the police station and were about to enter the building, pausing to wait for the person coming out. Redvers realized that the individual was someone we knew well before I did—I was quite focused on getting inside and gearing up for an argument with Fizzoli on being allowed to speak with Clara.

"George!" Redvers said. "Are you here to see Clara?"

George Kelley paused, hat still in hand as he let the door close behind him. He was clearly surprised to see us but not displeased. "Mr. and Mrs. Wunderly, what are you doing here?" he asked.

Redvers glanced around, then nodded to a nearby café at the end of the block with his head. "Can we buy you a coffee?"

George considered for only a moment before he agreed and the three of us strolled over to the café Redvers had indicated and sat at the table outside. We waited until we had our drinks in hand before we started discussing why we were all at the *polizia* station.

"I assume you were there to visit Clara?" Redvers asked.

George nodded. "I was trying to convince her to be honest with the police, but that woman is so stubborn."

"Honest in what way?" I asked.

"There's no way she killed D'Annuzzio or sent Catral that poisoned bottle of wine, which is what she's claiming. She's taking the blame for someone."

"Do you know who?" Redvers asked.

George shook his head. "She wouldn't tell me that either. All she would say is that this was the only way." He rubbed the bridge of his nose. "That *woman*," he muttered. "At least she has an excellent lawyer. I imagine she'll be home before the end of the day." He paused. "Well, not home, but back at her palazzo."

I thought that was an interesting distinction. "Does she not consider the palazzo home?"

George frowned. "She might, but she's really only here in the summers. She winters in Rome."

That wasn't as interesting or useful as I'd hoped, so I turned my mind to why Clara would avoid telling George the reason she'd taken the blame for the murders. Was it because she thought someone close to her had actually done it? It was the most reasonable explanation. Especially if she thought the culprit was Helen. It would explain several things, actually.

Redvers had moved on to his next question. "Did you happen to talk with D'Annuzzio the night of the party?"

George shook his head vehemently. "No, I was actually doing my best to avoid the man. I can't stand him, or couldn't rather, and not because he was married to Clara. No, I simply couldn't bear being in the same room as him because he was entirely arrogant and seemed to have no basis for it." He paused, letting his steam run out, then sighed. "Or perhaps I just don't understand the appeal of poetry."

I gave him a sympathetic smile. I had never understood poetry either. But more importantly, it seemed that George had good instincts about D'Annuzzio. I hadn't met the man, but from all accounts he *had* been baselessly arrogant, especially for someone who was an utter fraud.

"Can anyone vouch for that?" Redvers asked.

George gave him a long, searching look before answering. "I assume you have good reason to ask these questions." When Redvers gave a brisk nod, George answered. "Helen was with me most of the night. I suppose my own daughter doesn't make a solid alibi, though."

"I'm afraid not," Redvers said. "There's no one else?"

"I did have my cards read at one of the tables," George said.

"The tarot card reader?" I asked. That would have been Deanna; we would be sure to ask her about it when we returned to our hotel.

George shrugged. "I suppose that's what it was. A lot of foolishness if you ask me."

This wasn't a surprising reaction in the slightest. But what came next certainly was.

"She did pull the death card, though," George said with more than a little reluctance. "Twice."

Chapter Thirty-nine

Redvers and I wore matching expressions of surprise. I was surprised both that Deanna had pulled that particular card the very night that someone died and that George had admitted to it.

George shifted uncomfortably in his seat. "She said a bunch of things after she showed it to me the second time, but I wasn't really listening. I'm sure it was just a trick, designed to shock the person on the other side of the table. Or at the very least, simply a coincidence."

"Did you happen to mention this to the police?" I asked.

George's dark brows furrowed. "Should I have?"

I quickly shook my head. "No, I don't think so. I'm sure it's as you said, just a coincidence. The cards don't really mean anything." I didn't necessarily believe that was true, but I didn't want there to be any reason for Fizzoli to rearrest Deanna.

Although there was now a little voice in the back of my head asking if I'd been wrong in ignoring Deanna as an actual suspect just because we were friends. What did I really know about the woman anyway? Weren't we really just acquaintances? Could my gut be wrong about the type of person she actually is? And what about Charlie, who'd suddenly taken off?

I did my best to push these sudden doubts to the back of my mind. They weren't useful right now, and I could discuss them with Redvers later, when we were alone.

But I found it difficult to pay attention to the rest of the conversation. I went inside, ordered myself a cappuccino, and returned with it, still struggling with my doubts about the Parks when George stood to leave. We bid him good-bye, and I took my seat again.

"Where did you go?" Redvers asked, watching me sip my drink with a bemused look on his face. "I got the feeling you were very far from here."

"I suddenly became very worried that I'd made the wrong decision in trusting that Deanna and Charlie aren't responsible for these murders."

Redvers cocked his head. I appreciated that he never laughed at me when I had these types of reactions but was instead willing to talk things through with me. "Is this because Deanna pulled that card?" he asked.

I nodded. "Twice."

"You know how I feel about this type of thing," Redvers said. And it was true, I did know how he felt about things like the tarot and spirits—he thought they were a lot of foolishness with not a lick of truth to any of it. "But I understand why it would make you nervous." He leaned forward in his seat, holding my gaze. "But Jane, your instincts about people are good."

"Not all people," I mumbled.

He chuckled. "No, not all," he agreed. "But most. And truthfully, Charlie and Deanna don't have nearly as good a motive for killing D'Annuzzio as the rest of this crowd has."

I let out a breath. He was right on that account at least. Beyond D'Annuzzio being inappropriate with his hands and Deanna's person—which he'd quickly paid for—the Parks didn't have a good reason to kill the man. Or Catral, for that matter. The tension that had taken hold of my shoulders released, and I breathed a little easier. The killer had to be someone else, we were just missing who that someone might be.

"Do you think it actually might have been Clara?" I asked. I didn't, despite my mixed feelings about the women. I was nearly certain that she was taking the blame for someone else.

"I don't. But let's go talk to her and find out."

It took quite some convincing, but we were lucky that Fizzoli wasn't in his office, because the officer in charge eventually gave in and had us escorted over to the cell block to speak with Clara. I hadn't understood most of the conversation between Redvers and the *polizia* since it was in Italian, but I did know that my husband could be quite convincing when he wanted to be.

Clara was seated on the metal bench in her cell with her head in her hands when we appeared at the bars. "Clara," I said. When she didn't look up, I tried again, but louder. "Clara!"

That finally got her attention, and she shot up off the bench, hand to her forehead. "You've come to save me," she said dramatically.

"Uh, I wish we could say that we were getting you out of here, but I think you'll need your lawyer for that," I said. I didn't mention that I thought she would also need a wheelbarrow full of money, lira probably.

"Oh," Clara muttered, all dramatics gone from her manner and voice. "Why are you here then? And when is my lawyer coming? This has been interesting, but I would like to go home now."

I blinked at her. What did she think would happen when she confessed to murder? That she would spend the night in jail and then get released back to her normal life? I nearly asked, then decided it wasn't worth wasting our limited time on. "Did you ask Christopher to pick something up for you while he and Catral were in Australia?"

Clara frowned. "Yes, I asked them to bring me a baby kangaroo, and they failed to do it."

"No, not the kangaroo," I said. "Something else. Anything else, really."

She took a moment to consider the question. "No, I don't recall asking that. Why do you ask?"

"It's not important." It was important, but I wasn't going to tell her about the venom—if I did, there was zero chance of us keeping it quiet to unmask our murderer. Besides, I had more important things to ask the woman. "Who are you covering for?"

"Whatever do you mean?" Clara asked, now examining her nails.

"Clara," I said, using my most strident voice. "We all know that you didn't kill anyone. So who are you taking the blame for? Who do you think did this?"

She sighed and retook her seat on the bench. "It could be any number of people that I care about. And honestly, they're more likely to hang than I am. I figured if I confessed, I could be out of here in a few hours, and a jury will never convict me."

I thought the woman sounded awfully confident. Something I would not be if I were in her shoes. "Who, Clara?" I asked again.

"Well, Helen for one. My daughter clearly has a homicidal streak in her, I'm not sure where she got that from. Her father's side of the family, surely."

I didn't bother to respond to this, although I heard a snort from Redvers behind me.

"Kate of course, because Christopher ruined her art career."

We already knew about that one.

"And then there's George. I learned that Christopher was behind the failure of George's mining operation."

"What?" This was truly surprising information. "How did you learn this? And how did Christopher manage that?"

"Christopher left some letters tucked away in my bedroom. Not well hidden, frankly. I think he wanted me to find them. In any case, one of them was correspondence with someone in America who was being paid by Christopher to sabotage the mine."

"Does George know about this?" Redvers asked.

"I certainly hope not," Clara said.

I pursed my lips. I wished now that we'd spoken with Clara before sitting down with her first husband. Then we could have confronted George with this information over coffee.

I cocked my head. "Why would you confess to murder to save your ex-husband?"

Clara shrugged. "I still love the man. I don't want to see him hanged for this."

"Do you think he might have actually done it? Or the other two?" Redvers asked.

Clara actually thought that over before answering. "I really don't know. I can only hope they didn't."

I thought that was the most honest response I'd ever heard from the woman. It seemed she might have actually realized the severity of her situation and was setting aside the dramatics for once.

"What about the bottle of wine that was sent to Catral? The police have the note that arrived with it, and it appears to have been written by you," I said.

Clara wrinkled her nose. "I've seen the note, the beastly *ispettore* showed it to me. It *is* my handwriting, but I didn't send that bottle of wine. Why on earth would I spend even more money on that musician? I was willing to pay for Christopher's whims, but honestly. Now that he's gone, I have no more use for Ignacio." She waved her hand as if brushing the man away.

"So who did you send the note to?" I asked.

She shrugged. "I've been trying to remember, but I can't. I do send gifts to those I care about."

Which narrowed things down not at all.

"I hope I don't expire from hunger in here," she said. "They haven't sent me anything the least bit edible. Do you think my lawyer will rescue me soon? Or perhaps someone can send a basket of food. With a nice champagne, a good year, please."

So much for Clara Morton setting aside her dramatics. Our time was up, so rather than respond to her requests, we bid her goodbye and said we would speak to her soon. The officer was already leading us out the door, and I could still hear her call after us "don't forget the champagne."

Back on the street, Redvers and I looked at each other, then we each shook our heads.

"She's quite something," Redvers said.

"I think I'm starting to understand why she and Aunt Millie get along," I replied.

"You think Millie would have champagne sent to jail?" Redvers teased.

"No, I think she would have a barrel of Scotch sent in."

Redvers threw his head back and laughed, and I paused for a moment to appreciate my husband. Making him laugh like that filled me with a warm glow, especially since it was such a rare occurrence.

I allowed myself to bask in the glow for a while, both of us walking along the cobblestone and smiling, before becoming serious and asking Redvers what our next logical step should be.

"I think we should go back to the hotel and check on Deanna," he said. "From there we can decide what our next steps should be."

I agreed and mentally kept my fingers crossed that with any luck, Charlie would have returned as well. I didn't want to think about the possibility that he might never come back, either by his choice or someone else's.

Chapter Forty

Back at our hotel, we went straight up to Deanna's room. We could hear raised voices behind the door, and Redvers and I exchanged a glance before I knocked. There was silence for a beat before the door opened by Deanna, who looked positively ready to spit nails.

I was about to say that we could come back and speak with her later, but she swung the door wide and gestured for us to come in. "I'm glad you're both here. Please come in and join me in giving my husband a dressing-down for all the stupid things he's been up to."

Redvers and I looked at each other again, but since I couldn't think of a way to extricate ourselves gracefully, I slipped past Deanna and headed into their tiny sitting room. Charlie was standing near the window, his hair standing on end—he'd clearly been pulling it. I gave him a greeting, and he mumbled something in return.

Neither Redvers nor I took one of the available seats, choosing to stand and hopefully make our excuses instead of staying for what was clearly a domestic squabble. But Deanna began to cry, and I went to give her a hug.

"I was so worried about him the whole time I was in jail." Deanna hiccupped. "And he was just gallivanting around Rome."

I gave Charlie a dark look, although Redvers merely cocked his head at our friend. "What was in Rome, Charlie?" he asked.

"Nothing," Charlie mumbled.

I gritted my teeth. "Just come clean and tell us. It can't be worth making everything worse, which is clearly what you're doing by not coming clean about where you were and why."

"Fine," he said, his tone defeated. "I was meeting with a friend in Rome." He glanced at his wife. "Someone she doesn't like."

Deanna sighed and sank down into a chair. "Was it Jonathon?"

Charlie nodded guiltily. "I know how you feel about him, and I didn't want you to know we were still in touch. That's why I've been trying to avoid telling you."

"Who is Jonathon?" Redvers asked.

Charlie looked reluctant to say, so Deanna answered the question. "He's an old friend of Charlie's from our vaudeville days. But Jonathon is a grifter. He always has some scheme and is always trying to get Charlie involved in whatever he's up to."

It was obvious that Charlie couldn't argue any of that. "We've still been in touch, that's how I knew he was also in Italy."

"Been in touch how? I've never seen anything from him," Deanna asked, then stopped and shook her head. "You know what, I don't want to know. What terrible advice did Jonathon have for you this time?"

Once again, Charlie didn't seem able to argue the charge, leading me to believe that this friend was indeed bad news.

"He didn't have any advice, and that's not why I went there. You know he likes to target folks who . . . have a little too much money of their own. Or might have a little bit to spare without it hurting them. I thought he might know something about Clara or that D'Annuzzio fellow," Charlie said.

This at least seemed like a reasonable excuse to put himself in danger and travel to Rome. To me, anyway. I wasn't so sure that Deanna felt the same way based on her eye roll, but it did sound as though Clara and D'Annuzzio would have been ideal targets for Charlie's friend.

"Is that the real reason why Jonathon came here?" Redvers asked.

Charlie looked guilty. "I may have mentioned in one of my letters that Deanna got a job working for Clara."

Deanna closed her eyes, lips pursed. I could tell she was angry with her husband, but I thought she was doing an admirable job keeping her temper under control. Of course, I couldn't speak to what would happen once Redvers and I were able to extricate ourselves from the room.

"And?" Redvers asked. "Did you learn anything?"

Charlie tipped his hand back and forth. "Yes and no. He told me a lot of the same things you already learned—that D'Annuzzio was a grifter of sorts himself."

I glanced at Deanna, unsure about whether she'd heard this already, but she looked unsurprised.

"Jonathon also mentioned that Clara and D'Annuzzio—the fake D'Annuzzio, anyway—fought a lot."

"How did he know this?" I asked. It wasn't news, but I was still curious.

"My friend bumped into them in Rome and heard them arguing—everyone in the hotel heard them."

"Bumped into them, meaning he was following them, looking for an opportunity to bilk some money out of them," Deanna muttered. Charlie just shrugged, clearly not able to argue her point.

But then he continued. "He also said that one time Clara had a black eye and some other bruises. Pretty bad ones."

I could feel my body tense at this description; my gut

knew exactly where those marks had come from, having lived through a marriage where those things were the norm. I also felt a measure of guilt—I'd known that Clara and Christopher had a somewhat volatile relationship, but I'd never once considered that it had taken a step toward violence. It was something that I should have considered, since I personally knew not only the damage such a husband could inflict but also how hard it was to leave.

Of course, Clara *had* left, and she'd divorced the man. But she was still attached to D'Annuzzio, still subject to his whims, so I didn't know what to make of that. I was, however, conscious that Redvers had taken my hand at the first mention of Clara's bruises and was quietly supporting me. He was obviously aware of my inner turmoil, because he gave my hand a gentle squeeze and took over asking further questions.

"Deanna, did you ever see any evidence of injuries?" Redvers asked.

Deanna shook her head but looked thoughtful. "Not while I worked there, but that doesn't mean that there weren't any." Deanna cocked her head.

"I don't understand why she stayed with him, though, if he was beating her. Although it makes sense why she would have done him in."

Was I completely off base that Clara was innocent? Deanna was right, this gave her plenty of motive to kill D'Annuzzio, especially if the man wouldn't leave her alone even after the divorce.

Conversely, despite everything, it seemed that Clara really had cared about D'Annuzzio. Everything we'd heard from Clara indicated that she had divorced him only because he'd been siphoning off her money. I didn't think Clara would be shy about announcing a little domestic violence, but perhaps she was more embarrassed about that than I could anticipate. Clara seemed happy to air all her dirty laundry, but perhaps there *were* some secrets she kept to herself.

I sighed. I didn't know what to think, especially since the woman herself was such an enigma. But it seemed a good time to revisit the one person who might really know what had been going on between Clara and D'Annuzzio.

"I think we should speak with Kate Conrad again," I said.

We left Charlie and Deanna and headed to Clara's palazzo. I half expected to find Clara there, so sure was she that her money and her lawyer would get her released from jail. Instead, the door was answered by a member of the kitchen staff, who told us that Kate Conrad was in the garden.

We walked across the room and down the stairs leading out to the garden. As soon as we hit the cobblestones, we both stopped short—Kate was indeed here, but so was Clara's pet cheetah, lounging on the low rock wall. It looked as though Kate was trying to paint a portrait of the animal.

"Ah, Jane, Redvers. What can I help you with?" Kate asked. She glanced over her shoulder at us, but then returned to her work on the easel. "I'd offer you a seat, but there aren't many out here. Unless you want to cozy up with Carmine, of course."

Redvers and I were both more than a little wary of the big cat. It wasn't as big as a tiger, but it was still intimidating, and hardly a house cat. We stayed where we were, neither of us taking our eyes off the animal.

"We came to talk to you about Clara," I said. Out of the corner of my eye I saw Kate go still and carefully set her brushes on the easel ledge.

"Of course," she said. "I imagine you're concerned about her being in jail, as I am."

"We are concerned about that. Do you know why she would have confessed to a murder she didn't commit?"

Kate shook her head, but she still wasn't looking at us, instead wiping her hands with a paint-smeared rag and focusing her attention entirely on that task. "I don't know, although I told her it was a foolish idea."

I looked at Kate and wondered if I'd gotten her wrong. I'd eliminated her as a possibility because she'd been up front about her motive for killing D'Annuzzio. But what if that was a decoy? What if Kate had an entirely different reason for killing the man, one that had to do with black eyes and a bruised body?

"I know why you killed him, Kate," I said quietly. I could feel Redvers give me a surprised look before turning his attention back to the cheetah. "I know it's because he was hurting Clara."

It looked as though my arrow had struck true, because Kate turned slowly, her eyes full of tears. "He was a terrible brute," she said. "Clara was afraid of him. Even after she managed to divorce him, she was afraid of him. I thought we would never get rid of that man."

"So you had him pick up the poison in Australia while he was there," I said, filling in the parts of the story we'd been missing.

She nodded. "I thought there was a kind of justice in making him pick up the very venom I was going to kill him with."

"It's too bad he was lazy and had Catral do it instead," I said.

Kate sighed. "I didn't know that, but I should have figured he wouldn't do the thing himself. I was hoping there'd be no record of it, but he was such a lazy fool."

I thought the language was quite tame for what that man had actually been.

"And you're letting Clara take the blame for his murder?" I asked.

"I've been struggling with that," Kate said, her face anguished. "I went to see her and told her that I should be the one to confess, but she told me that she loves me and I should do no such thing. She said that her lawyer would get her out of jail, and then we would leave Venice, head somewhere else, somewhere new."

I just looked at her, trying to judge whether she actually believed what she was saying was true, or if she'd been trying to convince herself in order to keep from confessing to the murder. She must have been able to read it in my face, because her own face hardened, and she stretched out her arm, pointing at us.

"Carmine, attack!"

Chapter Forty-one

Redvers and I both froze at the command, terrified that the cheetah had been trained to attack strangers. But the animal yawned and stretched, then stepped off the wall, taking a seat on the ground and cleaning one paw. Carmine clearly had no intentions of attacking anyone.

"You stupid animal," Kate muttered, then took off running toward the back of the garden.

Redvers did a stutter-step, clearly wanting to chase after Kate but also not wanting to startle the cheetah into chasing after him. I was frankly surprised that the cat hadn't taken off after Kate, like a greyhound chasing a rabbit, but the big cat had sauntered over to me and was bumping my leg with his head. I tentatively reached down to scratch him, whispering to Redvers "go." If the cat moved in my husband's direction, I would now be able to grab his collar. It would likely dislocate my arm, but I could hopefully stop the cat from chasing Redvers if it was inclined to follow him.

My husband bolted, and I hoped that he would be able to catch Kate before she was able to escape the palazzo. It was working in our favor that we were surrounded by canals, and unless Clara had a private gondola hidden away, Kate would have a hard time leaving.

Meanwhile, Carmine the cheetah was rolling on the ground by my feet, batting at my shoes. "You're just a big kitty, aren't you?" I asked the creature before bending down to take its leash. As though it knew we were going somewhere, Carmine got up, nudging me once more. I petted its head, then urged it to follow me in the direction that both Kate and Redvers had gone.

At the back of the garden, I found a rusty iron gate that had been left hanging open. I stepped from the garden and found a narrow alleyway, although it looked as though it came to a dead end between the neighboring buildings. "Redvers?" I called out, but heard no reply. I paused long enough to hear some distant shouts and a splash, so I hurried back through the garden and up the stairs into the main room, cheetah loping happily alongside me. I calculated where I'd heard the sounds and moved in that direction, pushing open the nearest shuttered window and looking down to the canal just below me. Redvers, dressed only in his undershirt and trousers, was cutting through the water toward Kate, who was floundering in the water. I scanned the canal and was relieved to see there weren't any boats coming toward them, not at the moment anyway. With any luck, Redvers would be able to pull her safely back to the pier.

I was able to hand Carmine off to the kitchen staff, who promised in broken English to give the big cat some treats. My interactions with the animal felt surreal, to say the least, and while he'd been a friendly cat, I was more than happy to pass him off to the staff. I then went to the phone and made a quick call to Fizzoli, telling him to come to the palazzo as soon as possible.

In the meantime, it looked as though Kate had swum from the side canal out to the front of the building, where Redvers was now struggling with her. She was now fighting

Redvers off, shouting that she wanted to be allowed to drown herself, and Redvers was doing his best to keep her from doing that. I joined them, kneeling on the edge of the marble platform. I did my best to grab her shirt and tried to pull her to safety, but she started fighting me off as well, and I nearly ended up in the water beside my husband. It appeared that she was trying to get out to the deeper water, where there was regular boat traffic, but Redvers was doing his best to stop her from getting any farther than she already had.

It was probably only fifteen minutes before I spotted the police boat speeding toward us, and when she heard the sirens, Kate finally gave up, allowing Redvers to drag her to the edge of the landing. I still kept a close eye on her until Fizzoli and his men were able to secure her, afraid that she would make a second attempt to toss herself into the canal, possibly in front of a boat, but the *polizia* arrested her without any further incident.

Redvers was lying in a sodden lump on the marble landing, and I checked to ensure that he was alright. "I'm exhausted. That woman fights bloody hard." I stifled a smile and went into the palazzo to find him something to put on. The best I could find that might be both warm and long enough for him was a fuzzy pink robe from Helen's trunk, but Redvers didn't complain, excusing himself to a bathroom to remove his sodden clothing and slip into the warm robe I offered.

"It's a good color for you," I said when he came out.

He narrowed his eyes at me, then looked down at himself. "I won't be buying any new suits in this shade, I can assure you of that."

There was some commotion behind us, and I realized that George Kelley and Helen had returned to the palazzo from wherever they had been.

"That's my robe!" Helen cried. "You're going to stretch it out, you're too big."

Redvers gave her a dark look. "I'm sure your mother can buy you a new one."

We stopped by our hotel so that Redvers could have a quick hot bath and change into his own clothes before heading to the police station. On the way to our hotel, he'd begun shivering, his teeth chattering together with some violence. The canal was awfully cold, and both he and Kate had been in it for quite some time. Sure, they'd been struggling with one another, but the water was still a shock to the system, so I made sure Redvers was well and truly warmed back up before we left the hotel again.

Of course, this meant that Aunt Millie and Lord Hughes were able to track us down in our room and insisted on accompanying us to the police station. While Millie was quite annoyed at having missed the final showdown with Kate Conrad, she was pleased that her friend Clara was going to be cleared of suspicion and released.

"I don't know what she was thinking, confessing to a murder that she wasn't responsible for," Millie said. She thought for a moment. "I am sorry that it looks like Kate will be hanged, though. She was quite a talented artist." It looked as though my aunt was going to say something else but changed her mind. I decided I didn't want to know what her afterthought had been—it was likely along the lines of how much Conrad's art would be worth after all this.

There had been a sharp drop in my stomach at the thought of what Kate's fate might be. "I'm hoping it won't come to that. I think she actually had a fair reason for doing what she did. I'm hopeful that she'll avoid hanging once she explains about D'Annuzzio's penchant for violence toward his wife. Kate was trying to protect Clara, after all." The fact that the man had been a fraud would ultimately work in Conrad's favor as well.

Although it was likely that she'd tried to poison Catral as well, and *that* I couldn't excuse. But perhaps her other homicidal attempts wouldn't come up at trial.

Aunt Millie pursed her lips, then gave a single nod. "Clara and I will make sure she has the finest representation, and she'll only do some nominal time behind bars."

I didn't know Italian law and whether this was possible, but I did hope Millie was right.

By the time we arrived at the station, Clara had been released and reunited with her daughter and first husband. There wasn't room for anyone in Ispettore Fizzoli's tiny office, so our unwieldy group sprawled out across the reception area, the young *polizia* behind the desk gaping at the lot of us. Most of us stood, but Aunt Millie and Clara had scrounged up some chairs, and the two of them were holding court.

Fizzoli looked as though he was going to have heart palpitations, and I would have bet money that he was more than anxious for this case—and Clara Morton—to be far behind him. Fizzoli glanced at my husband. "Mr. Wunderly, thank you for pulling Miss Conrad from the canal. She's being taken care of in the infirmary. Did she give you a reason for jumping into the canal? She refused to speak with us."

Both Clara and Aunt Millie looked quite approving of Kate's refusal to speak with the *Polizia di Stato*.

"She admitted that she was responsible for killing D'Annuzzio—or rather Giovanni Marchesi—but that it was due to the physical violence he inflicted on Clara Morton," Redvers said.

"Is this true, Mrs. Morton?" Fizzoli asked.

We all turned to Clara, clearly expecting a dramatic answer, but were pleasantly surprised when she gave the *ispettore* a simple, "It is true."

I looked at George and Helen, both of whom looked shocked, although I couldn't tell whether this was because of Clara's admission about D'Annuzzio or at the news that D'Annuzzio wasn't his real name.

George quickly answered that question. "Who the hell is Giovanni . . . what did you say the name was?"

Fizzoli huffed, impatient. "Someone can explain that to you later." George looked around, and Redvers nodded at him. Fizzoli continued. "And you'll be finding an *avvocato* for Miss Conrad?"

Clara frowned, then her expression cleared. "You mean a lawyer. Yes. Likely we'll hire the same man that represented me." She looked at George. "Call him, will you?"

"I already did," George said. Clara beamed at him, and Helen rolled her eyes at her mother.

I was looking forward to putting some space between myself and these three.

We finished giving our statements to Ispettore Fizzoli, who seemed delighted to throw us out of his station when we were finished. I suspected he felt very similarly about Clara Morton and the rest of our group—happy to never lay eyes on us again.

It was supper time, and I was hungry when we found ourselves on the street. This was announced by my stomach, which Aunt Millie found very rude and made sure to tell me so. Clara Morton suggested we all have dinner at her palazzo, but Redvers and I excused ourselves.

"This is our honeymoon, after all," Redvers said. "So thank you for the offer, but Jane and I will say goodnight instead."

Aunt Millie did some grumbling, but it seemed as though Clara had already forgotten about us, making plans for both food and champagne to be sent to the palazzo, enough to feed the rest of the group and probably a small army besides. Redvers and I grinned at each other and slipped away, hopping into our boat, and heading straight for our favorite restaurant. I sighed with relief when I saw the place, and especially when we saw Pietro's delighted face. "*Allora!* I thought you abandoned us! Left without an *arrivederci*!" Pietro cried.

"We would never," I assured him, and he smiled widely, then led us to a table at the back. He didn't even bring us menus, he simply brought us a carafe of wine with glasses and told us that he would take care of everything. I gave a happy little sigh as I sipped my glass of red wine.

"Happy that everything is sorted out?" Redvers asked.

"To some extent. I'm sorry that Kate Conrad went to the lengths she did, although I suppose I understand why she did it," I replied.

Redvers nodded seriously. "I also understand—at least I understand her impulse to protect Clara. I'm not sure I understand the other poisoning. But even still, I hope she receives a light sentence."

I did, too, and I would be sure to follow her case through my aunt. I thought about the other attacks, the ones done by Helen Morton. "I hope Helen gets some help."

Redvers nodded seriously, before taking a sip of his own glass of wine. "I hope so, too. Perhaps we could mention that to Millie as well, since it seems as though she's going to stay here for a bit."

I imagined my aunt would stay for as long as it suited her, and right now Kate Conrad was a cause that seemed to suit her. Mentioning help for Helen was a good idea, though, and I said as much.

"But I'm mostly relieved that Deanna and Charlie are safe and out of jail."

Redvers nodded. "Do you think they'll be alright?"

I knew precisely what he was getting at. "You know, I do think so." When we'd left them at the hotel, Deanna had been telling Charlie that she really needed him to make some changes, and that they both needed to find a different way of life. He'd actually seemed amenable to it—I suspected he would do whatever it took to ensure he didn't lose Deanna again. And I intended to keep in touch with the pair, regardless of where they ended up, although right now that looked to be very much up in the air. But I believed in my heart that they would be fine, especially since it was obvious that they truly cared for one another.

"My only other question," Redvers said, biting into a piece of crusty bread, "is what happened with that cheetah?"

I chuckled. "I was quite surprised when I realized he's just a big kitty. He wanted head scratches and was quite happy to follow me through the house. I left him with the kitchen staff—they were going to give him a treat. Probably a piece of steak."

Redvers grimaced. "I was certain we were about to be a kitty treat. Again."

"You know, I thought that too. But Carmine is tamer than one might think."

"I'll be happy if we never run into another cat ever again," Redvers muttered.

I opened my eyes wide. "But dearest, I was thinking about getting one for ourselves. A nice attack house cat. You can take it for walks in the evening after supper."

Redvers threw a bit of bread at me, and I laughed. I hadn't been serious, and he knew that. Besides, who knew where we might be staying a month from now? I knew neither of us was interested in going back to London, which meant that where we landed next was likely to be a surprise to us both.

For now, I was looking forward to the rest of our trip and the chance to actually enjoy our honeymoon and this lovely city. Of course, once we were finished in Venice, I had no doubts that the place we wound up next would present us with some new adventures. And the two of us would tackle whatever we encountered as we always did. Together.

Author's Note

The nonfiction book that I found most helpful when researching Jane's adventure in Venice was *The Unfinished Palazzo* by Judith Mackrell. It covers three very interesting women who owned (or rented) the same palazzo on the Grand Canal.

I took a lot of what I read about Luisa Casati in Mackrell's book to create the character Clara Morton. Luisa Casati was a real-life Italian heiress who was incredibly eccentric. She did in fact walk her cheetah at night in Venice while nearly naked, threw elaborate parties, and owned several snakes. It seems that Luisa thought of herself as a walking work of art—she was a really interesting woman. Unfortunately, she also had zero concept of money and spent her entire fortune, dying nearly penniless. Luisa had a long-running affair with the real D'Annuzzio, who was a celebrated writer in Italy. I used only a very little bit about the real-life D'Annuzzio, and far less than I did with Luisa.

The hotel Redvers and Jane stay at is based on the hotel that I stayed in during my recent trip to Venice, although I don't believe it was a hotel in the 1920s and couldn't find much information about it during that time. It was a lovely little place, though, tucked away from the tourist madness, and I would certainly go back.

Acknowledgments

Huge thanks to John Scognamiglio, my editor extraordinaire, as well as to Larissa Ackerman and Sofia Szyfer, my outstanding publicists. Thank you to Robin Cook, Lauren Jernigan, Susanna Grüninger, and Sarah Gibb. Further thanks to the rest of the Kensington team who work so hard to get books into your hands.

Huge thanks to my agent, Courtney Paganelli, who is an absolute rock star.

Thank you and all my love to Ann Collette. I'm so grateful for you and for our continued friendship—you bring me joy.

Special shout out to Orsola Chini, the lovely Venetian guide who is not at all like the character in this book, I assure you. Thanks for answering my questions and believing that I had valid reasons to ask about murder and floating hearses.

Immeasurable thanks for the friendship, love, and support to Tasha Alexander, Ed Aymar, Gretchen Beetner, Lou Berney, Mike Blanchard, Keith Brubacher, Kate Conrad, Hilary Davidson, Dan Distler, Steph Gayle, Daniel Goldin, Juliet Grames, Andrew Grant, Glen Erik Hamilton, Carrie Hennessy, Tim Hennessy, Chris Holm, Katrina Niidas Holm, Megan Kantara, Steph Kilen, Zoe Quinton King, Elizabeth Little, Jenny Lohr, Erin MacMillan, Joel MacMillan, Dan Malmon, Kate Malmon, Marjorie McCown, Mike McCrary, Catriona McPherson, Katie Meyer, Trevor Meyer, Lauren O'Brien, Roxanne Patruznick, Margret Petrie, Nick Petrie, Bryan Pryor, Andy Rash, Jane Rheineck, Kyle Jo

Schmidt, Dan Schwalbach, Marie Schwalbach, Johnny Shaw, Jay Shepherd, Becky Tesch, Tess Tyrrell, Bryan Van Meter, Luis Velez, and Tim Ward.

Thank you to the amazing booksellers and librarians who've supported this book. You make what we do possible. Special shout-outs to Daniel, Chris, and Rachel at Boswell Books. Love you guys.

Thank you and big love to my amazing family: Rachel and AJ Neubauer, Dorothy Neubauer, Sandra Olsen, Susan Catral, Sara Kierzek, Jeff and Annie Kierzek, Justin and Christine Kierzek, Josh Kierzek, Ignacio Catral, Sam and Ariana Catral, Mandi Neumann, Andie, and Alex and Angel Neumann, Finn and Milo Blanchard.

Love and thanks to John and Gayle McIntyre for their many years as a second family. And all the love and thanks to Beth McIntyre. Peach emoji to infinity.

Special thanks and love to my dear friend Gunther Neumann, who is truly a rock.

And finally, much love, gratitude, and thanks to Mike Blanchard for being the amazing person that he is. To the bones, babe.